Mary Jo Putney

A Kiss of Fate

A Novel

BALLANTINE BOOKS • NEW YORK

2005 Ivy Book Mass Market Edition

Copyright © 2004 by Mary Jo Putney

Excerpt from *Stolen Magic* copyright © 2005 by Mary Jo Putney

Published in the United States by Ballantine Books, an imprint of The Random House Publishing Group, a division of Random House, Inc., New York.

IVY BOOKS and colophon are trademarks of Random House, Inc.

Originally published in hardcover in the United States by Ballantine Books, an imprint of The Random House Publishing Group, a division of Random House, Inc., in 2004

This book contains an excerpt from *Stolen Magic* by M. J. Putney. This excerpt has been set for this edition only and may not reflect the final content of the edition.

ISBN 0-345-44917-7

Cover illustration: Jon Paul

Printed in the United States of America

www.ballantinebooks.com

OPM   9   8   7   6   5   4

To Hilary Ross, who had the vision and/or the faith to buy my first book when I hadn't the foggiest idea what I was doing!

Acknowledgments

My thanks to all the usual suspects, including John, for his tolerance when my brain was lost in the eighteenth century, and my sister, Estill, and my friend Pat Rice, who were very patient with my whimpering when the book wasn't going well.

Thanks also to my editors, Shauna Summers and Charlotte Herscher, for their willingness to see a dash of fantasy added to historical romance.

Very special thanks are due to Susan King and Julia Ross, fine writers of historical romance, for their guidance on matters Scottish. I owe ye both a wee dram!

The skies wept with autumn rain, perfect for burying the dead. Gwyneth Owens was grateful that custom banned females from the graveside, for she would have been unable to maintain her composure as her father was laid beneath the damp sod.

As always, she sought refuge in Lord Brecon's library. Her father, Robert Owens, had been his lordship's librarian for almost thirty years, and Gwynne had grown up among these treasured volumes.

Lightly she skimmed her fingertips over tooled leather and stamped gold titles in the travel memoir section. Her father had always said that a well-furnished mind was proof against loneliness. She hoped he was right, for she needed that comfort now.

As she moved along the south wall, she caught a glimpse of her reflection in the mirror above the fireplace. She turned away, avoiding the sight of her too tall figure and garish, unfashionable hair. Such a pity that she had inherited neither her father's power nor her mother's beauty.

Perhaps riding breakneck across Harlowe's hills would relieve her restless tension, but that wasn't possible since soon she would be summoned downstairs to act as chief mourner at the solemn gathering that would be held in her father's honor. Needing to be active, she unlocked the adjacent gallery, which contained the private library as well as her father's office.

A faint, almost indiscernible frisson of energy flickered over her skin when she stepped inside. The long, high-ceilinged chamber contained Britain's finest collection of books and manuscripts about magic. The volumes also represented the history and wisdom of the ancient Guardian families of the British Isles.

The Guardians, her father's clan. Human but gifted with magical powers, they had lived clandestinely among mundanes since time immemorial. Gwynne had been raised as a Guardian by virtue of her father's blood though she had no power of her own. She was grateful to be part of the Families since women had a degree of equality unheard of among mundanes. That custom had evolved early since in the realms of magic, females could wield powers that matched or surpassed those of men.

Guardians took their name from the oath all swore to use their power to protect and serve their fellow man as best they could. Because of that mission, Guardians revered history in the hopes that it would prevent them from repeating earlier mistakes.

Occasionally it did.

As Keeper of the Lore, the Earl of Brecon was responsible for these precious books and manuscripts. At the age of six, Gwynne had started to assist her father in maintaining the books. She had started with dusting, handling the volumes as carefully as if they were fine porcelain. Later she had copied crumbling texts onto new parchment and learned the secrets of preservation.

She scanned the shelves with regret, knowing she

would miss the books fiercely if she left the estate. Given the importance of the collection, a new librarian would be engaged soon, so she must prepare for the change by removing her father's personal possessions.

At least she would not be turned penniless into the world—the Guardians took care of their own. A position of some sort would be found for Robert Owens's unimpressive daughter. With luck, that position would be at Harlowe, the only home she had ever known. More than that, she scarcely dared hope for.

With a soft feline sound, her plump tabby, Athena, jumped onto the desk and curled into a ball. Comforted by the cat's presence, Gwynne settled at her father's desk and began searching the drawers for personal items. Keeping busy was essential if she was to prevent herself from mourning the past or brooding about her future.

She blinked back tears when she discovered her mother's locket in the small central drawer. Inside the oval case were miniatures of her parents painted at the time of their betrothal. They looked young and very much in love. Her father must have kept the locket here so he could study the picture of his wife and dream of happier times.

A reserved, scholarly man, Robert Owens had lived a quiet life at Harlowe Place. His one act of rebellion had been to marry Anna Wells against the wishes of both families. Her family had disowned her. The Owenses had accepted the match, though reluctantly. Guardians were encouraged to marry other Guardians, and Anna had been a mundane. Though beautiful and sweet-natured, she had no magic in her soul.

But the marriage had been a happy one, and Anna's death of a fever two years before had devastated her small family. Now Robert was gone as well, and Gwynne was alone. A pity she had no brother or sister to mourn with her.

The last drawer was almost empty when the door opened. The tapping of a cane told her that Emery, Lord Brecon, was approaching. She rose at the sight of his spare, splendidly garbed figure. Tall and distinguished, he had hair so thick and naturally white there was no need for powder. The earl was the center around which Harlowe revolved. His courtesy and learning were legendary, and he had always been kind to a little girl who loved books.

Seeing her, he said quietly, "It is done, my dear."

"My parents are together now, and at peace." As Gwynne spoke, the truth of her words resonated inside her. Occasionally she had such flashes of absolute knowledge, her only trace of Guardian power. It was not the same as calling the winds or scrying the future or healing the sick.

"We are both expected in the blue drawing room, but I hope you don't mind if I rest here for a few minutes before we go down. A bitter wind was blowing." Wearily the earl settled into the leather wing chair by the coal fire.

"I'm glad for the rain. A beautiful day would have been wrong for a funeral."

"There are no good days for funerals." His gaze touched the willow basket that she had filled with her father's eclectic mix of notes and objects. "You've been diligent, I see. The library will be the poorer when you leave."

So she was to be sent away. The shock of that made her dare to make a request that was her only chance to achieve her secret dream. "I have always loved working in the library. Indeed, my lord, I . . . I have hoped that you might engage me to act as librarian in my father's place. Though I have not his formal education, he tutored me well. I have worked with the books my whole life. My father said that no one was better at preservation, and I write a fine clear hand when copying fragile manuscripts. Or if not as the chief librarian, perhaps I might continue here as an assistant?"

"You are only seventeen, child," the earl said, startled. "Too young to bury yourself among books. Life must be lived, as well as studied between dusty pages. You will never marry if your beau can't find you."

She almost laughed aloud. His lordship could not have looked at her closely if he thought her marriageable. She had neither fortune nor beauty, and few of the local lads even noticed her existence. "I've met no young men who interest me as much as a good book or a good horse, my lord."

His bushy brows drew together. "I had thought to have this discussion with you later, but apparently now is the time. What are your plans and desires for your future?"

She raised her chin a fraction. "Nothing is set yet, but don't worry, I shan't stay and be a burden to you."

"As if you could be. Harlowe is your home, Gwynne, and you are always welcome here. Though if you prefer to leave . . . ?"

"A cousin of my father has written to offer me a home." She hesitated, then decided it behooved her to be honest, since she was determining the course of her whole future. "I don't mind working for my keep, but I would rather assist your new librarian than be an unpaid nursery maid to my cousin's children."

"You deserve more than to be a servant or to bury yourself in books." His pale blue eyes studied her with uncomfortable intensity. "Yet you are not ready for marriage. It is too soon."

Hearing the deeper meaning in his words, she said eagerly, "You have seen my future?"

"Only in the most general terms. Your path is clouded, with many possibilities. But my sister, Bethany, and I both sense that a great destiny awaits you. Great, and difficult."

A great destiny. "How can that be true when I have no power?"

"Destiny is quite separate from power—mundanes without a particle of magic have created most of the world's history. Not that you are without magic, Gwynne. Like a winter rose, you are merely slow in developing."

"I hope you are right, my lord." She closed her eyes for a moment, blinking back the tears that were near the surface today. As a child she had dreamed of being a great mage, a wielder of magic. When she reached womanhood, she awoke each day eager to see if power had blossomed within her, but in vain. She had only the kind of intuition that any mundane might claim.

"With or without magic, you are a rare and precious being. Never forget that."

As a man past seventy, he idealized youth, she guessed. But his words were warming. "You have taught me that all human life is rare and precious, Guardian and mundane alike. I shall not forget."

He linked his hands over the golden head of his cane, frowning with an uncertainty she'd never seen before. "There is a possibility that will not leave my mind no matter how I try to dismiss it. At first glance it seems absurd—and yet it feels right."

"Yes?" she said encouragingly. The idea that the lord of Harlowe had been thinking about Gwynne and her future was gratifying.

"I have considered asking you to become my wife."

She gasped, stunned speechless.

"The thought shocks you." He smiled wryly. "And well it should. Over fifty years of age lie between us. Marriage would be scandalous. Women would despise me for taking advantage of your innocence. Many men would be envious, and with justice. If the idea disgusts you . . ." He reached for his cane to stand, and she realized that he was embarrassed, even shy.

"No!" She stopped him with a quick gesture. "The idea is startling, but not . . . not disgusting." She studied his familiar face with fresh, amazed eyes. "You have been like the sun, stars, and skies over Harlowe, and I no more than a sparrow. I have trouble believing that you are not jesting."

"This is no jest. You need to learn more of the world before destiny sweeps you up." He fidgeted with his cane again. "It would not be a conventional marriage. I will not live many more years, so you would soon become a young widow of fortune and independence."

"Surely your children will object to you remarrying. They will consider it an insult to their mother, and they'll resent any legacy you might bequeath me." She thought of the earl's three grown children. They were pleasant enough to her as a minor member of the household, but the idea of young Gwynne Owens as their stepmother was indeed absurd.

"I am still the master of Harlowe House and may do what I choose," he said dryly. "But after I have spoken to them, they will not object. Marrying you would serve

Guardian interests, if you would be willing to accept me."

She tried to conceal her disappointment. "You are proposing because it is your duty to the Families, Lord Brecon?"

"While preparing you for your destiny benefits our people, I could do that without wedding you. I . . . I have always found pleasure in your company, Gwynne," he said haltingly. "The years since Charlotte died have been lonely. Your wit and warmth and grace would be a blessing beyond what an old man deserves. I would be honored and grateful if you would become my wife."

He meant it, she realized. This wonderful man of power and wisdom truly wanted her to marry him. For the first time in her life, she felt the presence of power—not the power of magic, but the even more ancient power of a woman to please a man.

Glowing with delight, she rose and offered him her hands. "You do me honor beyond anything I've ever imagined, my lord. If you truly wish it, I will gladly be your bride."

With a smile that took her breath away, he clasped her hands. "This is right for both of us, Gwynne, I know it."

So did she, with a certainty beyond reason. Impulsively she raised their joined hands and pressed a kiss on his gnarled knuckles. Already she was saddened to know how short their time together would be. But she would make sure that he didn't regret this decision.

Destiny could take care of itself. For now, she would concern herself with being a good wife.

Part One

Lord of Thunder

uncan Macrae inhaled deeply, intoxicated by the rampant scents of summer. Having arrived in London the night before after a long, grueling tour of the Continent, he would have preferred to spend the day sleeping, but his friend Lord Falconer had insisted on dragging him from London to Richmond. Now Duncan was glad he had come.

As they rounded the corner of their hostess's mansion, he scanned the women in gorgeous gowns who drifted across the emerald grass, flirting outrageously with even more gorgeous gentlemen. "The ladies of London are like a bouquet of exotic flowers."

Simon Malmain smiled lazily. "You'll find no females so exquisite in those wild Scottish hills of yours."

"Scottish lassies are just as lovely, and with far less artifice." Duncan glanced at the sky. "Lady Bethany chose her day well. Britain at its best."

"As you know, she has some Macrae blood. Enough to always choose a fine day for her entertainments despite our chancy English weather." Simon lovingly smoothed a wrinkle from his blue brocade sleeve. "If rain threatened, I'd not have worn this new coat. It was damnably expensive."

Duncan grinned. His friend mimicked the manners of a fop so perfectly that even Duncan, who had known him since the nursery, sometimes had trouble remembering that Simon was the most dangerous mage in Britain. Except, perhaps, for Duncan himself. "Where is Lady Bethany? I should pay my respects to our hostess. It's been years since I've seen her."

Simon shaded his eyes to scan the crowd. "Over there, below the gazebo."

The men turned their steps toward their hostess. Duncan eyed the lavish refreshment tables with interest, but eating must wait upon manners. As they neared the gazebo, he heard a string quartet inside, playing music as lighthearted as the day. "It's hard to believe that the shadow of civil war lies over Britain," Duncan said softly.

"That's why you're here," Simon said with equal softness. "And it's why I and others have spent so much time in Scotland. The future isn't fixed. If we Guardians build enough bridges between our nations, perhaps war can be averted."

"Perhaps, but the Scots and the English have been fighting for centuries, and such bloody habits are not easily broken." Duncan gave his friend a slanting glance. "The first time you and I met, we did our best to beat each other unconscious."

"Yes, but that wasn't based on the fact that you were a barbarian Scot," Simon said promptly. "I hated you because you were brought to the nursery during my lessons, and immediately proved that your Greek was better than mine."

Duncan smiled wryly as he remembered that first encounter. "I suppose that's better than hating each other for our nationalities."

The group they were approaching included half a

dozen men and women, with the rounded figure and silver hair of Lady Bethany Fox in the center. Though past her seventieth year, she had the posture and fine bones that had made her an acclaimed Beauty her entire life. She was a passionate gardener, a doting grandmother, and the most powerful sorceress in Britain.

Lady Bethany laughed at something said by the woman at her side. Duncan shifted his gaze, and stopped dead in his tracks, entranced by Lady Beth's companion. Tall and elegant, she wore a creamy gown of modest cut, yet her demure garb couldn't disguise a lushly curving figure designed to drive men mad. As if that wasn't alluring enough, her straw bonnet accented a classically featured face that sparkled with humor and intelligence. This was a dangerous woman.

"Dear God," he breathed as thunder cracked in the distance. "Helen of Troy."

"I beg your pardon?" Following Duncan's gaze, Simon said, "Ah, Lady Brecon. A lovely lass, but launch a thousand ships? I think not. Five or six at the most."

"Ten thousand ships. More. She is like an ancient enchantress whose glance could drive men to madness." Duncan gave thanks that Lady Brecon was unaware of his devouring gaze. In the full flower of her womanhood, she was so compelling that he could not have looked away to save his life. "Lord Brecon's wife, you say? The earl has good taste."

"She's not wife to the present Brecon, but widow to the old one. You were on the Continent when they married, but it was something of a scandal since she was only seventeen and Brecon was over seventy. She seemed rather a plain girl at the time."

"Plain?" Duncan watched as the lady turned her attention to a languid young fop in gold brocade. The pure curve of her throat mesmerized him, and that luminous skin begged to be caressed. *"Her?"*

"She blossomed during the marriage—a wealthy husband often has that effect. But she and Brecon seemed most sincerely devoted."

Trust Simon to know all the gossip. Absurdly grateful to learn she was a widow, Duncan tried to remember when the fifth Lord Brecon had died. A little over a year ago, he thought. "She must have legions of suitors now that she's out of mourning."

"She has many admirers, me among them, but I've never seen her favor any in particular." Simon cocked one brow. "I haven't seen you like this since we went to the gypsy horse fair and you spotted that gray hunter."

His friend was right. Duncan had been sixteen when he saw that horse, and his reaction was the same as today when he saw Lady Brecon: He had to have her.

He drew a slow breath, reminding himself that he wasn't sixteen anymore, the lady might be a shrew, or she might find him as alarming as most women did. One might purchase a desirable horse, but women were more difficult. "If she was Brecon's wife, she must be a Guardian?"

"Yes, one of the Owenses. She has no power to speak of, but she grew up in the library at Harlowe and is a notable scholar of Guardian lore. Since her husband died, she lives here in Richmond with Lady Bethany." Simon grinned. "Hard to believe they're sisters-in-law. The dowager countess looks like Lady Bethany's granddaughter."

If the lady was bookish, it didn't show. From her powdered hair to her dainty slippers, she was an exquisite confection designed to ornament the highest social circles.

Thunder sounded again, this time closer. Duncan's eyes narrowed. Directness was out of place in aristocratic

London, but it was the only way he knew. "Introduce me
to the lady, Simon, so I can learn if she is as perfect as she
appears."

*   *   *

Gwynne smiled at the appallingly bad sonnet Sir Anselm
White had recited to her. Though his heart was in the
right place, his verses were leagues away in the wrong direction. "You flatter me, Sir Anselm. My eyes are light
brown, not 'sapphires bluer than the summer sky.'"

His languid gaze came briefly into focus as he studied
the color of her eyes. "Golden coins that outshine the
sun!"

She guessed that a metaphor had fallen on the poor
man's head when he was an infant and he had never recovered. Since a small amount of Sir Anselm's poetry
went a long way, she was glad to hear Bethany say, "Lord
Falconer, how good to see you again."

Giving Sir Anselm a last smile before turning away,
Gwynne greeted the newcomer warmly. "Simon, my favorite fop!" She extended her hand. "You've been ne-
glecting me, you rogue."

One of the handsomest men in London, Falconer was
always worthy of admiration. Today his fair hair was
tied back with a blue riband the same shade as his brocade coat, both an exact match for his azure eyes. That
embroidered silver waistcoat was more deserving of son-
nets than any part of Gwynne's body. He could give Sir
Anselm lessons in languid elegance—and underneath the
elegance, he was a glittering blade sheathed in silk.

"A fop?" He sighed dramatically. "You wound me, my
lady." He bowed over her hand with consummate grace,
looking not at all wounded. "Allow me to present my

friend Lord Ballister. You'll have heard of him, I think, but he's been traveling abroad for some time and says you've never had the opportunity to meet."

All Guardians had heard of Lord Ballister. Chieftain of the Macraes of Dunrath, among the Families he was known as Britain's finest weather mage. Some said he was even more powerful than his ancestor, Adam Macrae, who had conjured the great gale that destroyed the Spanish Armada.

Since he stood with the sun behind him, she could see little except the silhouette of a powerful, commanding figure. "It's a pleasure to meet you, Lord Ballister."

"The pleasure is mine." Ballister bowed.

A cloud darkened the sun as he straightened, enabling Gwynne to see his face clearly. His storm gray gaze struck her like lightning. *Destiny* . . . The word echoed in her mind, along with a dizzying sense that the world had changed irrevocably.

She scolded herself for too much imagination. The world was exactly as it had been. The grass was green, Bethany was composed, and Falconer his usual exquisite self. As for Ballister, he looked normal enough. Though his height and broad shoulders drew attention, his face was too craggy to be called handsome, and his navy blue coat and buff waistcoat were plain by the standards of aristocratic London.

Only his intense gray eyes were remarkable. She remembered a natural history demonstration she had once witnessed. The lecturer had said that electricity was a wild, mysterious force that could not be controlled and which no one understood. Surely that was electricity in Ballister's eyes, and in the very air that danced between them. . . .

She had spent too much time listening to Sir Anselm—

his metaphors were contagious. "You have been on the Continent, Lord Ballister?" she asked politely.

"I arrived back in London only yesterday. This morning Falconer dragged me from my bed, swearing that Lady Bethany wouldn't mind if I came uninvited."

"The lad would have been in trouble if he hadn't brought you," Bethany said severely. "I hope you'll be staying in London for a time, Ballister?"

"Yes, though I do long to return home to Scotland." After a moment's hesitation, he said gravely, "I was acquainted with the late Lord Brecon. In learning, wisdom, and gentlemanliness, he was an example to us all. Despite the time that has passed, I hope you will both accept my condolences on your loss."

As Lady Bethany murmured thanks, Gwynne swallowed hard, unexpectedly moved by his sympathy. "Thank you for your kind words. I was very fortunate to have shared my lord's final years."

Ballister inclined his head in respectful agreement before saying, "Lady Bethany, may I steal your lovely companion to show me the gardens?"

"Please do," Bethany said, her expression thoughtful. "That will leave me free to flirt outrageously with Falconer. Gwynne, be sure to show Ballister the parterre."

Glad for the chance to talk more with the Scotsman, she took his arm. Though she was a tall woman, he made her feel small and fragile.

The parterre was lower on the hill, near the river. As they crossed the velvety lawn, he said, "I understand that you live here with Lady Bethany?"

"Yes, she invited me to join her after Brecon's death."

"It was too difficult to stay on at Harlowe?"

Surprised at his understanding, she glanced up, and was caught by his eyes again. The gray was changeable, warm now rather than intense. "Yes, though not because of the new earl and his wife. I have the use of the dower house whenever I wish to be at Harlowe, but Lady Bethany and I were both in need of companionship, so I was pleased to accept her offer." Despite the difference in their ages, they had been new widows together. It had deepened their existing bond.

As Gwynne and her companion entered the parterre, an elaborate pattern of carefully cropped shrubs, Ballister halted and studied the pattern with narrowed eyes. "This isn't only decorative, is it? The pattern is designed to magnify power."

Gwynne automatically glanced around to see if anyone was within earshot. The Families had survived through the centuries by not drawing unwelcome attention to their abilities. To be different was dangerous. One of the first things Guardian children learned was to preserve secrets; never must they mention power in front of outsiders. But Ballister had been well trained, and there was no one near. "Yes, there's a power point here. That's why Lady Bethany and her husband bought this property. The circle in the center of the parterre can be used for rituals."

"I can feel the earth energy tugging at me. Can you?"

She knew what he was asking. "I have no real power. I can sense atmosphere and energy and emotion a little, but no more than any sensitive mundane." Even the happy years of marriage and her acceptance into the Guardian community had not eliminated her wistful regret for what she lacked. "What of you, Lord Ballister? You're called the Lord of Thunder, the Lord of Storms. Did your power manifest early?"

"Not until I was on the brink of manhood, but I always loved weather—the more dramatic, the better. When I was barely old enough to walk, my mother found me on top of the castle tower in the middle of a thunderstorm, my arms flung out to the sky as I howled with laughter." He smiled reminiscently. "I found that a mother's anger was another kind of tempest."

Gwynne laughed. "Since you're a Macrae, I assume your parents recognized early that you were a weather mage."

"Aye, it runs in the family, and where better for us to learn than in Scotland, when the weather changes every five minutes with or without a mage's help?" He smiled wryly. "No one even noticed my successes and failures when I was learning."

"I wonder if the Scottish climate is why the best weather workers are always Macraes?"

"Perhaps. There may be something in the air of Dunrath that enhances that kind of magic." He grimaced. "It enhances our weaknesses, too. The stronger a weather mage, the more we are weakened by the touch of iron, and a damnable nuisance it is. Most of the weapons in our armory have hilts of wood or brass."

"I've read about the connection between weather-working and sensitivity to iron. Does iron produce a general weakness, or does it merely block your power?"

"It varies." Changing the subject, he said, "Falconer told me you're an expert on Guardian lore."

"Since my father was the Harlowe librarian, I learned early to catalog and read the archives and write essays about obscure facts and correlations." She smiled wryly. "I know everything about power except what it feels like to have it."

"Knowledge is as important as power," he said seriously. "It is knowledge of history and of our own mistakes that gives us what wisdom we have. The work of Guardian scholars like you is the framework that helps us fulfill our vows."

"What a nice way to think of my work." Curious about him, she asked, "Do you travel a great deal, Lord Ballister? I gather you have been away from Scotland for some time."

"Too long." They had reached the riverbank, where a short pier poked into the Thames. "Three years ago the council requested that I act as envoy to Families in other nations. My journeys were essential and interesting, but I missed my home."

The Guardian Council was formed of the wisest, most powerful mages in Britain. Lady Bethany was currently its chief, the first among equals. Its suggestions were not refused lightly. "Did experiencing the weather of other lands compensate for being so long from Dunrath?"

"The basic principles of wind and cloud and rain are the same everywhere, but the patterns and nuances are different. The winds sing with different voices." His voice deepened. "I would like to show you the winds of Italy, my lady. Warm, sensual, soft as a lover's sigh."

A gust of wind snapped around them, swirling Gwynne's skirts. She had learned much about flirtation since her marriage, for many men offered gallantries to the young wife of an old earl. She knew when flirting was a lighthearted game, and when a man had more serious aims.

Lord Ballister was deeply, alarmingly serious.

She released his arm under the pretense of straightening her skirts. "I had hoped that my husband and I would travel, but his health did not permit it."

"Imagine yourself in Paris or Rome or Athens, Lady Brecon, and perhaps that will help your vision come true." He gazed at her like a starving man who eyed a feast. Her breathing quickened. Who would have thought that being devoured might be an intriguing prospect?

The wind gusted again and strands of his raven black

hair broke free of their confinement. Gwynne felt an impulse to brush the tendrils back. It would be pleasing to feel the texture of that strong, tanned cheek. . . .

Abruptly she recognized the electric pull between them as desire. She had loved her husband deeply and she was woman enough to appreciate a handsome man, but this hungry urgency was entirely different, and not at all comfortable.

A blast of rain struck her face and half soaked her gown. Breaking away from Ballister's gaze, she saw that a low storm cloud was sweeping over the river, the leading edge of rain as sharply defined as the wall of a building. "Where did this come from? Lady Bethany said the weather would be fine all afternoon." She caught up her skirts and prepared to bolt for cover.

"Damnation!" He looked at the sky, rain pouring over his face. "I'm sorry, my lady. I haven't been paying sufficient attention to our surroundings."

She almost laughed when she realized that the Lord of Storms hadn't noticed the change in the weather. The guests farther up the hill had seen the advancing rain and were racing for shelter or crowding into the gazebo while servants attempted to cover the food. "Nor have I, and my gown will pay for my carelessness."

"Don't leave." He held up a commanding hand.

On the verge of flight, she hesitated when his eyes closed. Despite his saturated hair and garments, his concentration radiated like heat from a fire.

She caught her breath as the storm cloud split and rolled away to both sides, avoiding the garden. Within seconds the rain stopped. Amazed, she watched as the clouds dissipated. The sun reappeared and for an instant a rainbow arched over Ballister's head. She caught her breath. This was the Lord of Storms indeed.

The rainbow faded, even more ephemeral than the storm. On the hill guests laughed and stopped retreating, ready to enjoy the party again.

Ballister wiped water from his face. "The weather here is not so chancy as in Scotland, but it's unpredictable enough that a bit of rain never calls attention to itself."

His tone was too casual. Making an intuitive leap, she said, "You didn't overlook that storm. You caused it, didn't you?"

He looked embarrassed. "If I'm careless, I can attract ill weather when my attention is otherwise engaged."

Amused, she brushed at her hair, where the wind and rain had pulled a lock loose from her restrained hairstyle. "What could be so interesting at a lawn party as to attract such a fierce little tempest?"

His gaze darkened. The full force of those eyes was . . . dangerous. They could make a woman forget herself, and all good sense.

"You, of course. There is power between us. You feel it also, I know you do." He touched her wet hair where a few bright glints showed through the powder. His fingertips grazed her bare throat as he caressed the errant lock. "What is the natural color of your hair?" he murmured.

Her breathing became difficult, as if the laces of her corset had been drawn too tight. The sensation was as unnerving as his powerful masculinity. As a widow and a Guardian, she had more independence than most women, and she had developed a taste for it. Ignoring his question, she said, "Power sounds like no more than another name for lust, Lord Ballister."

Deliberately she turned away, breaking the spell cast by his eyes. "I've enjoyed talking with you, but I have no wish for an affair. Good afternoon, sir. It's time for me to go indoors and change to dry clothing."

"Wait!" He caught her wrist, and lightning tingled across her skin.

Part of her wanted to turn back, but the part that needed to escape was much stronger. She jerked free of his grip and raced away, skimming up the hill and hoping he would not pursue her.

He didn't. When she neared the house, she turned and saw that he still stood on the pier, his brooding gaze following her. She had a moment of absolute knowledge that he was not gone from her life.

Expression set, she entered the house and climbed the stairs to her rooms. Now that she was away from Ballister, it was harder to remember why she found him so disquieting. His behavior had not been improper. It was his forceful *self* that had sent her haring off to safety.

She entered her bedroom, and was stopped in her tracks by the image reflected in her tall mirror. Over the years of her marriage, she had become a lady worthy of her husband: modest, discreet, as well dressed as a countess should be. Emery had taken pride in her appearance as surely as he had enjoyed their companionship and mutual love of books.

But the woman in the mirror was no longer that demure wife and widow. Her eyes were bright, her color high, and her wet gown clung wantonly.

She touched a lock of damp hair that fell across her shoulder, disliking the heavy pomade used to make the powder stick. She had never enjoyed powdering her hair, but she started doing it after her marriage because her natural hair color was too brash, too vulgar, for a countess. Powdered hair made her look more refined and mature. More suitable to be her husband's wife.

Ballister's very presence brought color into her life. He was a magnetic, intriguing man, and he looked at her as if she was the most beautiful woman ever born. His regard had been exciting, and yet . . .

Athena jumped from the bed and trotted over to press herself suggestively against Gwynne's ankle. She scooped up the elderly cat and cuddled her close, scratching the furry neck and belly. "Athena, I just met a man who made me feel like a mouse pursued by a cat. And not a sweet, friendly cat like you, either." More of a tiger.

She drifted into her sitting room, where a dozen or more books awaited her attention. There were more books in this one room than in some manor houses. On her desk lay the journal of an Elizabethan mage, a Latin treatise on spell craft written by a Flemish sorceress, a partially burned herbalist's workbook that she was trying to reconstruct. All her projects required slow, painstaking care. It was hard to imagine her work in the same breath with Ballister.

She could feel the passion burning in him, and like a moth, she was drawn to the flame. But his fire had the power to destroy the calm, ordered life she loved. A widow could have affairs if she was discreet, but an affair with Ballister would change her in ways she couldn't even imagine. She must keep him at a distance. Soon he would return to Scotland, and he would take his storms with him.

Yet as she rang for her maid, she thought she heard again the whispered word, *"Destiny . . ."*

Two

*M*ind whirling, Duncan walked slowly up the hill, barely aware of the chattering guests around him. All his thoughts were centered on Lady Brecon, who was as charming and intelligent as she was beautiful. Though she was wary of him, she wasn't repulsed. On the contrary . . .

Simon's dry voice sounded at his shoulder. "Now that you've driven the lady away, it's time to return to London."

Duncan nodded, glad Simon was ready to go. He had too much on his mind to socialize, and he had been drained by the surge of power needed to divert the storm. He'd been a damned fool for becoming so lost in Lady Brecon's smile that he hadn't even noticed he was drawing storm clouds.

As they took their leave of Lady Bethany, she murmured, "Careless of you, Ballister. A good thing you cleared that storm. I would have been most displeased if you had ruined my lawn party."

He flushed under her shrewd gaze, suspecting she knew exactly why he had committed such a faux pas. After bowing, he followed Simon to the Falconer carriage. He took the backward-facing seat, but before he could start asking about Lady Brecon, his friend snapped, "What did you do to Gwynne that sent her racing away like that?"

"Lady Brecon's given name is Gwynne?" Duncan tried out the name. It was different, like she was, with a sound both smooth and definite.

"Short for Gwyneth, and don't try to change the subject." The carriage lurched and Simon grabbed a handle to steady himself. "If you made some vulgar proposal, you're fortunate she isn't the sort to push a man into the river. I might be less tolerant."

Too late Duncan remembered that Simon was one of the widow's admirers, and his use of her given name suggested a degree of intimacy. "I'm sorry. I didn't realize you were seriously interested in her." Though he realized uneasily that even if Simon wanted the lady for himself, Duncan would be unable to step back.

"I'm not courting her, but she is a friend and a gentle lady. I will not see her debauched by any man, much less one I consider a friend."

Duncan's own anger began to rise. "You should know better than to think that of me. My intentions are entirely honorable."

There was a stunned silence before Simon said incredulously, "You wish to marry a woman you've barely met? Surely even you are not so impulsive."

The words stopped Duncan cold. Marriage? He hadn't thought that far—merely seen her and pursued her like a mountain storm. Marriage?

But he didn't want a casual affair or a bloodless friendship, and dishonoring her was out of the question. Which meant— "I believe that I do. Is the idea so outrageous? The elders have been urging me to marry for years. Lady Brecon and I are well suited by birth, age, and fortune. Why shouldn't I offer for her?"

Simon's anger was gone, replaced by a frown. "A mage of your power is encouraged to marry a woman who has power of her own, to strengthen the blood."

"Encouraged, yes, but it's not compulsory. You said yourself that Lady Brecon—Gwynne—is an accomplished scholar of Guardian lore, a respected member of our community. It's not as if I want to wed a mundane."

Simon gazed out the window of the rocking carriage, still frowning. "Even if she is mad enough to accept you, I have trouble imagining an English gentlewoman in the wilds of Scotland. Would she be willing to live at Dunrath? Would your clansmen accept an English mistress?"

Simon's points were legitimate, but Duncan refused to be swayed. "You're thinking with your head. Use your inner senses."

"Have you done so?"

"I don't think I can," Duncan said frankly. "I've no great talent for scrying. Even if I did, my emotions would get in the way of a clear reading on this subject. As soon as I saw her, I felt that we belonged together. I don't think that was a delusion." He paused, then said reluctantly, "Though it's possible I'm fooling myself."

"I'm glad you're still sane enough to recognize that." Simon pulled a watch from his waistcoat pocket. The massive gold timepiece and chain were handsome, a legacy from his father, but the real value was hidden. Instead of snapping open the front to reveal the time, he pushed the stem down and clicked it to the left.

The back sprang open to reveal a disk of pale, shimmering opal. It was a scrying glass, and the subtle, shifting colors and shapes could suggest images from past, present, or future to someone with the skill to read them.

Simon had a great deal of skill. His expression became remote as he relaxed and opened his mind to what might come. Duncan watched with hawklike intensity, eager to hear what his friend might see.

"There's certainly a great deal of energy around this meeting," Simon said at last. "Gwynne will be very important to you, though I can't say if it will be as your true love or your mortal enemy." His brows drew together. "Perhaps both."

"That sounds splendidly ominous." Gwynne might be his mortal enemy? Impossible. "Do you see us marrying?"

Simon contemplated the scrying stone again, then sucked in his breath sharply. "I see the shadow of war over you both. Another Jacobite rebellion, I think. And soon."

"Surely not," Duncan protested. James Francis Edward Stuart was considered by his followers to be the true ruler of Britain, but almost sixty years had passed since his father had been driven from the throne. "The Jacobites tried to restore the Stuarts thirty years ago, and failed miserably. Even if the Old Pretender's son wants to play at rebellion, he won't find the support he would need."

"Perhaps the French or Spanish will lend him troops and ships to see what mischief can be raised at England's back door. Even without foreign aid, I suspect that if Prince Charles Edward raises his standard in Scotland, thousands of Highlanders will follow him from sheer bloody-mindedness."

"Highlanders aren't bloody-minded." Duncan fell silent, thinking about Simon's words. "They care little for who sits on the throne in London, but Highlanders are loyal. If the chiefs declare for the prince, the clans will follow."

Simon studied the scrying stone again, his expression deeply troubled. "I've sensed the possibility of civil war for some time, but never so clearly as now. And . . . if there is another Jacobite uprising, I think you and Gwynne will play key roles."

"I can't imagine how," Duncan said, surprised. "Gwynne is English, and even though I'm a Scot, I'm no Jacobite. If there is another rebellion, I will support King George against the Stuarts. What sane man wouldn't?"

Simon regarded him gravely. "You speak with your head, not your heart. Though we are trained to be objective, we are still human, with the passions of our kind. Be careful, Duncan. A storm is coming that even you will not be able to tame."

Duncan shifted uneasily, knowing there was truth to his friend's words. Though in the long run Scotland's future lay with England, he was a Scot, proud of his nation's ancient heritage of freedom and independence. "If such a storm strikes, I know where my duty lies. For now, I'm more interested in affairs of the heart."

His friend's expression eased. "Gwynne will not be easily won."

"If I fail, it will not be for lack of trying."

"It is not enough to try hard. You must also try well." Simon closed the watch and tucked it back inside his waistcoat. "Under Gwynne's mild demeanor, she has a mind of her own. I understand that Brecon left her a comfortable income so she had no need to take another husband. I've never sensed that she wanted one." His mouth twisted without humor. "If I had thought she was available, I might have . . . reconsidered my relationship with her."

Simon's description made Gwynne seem like a cool woman, which was not the impression Duncan had received from her. But then, Simon was a cool man. Perhaps that was why he and Gwynne had struck no sparks together. "Do you have any suggestions on how to win her?"

Simon's smile became genuine. "That's easy. Court her with books."

"An excellent idea. I have some rare volumes I found

on the Continent." Mentally he reviewed the titles he'd acquired, wondering which would be the best.

"Just don't try any love spells. I suspect Gwynne has enough power to sense if you tried that, and she would not like it."

"No magic," Duncan promised. Besides, love spells could only enhance what already existed. The attraction between them was powerful, so no enhancement was needed, particularly since Gwynne seemed skittish about that pull. He would court her with books, flowers, poetry, and patience—the gifts of a civilized man.

Not that he was truly civilized—but if that's what it took to win the lady, he'd do his best.

*   *   *

Lady Bethany glided into the breakfast parlor, delicately concealing a yawn behind one small hand. "Good morning, my dear. Are you going riding after you break your fast?"

Gwynne filled a porcelain cup with tea and set it at Bethany's place. "After being with so many people yesterday, I've a desire for a good gallop."

The older woman took her seat and sipped at the steaming beverage. "Another fine day. I would have been most provoked with your new admirer if he hadn't dismissed his storm so efficiently. He's certainly smitten with you."

"He will have to recover without my help." Gwynne placed a bit of egg under the table for Athena, who was waiting patiently to be spoiled.

Bethany's silvery brows arched. "I had thought the interest was mutual."

Gwynne started to protest, then stopped. It was impossible to lie to Bethany, though she didn't know if it was the older woman's Guardian power or simply age, wisdom, and having raised four children. "He is intriguing, but he has too much power. I found him . . . oppressive. Perhaps if I had power of my own . . ." She shrugged. "But I don't, so Lord Ballister shall have to find a new object of admiration."

Bethany looked stricken. "I hadn't realized I've been oppressing you with my power for all these years. I offer you my deepest apologies."

Gwynne laughed. "You are never oppressive. Your power is female, and subtle as the first flowers of spring."

"You find Falconer alarming? He has enormous power, yet I had thought you were friends." Bethany added a sliver of ham to Athena's breakfast and was rewarded with an audible purr.

"Very well, it isn't power in general that overwhelms me, it's Ballister himself," Gwynne admitted. "He is . . . compelling, but also disturbing." She hesitated, wondering how to explain. "I am very happy in my life. I don't want to give that up for the highs and lows that would accompany a man known as the Lord of Thunder."

"Your life with him would certainly be different." The older woman's gaze was compassionate. "Would that be all bad? Perhaps you would have children."

Gwynne's gaze dropped and she buttered another piece of bread. "How absurd it is to talk about marriage with a man I've scarcely met. I doubt that his interest in me is matrimonial. When he weds, he'll choose a lady who is a better match for him."

"Don't be so sure that you aren't. You have strengths of your own." Bethany smiled fondly. "Guardians often know quickly when they meet the right mate. My dearest Matthew offered marriage before we had finished our first dance. And if he hadn't asked me, I would have asked him!"

Gwynne concealed her wistful envy. Though she would like power for its own sake, even more she yearned for the profound closeness that some Guardian couples found together because of their heightened sensitivity to emotion. Bethany had known that with her husband, just as Emery had known it with his first wife. He had been a kind and loving husband to his child bride, but she had yearned for a deeper intimacy.

She was casting about for a different topic when a footman entered. On his silver tray rested an elegantly decorated box with a small nosegay fastened to the lid. "This has just arrived for you, Lady Brecon."

She accepted the box, wondering who might have sent it. After sniffing the fragrant blossoms, she opened the box and found a book with a note resting on top. "It's from Ballister," she said, bemused. "He apologizes for his ill-bred behavior yesterday, and begs me to accept this small gift as a token of his regret."

"Handsomely done. He must have sent his messenger at dawn for you to receive this at breakfast."

"You see how overwhelming he is? He did nothing ill-bred yesterday, and certainly no gift needs to be sent as an apology." Setting the note aside, she took out the book, then gasped. "Dear heavens, it's Runculo's *Dissertation on Shape Shifting*! I've always yearned to read it, but I don't think there's a copy in England."

"Ballister might be overwhelming, but he's no fool," Bethany said with amusement. Finishing her bread and tea, she rose from her seat. "I'll send a message to the stables that your ride will be delayed."

Gwynne scarcely heard the older woman leave because she was already pulling paper and pencil from a drawer in the sideboard, as well as spectacles to help her with the faded lettering. Since she never knew when the urge to make notes would strike, she liked having writing materials at hand.

Scarcely able to control her excitement, she opened the slim volume, which was bound in scarred red leather. Almost two hundred years old, it was written in Latin. Luckily she read that, as well as several other languages. A scholar of magic needed diverse skills.

She began to take notes. Shape shifting was a very rare magical talent, and little had been written about it. Fascinating observations Runculo had made. . . .

She returned to awareness with a start when the footman entered. "My lady, you have a most insistent visitor."

Following the servant was Lord Ballister. Athena took one look at the newcomer and vanished under the sideboard. Even dressed as a country gentleman rather than a lord and sorcerer, Ballister drew the eye, and not only because of his splendid physique. Perhaps it was his confidence. He looked as if he would be at ease anywhere, secure in the knowledge that his strength and intelligence were equal to any challenge.

With surprise, she realized that confidence was what she had seen as arrogance the day before. Perhaps being in the middle of a crowd had made her oversensitive and she had judged him too harshly.

She glanced at the mantel clock and saw that almost two hours had passed since she had opened the book. Time to remember that she was a lady.

She took off her spectacles and rose to her feet, "Thank you for your gift, Lord Ballister. I should not accept anything so rare and valuable, but I don't think I can bring myself to give it back."

His return smile was so admiring that it warmed her to her toes. "I'm glad the book pleases you. Did I give you enough time to sample its contents?"

"You brought the book yourself instead of sending it by messenger!" she said as realization struck. "Why didn't you give it to me in person?"

"I suspected that as soon as you discovered Runculo, you would forget all else." His smile deepened, inviting her to laugh with him at the giddy madness of book loving. "After delivering the book, I rode up Richmond Hill and breakfasted at the Star and Garter so I could admire the view of the Thames Valley."

"I fear that you're right," she said ruefully. "If you had handed me the book, I would have opened it and forgotten your existence. Now that I've read enough to slake my first thirst, I can remember my manners. Shall I ring for fresh tea, or perhaps a pot of coffee?"

His glance touched her riding habit. "If you are going for a ride this morning, may I join you?"

Gwynne hesitated, realizing that if she accepted his offer, she would be agreeing to further their acquaintanceship. She had decided yesterday that would be unwise. But her mare needed exercise, and Ballister seemed less alarming today. Less . . . predatory. How dangerous could a fellow book lover be?

"I can tell you of other books I found on the Continent," he said coaxingly.

She laughed. "How can I refuse such an offer?" She glanced out the window and saw that the morning had clouded up. "Particularly if the sun is going to come out and make this a perfect day for riding."

He grinned. "I have a feeling that the sky is about to clear over Richmond."

Chuckling, she placed the book, spectacles, and writing materials back in the sideboard drawer. There were advantages to keeping company with a storm lord.

Three

*D*uncan had known that Gwynne loved books, and she had been an enchanting sight as she peered over her spectacles when he entered the breakfast room. He wasn't surprised to see that she was equally enchanting on horseback. Her seat and posture were perfect and her flowing green habit as stylish as it was flattering.

What he hadn't expected was that she would be a bruising rider. As soon as they entered the royal park of Richmond, not far from Lady Bethany's home, Gwynne called out, "Race you to where the trail bends."

Then she was off. Her pretty mare was as swift as she was decorative. It took a moment for Duncan to collect himself and take off in pursuit. Full skirts snapping in the wind and laughter floating behind, Gwynne set a pace that any man would envy.

He had half expected that when he saw her again she would be less dazzling than his memory. But he was wrong—she was even more alluring than the image that kept him tossing and turning half the night. When he walked into the breakfast parlor and saw her bending over the Runculo, his heart had twisted with yearning.

As he urged the gelding faster, he wondered what made her so irresistible. Certainly she was beautiful, with a lush feminine figure and features that were just imperfect enough to be entrancing. But he had never been a man to be unbalanced by mere beauty. Intelligence had always attracted him, and that she had in full measure, and charm as well. Yet she was more than the sum of her parts.

Gwynne reached the bend in the trail and slowed her mount, her expression radiant and her cheeks pink from her gallop. "I'm so glad Lady Bethany's home is in Richmond. I would hate to live in town and not be able to do this."

He fell into place beside her as they proceeded around the bend. "You ride like a champion, Lady Brecon."

Her brows arched. "You and that long-legged gelding could have overtaken us, I think, but you chose to be gallant and let us win."

What a remarkably direct woman she was. And how refreshing he found that. "Perhaps we might have won, but I'm honestly not sure. Your mare has hooves of fire."

"Bella likes the sound of that." Gwynne patted the horse's neck affectionately.

He gave her a sharp glance. "Can you sense your mare's moods?"

Gwynne's animation dimmed. "Not really. It was only a manner of speaking."

Even as a small child Duncan had been absolutely sure that he would be a great mage. What if he had reached manhood and discovered within himself . . . nothing? What if there had been no transcendent flowering of magic in his soul despite his youthful conviction that power was his destiny?

The thought was so disturbing that he wanted to enfold Gwynne in his arms to offer comfort for her crushing disappointment. But it was too soon to touch her, because when that happened he would have trouble letting her go. Though patience came hard, he must take the time to build a bridge of words and shared interests. Simon had been right about courting her with books. He would give the lady every rare volume he'd located on the Continent if that's what it took to win her.

It had also been Simon, the master of self-control, who had suggested that he deliberately tamp down his power before calling on Gwynne today. At the best of times he could be intimidating, and when they met he'd become so unbalanced he must have been a bonfire of searing energy. She was Guardian enough to sense that, even if not consciously. His strategy had worked, because she was much more relaxed with him today than the day before.

She glanced up at the sky. "It's still rather overcast."

"I do believe the sky is starting to clear." It was an easy matter for him to expand his power up into the clouds, dissolving some and sending others away. A thin ray of sunshine shafted to the ground around Gwynne, warming her skin to luscious cream before spreading over both of them like a canopy.

She raised her face to the sun, eyes closing with delight. "That's amazing. Is it difficult?"

"Compared to summoning a thunderstorm, it's child's play." An idea struck him. "I suspect that you can affect a small cloud yourself. Pick one and concentrate on it, willing it to vanish."

She obeyed, her brow furrowing with concentration. For several minutes there was no sound but the rhythmic thump of hooves on the soft trail. "The cloud is gone!" she gasped. "It just melted into nothingness. How did I do that? Not only do I have no power, but there's very little Macrae blood in my family. No Owens has ever been a weather worker."

"Everyone has at least a spark of power, even the most stubborn, unimaginative mundanes. You may not be gifted by the standards of the Families, but surely you have more than a spark of magic in you. Enough to touch a cloud."

"I *liked* doing that!" Her face glowed with excitement. "How wonderful it must be to wield power as easily as you. Though I shouldn't be encouraging you to use power frivolously. It's against all Guardian training."

"True, but this is only a very small misuse of energy." He smiled wryly. "And a man will do a great deal to impress a woman."

"Is that what you're trying to do?" Her gaze was very direct.

"You know very well that's my intent." He pulled his horse in a half circle and halted so that he was facing her. Their gazes locked and held, challenging, testing, judging. He could drown in those golden eyes, with their depths of wisdom and surprising innocence.

She broke the silence. "I'll not be seduced, Lord Ballister. The fact that I am a widow does not mean I'm ripe for casual bed sport."

"Why do you assume my motives are dishonorable?" He hesitated only an instant before following his instinct that directness was the best way to deal with her. "It's past time for me to take a wife, but until yesterday, I never saw a woman who I could imagine in that place."

She gasped, her hands tightening on her reins. The mare sidled nervously. "But you don't even know me!"

"Don't I, Gwynne?" He used his softest voice, as if he were luring a bird to his hand. "Surely you know that among Guardians, knowledge can come in an instant."

"I am a Guardian in name only. And I have not given you permission to call me Gwynne."

"Very well, Lady Brecon," he agreed peaceably. "But in my thoughts, you are Gwynne."

Looking impatient, she set her horse moving again. "I don't even know your given name, Lord Ballister. Not that I would use it if I did."

"It's Duncan, an old Scottish name." He grinned. "Not that you need use it."

A smile twitched at her full lips. "You honor me with your regard, sir, but you should find a different object for your affections. I have no desire to marry. If I did, I wouldn't choose a Scot who would take me so far from my home."

"Scotland is not so barbaric as you might think. Edinburgh is a city of learning and culture where you would find many friends." He could imagine her sparkling in the center of a salon of Scottish intellectuals, her wit as bright as her beauty.

"My work at Harlowe would suffer if I were so distant. It's awkward enough to live half a day away." Her lips curved up. "You're the one who pointed out how important it is to catalog and understand the lore of the Families."

"Dunrath has the finest library in Scotland, and I'd welcome a wife who expanded it. I found some amazing books on the Continent," he said temptingly. "And of course we would visit London regularly."

A flicker of interest showed before she made an exasperated noise. "Stop trying to entice me! You may think marriage a fine idea, but I don't."

"Why not?"

Her brows arched. "A lady need only refuse a proposal, I believe. Reasons aren't required."

"You care no more for such conventions than I do," he retorted. "Convince me that marriage is a bad idea and I shall depart with a bow and regrets, but you'll have trouble ridding yourself of me when I think we would suit admirably."

Her eyes narrowed. "The simple fact is that I have no wish to marry. My life now is exactly the way I want it. Why would I choose to be subjugated to a man's will?"

"Was Lord Brecon so demanding that you lost the taste for matrimony?" he asked, startled. "I would not have guessed that."

"On the contrary, he was the most indulgent of mates." She concentrated on guiding her mount around a soggy patch of ground. "But Brecon was a rare man. I doubt I would be so lucky again."

"Among the Families, women have always been equal—it's part of our Celtic heritage. Scotland is full of strong-minded females who can meet any challenge. I think you would be happier there than you've ever been."

"When a wife has power, she might be her husband's equal. But I don't, while you're one of the strongest mages in Britain," she said bluntly. "You would drown me with your force and strength."

Her stubbornness was making him uneasy. This was not mere female coyness, but a serious wish to remain unwed. What kind of woman truly wished to be single?

The kind who fascinated him, apparently. "You would be my honored wife, the Lady of Dunrath. I would never mistreat you."

"Not intentionally. Does a thunderstorm intend to crush a cottage? Does the wind think about the trees that fall before it?" Her smile was wry. "You are what you are, my lord. And I—I know my weaknesses. I like peace and solitude. In a stormy household, I would vanish like that little cloud. So enough of this discussion. Thank you for the book, and I hope you enjoy your time in London."

The finality in her voice alarmed him. Usually he was successful when he set out to win female favor, and he had been confident that Gwynne would be no exception. But this was a woman like no other, and it was impossible to doubt her resolve.

As she started to turn her horse, he leaned forward and grabbed the mare's bridle. "Don't dismiss me so quickly, Gwynne. We belong together—I know it."

"This is exactly what I meant!" Her composure shattered into outrage, and she slashed out with her riding crop. "You must have your own way, and be damned to what I want!"

Swearing as the leather whip bit into his wrist, he released her bridle. For an instant they stared in mutual shock. His surprise at her unexpected fury was swiftly followed by understanding. He had not been wrong about the passion that lay beneath her composed surface, for he raised powerful emotions in her without even trying. Since the line between love and hate was thin, he must hope that he would be able to transform her anger into a more pleasing form of passion.

Her fury vanished as quickly as it had appeared. "I . . . I'm sorry." She stared at the riding crop in her hand, as if unable to believe she'd lashed out. "I've never struck anyone before in my life."

"You're not the first person I've inspired to violence," he observed. "But I'm not a tree seeking to crush your pretty roof, Lady Brecon. I'm a man who genuinely wishes to win your heart. I can be impatient, but I'm not usually insensitive, I think. There is a connection between us—surely you must feel it, too. Or do I delude myself?"

She shook her head reluctantly. "The connection is real, but merely lust."

"Not lust. Passion."

"What is passion but lust by another name? Whatever you call this connection, it has made me violent and you a bully." A fallow deer darted across the trail. Her gaze followed the beast, as if envying its ability to flee. "I want no part of it."

Her words confirmed what he had suspected: her marriage had not been a passionate one—not surprising given Lord Brecon's age. As a virtuous wife and widow, she had not sought the embraces of other men. Since she had lived without passion, no wonder she found the prospect alarming. Passion *was* alarming, but it was also a great gift. He must convince her of that.

"The passions of the flesh often draw two people together," he said, choosing his words carefully. "But even the hottest fire soon settles into quiet coals. A true marriage is built on shared values and interests. Though I'm not a scholar like you, I do love books. And riding, too. What could be more pleasurable than riding through beautiful Scottish hills while we discuss some fascinating piece of Guardian history?"

Her mouth curved up again. "You are dangerously convincing, Ballister." She turned her horse back toward the park entrance, though at a social walk rather than a canter. "But have you ever really thought about the different ways men and women experience marriage? To a man, a wife is like a painting or a classical statue. He chooses one and takes it home and hopes it will fit in with his existing furnishings."

He had to smile. "That's a cold way to describe marriage, but I suppose there is some truth to it."

"Then imagine what it is like to be a woman. She gives

up her home and friends, even her name, to live among strangers."

"In Scotland, women keep their own names. And what is a stranger but a friend one hasn't met yet?"

"Glibness is not a solution," she retorted. "Though the Families have a tradition of equality, British law still says that a married woman can't control her own property, and she has few legal rights. Even her body and her children don't belong to her. She is chattel. Do you blame me for preferring independence? Would you be willing to marry me and live in England, far from Scotland and your family?"

He frowned. "I can't deny that the law is unfair, nor that I would be reluctant to live outside of Scotland. But your objections are of the mind, while marriage is a matter of the heart. If a man and woman love each other, they wish to please. Surely that helps balance the drawbacks of the wedded state."

"Perhaps, but love is not part of this negotiation. Lust and books are not enough. Accept that we have no future and go home to Scotland. Find yourself a strong, gloriously independent Scotswoman to be lady of your castle. That will be much easier than trying to turn me into the woman you would like me to be."

His mouth tightened. Though Gwynne rode almost within touching distance, she was farther away than if they had been on separate continents. "You say you have no power, but you're wrong. You can bring a man to his knees with a single glance."

"How poetic." Her golden eyes were as implacable as they were lovely. "Confess, Ballister. The greatest part of my charm is that I don't want you. Perhaps I should have encouraged your interest. That would have cured you quickly."

"Men enjoy the hunt, but when they meet the right woman, the game is over." He tried to keep his voice light and witty. "Nothing but victory will do."

"Then I hope you soon meet the right woman, and wage a successful campaign." She inclined her head, the plume in her hat fluttering gracefully, then urged her horse into a canter that took her through the park entrance.

He followed, abandoning conversation. If he were a reasonable man, he would take her at her word and withdraw from her life.

How fortunate that he was a damned stubborn Scot.

* * *

It was too much to hope that Ballister would allow Gwynne to ride home alone. A gentleman escorted a lady, even one who had just rejected him in the strongest possible terms. As he took his leave, he said, "Until next time, Lady Brecon."

"There will be no next time." Yet despite her firm words, she sensed they would meet again. She hoped that meeting was far in the future.

Frowning, she collected the Italian book and returned to her rooms to change from her riding habit. Guardian lore taught that the future consisted of an array of possibilities, not one single, unchangeable path. But some paths were far more likely than others, and some were so likely as to be almost impossible to avoid. That was when the word "destiny" was used.

If Ballister was her destiny, she intended to fight it tooth and nail. She had felt a disquieting mix of attraction and wariness from the moment they'd met, and both qualities had intensified during their ride. He had charm, intelligence, and—well, he was strikingly attractive. She'd be a liar if she claimed that his interest wasn't exciting. To have a powerful, sinfully appealing man propose marriage within a day of meeting her was the greatest compliment she'd ever received.

Nor was she as set against marriage as she had claimed. An English suitor with her late husband's kind, steady nature would be very appealing, particularly if he was a Guardian of only modest gifts. Ballister didn't qualify on any count.

She shivered as she remembered the rage that caused her to strike out at him. His stubborn refusal to take no for an answer had released a depth of emotion that had shocked her. Violence was not part of her nature, or so she had always thought. If passion turned people into knaves and fools, she could live without it quite happily.

She glanced at the book he'd given her. A pity that Ballister wasn't a civilized man like Emery.

But if he were, would she find him so intriguing?

Four

*H*aving returned Gwynne to her home, Duncan rode grimly down the long drive of Lady Bethany's house, wondering what he should do next. The first part of his visit had made him optimistic, not to mention even more entranced. Perhaps Simon might have more suggestions of how to proceed.

He was nearing the gates when an impulse made him glance to his left. Lady Bethany sat on a stone bench under a broad-limbed oak tree. Without a word being spoken, he knew that she wished to talk with him. He turned his horse, wondering what she wanted.

"Good day, Lady Bethany." He dismounted and tethered his horse to another stone bench. "Do you wish to encourage me in my courtship, or tell me to go away and leave Gwynne alone?"

"Since when have I meddled in the affairs of others?" she said with bland innocence.

He laughed. "Unless you have changed while I was away, you're the most notorious meddler in the Families. You only get away with it because you meddle so well."

Her eyes twinkled, the shrewdness belying her comfortable dowager appearance. "We had little time to talk yesterday, so I want to take advantage of this opportunity to ask about your travels."

He sat on the bench and obligingly told stories about his time on the Continent. Though sometimes national interests set different groups of Guardians at odds, overall they got along much more harmoniously than their governments. Their differences from mundanes bound them together. He finished by saying, "Of course, as head of the council I'm sure you've read the reports I've sent home."

"Yes, but the tastiest tidbits aren't usually written down." She gave him a slanting glance. "I sense that your courtship is not prospering."

Needing guidance, he said frankly, "Gwynne refuses to even consider me as a suitor. She doesn't want to marry, doesn't want to go to Scotland, and most particularly wants nothing to do with me. Is she so in love with her late husband that she will stay single the rest of her life?"

"Gwynne loved my brother most sincerely and she brought great happiness to his last years. But the love between an old man and a young girl is not the same as the love between two people in the prime of life. Continue your pursuit, Ballister, but gently."

"I'm not sure she'll receive me if I call again." His mouth twisted wryly. "I could kidnap her as one of my Highland ancestors would have, but I doubt that would achieve the result I want."

Lady Bethany laughed. "You are learning something about my Gwyneth, I see. She has more strength than she knows, and a stubborn streak equal to your own. But she has a generous and loving heart, and she'll make a wife without equal."

A note in the older woman's voice caught his attention. "Are you seeing that we will marry, Lady Bethany? I've felt that Gwynne and I are meant for each other, but perhaps infatuation is clouding my mind."

"Gwynne has been under the hand of fate for years. I feel you are part of that fate, but I can't grasp the shape of it. All I know is that you must woo her, and woo her well." She rose. "Tomorrow night Gwynne will attend a masquerade at New Spring Gardens with friends."

He stood also. "Thank you! I shall be there. What costume will she wear?"

Lady Bethany smiled mischievously. "If you can't discover her, you're a failure as both lover and Guardian. Good day, Ballister."

He bowed as the older woman left, hardly able to control his excitement. When it came to an affair of the heart, he'd rather have Lady Bethany on his side than a Roman legion. A masquerade would be a chance to get close to Gwynne without setting her hackles up. The free atmosphere would surely create . . . opportunities.

He wasn't worried about locating her. Even if he weren't a Guardian, he could find Gwynne among a thousand masked women.

* * *

Gwynne let her hand trail over the side of her friends' boat, her fingers playing with the cool river water. She had been doubtful when she accepted the invitation to attend a masquerade with the Tuckwell family, her closest friends outside of Guardian circles. The couple was older than she, with children near Gwynne's age, but they had become good friends after her marriage, and had been especially kind and supportive after Emery's death. Every fortnight or so Anne Tuckwell invited Gwynne to dinner or some other entertainment.

Though her first impulse was to stay home with her books and Lady Bethany, usually she made herself accept, knowing how easily she might become a hermit. She invariably had a good time, too.

The torch-lit landing and steps up to their destination appeared ahead on the south bank of the river. Though she had attended concerts and other events at Ranelagh, which was a newer, more aristocratic, pleasure garden, this would be her first visit to sprawling New Spring Gardens.

Her initial doubts about the masquerade had been replaced by anticipation, for the excitement of the unknown might distract her thoughts from Lord Ballister. Her mind knew that she was right to dismiss him—but other parts of her were not so sure.

Their boat nosed into the jostling group waiting for a place at the landing area. When their gunwale ground against the adjacent boat, one of the occupants, a gentleman in a Roman toga, grinned suggestively at Gwynne. Uneasy that he was within touching distance, she turned away and concentrated on donning her gloves, glad for the concealment of her mask. She wasn't quite ready for half-naked Romans.

Gaily costumed people streamed from the boats and up the brightly lit stairs as strains of orchestra music sounded from the Grove in the center of the gardens. It was a warm night, almost sultry. Perfect for an outdoor masquerade, if it didn't rain. She refused to think about how convenient it would be to have the Lord of Storms with her.

"I have been so looking forward to this evening," her seatmate said dreamily. Sally Tuckwell, oldest daughter of the family, was nineteen and an unabashed romantic. "I wonder if William will be able to identify me in this costume and mask? I wouldn't tell him what I was wearing even though he begged to know."

Gwynne smiled as she regarded the girl's shepherdess garb. "With your lovely blond hair and graceful figure, I'm sure he'll find you soon. And if not, you can catch him with your shepherd's crook."

Sally laughed. "One reason I chose this costume is because the crook can both capture and defend."

"Now that you and William are engaged, you don't have to defend yourself against him with quite so much vigor," Gwynne said with twinkling eyes. "Perhaps he might even lure you down a dark walk to steal a kiss."

Sally's lips parted as she contemplated the prospect. In later years, when she and William were sober, long-married citizens, they would no doubt exchange private smiles when New Spring Gardens was mentioned, and remember what they had done when they were young and in the first flush of love.

Gwynne shook off a pang of envy that she had never had such moments. She had loved Emery and her only regret was that their marriage hadn't lasted longer—but it would have been pleasant to have had a chance to be as young and giddy as Sally. Though only a few years separated them, Gwynne felt much older.

Their boat finally pulled up to the landing. The boatman and Norcott, a Tuckwell footman, jumped out to steady the craft. Sir George climbed ashore, then assisted his wife up before extending his hand to Gwynne. "I'll be much envied for escorting such beauty," he said jovially. "Three lovely ladies! What gentleman could wish for more?"

Gwynne laughed as she stepped from the rocking boat to solid land. "That would be more true if we weren't heavily disguised."

"Ah, but disguise stimulates the imagination," Anne Tuckwell said. "Any woman in a domino becomes a mysterious, alluring beauty, and every man can be a handsome prince in disguise."

Gwynne smiled at Anne's imagination, but privately admitted that there was truth to her words. Not fond of fancy dress, Sir George wore his usual evening attire with only a mask, but Anne and Gwynne wore dominoes that completely covered their evening gowns with hooded cloaks of flowing silk. Anne was graceful in green, while Gwynne wore the shimmering scarlet domino that belonged to Sally.

When Gwynne had first donned the domino, she had thought it garishly bright. Yet in the festival night, she found that the sumptuous color made her feel like a sophisticated, worldly woman. Not like a book mouse at all.

After Sir George had paid their admissions, they walked through the arched passage that led into the gardens and stepped onto the tree-lined Grand Walk. Gwynne stopped in her tracks, her eyes widening at the sight of thousands of lamps that brightened the night. Revelers in costume and dominoes filled the long promenade that disappeared into the distance. The sounds of music and gaiety were all around her, and she felt as if she had stepped from the normal world into fairyland.

Laughing, Sally caught her arm to get her moving again. "It's far too soon to be wonderstruck. The park is filled with delights—cunning statues and bridges, cascades and temples, paintings and music. One could wander for days and not see everything!"

Gwynne resumed walking, the silken folds of the domino rustling luxuriantly. With the deep hood concealing her telltale hair and a closely fitted black half mask, she realized that tonight she had the freedom of anonymity. Her spirits bubbled up as she surveyed the laughing crowd, and for the first time since her mother died, she felt young. She could be as playful and giddy as

Sally if she wished. Flirting with mysterious strangers would help her forget that wretched Scot.

Sally said with a touch of anxiety, "With so many people here, perhaps William won't be able to find me."

"Your father won't be hard to identify," Gwynne said practically. "William will recognize him, and be at your side a moment later."

Sure enough, as their party prepared to take seats in the supper box Sir George had hired, a dashing, masked cavalier joined them. He bowed, the plumes of his hat brushing the ground as he swept his arm grandly. "What a perfect picture of rural innocence you are, my little shepherdess," he said in William's voice. "Perhaps I shall steal you away."

As Sally giggled, Anne said, "Very well, but see that you bring her back before midnight, noble sir. Or you'll have to face a mother's wrath."

He grinned and kissed her hand, then offered his arm to Sally. As the young couple vanished from view, Sir George said, "Gwynne, would you mind if I took my lady wife for a short stroll?"

The gleam in Anne's eyes demonstrated that it wasn't only the young who found the racy atmosphere exciting, but she hesitated when she glanced at Gwynne. "We shouldn't leave our guest alone."

"Nonsense," Gwynne said. "With Norcott to look after me, I'll be safe enough in the supper box until you return. I shall listen to the music and watch the passing crowd and enjoy myself thoroughly."

"If you're sure . . ." Anne said, willing to be persuaded.

Gwynne made a shooing motion with her hand. "Be off with you, and there's no need to rush back. I'll do very well."

The Tuckwells went off arm in arm. Gwynne expected that when they returned, there would be grass stains on

Anne's domino. Perhaps that was why the older woman wore green? Smiling to herself, Gwynne turned to the supper box, then hesitated. The box would be safe, but she had spent too much of her life as an observer. The pleasure garden called to her, encouraging her to move and explore and see life.

"Norcott, I believe that I shall take a walk myself. Will you follow far enough behind that no one will realize that you are watching over me?"

The footman, a solid middle-aged man, looked uncomfortable. "For a female to walk alone here suggests that she is . . . is seeking a companion."

"I'll come to no harm as long as I stay on the lighted walkways. And if someone attempts to force unwanted attentions on me, you'll be there."

He inclined his head but wasn't quite able to keep a note of disapproval from his voice. "Very well, my lady."

Even knowing that Norcott was behind her didn't interfere with Gwynne's glorious sense of freedom as she set out along the graveled walk. Had she ever been alone in a crowded public place like this? Not that she could remember. Glad that she had worn a comfortable round gown that was easy to walk in, she set off at a brisk pace, as if she had a destination. That way she wouldn't be confused with the languid ladies of the night who were trolling for customers.

Her strategy seemed to work. Though the scarlet domino drew speculative glances, no one accosted her. Safe behind her mask, she studied the gardens and her fellow merrymakers. As Sally had said, there were many sights to see, and she enjoyed every one of them. The Grecian temple that housed the orchestra was particularly splendid, with globe lanterns outlining the building's arches and columns.

Watching people was even more amusing. Most were obviously decent citizens out for an evening of pleasure. A toga couldn't conceal a solid merchant, nor did a domino turn a farmer into a prince. But there were a few male figures that stirred her imagination. Like the two lean, scarred men whose army uniforms were clearly earned, not costumes. Or the bored aristocrat whose lazy gaze surveyed the courtesans, as if looking for one worthy of his attentions.

Soon the orchestra that played in the Grove near the entrance could no longer be heard and the crowd was thinning out. She must be nearing the end of the gardens.

She was about to turn back when she reached an open area where a group of musicians on a canopied dais were playing. Below them, men and women were performing a country dance, the men lined up opposite the women. There was much laughter as they joined hands, spun apart, then came together again.

As the last couple clasped hands and skipped up to the head of the set, she halted, foot tapping in time to the music. Wistfully she wished that she was one of those merry dancers.

Against so much movement, her attention was caught by a solitary gentleman in a black domino who stood near the dancers with a stillness so intense it drew the eye. As she watched, she realized that his masked gaze was very slowly scanning the crowd, like a predator seeking his prey.

Abruptly he pivoted on his heel and walked away from the dancers, his movements smooth as a cat. Tall and powerful and clothed in night, he was a man to stir dreams. Maybe he was the prince Anne had suggested, or a rake in search of less innocent pleasures.

Perhaps she should find out. On impulse, she moved on a path that would intersect his. Though she had no skill at flirting, where better to practice than here, where no one knew who she was?

And perhaps he would dance.

Five

*D*uncan strode through the entrance to New Spring Gardens, then paused, disoriented. Years had passed since his last visit, and he had forgotten how busy it was on a fair summer night. The masquerade had drawn crowds of disguised revelers, and the grounds covered sixteen acres of woods and walks. Where the devil should he start?

If you can't discover her, you're a failure as both lover and Guardian. Smiling wryly, he stepped into a niche that held a large wooden lion and closed his eyes. Was Gwynne near? *Yes.*

How near? He visualized the layout of the gardens, with its groves and crisscrossing walkways. When his mind was calmed, he felt her as a moving pulse of light toward the far end of the gardens.

Hoping he would have need of it later, he reserved a supper box, then headed to the far end of the gardens, all his senses extended. Convenient that the domino and mask he'd borrowed from Simon were black. In this colorful crowd, he drew no attention.

He used both eyes and intuition to scrutinize the merrymakers he passed. Since Gwynne had come with friends, she would probably be in a group. Was she wearing a costume? Consulting his inner senses again, he decided not. But she was at least masked, and probably wearing a domino as well.

As he neared the end of the gardens, he found a dance area beside the intersection of the Grand Walk and one of the smaller crosswalks. She was very near, he was sure of it. Eyes narrowed, he studied the dancers and onlookers. Could she be the graceful woman in a blue domino who danced with a short, broad satyr? No. Or perhaps the masked woman sitting on a bench with a group of friends? She looked to be about the right height and build. He was ready to walk toward her when she made a gesture that immediately proved her a stranger.

He searched for Gwynne again, but she was too close, he couldn't get any clearer sense than the powerful knowledge that she was near. But where?

Frustrated, he stalked across the open area toward the crosswalk—and suddenly there she was. Even though the woman was masked and cloaked in scarlet silk, he knew instantly it was Gwynne. And she stood alone, her tall figure outlined by lantern light.

Now that he had found her, he mustn't drive her away again. He forcibly masked the power and passion she aroused until it was an ember instead of a bonfire.

Then he created a light spell of attraction—not strong enough to affect Gwynne's will, just enough that she would find him intriguing. With luck it would allow him enough time to capture her interest. Then he might attain his true goal—rousing her deeply hidden passions toward romance, not the anger that he had sparked in her before.

He must disguise his physical characteristics since Gwynne had seen him twice in the last two days. A French accent would conceal his faint Scottish inflections. He would also walk with his weight shifted forward to the balls of his feet, just enough to make his movements subtly different.

Hoping that her power wasn't strong enough to recognize him despite his precautions, he went in pursuit of his lady.

*   *   *

Gwynne gasped as the dark man turned toward her. Even though he was masked, she had the sense that his gaze had struck to her soul. She'd had a similar experience when she met Ballister. Was it possible . . . ?

Even before the thought had formed, she rejected it. As the man walked toward her with a warrior's balanced tread, she decided that he was even taller and broader than Ballister. Her judgment was confirmed when he extended one hand and spoke in a deep voice enriched by a husky, sensual French accent. "Will you dance, milady?"

"*Oui,* milord." She couldn't have refused if she tried.

He bowed with a courtier's grace, then clasped her hand and led her to a dance set. Heat burned through her kidskin glove under the pressure of his fingers.

Most dancers laughed and chatted with their partners. The dark man said nothing, but his gaze never wavered from hers as they performed the simple figures of the country dance. Perhaps that silence was why she was so intensely aware of him. She sensed the shape of his limbs under the domino, the controlled movements of long, honed muscles. And though she could not see his eyes, his gaze burned wherever it touched her body.

As they moved together and apart, turning and double-stepping through the dance, she felt almost painfully alive, like a tender bud threatened by a late frost. She tried to convince herself that she was only excited by the naughtiness of dancing with a stranger, but without success. There was some force in this man that compelled all her attention.

As she circled her partner, she caught a glimpse of Norcott. The footman had seen her accept the dark man willingly, for he sat on a bench with his casual gaze following her. It was good to know she was protected, though she felt no threat from the dark man. At least, no threat that she didn't welcome.

The music ended and the group leader announced that the musicians were taking a short break. Mutely the dark man crooked his arm toward Gwynne. She slipped her hand into his elbow, wondering where he would lead her. Charmed she might be, but she was not ready to head into the shrubbery with a stranger.

His hand rested over hers, warm in the cooling air. "Will you join me for refreshments, my fair lady?"

"It will be my pleasure." She studied his lips and chin, the only area of his face visible below the mask. It was a strong jaw. Familiar? She couldn't decide. She thought again of Ballister. But being with him made her wary, while this stranger attracted her like a needle to a lodestone.

"Are you here alone, milady?" he asked as they began walking back toward the central area of the gardens. Despite the crowds, she felt as if they moved in their own private bubble of mutual awareness.

Even if she were alone, she wouldn't be so besotted as to admit that. "I'm with a party of friends, and even now a guardian watches over me."

A smile sounded in his dark velvet voice. "Milady, angels will always protect you wherever you may go."

Why was a French accent so utterly erotic? She felt almost dizzy with attraction. She wanted to run her hands over him, feel the muscles and sinew that lay beneath his domino. Touch those lips, which held such promise. She drew a slow breath to steady her unruly mind. "Are you an angel or a devil, milord?"

"I am but a man. One who is entranced by beauty."

She had to laugh. "You go too far, flatterer. I could be the ugliest woman in Christendom and you wouldn't be able to tell, the way I'm disguised."

"One can sense beauty even when it is disguised. There was beauty in your standing proud and alone in the night." His fingertips skimmed lightly along the inside of her gloved wrist. "There is beauty in your posture and the free way that you walk and in the curve of your arm. Beauty in your soft voice, which soothes as it excites." He touched her throat delicately with his knuckles, and shivers ran through her. "You are a symphony of grace. Seeing your face and form could only enhance that by revealing the countenance created by life and laughter."

His compliments left her breathless. She had wanted to learn to flirt, but she was out of her class. The dark man was the world champion of flirtation. "You could lure an angel down from heaven to listen to your sugared words, milord. I do not know how to reply. I don't even have a fan to rap your knuckles for being outrageous."

His laugh was soft and rich. "I am grateful you lack such a formidable weapon. Better that we simply enjoy each other's company, and the magic of the night."

She wondered if he hoped to seduce her. The bushes were alive with misbehaving couples, but it was presumptuous even for a silver-tongued Frenchman to think he might be able to coax a woman he'd just met into the shrubbery. Unless her scarlet domino had misled him? But he was making no improper overtures. His behavior was tenderly solicitous, as a true gentleman should be.

He guided her from the main walk into a grotto that contained a fountain. Colored lamps illuminated a naked female with a writhing serpent strategically draped over her and water spurting from the serpent's mouth. "The decorations can be considered tawdry by the jaded, or delightful by the enthusiastic." He scooped a handful of water from the basin and let it trickle away between his fingers, the droplets sparkling with light. "Which are you, milady?"

"I've never been to New Spring Gardens before, so I choose to find everything delightful. How can so many people enjoying themselves fail to be charming? This statue might be vulgar by daylight, but by night it invites the imagination to soar."

"I have just discovered new beauties in you," he said softly. "Those of the mind and the spirit."

"It is fortunate that we are masked, milord, or you would know that I am quite ordinary. Reality can never match illusions."

"There I must disagree, my scarlet lady." He took her arm and guided her back to the Grand Walk. "Illusions are as gossamer as clouds and hold no more satisfaction. Reality can be a flame that consumes." Wry amusement crept into his voice. "Though I must be grateful that you hold illusions about me. I do not pretend to be ordinary. Perhaps it would be better if I were."

"No," she said positively. "Do not wish yourself less than you are. Even masked, you are extraordinary. Compelling. Enigmatic. A master spinner of words. A conjuror of dreams."

"Then it is best we never unmask, milady, for I shall never be able to maintain such high regard from you."

His words reminded her how artificial this interlude was. She was entranced by a man who was more a creation of her imagination than real.

A group of drunken young bucks stumbled past, taking more than their share of space. Smoothly the dark man changed positions so that he was between her and the rowdies, and she could see how narrowly he watched until they were safely beyond. He might be a stranger but he was real enough in his strength and courtliness.

They reached the colonnade of supper booths. The Tuckwell booth was still empty. She was about to suggest that they could use it when the dark man led her to a different booth that he must have already reserved. Had he come to the gardens tonight with the plan of picking up whatever lone female was willing? Wryly she acknowledged that he had reason to be confident. "Your voice is French. Do you live in London now?"

"No, milady." He sat beside her, close enough to touch, but not touching. "I am merely visiting your great city."

She scolded herself for feeling instant regret. Womanlike, she had met an attractive man—one whose name and face she didn't even know!—and wanted to think about a future. The only reality between them was this swift, ephemeral flirtation. She must accept that limitation and enjoy a situation too exciting to be real. If they did really know each other, the excitement would be less.

The dark man murmured an order to the serving man, and a selection of refreshments were delivered almost immediately. Gwynne examined the platter of shaved ham with interest. "These slices of ham are so thin they're almost transparent. What skill the carver must have!"

"They say that one ham can be cut so thinly that the

slices will cover the whole of New Spring Gardens." The dark man lifted a fragile curl of ham and rolled it into a cylinder. "It's a marvel, but the portions are designed to tease rather than satisfy."

He touched the rolled ham to her lips. She opened her mouth and took in the tidbit, the delicate salty slice as sensual on her tongue as a kiss. She felt delightfully wicked, though she was safe enough since the booth was open to anyone who cared to look in this direction. After swallowing, she said, "Surely teasing and anticipation are the best parts of eating, and of flirtation."

She was reaching for the ham so she could offer him a slice when he caught her hand. His gaze holding hers, he very slowly peeled off the glove. His warm fingers sent more shivers through her. When her wrist was exposed, he bent forward to press a kiss on the pulse point. "Desire can be both tease and fulfillment, milady," he whispered.

She gasped and pulled back, her heart pounding. She had not known that such arousal was possible. "You must content yourself with the former."

He smiled down at her. "For me, your company is a deep satisfaction. I need no more for this night."

"And there will be no tomorrow." She tried to sound matter-of-fact. Already she was missing him and he wasn't even gone.

Gently he tugged the glove from her hand, finger by finger. "There is always a tomorrow, even if we do not know the shape of it." The glove slipped away and he breathed a kiss into the sensitive center of her palm.

She felt an intoxicating blend of fierce desire and pliant yearning. Instinctively she cupped her hand around his chin, feeling warm, firm flesh spiced with the provocative prickle of hidden whiskers. He inhaled sharply at her touch. She let her palm trail down his bare throat, absurdly pleased that she could affect him as powerfully as he affected her.

To maintain her advantage, she peeled off her other glove and rolled a sliver of ham for her companion. He took it neatly, his teeth just grazing her fingertips. She gasped, realizing that she should have known she could never best him at erotic games. Though in this game, there were no losers.

He offered her a sip of wine, then turned the goblet and deliberately drank from the place her lips had touched, while his gaze held hers. His eyes behind the mask seemed light-colored, though the strands of hair dancing beside his face were dark.

She licked his fingertips when he gave her the next slice of ham. He laughed softly and stroked the inside of her wrist where her pulse beat swift with excitement. Then he skimmed his hand up inside the loose domino until he reached the edge of her sleeve. He caressed her bare skin, his fingers warm, knowing, indecently provocative. "Ah, milady, how can you imagine that you are ordinary?"

She laughed softly, drunk with sensuality and the power of his presence. He offered her a marzipan disk imprinted with the image of a ship. She took the sweet with her teeth, and the taste of almonds and sugar melted across her tongue. Feeling wanton, she nipped at his fingers. "I am ordinary, but the night is not."

He placed another marzipan in his mouth and leaned forward in silent offering. Giddily she lifted her face and took the sweet. His lips were rich with the taste of wine and spice. She swallowed the dissolving marzipan, then nibbled delicately at his lips.

He made a rough sound in his throat and put his arms around her, his mouth opening on hers demandingly. Heart pounding, she closed her eyes, wholly in the pleasure of the moment. For an instant she felt rapture.

The moment shattered in a kaleidoscope of images. *Fire, blood, death! Homes consumed by flames, screaming children stumbling over the bodies of the dead. Horror beyond imagining . . .*

She gasped and shoved him away as devastation seared her mind. Passion and danger were inextricably interwoven with this man.

And she knew who he was. She ripped off his mask and stared at the familiar craggy face, wondering how she could have been fool enough to be deceived. "Damn you, Ballister! How *dare* you!"

After an involuntary flinch at being exposed, he said calmly, "I needed more time with you, Gwynne. From the beginning, I have alarmed you. Some of that, I think, is because of my reputation. I hoped that if you had a chance to spend time with me as a stranger, not the Lord of Thunder, you would relax enough to feel what is between us instead of always running away." He reached toward her with the warm, strong hands she had found so enticing. "Now that you and I have spent an hour together as a man and woman rather than as Lord Ballister and Lady Brecon, can you deny that attraction?"

No, nor could she deny the ghastly visions triggered by his kiss. Too upset to think, she scrambled sideways across the bench seat and stumbled to her feet. "Don't ever come near me again!" she said, voice shaking. "Ever!"

She hurled his mask to the ground, then bolted from the booth even though her knees were almost too weak to hold her. She was halfway to the Grand Walk when a familiar voice called, "Gwynne? What's wrong?"

She turned to the left and saw the green dominoed figure of Anne Tuckwell, her husband beside her. At the same time Norcott sprinted toward her from the right. "My lady, are you hurt?"

"No, only . . . only upset." Gwynne went gratefully into Anne's maternal embrace. She yearned for Lady Bethany, who would help her understand what had happened. Struggling to compose herself, she said, "I must go home now, but there's no need for you to leave. If you walk me to the river, I'll hire a boat. . . ."

"Nonsense, Norcott and I will take you home. George, wait in our booth for Sally and William to return." A protective arm around Gwynne's waist, Anne turned toward the river landing. "Can you talk about it?"

What, after all, had happened? Gwynne had flirted with a man, and now regretted it. "It was . . . not a great matter, except to me. I am not suited to adventures, I think."

She glanced back and saw Ballister standing in the supper booth, a blacker shape against the shadows of the night. Even at this distance she could see the tension in his cloaked figure, and knew that he wanted to rush after her. Those clever, provocative hands would be clenched with the effort of controlling that impulse.

The pull between them was undeniable—despite the horror of her visions, she yearned to return to his arms. She wondered if he had bespelled her, for she had never felt such a compulsion before.

Deliberately she turned away and concentrated on the walk back to the river landing. Ballister was mysterious, compelling, the most fascinating man she had ever met— and tonight it had been made blindingly clear that he was even more fearsome than she had imagined.

* * *

Aching, Duncan watched Gwynne flee to her friends. He supposed he should be grateful that she didn't send the two men to beat him. Perhaps she thought that a mage might do her friends an injury.

As she left, she glanced back at him. Her burning gaze was implacable.

Then she was gone. He retrieved the mask from the ground. She had yanked it from his head with such force that one of the ties had broken. Numbly he removed the domino and folded it around the mask. Now that he had alienated her forever, there was no point in disguising himself.

He dropped a handful of coins on the table and headed for the river. His thoughts circled obsessively all the way back to Falconer House. He had hoped to charm Gwynne into accepting their mutual attraction, and at first it had worked. She had been as warm, playful, and responsive as he had known she could be.

Why had that kiss destroyed the very human magic that bound them? He would swear that she was as eager as he. It wasn't only that she recognized him and was furious over his deception. He had seen fear in her when she cursed his name and ran away. How could she think he would ever hurt her? Ordinary women might find him fearsome, but she was no ordinary woman.

Her kiss would haunt him forever.

He had hoped to be able to retire without being seen, but when he entered the foyer of Falconer House, he saw that the door to the sitting room was open and Simon was sprawled in a chair by the fire. His friend glanced up and made a lazy gesture. "Join me for some brandy and tell me how your night's hunting went."

Duncan grimaced and entered the sitting room. After laying the bundled domino and mask on a table, he accepted brandy and folded into the chair on the opposite side of the fire from his host. He took a sip of the brandy, then another, glad to have the spirits burn through his numbness. "My hunt was a disaster. It's time for me to return home."

Simon's brows arched. "Without Gwynne? I thought you were determined to win her, whatever the cost."

Duncan's laughter was bitter. "I've destroyed whatever hope there was." Succinctly he described the events of the evening, and the catastrophic ending. "She'll not forgive me for deceiving her—that I'm sure of."

"Perhaps she won't, but the two of you aren't done with each other. Though that kiss triggered an explosion, it's also a sign of the incredible amount of energy between the two of you. You're like opposite poles of a magnet, inexorably drawn together." Simon closed his eyes and frowned. "When I imagine the two of you together, the energy is like a city burning. Fate will draw you together again. That I guarantee."

Duncan rubbed his aching temples. After this disastrous night, he wasn't sure whether Simon's prediction was a source of hope—or of threat.

$\mathcal{G}$wynne managed to regain a semblance of calm on the boat ride back to Richmond. Once they were safe in Lady Bethany's drawing room, she dismissed Anne and Norcott with assurances that she was fine, and many thanks for the exciting evening.

Lady Bethany wasn't fooled, of course. Eyes narrowed, she waited until they were alone before saying, "You look as if you've seen your own ghost, my dear."

Gwynne sank into a chair, trembling, and was grateful when Athena jumped into her lap. The cat's purring warmth helped her keep her voice steady as she described her encounter with Ballister, including the visions of doom. She ended by asking, "Is he evil, Bethany?"

"Not at all, but good men can cause evil without intending it." Expression troubled, the older woman rose. "Get ready for bed. I'll prepare a posset that will help you sleep."

Knowing her friend's skills, Gwynne asked, "Is it more than a sleeping draft?"

Bethany nodded. "I'll use a potion that will calm you enough for me to ask questions without upsetting you again. I need to know more about those visions."

Gwynne needed to know more, too. Athena in her

arms, she returned to her room and rang for her maid, glad to exchange corset and petticoats for a cambric nightgown. She brushed out her hair and was braiding it for sleep when Lady Bethany appeared with a gently steaming goblet. Gwynne tied the end of her braid with a ribbon, then took a sip of the spicy drink, wondering what it contained besides warm milk and wine.

The heat of the posset curled through her, easing the tension that had knotted her ever since that shattering kiss. She drank more deeply, trying not to remember the food and drink she had shared with her deceiver. "I don't understand why I didn't recognize Ballister. Do you think he cast a confusion spell over me?"

The older woman's gaze became unfocused as she studied the question in ways Gwynne could only imagine. "If he had, I would be able to see traces of it around you. I think he might have used a mild attraction spell—just strong enough to overcome any reluctance you might feel about dancing with a stranger. Since you've felt attraction and wariness since you met him, he merely cloaked that part of his nature that alarmed you, then disguised his physical appearance with simple tricks of costume and accent."

Whatever combination of spells and artifice he'd used, it had been very effective. Gwynne remembered the first rapturous instant of their kiss and felt a wave of heat that was followed immediately by icy rage. "Using his power to deceive me was wicked."

"I doubt he needed even that small spell. You were ripe and ready, my girl. All you needed was an excuse not to recognize him." Bethany's voice held a shade of tartness as she turned down the bedcovers. "Finish the posset and lie down. When you're comfortable, I'll see how much you remember."

Gwynne obeyed, grateful to sink into her feather mattress. Bethany pulled the covers over her and extinguished the lamps until only a single one burned. Then she sat beside the bed and began asking soft questions about the evening.

Arm curled around Athena, Gwynne elaborated on how she met Ballister, the dancing, their conversation, the refreshments. Her peaceful state removed much of the anger and embarrassment. She felt detached, as if standing outside her body and watching the actions of a besotted stranger.

Deftly Bethany coaxed Gwynne along to the moment of the kiss. "When you saw your vision of disaster, did you witness Ballister committing violence?"

Even the posset could not eliminate the memory of horror, but at least Gwynne could now view the images calmly. "I . . . I see him with a sword. The hilt is brass or gold, I think. But he's only holding it in readiness, I don't see him striking anyone."

"Very good," Bethany murmured. "You saw fire. What was burning?"

"First a cottage. It was crude and solitary—rough stones and a thatch roof. I . . . I think it was in Scotland. Then there were villages burning, and finally a great city. There was a particular woman fleeing with her child in her arms." Panic flared again, and she clenched the edge of the coverlet. "The woman stumbles and falls, and her child begins to scream. The flames are closing in and she can't escape. Embers fall on her gown. . . ."

Bethany's hand gripped hers, pulling her from the vision. "The images didn't necessarily show real fires. I think they were symbols of increasing catastrophe, going from small to large. What other images did you see?"

Gwynne inhaled deeply and forced herself to relax

again. "There was—I think it must have been a battlefield. There are bodies everywhere. Some are wearing
scarlet coats, others in . . . in Highland dress, I think. It's
dusk and very quiet except for . . . for the buzzards
and—oh, God, that dog has a severed arm in its mouth!"
Her stomach heaved.

Once more Bethany's touch drew her back to her safe,
clean bedroom. "The fact that you had visions when you
and Ballister kissed suggests that he is involved in some
way. Do you have any idea how?"

Stilling her mind so that it was like a silver pool,
Gwynne waited to see if an answer would come. "He is
not the instigator, but rather is like . . . like a spark to tinder. He changes the balance." She turned her head toward
Lady Bethany. "He has so much power that it overflowed
into my mind. For the first time, I'm glad that I have no
power of my own. Do you think I'm seeing true visions?"

Bethany frowned. "I think that you're seeing possible
futures. Those horrors may not all come to pass."

Gwynne thought of the fire consuming that frantic
mother and child, and shuddered. "But some will?"

"You saw a battlefield. You've heard the rumors of another Jacobite rising. If that happens—and I fear it will—
the rebellion could lead to another civil war. Certainly
there would be fierce fighting." The older woman sighed,
her age evident. "But the outcome is uncertain. Some of
the possible paths are . . . very dark. I feel that you're
right—Ballister is critical as to how the rebellion will un-
fold. But in what way?"

"Is Ballister a Jacobite? I thought all Guardians support
the Hanoverians because of the peace and prosperity they
have brought."

"We do, for exactly those reasons. Ballister is no Jacobite, but he is a Scot. In the forge of war, who knows

what might happen? He is a man of great power, which means he has the potential to cause great harm."

"Then I am right to avoid him."

"Perhaps. Or perhaps not. This is not a simple matter." Bethany stood and kissed Gwynne's brow. "Sleep, my dear. We can discuss this more in the morning."

Gwynne hesitated, then asked a wistful question. "Do you think that the visions mean that I am developing power?"

Bethany's gaze became vague as she considered the matter. "I wish I could say yes, but I simply don't know. Though it's possible that a latent talent is finally manifesting, the most likely explanation is that Ballister's power and the intensity of your connection caused images related to him to spill into you."

Gwynne sighed. "I rather thought that it was too much to hope that I'm finally turning into a mage." After Bethany left, Gwynne turned onto her side and curled around Athena, promising herself that she would not dream of the sensuality and excitement of the time she spent with the man in the black domino before she learned his identity.

But dream she did, and in the night she burned for her loss.

* * *

Wearily Bethany considered her own bed before she turned and made her way to her workroom. She had chosen the large, airy chamber because its southern exposure allowed sunshine to warm her aging bones. There would be no warmth there now.

She turned the knob and entered. The door was never locked. There was no need for locks because the door was spelled and would open only for Bethany, Gwynne, or the lady's maid who had been Bethany's friend and companion since they were both girls. It would have opened for her brother or husband if they still lived. Now only women came to this chamber of mysteries.

A draft caused the light of her lamp to flicker eerily over the books and equipment of her private magical laboratory. Scented bunches of drying herbs hung in one corner, and a large cabinet contained the glassware and tools she used for compounding potions. She liked to think that over the years, she had produced original work that would be of value to future Guardians.

A fire was laid, so she snapped her fingers to start the coals burning. Simple heat would not eliminate the deep chill that had come over her when she listened to Gwynne's visions, but it would help her tired body.

Settling at her desk, she removed an ebony box from the lower drawer. The dense wood had been chosen to protect the treasure within. She lifted the lid, revealing a velvet-lined interior and a quartz sphere about three inches in diameter.

There were nine such spheres, one for each member of the Guardian Council. To be on the council required maturity, wisdom, and the ability to use a sphere. Not everyone had the gift. Her brother, Emery, had possessed as much power as she, but he didn't have the knack for communicating clearly through the sphere, and communication was vital for keeping the Families in harmony.

Absently she contemplated the planes and occlusions inside the translucent stone as she warmed it between her palms to wake the energy. The talking spheres had been made by Lady Sybil Harlowe, an ancestress of Bethany and one of the greatest mages of the sixteenth century. Bethany could feel Lady Sybil's power even now, as well as traces of every council member who had used it since.

The last before Bethany had been her father. Family legend described how at the age of three, Bethany had found the ball and engaged in an earnest conversation with the bemused head of the council, who had been in Newcastle at the time.

Tonight she craved a discussion with another council member, but most would be sleeping at this hour, and the matter wasn't quite urgent enough to disturb them. Who might be awake? Ah, Jasper Polmarric, the eldest mage of the Cornish Families. He was a creature of the night, as was she.

The sphere was pulsing with power now, so she visualized seven of the other eight council members, then sent her message. *I summon the council on a matter of great urgency. Noon today.* She framed the request so that it wouldn't be noticed until the recipients awoke the next morning. The summons would tell them to go to their sphere. When they touched it, they would receive the full message.

There was no need to use her name. Each member of the council had an energy imprint as distinct as a voice. Those who lived in the London area would come to her home. More distant members would contribute by means of their spheres.

To Jasper Polmarric, she sent a different and more immediate call. *Are you available to talk?* If he was awake, she would hear from him soon.

Within minutes, she felt words forming in her mind with the dry humor that was characteristic of Jasper. *Up to some mischief, my dear Bethany? Or having trouble sleeping?*

She let him feel her fatigue and anxiety. *If only that were true, Jasper. You know how every mage in Britain has been sensing an approaching cataclysm? It's almost here, and when it breaks, the whole nation will be rocked to its foundations.*

* * *

Gwynne awoke feeling surprisingly rested. She wondered if Bethany would part with the recipe for the sleeping potion. If no magic was required in the preparation, she could make it herself.

She yawned and swung her feet from the bed, feeling a guilty twinge when she saw the position of the sun. It must be midday. No wonder she felt rested.

After washing up, she rang for her maid, Molly, who appeared with a breakfast tray. Lady Bethany's household always ran like clockwork. Gwynne poured herself a cup of hot chocolate. "Do you know if Lady Bethany is available to join me? I'd like to speak with her."

Molly shook her head. "Her ladyship has company and can't be disturbed."

Gwynne's brows arched. When Bethany said she couldn't be disturbed, it usually meant Guardian business of some sort. No matter. They could speak later.

After Molly left, Gwynne poured more chocolate and settled at her desk to work at deciphering a two-hundred-year-old journal that included numerous spells and recipes. It was written in a code that had taken time to solve. Codes were so much simpler to understand than men. . . .

Absorbed in her work, she was startled when Molly returned and said, "Lady Bethany wishes you to join her in the small salon, my lady."

Gwynne blinked at the mantel clock and realized that over three hours had passed since she breakfasted. What an odd day this was.

She stood and stretched her tight muscles, glad for a break. "Thank you, Molly, I'll go right down."

When Gwynne reached the salon, she knocked lightly to warn Bethany that she had arrived, then entered. Surprise jolted through her. She had just walked into a full Guardian Council meeting, and the energy was so powerful that a rock would take notice.

All council members maintained homes in the London area, and at any given moment at least four or five of them were in residence. That was not an accident; they took care to ensure that everyone didn't go to the country at the same time. If important events transpired, London was the crossroads of Britain, which meant that if Guardian intervention was required, no time would be wasted.

Today's meeting included Bethany and four others. They sat around the circular table which was usually used for cards. Guessing that this gathering involved Ballister and perhaps her as well, Gwynne curtsied deeply. "Good afternoon. How may I serve you?"

Perhaps they wanted her to take notes or write a letter, since she had a fine hand and could be trusted with Family business. But she doubted it would be so simple.

"Please, sit down," Bethany said gravely. "You know all of my colleagues, don't you?"

Gwynne sat, taking a chair several feet from the table. To sit with the great mages as an equal would be presumptuous.

Small, bald Jasper Polmarric, who was a particular friend of Bethany's, turned his wheeled chair so that he faced Gwynne. "You know that this meeting was called because of you and Ballister."

Gwynne nodded. She would not have been invited otherwise. "He did nothing that requires censure, sir. It was I who lacked propriety."

Polmarric made an impatient gesture. "We are not concerned about young people stealing kisses in a pleasure garden. But sometimes an event that seems small on the surface is like the thread that will unravel a tapestry once it is pulled. That kiss was more than just a kiss."

Gwynne could feel the heat in her cheeks, and wished that her private life had not become so public. But Polmarric was right; more was involved than flirtation.

"As I said last night, all of the senior mages have been concerned about gathering events, but the shape of the future has proved maddeningly elusive." Bethany touched her fingertips to her scrying glass, which lay on the table before her. "Until now. I described your visions. Then we had a meeting of the minds."

Lady Sterling, a tall woman whose blond hair was shading into silver, asked, "Are you familiar with the process, Lady Brecon?"

Gwynne noticed how Lady Sterling's palm was firmly cupped over her talking sphere. That contact was how the absent members "heard" Gwynne—whatever she said was channeled through Lady Sterling, who was the strongest communicator on the council. "As I understand it, a question is posed and everyone is encouraged to share ideas and insights. Several strong mages working together will spark one another's ideas, and it's usually possible to develop a much clearer picture of the matter at hand."

Bethany nodded. "Often such sessions lead to places most unexpected. The political situation is rapidly becoming critical. If we are to have any effect on the outcome, we must act immediately." She caught Gwynne's gaze, her eyes blazing with Guardian power. "Which is why we want you to marry Lord Ballister."

It was fortunate that Gwynne was sitting down. "You want me to do *what*?" Her voice made an undignified squeak. "I'm not going to marry a barbarian Scot!"

"Not such barbarians as all that," Sir Ian Macleod said dryly. The dean of Scottish Guardians, among the Families he was called the Lord of the Isles.

"Forgive me, Sir Ian. I meant no insult." Gwynne's gaze skipped from face to face. This was no joke—they watched her like cats eyeing a mouse. "Duncan Macrae is a powerful mage. Someday he might sit on this very council. If he represents a danger to the nation's stability, what can *I* do about it? Assassinate him if he goes awry?"

Bethany clicked her tongue. "Don't say such a thing even in jest, Gwynne! Duncan has talent, integrity, and a deep respect for our traditions, but circumstances might lead any of us astray."

"It's difficult for a Scot to resist a call to freedom," Sir Ian observed. "If not for my age and the fact that I remember the Rising of 1715 too well, I'd be tempted to fight for Scottish independence myself. Those Acts of Union . . ." He shook his head dourly. "They're bitter unfair."

His words startled Gwynne, but also gave her greater insight into how a Jacobite rebellion would cause Scottish Guardians to feel the pull of divided loyalties. If even Sir Ian was tempted by the siren call of freedom, Duncan was vulnerable, too.

"Remember what I said last night?" Lady Bethany asked. "Ballister has a potential for harm, but an even greater potential for good. Our people are few in number, Gwynne—we cannot afford to lose one of the best men of your generation. We think that you might be able to prevent him from causing harm. You two are profoundly connected. If you marry him, you will have great influence over his actions." The older woman's eyes twinkled. "It's not as if doing so would be unrelieved misery."

Hugh Owens, a distant relative of Gwynne's, gestured and a small set of silver scales appeared on the table. Gwynne caught her breath. The scales must be an illusion, not a physical object, but it was still an impressive trick.

"Imagine these scales are Britain today," Owens said. "Though many forces are in play, overall the nation is reasonably peaceful. In equilibrium. Then imagine Ballister as throwing his considerable weight onto one side of the scales."

He snapped his fingers and a red spark appeared in one pan. The scales tipped violently, causing the whole mechanism to shake. "You and he have a fated relationship, which means that only you have the power to balance him." Another finger snap and a white spark appeared in the opposite pan. Slowly the scales returned to equilibrium.

A fated relationship. She had half forgotten Emery's words about destiny the afternoon he had asked her to marry him. Was this what he had foreseen that day?

Trying to sort her whirling thoughts, she said, "You are

asking me to leave everything and everyone I love and go among strangers."

"Do not think that we ask this lightly." Bethany sighed. "You are dearer to me than my own granddaughters, and I had thought I would have the pleasure of your company through my last years. But apparently that is not to be."

Gwynne shivered when she thought of Ballister's power. She would be intimidated by any suitor with such strong magic, she guessed, but Ballister was particularly fearsome. "You can't force me to marry him."

"No, we can't," Lady Sterling said coolly. "We request, not compel. Yes, it's difficult to go to a new land among strangers, but women have done that from time immemorial. You are too young to settle into the rut of the familiar. More important, you have a duty as a Guardian. Though you are no mage, when you reached womanhood you swore a solemn oath to serve and protect. You have enjoyed the privileges of being one of us. Now it is time for you to fulfill your responsibilities."

The words were like a splash of icy water. Lady Sterling was right; Gwynne had been cared for and protected her entire life, and this was the first time she had been asked to put aside her own desires for the greater good. An oath to serve was also a promise to sacrifice oneself if necessary.

Strangely, she didn't resent the council's coercion. Instead she felt pride that finally she had something to contribute: her life.

More gently, Bethany said, "We are not asking you to cast yourself from a cliff, my dear. Think of our request as a good excuse to give in to the part of yourself that has been yearning for Ballister."

That surprised a laugh from Gwynne. "It's true that I find him . . . very attractive. But how can I be his balance-mate if I am overwhelmed by his power and become a docile wife with no will of my own?"

Jasper Polmarric snorted. "I guarantee that you'll never be a docile wife. Your aura pulses with strength."

Easy for him to say—he had lived with great power most of his life. "If I marry Ballister, what will I do? Am I to be a spy reporting on his activities? How am I to know when he is going to cause this great harm you fear?" Her stomach clenched at the magnitude of the task she was being given, and how ill-qualified she was to perform it.

"Simply be yourself," Bethany said soothingly. "You are an archivist and keeper of the lore, which gives you an objective mind. You will always be capable of judging his actions. And if some great deed is required of you, you will recognize it, I think."

Gwynne didn't want to think what kind of great deed might be necessary. Though Bethany had said that the council would not want to move against one of their own, such things did happen when a mage turned renegade and used his power in menacing ways. Since she could never destroy another living being, much less her husband, she must pray that she really would be equal to the task she was accepting.

She stared down at the hands locked tightly in her lap. If she married Ballister, her entire life would change. Yet what choice did she have? Her Guardian oath had been invoked, and she could not in honor refuse. It was characteristic of the Families that a woman's honor was considered as vital as a man's; she did not want to prove unworthy.

If she was to survive, she must concentrate on the good

of the situation. She would be marrying a man who doted on her, at least for now. He'd said that Dunrath had a good library and that she could add to it. There might, please God, be children.

And he was the most wickedly attractive man she had ever met.

"Very well," she said in a low voice. "If Duncan Macrae of Dunrath will have me, I will marry him."

She could feel the council members relax as clearly as if they were exhaling with relief. Looking up, she blurted out, "And I hope that you are all as wise as your reputations say you are!"

*   *   *

Duncan faced Simon in the front hall of Falconer House, neither of them quite ready to say good-bye even though Duncan's carriage was waiting.

Simon said, "I had hoped you would stay longer."

Duncan shook his friend's hand, hard. "If all hell is about to break loose in Scotland, I need to be home and taking up my responsibilities." He tried to suppress the images of Gwynne at Dunrath that persisted in haunting his imagination. "You should come visit me. Some fresh Scottish air would be good for you."

"If all hell breaks loose, perhaps I shall. Disaster is my business, after all." Simon stopped suddenly, his attention wrenched away from the present.

"Has something happened?" Duncan asked quickly.

"I . . . I'm not sure. I'll think about it." With visible effort, Simon focused on his guest. "At least when you're no longer brooding about my house with a broken heart, the London weather may improve from this gray and gloomy dampness."

A knock sounded at the front door a few feet away. Not waiting for his butler, Simon swung it open. A neatly dressed groom offered a sealed letter. "A message for Lord Ballister, sir."

Duncan moved forward to take the letter and give the messenger a coin. "Is a reply expected?"

"No, sir." The groom bowed and returned to his waiting mount.

After closing the door, Duncan broke the wax seal curiously. Few people even knew he was in London. His face stiffened as he read the polite words of the message.

Catching his expression, Simon asked, "What's wrong?"

"Lady Brecon requests the honor of my company at my earliest convenience." Duncan grimaced. "A pity I didn't leave five minutes earlier."

The other man's brows arched. "I would have thought you would be happy to hear from her."

"Considering her fury when she bolted from our last meeting, I suspect she wants to spell out in greater detail how utterly ungentlemanly I am." Duncan paused, distracted by the memory of their one kiss. . . . "I'll call on her on my way north."

"If you'd rather not, I can send a message saying that you've already left town."

"She has the right to castigate me. I shall confess my sins, apologize profusely, and leave." It would be worth harsh words to see her one last time.

What a thrice-damned fool he was.

*   *   *

By the time Duncan reached Richmond, he had his emotions well in hand. The finality of their last meeting made the situation easier, for he no longer had to worry about wooing Gwynne. This would be a chance to say goodbye and wish her well for the future, no matter how angry she was.

Since he needed a wife, a good ending might make it easier to look elsewhere when the worst pain of loss wore off. The Macleods of Skye had a quiverful of attractive daughters, all of them magically talented. Perhaps one would catch his fancy. Wedding a fellow Scot would be altogether better than a reluctant Englishwoman.

Lady Bethany's butler recognized him. "If you will wait in the small salon, my lord, I shall inform Lady Brecon that you are here."

Duncan stepped into the salon and was hit by a blast of psychic energy that would have curled his whiskers if he were a cat. What had Lady Bethany been up to?

Since Gwynne would probably keep him waiting, he decided to use the time to sharpen his analytical skills. He paced around the room and tried to sort out the different energy signatures. Interesting—there were clear traces of several council members. They must have used this room for a session, and recently.

He tried to determine what subjects they had discussed. There was a heaviness in the atmosphere that suggested concern about impending war, but there had been other topics as well. He had a distinct sense that his name must have come up. . . .

"My lord Ballister."

He was so involved in his analysis that Gwynne's voice startled him. He spun about to see her poised in the doorway, as if ready to take flight. Her powdered hair was pulled back severely and she wore a simple green-striped cotton morning gown. The very chasteness of her appearance was almost unbearably provocative.

He took refuge in a deep bow. "Your messenger caught me just before my departure to Scotland. I am grateful for this opportunity to take my leave, and to offer you my deepest apologies. It was wrong of me to deceive you at New Spring Gardens. My only defense is—" He hesitated, realizing it was hard to defend the indefensible. "—it seemed like a good idea at the time."

His honesty won a slight smile from her. "That thought is surely at the root of most human folly. Pray take a seat."

He settled in a chair warily, thinking this would be easier to understand if she were more obviously angry. Instead, her mood was conflicted and . . . determined?

She stayed on her feet, moving about the room with a restlessness that belied the serenity of her face. "Our relationship has been as fraught as a summer storm, my lord."

He thought of the squall that had blown up on the day they met because he had failed to control his reaction to her. "You are a woman who inspires storms of passion, not tepid breezes of mild affection."

"You are the only man who has thought so."

Her pacing temporarily halted while she gazed out the window. The silhouetted curves of her lush figure made him swallow hard. "If you haven't been besieged by suitors, it's only because they didn't know to seek you in your library."

She turned to face him, her expression somber. "Why are you so interested in me? Is it something about my appearance? That's a shallow reason for deciding that you must have me. Or do you just enjoy conquest and my resistance is a challenge?"

He could fall into those golden eyes and never come out. . . . He forced his attention back to her words. "Acquit me of such shallowness. Yes, I am a man and enjoy feminine beauty, but I am also a Guardian. When we met I saw not only your beauty but your intelligence, your integrity, and your warmth. I knew as surely as I know the shape of the wind that if you honored me with your hand, I would be entranced and in love for as long as we both live."

She blushed and looked away. This time it was the pure line of her throat and profile that caused his heart to beat faster. He would think she was deliberately teasing him with her beautiful self to torment him, except that such behavior was not part of Gwynne's nature. But there were strange undercurrents swirling through the room, and their conversation certainly wasn't following the course he had expected.

Visibly steeling herself, she faced him again. "Are you still sure that you want me, and only me, as your wife?"

He didn't understand this, but his pulse began quickening. "I am sure."

"Then if you wish it . . . I will marry you."

Her words dizzied him. He must be dreaming. It was the only explanation.

But the world was too sharply real for a dream. He could feel the breeze rippling through Lady Bethany's trees and count the swift pulses beating in Gwynne's slender throat. "If you are serious . . . *yes!* A thousand times yes." He drew a shaky breath. "And I hope to God that you are not saying that to torment me."

She smiled a little. "If I'm the paragon you think, I would never behave so badly."

There was a moment of uncertain silence. Pulling himself together, he used his inner senses to read her. Unless she could control her emotions like a master mage, she was completely sincere—and as frightened as a kitten menaced by a wolf.

"Gwynne." He closed the distance between them and enfolded her in his arms, forcing himself to be tender rather than giving in to crazy exhilaration and frightening her even more. "My matchless, indomitable lady. Please don't fear me. I'll never hurt you. I would strike off my right arm first."

For a moment she was stiff as a statue. Then she gave a little sigh and softened against him, hiding her face against his shoulder. He wanted to talk, kiss, laugh, make love to her—preferably all at once. "You won't regret accepting me, Gwynne. I swear it on my honor as a Guardian."

"I hope you're right."

She raised her head, and he was shocked to see tears glinting in her eyes. Not tears of joy, either, unless he had become deaf to emotion. "What's wrong? Are you already regretting the thought of marriage?" The question that should have occurred to him immediately struck. "The last time you saw me, you wanted my guts for garters. Why did you change your mind?"

She blinked back her tears. "Lady Bethany said that I should marry you. After considering the matter, I agreed."

"You'll marry me against your will because she ordered you to?" Anger surged. "Sweet Jesus, Gwynne, what kind of marriage would that be? We are not children to tamely agree to arrangements made by our elders. I will not take an unwilling wife."

He started to pull away. She caught his wrist. "I did not accept you against my will," she said tautly. "Bethany said that . . . that I would balance you. That I should surrender to the part of me that catches fire whenever we meet."

He wanted to be persuaded. Dear Lord, how he wanted to be persuaded. But he wasn't quite witless. Trying to read into her soul, he said quietly, "Is that true, Gwynne? For we must have truth between us, or we are better off apart."

"The bald truth is that from the beginning I have found you equally attractive and intimidating. Cowardice was winning until Bethany decided to take a hand." Gwynne's smile was tremulous. "I'm still afraid—of leaving my home and friends, of going to a strange land. Most of all, I fear marrying a man who has such great power when I have none, even though you have given me no reason to fear you."

He caught her hands and raised them for a tender kiss. "You underestimate your own power, Gwynne. Eve's magic is even more ancient than that of the Guardians."

"I hope you're right." She smiled with wry surrender. "I do know beyond doubt that with you I can reach heights I have never before imagined. That is worth facing my fears."

This was the strangest proposal and acceptance he'd ever heard of, but honesty was a good beginning. Perhaps she had felt guilt about marrying again, and permission from her late husband's sister freed her to risk her heart once more.

Whatever the path that had brought her to accept him, she was committing herself to be his. Nothing else mattered.

Eight

Gwynne leaned into Ballister's embrace, shaking with reaction. She had done it—she's asked the man to marry her, and he had accepted. Earlier, she'd been petrified with nerves, wondering if he would call, and if he did, whether she would have the courage to speak. Now the die was cast, and the relief from uncertainty was enormous.

"My sweet Gwyneth. My lady of sunshine." He cupped her chin between his hands and raised her face for a kiss.

For an instant she felt the terror of blood and death that she had experienced before, but this time she was prepared. Earlier in the day Bethany had taught her a mental trick for dealing with painful thoughts, so she visualized tossing the horrific images into a lead casket, then slammed the lid of the casket shut to confine the horror.

To her surprise, after a moment of disorientation, the trick worked. She was no longer paralyzed by shock, and from what Bethany said, she should be able to train her mind to automatically channel away the images.

That left her free to experience the passion of the man

she was taking as her husband. His mouth was warm, compelling, and the hardness and power of his muscular body sent languor melting through her limbs. Odd to think that this newness and exploration would soon become known and familiar. But never ordinary.

As she slid her arms around his neck, she sensed the control behind his hungry embrace. She was grateful for that, because his unbridled passion might have incinerated her. She wondered if her desire could ever match his. Surely not—the intensity of his nature was part of what both attracted and intimidated her. Even restrained passion weakened her knees and dazed her mind. Never had she experienced such intense aliveness, or such blinding need.

She wasn't even aware that they had moved until he ended the kiss and she realized that they were sprawled on the sofa, her body lying across his with embarrassing intimacy. His voice husky, he whispered, "How soon can we be married? I'd wed you today if I could."

Returned to her senses, she pulled away and tucked herself into a corner of the sofa, not touching him. "I . . . I will need more time. Perhaps in a month. Or two?"

He clasped her hand, his thumb caressing the sensitive flesh of her inner wrist. "I don't want to rush you, and not only because I fear that you will change your mind." He smiled ruefully. "But I must return to Scotland as soon as possible. Falconer is one of the best scryers in Britain, and he says rebellion is imminent. I must be there to lead and guide my clansmen."

As she considered how long it would take to organize a wedding and pack her belongings, she brushed back her damp hair, thinking it was uncomfortably hot. Then she realized the heat wasn't only from that scalding kiss. The sun had come out and was pouring through the window to warm the sofa. "Did you make the clouds disappear?"

He looked out the window, startled. "I believe I did. I was so happy that I probably burned away every cloud in the Thames Valley. You have an alarming effect on me, Gwynne. If I'm not careful, after our marriage I'll turn Scotland into a desert."

She laughed, then turned serious. "I know so little about your homeland. Nothing about your family, your home, what my life will be like."

"Dunrath is quite possibly the most beautiful place on earth. Not that I'm biased, of course." He gave her a teasing smile. "The castle is ancient and impregnable. In more turbulent times, it was besieged often but never conquered. The glen lies between Highlands and Lowlands, not quite belonging to either. That suits us, I think. As Guardians, the Macraes of Dunrath try to maintain loyalty to a larger cause than just the clan. It's not always easy."

"I've heard that Scots are loyal to the death."

"And often loyal to a fault." He sighed. "Too many of my stubborn countrymen will let themselves be flayed alive rather than admit that they might be wrong, or that there might be a better way to resolve a problem. I try to provide an example of common sense."

"A man who lives in a drafty, ice-cold castle talks of common sense?"

He grinned. "It's not so bad as that. Some of the rooms have been fixed up to be quite comfortable."

She suspected that what seemed comfortable to a Scot would have her wrapped in blankets and shivering by a fire. No doubt she would get used to it. "I've read of Dunrath in Guardian memoirs. It's exciting to think that I shall be living in the home of Isabel de Cortes. She has long been my heroine, you know. I've read that when she and Adam Macrae quarreled, all of Scotland rocked."

"She and Adam were my three times great-grandparents."

Ballister raised his hand to show a massive sapphire ring. "Queen Elizabeth gave them both rings as recognition of their service against the Spanish Armada. This ring was Adam's and is always worn by the chieftain of the Macraes of Dunrath. Isabel's ring is set with a ruby. It will be yours after we are wed."

"I'll have Isabel's ring?" Gwynne exclaimed, surprised and delighted. Isabel de Cortes had been a London merchant's daughter of Spanish Marranos stock. Despite her mundane origins, she had been one of the great mages of her era. Not only had she studied with John Dee, Queen Elizabeth's legendary alchemist, she had brought fresh wild magic to the British Guardians.

Gwynne recognized that Ballister should have found a woman like Isabel—a wife who was his equal. But since he wanted Gwynne, she must hope that Isabel's ring would lend a little strength. "If you had told me of the ring earlier, I might have accepted you at once," she said with a smile.

"I wish I'd known. That would have saved me much grief." His gray eyes were full of warmth. "I am so proud, so honored, that you will be my wife. Even if you did have to be talked into it by your sister-in-law."

"She thought that all I needed was an excuse to abandon my anxiety, and I think she was right, Ballister." That was the truth, if not the whole truth.

"Call me Duncan."

"Duncan," she said, trying to include a faint Scottish lilt in her pronunciation. The hard edge of the name suited him.

"Well done! May I call you Gwynne now?"

"I think I might allow that." She felt breathless and silly and happier than she could ever remember. It would be so easy to fall in love with Duncan Macrae. She was already halfway there. . . .

A cool thread of reason interfered with her happiness. Her task was to balance Ballister—Duncan—and prevent him from triggering a disaster. That would be impossible unless she kept a small part of herself reserved from him. She must not become a dazzled bride. She hadn't realized how hard a task that would be.

Not wanting Duncan to sense her withdrawal, she asked, "Was Isabel de Cortes vital to Adam Macrae's success at destroying the Armada? I've seen no suggestion in the chronicles that she was a weather worker."

"She wasn't, but she was able to channel some of her tremendous power to Adam. Otherwise, he could never have conjured a tempest so immense." He touched her hair. "Now that I can call you Gwynne, when can I see you with your hair unpowdered? I've been longing to admire your natural beauty."

"It is not beautiful hair, but I suppose that you must see it sooner or later. You will understand then why I powder it." She frowned, thinking of all that must be done. "I'll speak to Bethany about how quickly a small wedding can be organized. Will you allow me a week?"

He hesitated. "I can feel Scotland tugging, but less time would not do the occasion justice. A week from today, then?"

She nodded, excited and a little dazed. In a week she would be wed again, and she didn't need scrying ability to know this marriage would be very different from her union with Emery. "Who has taken care of Dunrath during your travels?"

"My sister, Jean. She's much younger than I, only twenty-one, but already she's a better steward of the land than I will ever be. You'll like her, I'm sure."

"Is Jean a mage?"

"She has her share of power, but she hasn't spent the

time needed to develop her gifts to the fullest." He released Gwynne's hand and began trailing his fingers up her arm, sparking tingles of excitement.

Gwynne hoped fervently that Jean would marry and leave Dunrath as soon as possible; the last thing the new lady of the house needed was a magically gifted sister-in-law who might resent relinquishing power to her brother's wife. "There will be so much to learn. I know how to run an English household, but not a Scottish one."

"Scots tend to be less formal. Clans are family groups, after all, so there's a natural equality not found in England." He grinned. "I'm told that when Mary Queen of Scots returned from France to take up her throne, she was shocked by clan chiefs who called her 'Lass.' You are warned."

"I'm not royal, and I neither want nor expect deference. I like the idea of a society of natural equality." She had never become comfortable with the subservience she received after marriage made her a countess. In her heart, she was still the librarian's daughter. Perhaps Scotland really would suit her, as Duncan had once said.

She hoped so, given that she would be spending the rest of her life there.

"Before we announce the happy news to Lady Beth, shall we have another kiss?"

Not waiting for Gwynne to reply, Duncan closed the space between them and drew her into his arms again. She had just enough time to ready her defense against the blast of painful images. Then she let herself tumble into the kiss. The world disappeared, leaving only the sensuality and the sweet rush of desire. With this much passion, there would be no need to worry about freezing in a Scottish winter. . . .

"Excuse us." The words were apologetic, but the voice wasn't.

Gwynne blushed and pulled from Duncan's embrace. He gave her an intimate smile before turning in an unhurried fashion. Entering the room were Lady Bethany and Lord Falconer, their expressions grim. Surely not because they disapproved of a kiss?

Duncan stood, keeping one of her hands in his clasp. "It is fitting that you two are the first to know that Gwynne has honored me by agreeing to be my wife."

"My felicitations. I wish you both happiness." Simon sighed. "I wish I weren't the bearer of bad news. Prince Charles Edward Stuart has landed in Scotland."

Nine

"And so it begins." The news was an icy wind that drained away Duncan's excitement and pleasure. For years, he had been sensing a dark and possibly disastrous future, one of war and destruction. Why did this have to happen now, on the happiest day of his life? "Though we've expected this rebellion, now that it has arrived . . ." He shook his head. "How did you find out?"

"This morning I had a strong sense that some great event was unfolding. After you left, I began seriously scrying." Despite Simon's fair coloring, there was darkness in his gaze. "I saw the prince and his companions stepping onto Scottish soil, and it sent a drumbeat through the whole of Britain. I came here to see if Lady Beth could confirm what I saw."

"Simon was right. Unfortunately." Lady Bethany took a seat, her usual sparkle absent. "The prince will start by raising support among the Highland chiefs, I think."

"Do you know if he has French backing?" Duncan asked. "It was only last year that the French were set for a full-scale invasion of England."

"An invasion that was blocked when unexpected

storms dispersed the French fleet." Simon smiled faintly. "That was well done of you, Duncan. I'm not sure where the French stand now. The prince arrived in a French ship, but that doesn't necessarily mean they are supporting this adventure with men and weapons."

"I must go home immediately." Duncan turned to Gwynne, whose hand he was holding too tightly. The thought of leaving her was a blade slicing his heart, but he had no choice. "We shall have to postpone the wedding. If the prince doesn't have French support, the rebellion will collapse quickly. I'll come back for you then and we can have a proper wedding."

"No." Gwynne rose, not relinquishing his hand. "A marriage vow is for better and worse, and surely that means I should not hide here in England. You said Dunrath Castle is impregnable, so I should be safe enough if I come with you."

"Gwynne . . ." She was so lovely he could hardly bear it. He wanted desperately to keep her close, but there was danger ahead for both of them. He could see it as clearly as he could see her golden eyes.

"Duncan, marrying at once is not a request, but a requirement." Her voice was steely. "If you want a compliant bride who allows herself to be set aside like a pair of gloves until a more convenient time, you must look elsewhere. We can be married tomorrow. Surely one day's delay will not be critical."

He hesitated, admiring her courage but hating the thought of risking her in the uncertainties of a rebellion. Yet she was right—she was a woman grown, not a child to be kept in the nursery. And some deep, intuitive part of his soul said it was more important to have her with him than to keep her safe in the south. "You win, my love. I can't be wise if it means losing you."

"Two days," Lady Bethany said. "The wedding can be held day after tomorrow. I guarantee that the delay will not be harmful, and for both your sakes, the wedding should be done with the dignity it deserves."

Despite his impatience to return to Scotland, he deferred to the older woman. If she said another two days would cause no harm, it was surely true. "Very well, Lady Beth. Simon, will you stand up with me?"

"Of course. But for now, you must bid your lady goodbye. We need to put our heads together and see what more we can learn about this rebellion. As for Gwynne—" He smiled and kissed her cheek. "—she needs to plan her wedding."

Duncan hated to leave Gwynne, but Simon was right. As he gave her a sweet, taut kiss of farewell, he reminded himself that his wedding night was only two days away. He must keep himself busy till then, or he risked perishing of anticipation.

* * *

For Gwynne, the next two days passed in a blur. Not only did she have to prepare for her wedding, but she had to sort her possessions and decide what must be sent to Scotland. She would have succumbed to strong hysterics if not for Lady Bethany's calm good sense. Anne Tuckwell also sent her daughter Sally to help, and Sally was most knowledgeable about what was important to a bride.

The baggage coach that would travel separately could take the most important of Gwynne's books, but sadly, her cat was too old to make such a long journey. Duncan had also advised that her pretty mare was not well suited to Highland life. He had promised to buy her a more suitable mount in the north.

Now, suddenly, it was time for the wedding. Gwynne held still while Molly, the middle-aged maid she and Bethany shared, fussed with the hooks and eyes at the back of her bodice. The gown was new and fashionable, and Gwynne had not yet worn it, so the garment was a good choice for a day that would change her life.

She glanced across the room to inspect herself in the mirror. The bodice and overskirt were made of cream-colored silk delicately embroidered with blossoms and birds. The fabric shimmered over her hoops, set off by an underskirt of ice white satin and sleeves that ended in a foam of creamy lace. She had chosen the garment to be richly attractive but discreet, and it made an admirable wedding gown.

Bethany stepped back and viewed her critically. "You are lovely, my dear. I'm glad you decided to wear your hair loose and unpowdered. It makes you look young and eager for life, the way a bride should be."

"Now for the flowers in your hair." Molly placed a chaplet of pale blossoms on Gwynne's head, then blinked hard. "You have never looked better, my lady. I will miss you, I surely will."

"Oh, Molly, I shall miss you, too." Gwynne hugged the maid. "I wish I could take you with me, but you wouldn't go and Lady Bethany would never forgive me if I stole you away."

"It will be better if you choose a local girl as a maid," Bethany said practically. "She can help you learn Scottish ways."

Athena, who had been sleeping on the bed, jumped down and strolled over to Gwynne, batting at the lace trailing from her right sleeve in passing. Ignoring the delicate fabric of the gown, Gwynne bent and swooped the cat into her arms. "I'm going to miss you, sweet puss."

Athena rubbed her whiskered muzzle against her mistress's cheek while Gwynne fought tears. She did not want to go to her wedding with puffy eyes and a red nose.

"I shall take good care of Athena," Bethany said. "You'll see her again when you visit London."

"I know that she'll be perfectly happy here with you. I'm the one mourning." Reluctantly Gwynne allowed Molly to take the cat from her arms. "No doubt there are cats in Scotland, but none will be such splendid library cats."

"Never say never, my dear." Bethany approached and gave her a light kiss on the cheek. "And now it's time for you to be wed."

Gwynne nodded and followed the older woman from the room. Her formal gown was so wide she barely managed to get through the door without turning sideways. She was almost dizzy with nerves. This would be in all ways different from her first wedding. Though she had also been nervous when she married Emery, at least then she had stayed in her childhood home.

Though part of Gwynne still wanted to cling to her safe, familiar life, it was too late for that. Ever since the council had asked her to marry Duncan, she had felt a sense of rightness. That was why she had insisted they marry immediately: that same inner sense whispered that her influence was needed now, during the rebellion. If she delayed the wedding until peace returned, it would be too late.

Prayer book clenched in her hands, she left her home and climbed into the coach that would carry her to her destiny.

*   *   *

Duncan had hardly slept for two days as he and Simon and other senior mages had attempted to probe the future to learn what the rebellion would portend for Scotland and England. The answers had been frighteningly vague, with far too many possibilities.

The process had been disquieting because he had sensed that his own actions would be significant in unexpected ways. Perhaps that was why several of the older mages, particularly Lady Sterling, had seemed wary of him.

The thought was outrageous, and made him wonder if anti-Scottish prejudice could exist among a group that was supposedly enlightened. As a man whose home was in the center of Scotland, he was bound to be involved in the rebellion in some way, but he would never be disloyal. He had always honored his Guardian oath and supported King George, even though the Hanoverians were an unappetizing lot.

There were times when it was a nuisance to be a Guardian and be unable to avoid sensing what your peers were thinking about you.

But that was behind him. Today was his wedding day. The ceremony was being held in the Richmond parish church of St. Mary Magdalen, with a wedding breakfast at Lady Bethany's afterward. About thirty guests waited. He noted Gwynne's friends from New Spring Gardens as well as several Harlowes and half a dozen members of the Guardian Council. It was a good gathering for such short notice.

Surely it was past the time the bride should arrive. He shifted uneasily, not absolutely sure that she might not change her mind. As the minutes stretched, it was hard not to wonder.

"Stop worrying," Simon murmured. "It isn't that late, and she will come."

Duncan managed a smile. His friend had always been something of a mind reader, and today Duncan's feelings must be blindingly obvious.

He tried not to fidget with his cuffs. If they were marrying in Scotland, he would have worn a belted plaid, but here in England he had donned the elaborate costume that he'd worn to the French court at Versailles. A Parisian tailor had cut the deep violet silk coat embroidered in silver, the brocade waistcoat, the silk breeches. He was so grand he hardly recognized himself.

Simon said quietly, "The bride is here."

Duncan turned to the doorway, and almost stopped breathing as the bride's party entered. As Gwynne stepped inside the church, sunlight touched her hair into a blaze of brilliant color, all red and gold like sunrise in the Hebrides. She glowed like a lit candle.

He watched, enraptured, as she approached the altar. Her hair swooped upward before cascading over her shoulders in molten waves. Her flowered wreath made her look like a pagan goddess of life and love, yet there was an innocence in her expression and in the pale shining silk of her gown.

"Be careful your eyes don't fall out," Simon whispered with a hint of laughter.

Gwynne's stepson, the present Earl of Brecon, was giving her away as a signal of his approval. There would be no hint that this wedding was anything less than welcomed by her first husband's family.

She gave Duncan a shaky smile when she reached the altar, looking very young and vulnerable. Her waist was so tiny that surely he could span it with his hands.

His emotions flooded so powerfully that it was almost

painful. Silently he pledged that she would never regret accepting him. Aloud, he said softly, "You are as magnificent as the dawn." He took her hand, and distant thunder sounded.

"And you are the storm that carries all before it," she said in a voice so low even the vicar couldn't hear.

As they turned to face the altar, he knew with absolute certainty that this marriage was the most wondrous thing that had ever happened to him.

*   *   *

As rose petals showered over them, Gwynne accepted Duncan's hand and climbed into the waiting carriage. He followed and settled beside her as the door was closed, and they set off from Lady Bethany's house followed by a chorus of good wishes.

The wedding breakfast had been lively with toasts and laughter. She had deliberately kept herself busy chatting with guests and had hardly spoken a word to her new husband. Her nerves were on edge as she wondered whether he would be able to read her mind once they were truly wed. Everyone needed privacy in their own minds.

Finally they were alone. She was acutely aware of his tall, masculine body, and how small and private the travel coach was. She took a deep, slow breath. She was now Lady Ballister, not Lady Brecon, and they were heading to Scotland. This was a great adventure. . . .

A strong, hard hand came to rest over her locked fingers. "You look ready to jump from the carriage and head for the hedges. Is marriage to me that frightening, Gwynne?" Duncan's deep voice was warm with teasing.

Praying that she had the ability to shield her deepest

thoughts from her new husband, she smiled back, enjoying the unruly dark curls that escaped the riband at the back of his neck. The more she saw of his craggy face, the more handsome he seemed. "I am accustoming myself to the idea of having a new lord and master."

"As if any Guardian woman would tamely submit to a man!" He laughed. "Certainly no woman with red hair like yours has ever been docile."

She glanced away. "I warned you that it was not good hair. I should have powdered it for the wedding."

"No!" He brushed her hair gently, his fingers lingering. "It's the most beautiful hair I've ever seen. To see it revealed today was a very special wedding gift." He leaned forward and kissed her throat through the silky strands.

She caught her breath, transfixed by the feel of his lips. There had been attraction from the beginning, and now desire was sanctified by God and man. Raising her hand, she stroked his thick hair. It was all the encouragement he needed.

"You are the most beautiful woman in the world," he breathed before claiming her mouth. His kiss melted her reserve. She felt like molten wax, flowing and yearning to mold herself to him. He cupped her breast, and she almost cried out at the exquisite sensation. How could she ever balance him when he had such power over her?

As if reading her mind, he said huskily, "Don't ever fear me, Gwynne. Don't you know that I would do anything for you?"

This magnificent, powerful man wanted her. Her wedding-ceremony tension melting away, she touched her tongue to his.

It was like setting a spark to tinder. His kiss deepened,

dizzying her, and the rocking of the coach moved their bodies together. "Gwynne, Gwynne," he groaned. "I wonder if there is enough space in this carriage to consummate our marriage? That would make an exciting memory for when we are old and gray."

His words were like a splash of icy water. She put her hands on his shoulders and pushed him away. "I don't think that's a good idea, Duncan." She drew a deep breath, knowing she must speak up. "Though I am a widow, I . . . I am also a virgin."

The change in Duncan's expression was so abrupt it was almost laughable. Gwynne gave him credit for how quickly he assimilated her announcement.

"I see." He sat back in the seat, putting space between them, though awareness thrummed. "Of course, Lord Brecon wed you when his years were much advanced."

She began to pleat the lace falling from her sleeves. "I do not believe that he was unfit. Rather, he . . . he chose not to."

She had been a willing bride. More than willing, for she had always adored the lord of Harlowe and she wanted to please him. She had been bitterly disappointed when he entered her bedchamber on their wedding night and gave her only a kiss. There had been desire in his eyes, she was sure of it. But not enough. "He . . . he said I had a destiny, and he should not interfere with that." And perhaps he wished no more children.

Duncan's eyes narrowed thoughtfully. "I would give much to know what Lord Brecon saw. But I agree that you are my destiny, as I am yours."

He accepted the idea of destiny so easily, but of course, he was a mage. In the heady excitement of his embrace, she was tempted to tell him that her decision to marry had been almost a command from the Guardian Council, not merely a suggestion from Lady Bethany. He was her husband and she wanted to be truthful.

Instinct said to hold her tongue. If she told him too much, it might alter his behavior in the future. Unless that was what she should be doing? She suppressed an unladylike curse. Being told to be herself wasn't very useful as a guideline to her new life, much less to her "destiny."

The wheels hit a hole and the vehicle rocked. He sat back in the seat and took her hand, lacing his fingers through hers. "A carriage is a poor choice for being initiated into passion."

She blushed, remembering how willing his kisses had made her. She'd been scarcely aware of their location. "Tonight I would prefer a proper bed. Will we be spending the night at some coaching inn you know?"

"Sorry, it's been so hectic that I didn't have a chance to tell you that Falconer has loaned us one of his estates for the night. It's only a few hours north and very close to the turnpike, so it will be convenient, and more private than a coaching inn. He's notified his servants to expect us. There will be a bedchamber and a supper waiting for us."

"Bless Simon." She smiled, glad that her wedding night wouldn't take place in a common inn. "Perhaps we might try the carriage at . . . some future time."

Laughing, he raised her hand and pressed a lingering kiss on her knuckles. "We shall find great pleasure in each other, Lady Ballister. I know it."

hough it was still light when they reached Buckland Abbey, Gwynne was grateful to arrive. Getting married was a tiring business.

The sprawling Tudor house was well proportioned and immaculately maintained. Much, much nicer than a coaching inn. "The ruins of the original abbey are behind the house," Duncan said as he helped Gwynne from the carriage. "They're very Gothic and mysterious. Perhaps we can walk through them in the morning before we leave."

She lifted her skirts to climb the front steps. "I thought you were in a mad rush to reach Scotland?"

He made a face. "I am, but Lady Beth informed me in no uncertain terms that there was no harm in spending some time enjoying the company of my bride on the journey home. So I will, since she's always right."

Gwynne laughed. "I've noticed that."

As Duncan raised his hand to the massive knocker, the front door swung open and an elderly butler bowed them into the house. "My lord and lady, welcome to Buckland Manor. May I escort you to your rooms so you may refresh yourselves?"

"Please do." Duncan glanced at Gwynne. "And have

our supper served immediately after we've freshened up."

Gwynne nodded agreement. "I spent so much time talking at the wedding breakfast that I ate very little, and now I'm ravenous."

A light sparked in Duncan's eyes, which were now the clear gray of early dawn. "An appetite is a fine thing in a bride," he said softly.

Once more, Gwynne blushed. Amazing how many comments were suggestive when one was in the mood. Though they had talked of unimportant things on the carriage ride, and she had even dozed a little with her head on Duncan's shoulder, a delicious tension had pulsed between them. Despite her uncertainties about this marriage, she was eager to be initiated into the mysteries of the marriage bed by a man who aroused her so thoroughly—and kissed so well.

"Let me take you both up now," the butler said. When they had ascended the stairs and walked to the west wing, the servant indicated the end of the corridor. "These three rooms have connecting doors. Lady Ballister, your chamber is in the middle, my lord's is to the right, and your private supper shall be served in the sitting room to the left. Ring if you have any special request. Your wishes are our commands."

"Lord Falconer has provided well for us," Duncan observed. He kissed Gwynne's hand. "Knock on my door when you are ready for me to join you for supper, my dear."

She nodded, then entered the center room. The chamber was beautifully appointed and clearly intended for a lady, with striking views of the sun starting to set over the rolling countryside. She had just finished washing up when a pretty young maid came in and bobbed a curtsey. "I'm Elsie, Lady Ballister. How may I serve you?"

Falconer's orders had definitely inspired the staff to exceptional efforts. Gwynne turned her back to the girl. "Thank you, Elsie. Will you unlace me, please? I've had quite enough of this corset for one day."

Deftly Elsie began unfastening her garments. "A nightgown and overrobe were sent here by a Lady Bethany Fox. Would you care to put them on now?"

Gwynne smiled a little mistily. Bethany had spared no efforts to make this wedding special despite the haste. And since she and Duncan would be dining quietly, why not don her nightwear now? It wouldn't be long until they were in bed, she was sure. "I would like that."

The maid opened the wardrobe and brought out the most amazing negligee set Gwynne had ever seen. The robe was many layers of sheer gauzy silk, with the outermost a pale leaf green and each underlying layer a darker shade. Tiny sparkles of gold thread floated like stars on the delicate fabric. The nightgown itself was a sumptuous emerald satin that shimmered a subtle blue where light struck the fibers. "How lovely! I shall look like a water nymph."

"You will be even more beautiful than you are now," Elsie promised.

The robe slid easily over Gwynne's head and clung to her figure with wanton sensuality, while the robe tied in front with a ribbon and drifted around her like sea foam. She regarded the low neckline warily. If it weren't summer, she would risk lung fever. But Duncan wouldn't mind, she was sure.

"Let me brush out your hair," Elsie said. "Don't look in a mirror until I'm done."

Gwynne obediently sat still while the maid brushed her hair into a shining mass, then tied it back loosely with an emerald velvet ribbon, leaving a few strands to curl around her face.

"Now you may look, my lady."

Gwynne turned to face the long mirror, then gasped. Proper Lady Brecon had been replaced by a creature of fire and water, all glowing color and voluptuous female curves. Was this how Duncan saw her? But this image was an illusion born of garish hair and expensive silks. She hoped he wouldn't be disappointed with the mundane reality of her bookish self. "Thank you, Elsie. I look better than I dreamed possible."

The maid beamed. "Now you must find a proper lady for Lord Falconer to marry. The household needs a mistress."

Gwynne felt one of her flashes of certainty. "In a year or two, he will bring you his lady. You will like her."

"Is he courting someone now?" the girl asked with interest.

"Mere female intuition on my part," Gwynne said lightly. "A man who has no urgent need to marry must ripen to the point of readiness to become a husband. I think Lord Falconer is approaching that state."

Elsie nodded thoughtfully. "I know just what you mean, ma'am. My Ned, the head groom, kept coming to me for months with no word about marriage, yet when he decided it was time, he rushed me to the altar as soon as the banns were read."

The women exchanged a conspiratorial smile. Duncan had been even quicker than Elsie's Ned. Had he been entranced by her in particular, or was he merely very ready to settle down after years of traveling? Well, whatever the reasons, he was her husband now. "Thank you, Elsie. I won't need you again tonight."

The girl curtsied, then left the room. Gwynne found the glass vial that held her favorite perfume. It had been made by the current Countess of Brecon, who was a noted perfumer, and it combined delicate floral notes with a deeper, more provocative scent. After dabbing a bit behind one ear and, self-consciously, between her breasts, she returned the perfume to her cosmetics case.

She looked in the mirror one last time, vibrating with anticipation. Though she knew in principle what happened in a marital bed, that knowledge was of the mind. Soon she would know the physical and emotional reality, and her teacher would be a man who affected her like no other.

How would their relationship change? She couldn't begin to imagine. But people had been marrying since the dawn of time, so she and Duncan should be able to manage it. Certainly she intended to be a good and loyal wife.

Praying that her Guardian oath would never clash with her duty to her new husband, she crossed the room and knocked on Duncan's door. His tense but willing bride was ready to face the thunder.

*   *
    *

Duncan supposed it was natural to be nervous on his wedding night. Thankfully Gwynne wasn't a flighty young girl, but she was an innocent, and he wanted so much for everything to be right. His blue velvet banyan robe swirling around his ankles, he stalked to the window and stared out, his hands clasped behind his back.

He wanted desperately to make love to Gwynne. Even more, he wanted to bind her to him. Though he didn't doubt that she would take her vows seriously, she'd had to be persuaded to marry him. He wanted them to merge, to be one in love, but he sensed a deep reserve in her. He hoped intimacy would dissolve that, because he wanted all of her—body, mind, and soul.

Needing calm, he reached into the dusk to sense the air

and the weather patterns. There were storms to the west in Wales, but overall it was a peaceful summer evening. He flowed his consciousness into a cloud that drifted over fields of ripening grain, and it slowed the impatient beat of his heart.

Nonetheless, he spun around and crossed the room in three strides when Gwynne tapped on his door. He opened it, and peace vanished. Dressed in a confection of gauzy green silks and with sunset hair spilling over her creamy shoulders, she was dazzling. A pagan goddess. "Each time I see you, you are more beautiful," he said huskily.

Her smile had a shyness he found ravishing. "I'm glad you think so."

He wondered how long it would take for her to believe in her own beauty. With luck, he would have her convinced by the next morning. "I owe Lady Beth a great gift for persuading you to marry me. Now . . ." He bent into a kiss. Her lips opened easily under his, and for an intoxicating instant they tasted each other. When he started to embrace her, she stepped away.

"First we eat," she said teasingly. "I didn't pay much attention at the time, but there were sounds coming from the next room, and a few delicious scents. Shall we see what the cook has provided?"

Knowing that anticipation would make fulfillment all the better, he kissed the bare hollow of her shoulder, enjoying her sudden inhalation of pleasure. She smelled of violets and provocation. "Your wish is my command, my lady."

He wrapped his arm around her waist and they crossed to the sitting room. Her strides were long, and the soft sway of her hip against his almost persuaded him to carry her directly to the bed.

Later. Dark events might be unfolding in Scotland, but tonight was theirs. They would savor every moment of it.

When they stepped into the sitting room, he scanned the porcelain and crystal and silver laid out on immaculate white table linens. "Excellent. I asked Simon to arrange a *souper intime*. He promised to send his French chef from London to prepare the dishes."

"An intimate supper? Does that term have some special meaning?" Gwynne went to investigate the covered silver dishes set on the sideboard, some of them steaming gently over canisters of hot water.

"The French invented the idea, I think. It's a meal designed specifically for seduction," he explained. "With chafing dishes and bowls of cracked ice to keep food and drink the proper temperature, there's no need for a servant to interrupt, so we can dress informally. The dishes are chosen to be light and exquisite, teasing the palate rather than making the body heavy and ready for sleep."

She gave him a roguish glance. "Is it seduction when husband and wife share such a supper?"

The brightness and humor in her eyes went to his soul. He drew a deep breath to compose himself. "This will be a seduction of sorts, as we take the time to become attuned and discover what pleases."

"I am glad for that," she said softly.

One end of the sideboard held bottles of red wine, plus two bottles of white wine set in a large silver basin filled with pieces of ice. One was champagne, so he poured them glasses of the sparkling wine. "To our marriage, my lady. May we never be less happy than we are at this moment."

She took the glass, but a small line appeared between her eyes. "It seems almost ill luck to wish for such an impossible goal. To our marriage, my lord, and may we suit each other even if we don't always agree."

As he sipped the champagne, he felt a small chill of premonition. There would be disagreements, some of them shattering. Yet he could not imagine wanting any other woman in her place. "Agreement isn't essential. Respect and honesty are."

"I can't imagine not respecting you." Her gaze moved away from his. "Shall I serve you some of this lovely clear soup? I think it has slivers of truffle in it."

"Please do." He took a seat at the elegantly set round table. "Truffles are said to be aphrodisiacs."

"From what I've read, anything that gives a person the strength to act upon desire has been considered an aphrodisiac at one time or another." She ladled the delicately scented broth into small porcelain bowls and set them on the immaculate white linen, then took her chair, layers of silk drifting around her enticingly.

Duncan sampled his broth. Yes, this had to come from a French chef.

Without haste, they consumed their meal. Each dish was chosen to complement the other offerings, and the superb food provided a source of easy conversation. They drank wine, enough to relax but not enough to become befuddled. They fed each other choice tidbits, sampling fingertips as well as lips.

He was delighted to learn that she had a hearty appetite, for the love of food often went with other fleshly appetites. By the time they reached dessert, he was in a sensual haze beyond anything he had ever experienced.

He dipped a succulent, perfectly ripened strawberry from the Falconer glasshouse into a silver porringer filled with an orange-flavored liqueur. She licked a drop from her lower lip. His groin tightened and his mouth dried with the heat that surged through him.

Forcing himself to raise his eyes from the cleft revealed by the loose neckline of her negligee, he took a sip of wine and broached a subject that must be discussed. "In your studies, you must have learned that intimacy between Guardians is exceptionally intense. There is an opening of the souls, a dissolving of barriers. It might feel unnerving the first time."

"Do you find it so?"

"I've never lain with another Guardian." Before she could voice her surprise, he popped another liqueur-dipped berry into her mouth. "Intimacy is too powerful to share lightly. Even with a non-Guardian, there are dangers. A cruel or malicious lover can poison one's spirit. That's why it's rare to find a rakish Guardian."

"I've read such things in my studies, of course, but the subject was of mere intellectual interest, since I had neither lovers nor power." She propped her chin on her hand and gazed at him with languorous eyes. "Have you experienced a malicious lover?"

He grimaced, remembering. "Once, when I was young and foolish. I was besotted by a pretty face and didn't take the effort to look more deeply. I suspect I didn't want to acknowledge the meanness of her nature. So I lay with her, and spent months feeling soiled. I took so many baths my valet thought I'd scrub my skin off."

Gwynne cocked her head, her hair catching red and gold highlights as it slid luxuriantly over her shoulder. "And here I had thought you were a vastly experienced man of the world."

He smiled wryly. "Is it worse for me to confess to decadence, or to admit that I am less worldly than you thought?"

She fed him the last strawberry, her fingertips brushing teasingly over his lips. "I am glad you're no rake."

The berry burst in his mouth with tangy sweetness. "And I'm glad you are a virgin even though I didn't expect it. Knowing that you are untouched is a rare and special gift." And it made it more likely that he could bind her with passion. He caught her hand and kissed the palm. "I shall strive to be worthy of it."

Her hand tightened over his. "A *souper intime* certainly puts one into an agreeable mood. I will agree willingly to whatever you desire."

Her words kindled the latent fire that had been searing his veins. He stood and took her hands and raised her to her feet. "Then let us wait no longer, my dearest bride."

Eleven

The pleasures of the dining table were nothing compared to the delights of Duncan's touch. Gwynne leaned into his embrace, both relaxed and tautly ready. The velvet of his banyan was a richly textured contrast to the sleek elegance of her silk. If she was fire and water, he was earth and air, solid and yet blazingly exciting.

As they kissed, his warm hands slid over her negligee, bringing her skin to tingling life. He murmured, "I feel as if I have been waiting for you for a lifetime."

"And I feel as if you're the lightning that struck from a clear blue sky, changing my life with no warning," she said honestly.

He bent to nip lightly at her bare shoulder. Her reaction was so intense that her knees weakened. As his arms tightened in support, he said, "It's time to seek our bed."

He claimed her mouth, and she was barely aware of how he guided her into the bedchamber. When the back of her thighs touched the edge of the mattress, he halted and untied the ribbon that secured her robe, then peeled the garment from her body. It drifted down into a gauzy cloud around her ankles.

"Better," he murmured as he cupped her satin-covered breasts and slowly circled his palms. The sensations shot straight to her core, creating heat and moist readiness.

"But then, no robe is as lovely as female flesh." When he started to pull down the shoulder of her nightgown, she tensed, embarrassed by the thought of being naked before him. With his preternatural sensitivity, he caught her reaction. "Later, then."

Effortlessly he swept her from her feet. "You're so strong," she said breathlessly. "I'm not a delicate sylph."

"No, you're a lush, sensual woman. Every man's dream of the perfect wife." He laid her full-length on the bed.

They had dined from dusk into night, and the bed-chamber was lit by only a single candle on the night-stand. Just enough to illuminate his craggy features, his powerful shoulders, his mesmerizing gaze.

She slid hungry hands inside his banyan and was startled to find nothing beneath the sumptuous fabric but warm skin over hard muscle and bone. Knowing he had been naked under his robe when they shared that sensual meal was powerfully arousing.

The robe was secured by silver buttons. One by one she unfastened them, revealing a haze of dark hair over his broad chest. Inspired, she reached up and untied the riband that secured his hair at his nape. It tumbled forward in an irresistible wave. "You, too, are beautiful," she whispered as she slid her fingers into his hair.

Her Lord of Thunder looked almost shy. "No male can match female beauty, my lovely Sassenach."

She recognized the Scottish word as meaning someone who was English. It wasn't usually an endearment, but his rich, smoky voice made it one.

When he kissed her breast through the emerald satin, she arched with shocked delight, her nipple hardening instantly. She had expected that even in passion she would retain her conscious will, but every kiss, every touch, triggered wondrous new sensations that dissolved coherent thought. "I . . . I don't know what to do," she said helplessly.

"You need do nothing but surrender yourself to pleasure, my love." He drew down the loose bodice of her gown so he could have full access to her breasts. She exhaled with a rich, purring sound.

Dizzily she recognized that as his caresses became increasingly intimate, she was becoming more attuned to his spirit. Merciful heaven, but the strength of his broad, muscular body was nothing compared to his powerful, disciplined mind. He stirred her emotions and senses as easily as he stirred the wind.

Her satin skirts slid upward as his strong hand stroked her exquisitely sensitive inner thighs. She cried out when he touched the moist, throbbing folds of intimate flesh. Her breath fractured into short, rough pants. "Please. . . . ," she gasped.

He yanked off his robe and tossed it aside, then moved over her. "This may hurt," he said raggedly. "I shall try to block that. Now relax. . . ."

As the insistent pressure increased between her thighs, she sensed his mind reaching into hers, easing discomfort with tenderness. When he suddenly filled her, there was only the briefest twinge of pain, and it vanished as the essence of his spirit swept through her like a rushing tide.

As he began moving slowly back and forth, her hands kneaded at his shoulders and chest like a tigress. She could feel his power in every fiber of her body, as if she were filled with light. "This is magic," she choked out.

"More than magic," he breathed. "A divine gift."

She locked her arms around his lean waist as he thrust harder and harder. Following him like a dancer, she enhanced his movements with her own.

As thunder boomed across the sky, she had the dizzy feeling that every secret she had must be visible to him. She could deny him nothing, nothing. . . .

He had meant to proceed slowly, to initiate her with patience and care, restraining himself so that all his attention could be on her, but her eager response was the sweetest of aphrodisiacs. Her urgent breath and rapt expression shattered control and turned him into a lover, not a teacher.

Though he had enough control to mitigate her pain, as soon as she rocked against him he was lost to reason. They were born to be together, mated as surely as the wind and rain that slashed this house, as the thunder and lightning that ripped the sky. Only a tempest was powerful enough to express the passion that blazed through him.

Searing lightning, thunder that hammered the air, passion that vibrated through marrow and bone as urgency rose to fever pitch. "I love you," he gasped, his words lost in the howl of the storm. "I love you. . . ."

Then he lost himself utterly in his bride.

*   *   *

The Lord of Storms had claimed his lady—or had she claimed him? In the dazed aftermath of desire Duncan drew her close, blood hammering through his limbs.

Now that his wits were returning, he recognized that the inner storm that had swept him away was echoed in the tumult of the sky. The violence of the tempest lashing Buckland Abbey reflected the vastness of their passion.

Despite his exhaustion, he forced himself to find the heart of the storm. It took all his trained will to disperse the energy before the lashing winds and pounding rain did too much damage to cottages and crops.

When the storm had faded to soft rain, he relaxed, so drained he wasn't sure he could even roll over. He *must* find a way to reduce the linkage between his passion for Gwynne and his weather magic, or the possibility of wreaking havoc in Scotland would be no joking matter. He looked down at her red gold hair, her face invisible as she burrowed against him. Tenderly he stroked her nape. His desire for her was unabated even though his ability to perform was temporarily nil.

Mentally he reviewed the spells he had learned and remembered an obscure one created by Adam Macrae. The spell was intended to temporarily isolate power, and it might suit his needs. Had his several times great-grandfather had a similar problem because of his passion for the magnificent Isabel?

Gwynne turned a little and gazed up at him, the centers of her eyes dark, dreamy pools of wonder. Truly, she was magnificent, a symphony of curves and soft, sleek skin. "Now I know why I found you so alarming," she murmured huskily.

He frowned, thinking this was not what a man wanted to hear from his bride. "What do you mean?"

"On some level, I sensed the terrible immensity of passion between us, and that it would change me forever." With gentle fingers, she smoothed the frown lines from his brow. "The girl that I was feared that, for don't we all fear the abyss? Yet now that I look back, I'm amazed. Lady Bethany was right to tell me I must surrender to the part of me that yearned for you."

Relief washed through him. He should have guessed why she had been so ambivalent about him. A transforming passion was indeed fearsome to contemplate, especially for a virgin who had led a sheltered life. Yet as they had found tonight, such passion was glorious when embraced. "We will both be transformed, *mo cridhe,* my heart. And be the better for it."

"I'm sorry, dearest husband, that I gave you such a difficult time." Gwynne shivered a little. "It's turned cold. Did you conjure that storm?"

"I'm afraid so. I've remembered a spell that might help me keep the weather magic under control in the future. For now, we must rely on blankets." He tugged the covers up around them, then deftly removed her crumpled gown so they could lie skin to skin. Amazed, he felt the first tremor of returning desire. He would have thought it would take him days to recover after such explosive lovemaking.

But she was cold and tired and new to the sport of Aphrodite. He wrapped himself around her for warmth. "Sleep, my dearest bride."

She gave a sigh of profound satisfaction, and within a few minutes her breathing had the regularity of deep slumber. He nuzzled her hair, thinking that she smelled like sunshine and spring breezes and sensual allure.

Yet though he was equally tired, he could not relax. He had wanted to make her so much his own that they would be bonded forever, but despite her wholehearted acceptance of the passion that bound them, part of her spirit remained elusive. Instead of him possessing her, she now possessed him.

Yes, this marriage would transform them both. And whatever the cost, Gwynne was worth it.

*   *   *

Gwynne awoke as the first hint of dawn lightened the sky outside their chamber. She stretched languidly, careful not to wake Duncan, who slept with a muscular arm around her waist. A stub of candle still burned, and by its light she could admire the rugged planes of his face. Though his strength was evident even in sleep, she no longer felt intimidated. Already it was hard to remember how alarming she had found him. That seemed a lifetime ago.

She understood now why Emery had chosen not to make her his true wife. He had married her to give support and guidance, and to groom her for her future destiny. His reward had been the rare companionship they had shared.

But now that she'd been initiated into passion, she recognized that if she and Emery had been lovers, the powerful bond of intimacy would have changed her in fundamental ways. She would have been a different woman when she met Duncan, and she suspected those differences would have influenced whatever mysterious destiny lay ahead. So Emery had suppressed his own desires in the interests of the greater good. He was a true Guardian to the end.

Overcome with tenderness, she caressed Duncan's bristly jaw with the back of her hand. How fortunate she was. Her first husband had been a wise scholar and the epitome of kindness. Her second husband—no, her last husband, she knew in her bones there would be no other—personified power, intelligence, and leadership, while also being passionate and devoted.

Merely looking at him began to rouse the desire she'd never known before they met. Lightly she skimmed her hand over his broad chest, wondering if he would be willing to teach her more about passion if she woke him. She didn't feel sore at all. Instead, she felt . . . ready.

He shifted a little and she moved her hand to his heart, thinking how easy it would be to fall in love with this man. She had loved Emery, but Duncan would call forth a different, wilder love.

His eyes opened, and he smiled up at her. As she smiled back, she had a sudden, horrifying vision of him shouting at her, his face contorted with rage and anguish.

And a cool voice in the back of her mind said, *"You will betray him."*

Part Two

Enchantress

*G*wynne gazed idly out the carriage window, admiring the way the late-afternoon light gilded the Northumberland hills. They had traveled fast on this wedding trip, but Duncan had taken the time to show her sights of interest. Every experience was new and wonderful—especially the nights.

But the days were also a pleasure despite the long hours rattling around in a carriage on rough roads. They had talked about topics large and small, deepening their knowledge of each other. He had described what it was like to wield power so vividly that she almost felt that she could do the same.

In return, she revealed theories she had developed from her researches but not yet published for other Guardians to read. Several times, his insights as a mage helped her crystallize her ideas.

Much of the time, it was almost possible to forget that uncanny mental voice warning that someday she would betray her husband. The idea was so painful that she couldn't bear to think about it. Since she was no mage, perhaps that ominous voice was wrong, a mere product of her anxiety. But there were times when she knew what would happen with absolute certainty, and this had felt like one of them.

A new hill came into view, a bold linear structure running along the ridge. She leaned forward eagerly. "Is that Hadrian's Wall?"

He nodded. "You can see it close up since we'll be staying with Lord Montague tonight. That section of the wall is on his estate." He glanced across her at the distant wall and said musingly, "The mighty Roman Empire ended here because the savage tribes of Scotland refused to yield their freedom. They fought so ferociously that Emperor Hadrian decided it was easier to draw a line and protect it with stone, ditch, and soldiers."

His expression revealed how much that ancient fight for freedom spoke to him. As when she'd listened to Sir Ian Macleod, her understanding of what it meant to be a Scot deepened. "You had indomitable ancestors," she said quietly.

"Freedom is worth a high price."

Did the Stuart cause whisper to his love of freedom? Hoping that wasn't the case, she asked, "Is the wall the special surprise you told me I'd have tonight?" She immediately recognized the double entendre. As she glanced across the carriage at her husband, his grin revealed that he knew exactly what she was thinking.

She'd learned that he couldn't read her mind, but he was uncannily accurate in reading her emotions, and lovemaking figured heavily in them. "What you are thinking is no longer a surprise." She fluttered her lashes extravagantly. "But it is a most delicious adventure. This whole journey is an adventure."

"Surely you've already tired of ruts and carriages."

"True, but since I've never been more than a day's

travel from London, this trip is marvelously exciting despite the rough roads."

"There are some good roads being built in the Highlands," he said dryly. "After the Fifteen, London wanted to be able to send troops in quickly to quell rebellion."

His words silenced her. At every stop on their road north, they heard more news about the uprising. Prince Charles had raised his standard at Glenfinnan in front of a thousand Macdonalds and Camerons, it was said. After declaring his father to be King James the VIII of Scotland and the III of England, the prince had set off for Edinburgh and he was swiftly gathering support.

Rumor said that three thousand clansmen from the west marched at his back, with more joining his army every day. He was being called Bonnie Prince Charlie, and he possessed the personal magnetism that his father had lacked when James had come to Scotland to lead the rebellion in 1715.

Breaking the uneasy silence, Duncan said, "Though you'll enjoy Hadrian's Wall, that's not the surprise I had in mind. I want to give you a horse as a wedding gift, and Lord Montague has the finest breeding stables in the north. There's a good bit of mountain pony in his stock, so they're tough and surefooted, with amazing endurance. The beasts are much better suited to conditions in Scotland than the horses you rode in the south. I hope to find a suitable mount for myself as well. Perhaps we can ride the rest of the way to Dunrath if you're up to such a long distance."

She almost bounced with excitement. "What a wonderful idea! I gather you've bought other horses from the Montagues?"

"Yes, my favorite mount, Thor, was bred here." Duncan smiled reminiscently. "When I left on my travels, my wee sister, Jean, told me that the price of her stewardship was Thor. I couldn't really object when I was going to be gone so long, but I'll feel better if I ride home on an equally splendid new horse. With luck, perhaps I'll find one of Thor's half brothers."

She took his hand. "I like the idea of arriving at Dunrath the first time on horseback. One sees so much more when riding, and since this will be my home, I want to see everything. The trails through the hills and glens you've described will be more romantic than having to keep to the carriage roads." Her smile broadened. "And since I'm with you, I won't even be rained on."

"If you're going to put me to work, I demand compensation." With a quick swoop of his powerful arms, he lifted her and deposited her on his lap, flouncing her skirts up so that she was straddling him with blatant intimacy. "You said right after our wedding that you would consider trysting in a carriage later. Has enough time passed?"

She caught her breath, startled and excited. "It's only been a week—"

He cut off her words with a kiss. The mental barriers she had constructed against the images of disaster rose instantly and she kissed him back, fierce with need. Had she really been a virgin a week ago? Already she and Duncan knew each other's bodies with uncanny intimacy.

She rolled her hips against him with wicked deliberation, and was rewarded as he hardened instantly. His eyes turned dark as storm clouds. "A week is obviously quite long enough, my wicked wench."

She gasped when his knowing hand slid between her legs. The lightest of his touches brought her to readiness. Daringly she reached down to find the fastenings of his breeches. "If we're buying horses, I need to practice my riding."

He swallowed hard. "Ah, Gwynne, you are pure delight." He clasped her hips to rearrange her position and suddenly they were joined, the rocking of the carriage adding to their ardent coupling.

As her body began spinning out of control, she hoped they wouldn't reach the home of the Montagues too soon.

*   *   *

Duncan climbed from the carriage, then offered his hand to help his wife down. Gwynne positively glowed with sensual excitement from their recent lovemaking. Softly he said, "You are ravishing, my dear."

She smiled wickedly. "And here I thought I was ravished, not ravishing."

If Lord Montague and one of his great strapping sons weren't descending the steps of the hall, Duncan would have kissed those soft, provocative lips. Instead, he said under his breath, "You may ravish me later," before turning to greet his host.

"Ballister, splendid to see you! This is my youngest, William. Pray present us to your lady." Montague, sturdy in worn riding costume, turned to Gwynne. His expression changed instantly, as if he had been kicked in the head by one of his prize stallions.

As Duncan performed the introductions, he thought wryly about how often he'd seen that dazed expression. The farther north they traveled, the more intensely men reacted to her. He supposed it was because northerners showed their feelings more freely.

At the moment, she looked as if she had just tumbled

out of a bed, which was close to the truth, and she radiated sensuality so intensely that a man would have to be three-quarters dead not to respond. Montague's young son William looked as if his eyes were about to fall out of his head. Even the coachman who had driven the newlyweds all the way from London watched Gwynne with quiet hunger.

Pulling himself together, Montague suggested, "Perhaps you would like to go to your rooms and rest until dinner."

"Actually, we'd like to look at your horses." Duncan glanced at his wife. "If we change into our habits, perhaps we could go for a ride? I'm thinking the Dunrath stables could use some new stock."

Montague's business instincts took over. "Then you need look no further. I have some exceptional beasts available now, if I do say so myself."

Their host's pride proved justified. After Duncan and Gwynne changed to their riding clothes, they met the baron and his son in the stable yard. William's gaze immediately locked onto Gwynne even though he was too shy to speak to her. Duncan guessed that the young man was about twenty. A susceptible age.

"Does Thor have any half brothers ready for sale?"

Montague chuckled. "You have the luck of the devil, Ballister. Come take a look at Zeus. He's a full brother to Thor, and as fine a horse as I've ever bred."

"I'll show Lady Ballister mounts suitable for a lady," William offered eagerly.

Gwynne gave her husband a laughing glance, then went off with the young man. Duncan hoped that William's heart wouldn't break too easily.

Montague led his guest to a box stall that held a magnificent dark bay. "What do you think, Ballister?"

Almost black, Zeus was tall and powerful, and his relationship to Thor was visible in every line of his magnificently proportioned body. Duncan knew instantly that this was the horse for him, but it wouldn't do to seem too enthusiastic. "He's a handsome fellow," he said noncommittally. "May I have one of those apples you're carrying?"

While Montague handed over the fruit, Zeus thrust his head out of the box curiously. Duncan stepped forward to introduce himself, mentally sending a message of admiration and affection. Horses didn't think like humans, but they responded to positive feelings. Zeus was no exception. Within moments, he was eating the apple from Duncan's hand. The horse had a fine opinion of himself, but Duncan sensed no malice. "I'd like to take him for a ride."

Montague signaled a groom to lead the horse out and saddle it. "Shall we see how your lovely lady is doing?"

Duncan wasn't surprised to see that Gwynne had bypassed the ladies' mounts and was stroking the elegant muzzle of a tall chestnut mare that was almost golden in the afternoon light. William said nervously, "Sheba is very lively, my lady. She is not a mount I would recommend to you. Perhaps this gelding in the next stall—"

"Not to mention that Sheba isn't for sale," Montague interjected. "I want to keep her for breeding."

The mare gave Gwynne's shoulder a friendly head butt that almost knocked her backward. Laughing, she stroked the glossy neck, then turned to Montague. "Please, may I at least ride her? She's the most beautiful mare I've ever seen."

Montague hesitated, then surrendered to his guest's lovely warm gaze. "Very well," he said gruffly. "A sidesaddle for the lady. But I warn you, Sheba is a rare handful. She might not be to your taste."

"We'll see. Thank you so much." Gwynne's smile was dazzling.

When the saddled horses were led out into the yard, Duncan personally helped Gwynne onto the saddle. He was afraid that if William had a chance to touch the object of his infatuation, the poor lad might never recover.

As Gwynne settled down and straightened her flowing skirts, Montague himself stood at the mare's head and held the bridle. "Be careful with her," he warned.

Gwynne nodded, but care wasn't required. When the stable owner released the bridle, Sheba walked around the yard as placidly as an aged cart horse. "What a light mouth she has," Gwynne observed. "Can we ride up to Hadrian's Wall, Duncan?"

He swung onto his own saddle. "Is that all right with you, Montague? It's a long enough ride for us to develop a sense of the horses' quirks."

"These horses have no quirks," the other man retorted. "They'll ride smooth as silk. Try to be back in time for dinner."

Duncan and Gwynne walked sedately out of the yard, but once they were clear of the farm buildings, he said, "That path will take us up to the wall."

"Now to see what Sheba can do!" Gwynne and the mare took off in a blaze of golden light.

The whip of her skirts reminded him of that ride in Richmond Park. Lord, was that only a fortnight ago? He gave Zeus his head and the horse leaped into a gallop, eager to run off his excess energy.

Just before they were out of sight of the stables, Duncan glanced back and saw that William was staring after Gwynne with blatant adoration. Now he could admire her superb horsemanship as well as her beauty.

The ride out to the wall gave them time to check the

horses' paces. Like all Montague mounts, these were beautifully trained and a pleasure to ride. They would cost a king's ransom but be worth the price for the blood-lines they would bring to Dunrath.

Duncan savored the ride, knowing that troubles would crowd in once they reached Dunrath. Fast-moving clouds danced across the sky, interrupting the late-summer sun-shine. Once he reached up to push away a rain-bearing cloud, quietly protecting his lady's splendid plumed hat.

As they reached the hill below the wall, Gwynne pulled her mount into a walk. "I must have Sheba!" she said, her face rosy from the fast ride. "It was the strangest sen-sation when I first saw her—almost as if our minds con-nected and I *was* her, seeing me and wanting to be with me. Do you think Montague will sell?"

"He will if you smile at him again," Duncan predicted. A smile and an outrageous amount of money would do the trick. "I feel the same about Zeus. As soon as I saw him, I knew he was the one. He's every inch Thor's equal."

"Then I shall buy Zeus for you as a wedding gift."

"There's no need to do that!" he said, startled. "You yourself are the greatest gift any man could want. Be-sides, Montague will charge a fortune."

Her brows arched. "There may be no need, but I want to. The marriage settlements left me in control of my own money, my dear. Haven't I the right to spend some of it on you?"

He couldn't deny the logic of that. "Very well, I accept with gratitude." He patted the glossy dark neck. "I look forward to our ride to Dunrath."

"So do I."

They reached the wall, which was built of great stone blocks and loomed twice the height of a tall man. Wordlessly they turned their horses to amble along the track that paralleled the ancient structure, Duncan imagining those distant days when Scots stood up against the greatest empire the world had ever seen, and won.

"It's even more imposing than I expected," Gwynne observed. "If we were to climb to the top of the wall, would we be able to see Scotland?"

"No, but a day's ride will bring us into the Lowlands. Which are not at all low, really. Dunrath lies right on the edge of the Highlands."

"That will suit me well. The farther north I go, the more alive I feel."

And the more beautiful she became. Despite their lovemaking the night before and in the carriage earlier in the afternoon, his desire flared with painful urgency. If they weren't expected back at the house, he would coax her from the horse so they could add life and laughter to the memories held in the ancient stone wall. Clearing his throat, he said, "Shall we ride back and start bargaining? Half the fun is in working out the price."

She grinned. "I shall leave that part to you, my lord and master."

"You need to practice being demure, lass," he advised. "You're not convincing."

With a peal of laughter, she set off down the hill. He followed, thinking he was the luckiest man in Britain.

Thirteen

Gwynne was glad it was still summer, because Montague Hall was drafty. Very drafty. In winter the halls would be icy as a north wind, but at this season a shawl was enough to keep her comfortable. As she entered the sitting room on Duncan's arm, she remarked, "I suppose it's time to accustom myself to drafts and cold rooms. How many residents of Dunrath die of lung fever each winter?"

He chuckled. "We Scots are a hardy lot. After a winter in Dunrath, you'll hardly notice the cold. You'll be a hale and hearty Scotswoman, vastly superior to the frail Sassenach ladies."

"I fail to see how being comfortable makes one inherently inferior," she said tartly. "If God had intended us to be cold, he wouldn't have given us fire and wool."

Duncan's grin deepened, but she saw that young William looked alarmed, as if her husband intended to keep her in misery. Very earnest was young William.

She gave the youth a smile, accepted a glass of sherry from a footman, then turned her attention to Lady Montague, whom she hadn't met before. The woman was a sturdy, no-nonsense Scot, fully capable of running a household full of horse-mad men. "I hear you've charmed Sheba away from my husband." Her ladyship gave him an affectionate glance. "He's always been daft for a pretty woman."

"That's why I married you, my girl. You were the prettiest lass in the North Country," her husband said with a twinkle. "And the bargain Ballister and I concluded gives us Sheba's first foal."

Duncan raised his glass. "A good bargain is one where both sides feel well satisfied. May all our bargains be good ones."

Everyone drank to that cheerfully. Then politics reared its ugly head. William raised his glass and said, "A toast to the king over the water!"

It was a common Jacobite toast to the exiled Stuarts, and the young man's words created instant silence. Duncan said peaceably, "I believe that George is in London now, not Hanover, but to the king's health wherever he may be."

The older Montagues would have been happy to let it go at that, but William said, "The Hanovers are not our true kings. They are coarse, stupid Germans, unfit to sit on a British throne. The Stuarts are our legitimate rulers."

"William . . . ," his father said warningly.

Ignoring the caution, William said defiantly, "Scotland has been treated abominably by the Hanovers. Surely no Scot can deny that."

William's words were treason, and his parents' tense expressions showed they knew it. Wanting to change the subject, Gwynne asked her host, "Have the Montagues always been horse breeders, or are you the first?"

Ignoring her feeble attempt at distraction, William said to Duncan, "To see the prince is to recognize true roy-

alty. The day will come when all of Britain will acknowledge him."

Uneasily Gwynne saw that this conversation wasn't
only about politics, but about her. William wanted to impress her and humiliate Duncan. The fool.

"The Stuarts had their chance," Duncan said dryly. "If
James II had ruled like a sensible man and not converted to
Catholicism, he could have kept his throne, but he was a
fool, and his heirs have been equally foolish. James Francis
probably could have had the throne when Queen Anne
died if he had moved quickly and turned Protestant, but he
let the opportunity fall through his hands and now the
time has passed. Though Charles Edward may be dashing,
he hasn't enough support to overthrow the government."

"Unfortunately, he has enough support to cause many
deaths," Lady Montague said with a frown. "Let us
speak no more of this. It's time to go into dinner."

Standing firm, William spat at Duncan, "Prince
Charles has only to set foot in England and Jacobites will
rise everywhere to support him, as they are doing in Scotland. How many men will rally to the Hanoverian king
once his troops start losing battles?"

"When you are older, perhaps you'll come to realize
that being dashing isn't a good trait in a king," Duncan
said with lethal coolness. "Especially not when paired
with a belief that royal blood gives him a divine right to
do any damn-fool thing he wants. A boring monarch who
keeps to his mistresses and spends much of his time on the
Continent may not be as exciting, but he's a safer ruler."

Fury flashed in William's eyes, but before he could offer another retort, his father snapped, "If you speak one
more word on the subject of Jacobites, I'll send you to
your room, young man! Now let us eat." He offered his
arm to Gwynne.

Gwynne winced inwardly as William's face turned scarlet. He had wanted to impress her, and instead he was being treated as a child. She gave him a swift, sympathetic smile. His expression eased and he inclined his head before spinning on his heel and stalking from the room, his back ramrod straight.

Thinking it would be a more relaxed dinner without the young firebrand present, Gwynne accompanied her host into the dining room.

"He's but a boy, Lady Ballister," Lord Montague said, his expression anxious. "His words aren't to be taken seriously."

His concern was understandable. William might be young, but he was old enough to be executed for treason, and perhaps bring his whole family to disaster. With a rebellion in Scotland, English authorities wouldn't be inclined to leniency. Gwynne said reassuringly, "It is usual for the young to be romantic about lost causes. There's no reason for us to mention it elsewhere."

Montague's expression eased. "I knew you for a sensible woman."

"I make no claim to politics, but like most females, I have no use for war."

His lordship sighed. "When I was William's age, I thought war a grand and noble enterprise. Fight for the right! Show your courage! Now I know better."

"Are you afraid he'll run off and join the Young Pretender?" she asked quietly.

His stricken expression was answer enough. She suggested, "Say you want to buy new breeding stock and send him off to India or America or some other distant place where he can have adventures that don't involve civil war."

An interested light showed in his eyes. As he pulled out

her chair, he said, "That's good advice, Lady Ballister. Perhaps I'll do just that. Thank you." His smile was so warm it was almost alarming, but he moved away to the head of the table without saying more.

Despite the tenseness caused by William's political proclamations, the dinner went well. Besides Gwynne and Duncan and the senior Montagues, there were half a dozen other members of the household, including the oldest son and heir, George, and his wife.

Tired by the long day, Gwynne was glad when Lady Montague rose and led the ladies off so the gentlemen could talk over their port. Gwynne wondered if the men would venture into politics again, or stay with the safer topic of horses.

She chatted with the ladies only as long as was polite before retiring to her bedchamber. After changing into her nightgown and braiding her hair, she pulled open the draperies at the windows and went to bed, wondering how long it would be before Duncan joined her. Ah, well, if she fell asleep he could always wake her. . . .

*   *   *

The hand on her shoulder brought Gwynne to sleepy awareness. She smiled, the darkness making her acutely aware that desire hummed in the air, along with a distinct scent of alcohol. "Come to bed, my dear."

She reached for Duncan, and touched a face that was unfamiliar. Snapping to full wakefulness, she asked, "Who's here?"

"Shhh . . ." The whisper was urgent. "We've come to rescue you."

"William?" Incredulous, she sat up in bed, clutching the covers to her. The faint light from the window showed the strapping form of her host's youngest son and an even larger young man dressed as a servant. "Is the house on fire?"

"No, no, I'm going to rescue you from that bullying Whig. Come with Jemmie and me, my lady." He opened the window of a lantern to release more light. After handing the lantern to his servant, he pulled the covers away and tugged Gwynne to her feet. "We must be quick, before we're discovered."

The floor was cold under her bare feet, but she hardly noticed because of the thunderstruck way the two young men stared at her. In her satin nightgown, she was a sight fit only for the eyes of a husband. Blushing furiously, she grabbed Duncan's banyan from where it was draped over a chair and wrapped it around her.

Once she was safely covered, she said in her best countess voice, "How dare you enter my bedroom! I have no idea what you think you're doing, but you're foxed. Leave my room this instant and I'll pretend this never happened."

William shook his head. His eyes were bright with some combination of drink and recklessness. "I can't let him have you. You're a brave lass to pretend all is well, but I heard him being rude to you. I saw how you smiled at me, as if you were pleading to be saved."

Dear heaven, he must have interpreted her smiles of sympathy as interest in his immature self! "You misunderstood everything. I consider myself blessed to have Ballister as my husband, and I need no rescue." She tugged the robe around her more tightly. "Now *go!*"

William's face hardened. "A craven Whig who is betraying his own people doesn't deserve you! When the prince has conquered Britain, there will be honors and riches for his supporters, and I will keep you like the queen that you are. Our lives will be a glorious adventure."

As she tried to edge away, William suddenly caught her in his arms and tried to kiss her. She managed to turn her head quickly enough so that his mouth landed on her cheek, not her lips. Revolted, she broke free but tripped on the trailing hem of the robe. She fell hard, banging her temple on the heavy bedpost.

As she lay dazed on the floor, a thick north country accent exclaimed with horror, "My God, mon, you've killed her!"

Frantic hands turned her over and explored the throbbing side of her head. She could see and hear, but couldn't quite move. "Nay, she's only stunned," William said with relief. "She'll be all right."

Swiftly he wrapped her in blankets and carried her out into the dark corridor. "Don't worry, my lady," he crooned. "I'll take care of you."

Immobilized by the blankets and the blow to her head, she couldn't even struggle as the young idiots abducted her. With all the concentration she could muster, she sent a cry for help to her husband, and prayed that she was Guardian enough to reach him.

*   *
*

Duncan enjoyed his discussion with Lord Montague and the other men of the household. They were sensible fellows, as alarmed by the prospect of civil war as he was. Perhaps this rebellion would die down quickly, before too many lives were lost.

The port was making another circuit when he felt a sharp tug in his mind. Gwynne? Used to disguising power, he finished what he was saying before analyzing what he'd felt. Was she having a nightmare? Fatigue might have sent her to bed early. Or was she with the other ladies and an argument had broken out?

Thinking it could be nothing serious, he continued with the evening's discussion, but anxiety gnawed at him. Finally, damning himself for an anxious bridegroom, he rose. "Having been married less than a fortnight, I think I shall seek out my bride."

George Montague, the heir, stood and raised his glass. "Here's to the fairest lady in the North Country!"

"The loveliest woman in Europe!"

"Aphrodite reborn!"

"The most beautiful woman in Christendom!"

Every man present leaped to his feet and raised his glass, booming another contribution to the toast. Duncan watched in amazement. Admittedly he thought Gwynne was the most beautiful woman in the world, but she was his wife. This fervent acclamation by responsible gentlemen, most of whom had attractive wives of their own, was downright unnerving.

After acknowledging the toast, he headed for the drawing room where the ladies were taking tea. He entered and glanced around the room, needing to see her.

"Your wife retired early," Lady Montague said with twinkling eyes. "No need for you to rush off—she'll be glad for your presence whenever you join her."

He managed to smile at the pleasantry, but his anxiety was increasing and he resented spending time in small talk. As soon as manners allowed, he withdrew and climbed the stairs three steps at a time. Surely when he'd felt that tug she had just been experiencing a nightmare. . . .

He strode into the bedroom, candle held high—and saw that the bed was empty and a shambles of tangled sheets. The blankets were missing. Instinctively he touched a spot on the bedpost, and knew that Gwynne had struck it forcefully. An image formed in his mind of Gwynne being abducted by that besotted young idiot.

For a moment, anguish and guilt paralyzed him. He had known something was wrong, and by his failure to act, Gwynne had been placed in danger. She was his wife, and he hadn't protected her.

There would be time for guilt later. Now he must concentrate on finding her. He stormed downstairs and burst into the drawing room. "Your damnable son has abducted my wife," he said harshly to his host. "Where would he take her?"

Everyone stared at him in shock. "That's impossible!" Montague exclaimed. "Your lady must have decided to take a late walk, perhaps to the kitchen or the library."

"The bedroom has been torn up and the blankets are missing. See for yourself."

The group surged upstairs after him and saw the mute evidence of the tumbled room. Lady Montague pressed her hand to her mouth, fear in her eyes.

"There must be another explanation," Lord Montague said as if trying to convince himself. "William is not so rash as to steal another man's wife. Perhaps . . . perhaps she wasn't unwilling. Or perhaps robbers broke in. . . ."

"If your son is innocent, produce him," Duncan growled. "Once you admit that he has committed this crime, will you help me, or must I go after my wife alone?"

Montague sent his oldest son off while Duncan paced, furious at the time that was being lost. He tried to reach out to Gwynne to assure himself of her safety, but he was too upset to get a clear reading. She was alive, that much he was sure of, and probably not seriously hurt, but beyond that he could not be sure.

After a handful of minutes which felt like hours,

George returned to report, "William and Jemmie are both missing, and it looked as if William did some hasty packing. Three horses are gone, including William's."

Lady Montague pressed her hand to her heart. "That foolish, foolish boy. Please, Lord Ballister . . ." Her voice trailed off miserably.

Her fear helped Duncan master his temper. "I'll try not to kill him, richly though he deserves it. Do you have any idea where he might take her?"

"There are half a dozen bothies up in the hills," George said. "Since there's little moon and riding would be difficult, he might take her to one and wait until daylight."

"Show me a map."

One was provided in Montague's study. As George pointed out the locations of the bothies, Duncan stilled his mind so he could sense where Gwynne might be. *There.* He stabbed his forefinger down on the map. "He's taking her to this one. I'm sure of it."

The Montagues stared at him. Inventing an explanation to justify his certainty, Duncan said, "My guess is that he wants to join the rebels. If so, that's along his route. Montague, will you lend me several of your men?"

His host nodded, his face gray. "I'll send a pair to each of the other bothies. George and I will go with you."

Duncan wondered if they could be trusted to deal with their villainous young relative, and decided that they could, for honor's sake. Though they would also try to protect the boy from Duncan's wrath. "Then we'll be off," he said grimly. "And if he's harmed a hair on her head—"

He cut off the words. As a Guardian, he shouldn't be thinking murderous thoughts. But if William harmed Gwynne, may God have mercy on his foolish soul.

Fourteen

G wynne came awake groggily. Male voices speaking in low, urgent tones brought back sharp memories of her abduction, so she kept her eyes closed as she evaluated her situation. The air was cool and smoky, and she lay on a rough surface. Hard earth padded by a folded blanket, she guessed.

Opening her eyes a slit, she saw that she was in a crude hut with stone walls and a dirt floor. A small fire burned in the center of the room. Most of the smoke wafted out through a hole in the roof, but enough stayed to sting the eyes and rasp the lungs.

William and his servant sat on the hard earth on the other side of the fire. They must be sobering up, because Jemmie said urgently, "We've got to take her back, mon, before they know she's gone! Ballister will hunt us down and cut off our balls for this."

"No!" William looked across the fire to his captive, his voice as stubborn as his stony face. "She's mine! Her husband is a coarse brute who doesn't deserve her. She smiled at me with her soul in her eyes. She wants me as I want her. Once we join the prince and his army, we'll be safe. With luck, Ballister will die in the fighting and I can take her for my lawful wife before the year is out."

Gwynne wondered how long it would take William to decide that murdering Duncan would be more efficient than hoping for him to become a victim of the war. When she first met the boy, she had thought him rather sweet and earnest and she sensed that he still was, under this strange obsession he had developed for her. How could the brief two smiles she had given him be interpreted as an invitation to elope?

Whatever had come over him, he was now potentially dangerous. If he could convince himself that a friendly smile meant that she desired him, how long until he decided that she was yearning for his embraces? She shuddered at the thought. With Duncan she had discovered the joy of the marriage bed, and the thought of her body being invaded by any other man was loathsome.

She knew beyond doubt that Duncan would come for her, but how long would it take? Not long, she guessed—a powerful mage should be able to locate a missing wife easily. Perhaps if she kept up the pretense she was asleep, he would be here before the situation turned ugly.

Too late. Even as she closed her eyes again, Jemmie said, "I think she's awake."

William stood, his head almost touching the roof, and came around the fire. "How do you feel, my lady? I didn't mean for you to be hurt."

Gwynne made a swift decision to behave with the hauteur she'd learned in the upper levels of English society. He must be persuaded that she was untouchable.

She pushed herself into a sitting position and wrapped herself in dignity along with Duncan's robe. "I am gravely disappointed," she said icily. "How *dare* you abduct me from under your father's roof! You dishonor your family."

He flushed. "I had no choice. I had to save you from that man."

"Of course you had a choice! And 'that man' is my husband. I need no saving from him." Her eyes narrowed with anger. "Ballister and I have been joined in the eyes of man and God. It is not your place to put us asunder."

He looked shaken by her vehemence. "Perhaps it is not, my lady." His hand fell to the dagger at his side. "But I will not give you up."

She was acutely aware of how large he was, and how unpredictable his moods were. Would Jemmie try to prevent any violence against her, or would he join in? She didn't want to find out. "Take me back to my husband, *now*. I have no more interest in your precious prince than I have in you."

William's expression changed. "Once you meet Prince Charles, you will come over to his side. He has such grandeur, yet such affability. Not like that rude, mean Hanoverian king who sulks in London." He bent and caught her hands, lifting her to her feet. "You will soon be grateful that I am taking you into a glorious new life!"

She tried unsuccessfully to tug her hands free. "I'm happy with the life I have!"

"Then I shall change your mind." He gazed into her face longingly. "You are so beautiful. So irresistibly beautiful . . ." His mouth crushed onto hers with hungry demand.

She gagged, struggling against him but unable to retreat since her back was against the wall. *Duncan . . . !*

The door slammed open and her husband swept into the hut like a thunderstorm, Lord Montague at his back and George Montague a step behind. Duncan's black cloak billowed about him as dramatically as his power filled the room. He was dark and commanding, as splendid as he was terrifying, yet the reassuring glance he gave her was full of tenderness. She had never been so glad to see anyone in her life.

Crossing the hut in two long strides, he thundered, "Damn you, boy! I should kill you where you stand!"

William snapped his head around while Jemmie prudently scrambled to the farthest corner of the hut. "She's better off as my mistress than your wife, Ballister," William blustered, but his voice was shaking.

"You're a stupid young fool who deserves to have your liver and lights cooked into haggis," Duncan growled as he yanked William away from Gwynne. "But for the sake of your parents, I'll spare you."

"You think me a poor adversary? I'll show you!" Humiliated, William whipped out his dagger and lunged at his tormentor.

Duncan dodged the attack, but the small hut limited his movement and the blade slashed along his left forearm. Though his face grayed, he caught William's arm and twisted it fiercely to crash the younger man into a stone wall. As Lord Montague caught his breath with fear, George grabbed his younger brother's dagger, then locked William's arms behind his back to prevent further attacks. Gwynne guessed that he hoped disarming William would keep Duncan from doing murder.

But Duncan had no more interest in William. He turned to Gwynne and she went into his arms with dizzying relief. "Thank God you're here," she said raggedly.

"Did he hurt you, lass?"

She shook her head. "When he came to abduct me, I slipped and hit my head on the bedpost, but that was an accident. He . . . he didn't have time to do worse."

Duncan's embrace tightened. It took her a moment to realize that he was on the verge of collapse. "You're hurt!"

His voice dropped until it was almost inaudible. "The dagger . . . iron."

She had half forgotten about his weather mage's sensitivity to iron because the subject hadn't come up since their marriage. Yet looking back, she remembered all the small instances of his avoiding iron. Having it pierce his flesh had to be painful and debilitating even if the wound wasn't serious. And perhaps even a slight injury was dangerous to him—she had never come across a discussion of the subject in her studies.

She turned him so that he was supported by the wall and examined the wound. Though it was bleeding messily, it looked shallow and shouldn't be serious unless the iron poisoned him in some way. "You must remove your cloak and coat so I can bind this until we return to the castle."

Under his breath, he said, "Place your hand over the wound and push down hard. That will counter the effect of the iron."

Though she worried about hurting him, she did as he said, pressing firmly on the injured flesh. Blood oozed between her fingers at first, but his color began to improve.

"Is the wound serious?" Lord Montague asked with concern.

"No," Duncan replied himself. "Gwynne is taking care of it." He glanced at William, whose hands were now secured behind his back. The boy was staring at the earthen floor, his expression equal parts fear and sullen anger. "The sooner you ship that lad to the colonies, the better. I don't want him within a thousand miles of my wife."

"You won't press charges?" Lord Montague asked with relief.

Duncan shook his head. "For the sake of you and your family, and because Gwynne is unhurt, I won't. I can understand anyone becoming enchanted by my bride, but keep William away from Britain until he learns that a real man doesn't act on all his impulses."

"It shall be as you ask." Lord Montague inclined his head to Gwynne. "If you agree, Lady Ballister?"

"I agree." Gwynne didn't want the boy dead, but she hoped never to see him again. Reaction was setting in, and her hands shook as she bound her husband's arm with a long neckcloth silently offered by George. The bleeding had almost stopped and Duncan's color seemed normal, but she must talk to him later about his reaction to iron. As his wife, she needed to know what to expect.

Montague turned to his son's servant, who was doing his best to look like part of the wall. "What about Jemmie?"

"He didn't hurt me," Gwynne said. "I think he was not happy to be involved in an abduction, but he did not want to be disloyal to his master."

Jemmie gave her a grateful glance as Montague nodded and turned away. With luck, the servant wouldn't be shipped off to the colonies with William.

George hauled his brother to his feet. "Time we headed for home."

Duncan draped his cloak around Gwynne's shoulders and led her from the hut. She avoided looking toward her young abductor. Bitterly she wondered if she would ever dare be friendly again.

* * *

Duncan and Gwynne hardly spoke on the ride back to the castle, but he kept a close eye on her. Though the lump on her temple where she hit the bedpost was turning alarming colors, she rode with her head high and her back straight. With his cloak rippling in the night air, she looked like a warrior queen returning from battle.

The summer sun rose early this far north, and the sky was pale in the east by the time they finally returned to their bedroom. The bed had been made up again with fresh blankets, and Lady Montague had sent a maid up with a tray of steaming tea and food. Presumably she was grateful to see her youngest son intact.

After the servant left, Gwynne tossed Duncan's cloak over a chair, then wearily touched the spot on the bedpost where her head had struck. "And to think that all I wanted last night was a few hours of sleep. Instead, I got an adventure."

He wrapped his arms around her and rested his brow against hers. "Adventures are overrated. I prefer a good night's sleep every time."

She locked her arms around his waist. "Thank God you found me so quickly. If you had been even a few minutes later . . ." She shuddered.

He hugged her back, hating to think how narrowly disaster had been averted. "Would you like some tea? Much as I long for our bed, we must talk."

"Agreed." She poured them each a cup of tea, steam rising in the cool dawn air. Even with tangled hair and draped in his shapeless banyan, her beauty made him ache.

After handing over his tea, she took a chair and cradled her cup between her palms. "Your reaction to iron was frightening. Were you in . . . in danger of your life?"

He sank into the opposite chair. "I am no more nor less likely to die by the sword than any man, but any touch of iron weakens me. Not only does it block my power, but it reduces my physical strength as well, even if the wound itself is minor, like this one."

She nodded thoughtfully. "No wonder you're so careful to keep iron out of your life, and why you didn't want to talk about your sensitivity. It wouldn't do to let enemies know of your weakness."

He gave a scowl of agreement. "The real danger is that in a situation like last night, iron would make me incapable of defending myself, or you."

She took a swallow of her cooling tea. "I could feel you wielding power when you came into the hut. Did you use a spell to control William?"

"I was so furious that if I'd used a spell directly against him, I might have done murder. Instead I used a calming spell so he and his servant wouldn't be inclined to fight. It worked on Jemmie, but William was too obsessed by you to be fully controlled." He sighed. "Despite his crime, killing him would have been wrong since he was not entirely responsible for what happened."

Gwynne straightened, her expression outraged. "Do you think that I encouraged that silly boy?"

It was light enough now to see the pure line of her profile against the window. "Not deliberately. You couldn't help yourself."

"Am I such a flirt?" she asked, unmollified. "I hadn't thought so."

"You behaved with complete propriety." He smiled without humor. "I'm the fool for not recognizing what was happening sooner. All of the signs were there. In fact, from the beginning I'd sensed that you had untapped reservoirs of power, but you were so sure that you had no magical ability that I disregarded my instincts."

She frowned. "I *don't* have any power, except a small amount of intuition and rare moments of foreknowledge. No more than many mundanes have."

"On the contrary, sweeting." He considered with weary curiosity the complications that lay ahead. "You're an enchantress. That's why William couldn't resist you."

Fifteen

Gwynne's mouth dropped open with disbelief. "You think I'm an enchantress who can dazzle men out of their wits? I've had a few admirers, but Lady Bethany has more, and she's fifty years older than I."

"There's more than a touch of enchantress in Lady Beth," Duncan agreed. "But in this area of power, she is nothing compared to you. You must have studied enchantresses. What is the most striking aspect of their power?"

She thought about what she'd read on the subject. "A dash of enchantress isn't uncommon among Guardian women, but true enchantresses are quite rare—only one appears every generation or two. Their power is dormant when they are maidens. It is only awakened after they first lie with a man." Those were the facts, but Gwynne couldn't connect them with herself. Plain Gwyneth Owens, an enchantress? Absurd!

Duncan's gaze became distant, and she realized he was studying her not as a husband but as a mage. "I sensed great passion in you from our first meeting, and even so, I was amazed at how sensual and irresistible a bride I'd taken. Ever since our wedding night, your power has caught fire. You fascinate every man who sees you."

"Not that I've noticed."

"Our marriage is recent and we've been traveling, so it hasn't been obvious. But I've seen how men look at you whenever our carriage stops. When we were drinking port last night, each man at the table cried out a fervent toast to your beauty and desirability." He smiled wryly. "It was damned unnerving. That's when I first began to suspect what you are. I realized the truth when William abducted you. He is just the right combination of youth, passion, and hotheadedness to convince himself that you needed to be rescued from me."

"How does his youthful foolishness make me an enchantress?" she asked, exasperated. "I'm glad that my husband finds me desirable, but I think you're imagining that other men admire me more than they really do."

"Granted, William is young, but he's never done anything remotely so foolish before. It took enchantress power to scramble his wits so thoroughly. But there is more evidence if you remain unconvinced." He rubbed at the new bandage that Lady Montague had applied. "When an enchantress's power wakens, it isn't only the ability to entrance men. When we approached the bothy, your mental screams for help had so much power behind them that they slashed my mind like the hunting cries of eagles. Damned unnerving. I'll wager you've felt other stirrings of power since our wedding."

Her eyes widened as she thought back. "You're right— my awareness has been increasing in many ways. I feel your power more vividly, and I . . . I know more about people around me. I didn't notice because marriage changed so many things in my life."

"The changes have just begun." Duncan set aside his

empty teacup, then stood and took off his coat and waistcoat, his tired fingers fumbling with the buttons. "We are going to have a wild ride, I suspect. I feel as if I invited a house cat into my parlor, and she's turned into a tigress."

Gwynne, a tigress? She rather liked the idea. "I really have power? How splendid!" She threw back her head and laughed with sheer, giddy delight. She wasn't a powerless mundane. She had magic!

"Splendid, but also perilous," he said softly. "Enchantress power is a double-edged sword. You have power over men, but if you don't learn to control it, you risk driving them mad with lust and becoming a victim, as happened with William."

His words chilled her exuberance. "I could be abducted again?" She thought of the young man's strength, and how easily he could have overpowered her while in the grip of his obsession. "What a horrible thought!"

"It's a very real danger. Or some handsome, charming fellow may seduce you rather than stealing you against your will."

His words were light, but she recognized that he was expressing a real fear. How strange that her storm lord could be so unsure about his own power to win a woman's heart. "The records are very clear that being an enchantress doesn't mean a roving eye," she said firmly. "You are my husband. How could I want another man?"

She watched, fascinated, as his unvoiced anxiety faded. No, not watched, exactly—it was more a sensing of his emotional shift. She'd always had some ability to sense emotions, most women did. Now that ability was much stronger.

He ran a weary hand through his dark hair. "Since I've never encountered an enchantress before, I know very little about them. What do your books have to say about this kind of power?"

"I've not studied the subject deeply since enchantresses are rare. I certainly never thought the information would be personally relevant." She drifted to the mirror and gazed into it. Was it her imagination, or did her reflection show a vivid woman who captured attention even though her features were still those of Gwyneth Owens? Yes, there was a difference, she decided. Even exhausted as she was now, her energy had a brightness that was new. A quality that would draw eyes whenever she entered a room.

Enchantress power is a double-edged sword. That had been proved conclusively the night before. Now that it was clear she had power, she must begin training as quickly as possible. "The library of Harlowe contains a journal maintained by an enchantress named Elizabeth Jameson, who died about a hundred years ago. I never read the journal because her handwriting was difficult to read and the subject didn't interest me particularly, but I'll ask Brecon to send it to me. Perhaps I can learn something about how she controlled her enchantress energy."

"You will need that, along with knowledge of how to master whatever other powers appear. Preferably before you start a war." He smiled faintly. "I suspect that Helen of Troy was an enchantress who hadn't learned control."

Gwynne made a face. "That's not exactly a comforting thought."

"To say the least. There's enough war in the wind without adding a Helen of Troy." Duncan's dark expression reminded her of the potential disaster that hovered over both their nations. Could her destiny have something to do with building peace?

What a grandiose thought! She was no mage, merely a woman with budding powers. But she might have some role to play in the rebellion. Heavens, what if she was supposed to seduce the prince and convince him to return to Rome? Surely not!

Destiny made her think of her first husband. She caught her breath. "This is the real reason why Emery wouldn't lie with me! Not because he didn't desire me, or because he wanted to avoid siring more children. He knew that I was a latent enchantress, and he didn't want my power to be awakened too soon."

"Lord Brecon was a wise man. Marriage protected you long enough for you to grow into your power. It must have been difficult for him to keep his distance knowing what you would become if he took you to his bed."

Gwynne nodded, throat tight. Would it have been such a great mistake for Emery to lie with her? She would have liked to have been his lover as well as his companion. Surely she could have given him pleasure in his last years. But she vaguely remembered reading that an enchantress bonded very deeply with her first lover, and Emery must have felt that would interfere with her destiny. Certainly she had a profound bond with Duncan despite her initial wariness about him.

Duncan's words pulled her from her reverie. "Do you have the energy to try a new test of your power?" he asked.

She nodded. "I'm horribly tired, but too excited to sleep."

He removed a small enameled box from his luggage while she admired the fit of his breeches over his muscular legs, and the way his shirt emphasized those broad shoulders. One of the pleasures of marriage, she was discovering, was the delicious intimacy of seeing her husband casually dressed.

He opened the box and took out a disk made of a smoky, transparent material and edged with worked silver. Wordlessly he handed the disk to her. It was a scrying glass. As soon as it touched her palm, she said, "This burns with your energy. Do you really want me to try to use it? Scrying glasses are so personal."

"If we can share a bed, we can share a scrying glass." He sat down opposite her again. "This one is polished obsidian and copied from Isabel de Cortes's own glass."

Gwynne had tried scrying many times, but had never seen anything. Tonight would be different, she sensed. Already she could see shadows moving inside the smoky volcanic glass. Ancient and powerful, formed in the earth's own fire, obsidian was said to be the best material for scrying. "What happened to Isabel's glass? Was it lost or broken?"

"No, it's still among the treasures of Dunrath, but it went dark after her death."

That fit with what Gwynne knew of the brilliant, head-strong Isabel. She'd probably cursed the glass to darkness as she lay dying. "I know the theory of scrying, but I'm not quite sure where to start. What should I look for?"

"Why not look at William Montague and his fate? That's a subject that surely has a great deal of energy around it."

She wrinkled her nose. "Indeed. Now I relax and calm my mind and think of what I'd like to see?"

He nodded, though it was hardly necessary. Every Guardian child knew the principles of scrying. For a painful moment, Gwynne remembered her many failures.

This time would be different. She closed her eyes and stilled her whirling thoughts. When she had achieved calm, she silently formed a question about William's emotional state. What was his future?

For the space of a dozen heartbeats, nothing. Then

light filled her mind. Opening her eyes, she gazed into the scrying glass and saw William. The image was not precisely in the glass, she realized. Rather, it was in her mind and the obsidian somehow brought it into focus.

"He's in a windowless room somewhere low in the castle—a storeroom, I think. There are shelves and sacks and barrels. His father locked him in so he can't run off to join the rebels, but his mother made sure he had food and drink and blankets."

"Can you see more detail?"

She concentrated, then bit her lip. "He's lying on his stomach on the blankets, weeping. He's sure that he has destroyed his life. He can't have me, he has shamed his family, he will be sent away in disgrace. Dear God, the poor boy! If . . . if he had his dagger, he would use it to cut his throat." The bleakness of his pain swept through her with punishing force.

"Don't let the emotional energy of what you're scrying poison your own emotions!" Duncan said sharply. "That's a very real danger. You must keep distance between you and what you are viewing. Shield yourself with white light so that the anger and despair of others can't touch you."

She breathed deeply once, twice, thrice, as she visualized the shield of light around her. Though she had studied all these techniques, putting them into use was a very different matter.

"Are you balanced again?" After she nodded, Duncan continued, "Try looking at William's future. If there is a strong chance he'll commit suicide, we must take steps to prevent it."

She quailed at the thought of perhaps seeing William's dead body, but Duncan was right—if suicide was a possibility that could be prevented, they must act. It would be tragic for a young man to throw his life away over one stupid mistake.

What does William's future hold? She exhaled with relief as she sensed that he would get through this dark time without attempting self-destruction. "Lord Montague is going to move very quickly at getting him out of Britain—within a fortnight, I think. He's going to . . . to a warm, tropical place." She frowned, asking herself where. "Jamaica, I think."

"Will he stay there long, or turn around and come back to join the new rising?"

Duncan's questions stimulated new knowledge. "He'll be tempted to return to support the prince, but his desire to redeem himself with his family is stronger. He will take over stewardship of a sugar plantation his father owns. He'll work very hard, and in time, he'll come to love the Indies."

"Will he recover from his obsession with you?"

"By the time he reaches the Indies, he'll no longer remember why he felt such a compulsion to abduct me—it will seem like a bad dream." Another image appeared: strapping young William and a pretty blond girl with wide, admiring eyes. "He'll meet a woman there—the daughter of another planter, I think." Her tension eased into a smile. "They'll be happy together. There will be children, and occasional visits to England to see family, but the Indies will be William's home."

"So what seems like disaster for the lad now will in the long run be a blessing." Duncan shook his head. "That was remarkably fine scrying. If you can see so clearly only days after the awakening of your abilities, you'll be one of the best scryers in Britain when you come into your full power."

The thought was unnerving. She handed the obsidian

disk back to her husband. "I was only that good because the subject concerns me so closely."

His eyes said that he knew better, but he didn't argue the point as he returned the glass to his luggage. "We'll start your training tomorrow as we ride into Scotland, but now it's past dawn and time we slept. Unless you're still too exhilarated?"

"No, the scrying drained what energy I had." She stood, smothering a yawn.

Despite her fatigue, she found herself exploring within. Now that she knew she was an enchantress, she recognized that a vast, powerful stream of sensual energy flowed around her like an invisible river. Already she could shape it and direct it to some extent, and in time her mastery would increase.

The most important lesson would be using that energy so that men would be awed or respectful rather than being seized by ungovernable lust. Better to be placed on a pedestal than slung over a saddlebow.

She eyed her husband speculatively, wondering if she could wield that sensuality despite her fatigue. Though there were many techniques for mastering power and creating spells, the basic principle of wielding magic was to visualize the desired goal, then direct the force of one's will toward that goal.

As she drifted toward the bed, she imagined irresistible passion, the currents swirling from her and around Duncan. She glanced over her shoulder, both feeling and imagining desire, hot and tender. . . .

He knew at once, of course. "You're a shameless witch," he said, but there was laughter in his voice.

He caught her shoulders and turned her around. There was lightning in his eyes, and his gaze triggered hot, liquid pulses deep inside her.

As he unfastened the oversized banyan she still wore, he continued, "You're learning the tricks of the enchantress with alarming speed."

"Is this bad when we both enjoy the results so much?" she asked breathlessly.

"I didn't say it was bad." He slid the garment from her shoulders. As the heavy fabric pooled around her ankles, he bent forward to kiss the bare hollow above the edge of her nightgown, sending shivers through her. "I am blessed and cursed that you are my wife, *mo càran,* my beloved. You are passion and fulfillment—but until you learn to master your powers, I will have to defend you like a dragon."

"The fact that other men desire me doesn't mean that I desire them." She linked her hands around his neck, her deep fatigue seared away by the onset of passion. "An enchantress is as affected by desire as the men around her. Teach me what I need to know, my dearest mate."

"You have already surpassed me, I think." He swept her from her feet and laid her on the bed, following her down so that his hard body trapped her against the feather mattress as he kissed the sensitive curve of her throat.

"Then I shall teach like a tigress." Laughing, she locked her arms around him and rolled him onto his back, reveling in the power she had to arouse him. It was truly a double-edged power, for it aroused her equally. She was frantic to join with him, to dissolve the fear, relief, and shock she'd experienced that night into blazing delight.

She nipped his neck, loving his salty taste and the tantalizingly male rasp of whiskers. He was all man, and all hers. She rolled her hips against his, feeling the hard heat of his response. Then she moved to claim his mouth with her own, sliding her tongue between his lips. . . .

Scenes of violence and death swept through her with blinding vividness. Instinctively she slammed her protective shields in place before she could say anything that would alert Duncan, for she knew in her bones that this was something she must not discuss with him until she understood it herself.

He stiffened, too perceptive not to recognize that something had happened. She buried the images deep in her mind and slid her hand down his body. He groaned when she clasped him, his momentary distraction vanquished by passion.

She helped him strip off her gown, then offered her breasts. He sucked at them ravenously, shattering her whirling thoughts. In her last remaining trace of rationality, she recognized that her newfound power and awareness also meant greater sensitivity to unexplained terrors.

But she would worry about the dark side of her gift tomorrow. For now, she would end this long night with love.

Sixteen

With Dunrath so close, Duncan had to restrain himself from pushing Zeus to go faster. Their new horses had been working hard enough these last three days as he and his bride rode through the hills of northern England and the Scottish Lowlands.

This last leg of the trip had been a very special kind of honeymoon. They'd had a degree of privacy that would be impossible once they reached Dunrath. Traveling rough, eating bread and cheese by the road, and sleeping in small, remote inns had shown him that Gwynne was as adaptable and good-natured as he'd hoped. He no longer worried that she would have trouble adjusting to life in Scotland.

Duncan had also used the time to tutor Gwynne on controlling her power. Since she knew the principles already, she caught on with lightning swiftness. At least once a day, the lessons had led to stopping in quiet places to explore new aspects of enchantress power. Just thinking of that caused his blood to quicken.

Gwynne was riding a half length in front of him, and he took the opportunity to study her. The lithe, sensual body he knew so well. The silky complexion which was so amazingly soft and smooth against his own tough hide. The bright glint of sunlight on the unpowdered hair that showed beneath her bonnet. Every day she seemed more beautiful. More enchanting.

Yet it wasn't mere physical beauty that drew him so intensely. Even when they were both old and gray, he would be unable to resist her. Luckily, she was learning how to transmute her enchantress energy into an elegant allure that men would admire, but which shouldn't drive them to madness like poor William.

He had mixed feelings about her newfound powers. He loved watching her joy as she discovered her abilities, and in most ways he was glad to have a wife with strong magic. But he had married her thinking that he was a mage and she had no power to speak of, and now that balance had shifted. He would be at her mercy if she ever chose to use her enormous sensual power to bend him to her will.

He didn't expect her to, any more than he would threaten his family with a gale. However, her power was so bound up with marital intimacy that she might influence him without intending to.

He smiled wryly. What nonsense he was thinking! He'd give her the moon if he could—she would never have to make special efforts to persuade him of anything. And if she did, he would surely enjoy them profoundly.

Ahead of him, Gwynne shifted in her sidesaddle. "How much farther? Much as I love riding and my dear Sheba"—she patted the mare's sleek chestnut neck—"I'll be glad to reach Dunrath."

"We'll enter Glen Rath as soon as we round the next bend." Duncan grinned. "At least I hope so. After three years away, I may not remember every turn in the road."

"I'll wager that you do." She smiled back fondly. "Though calling this a road is generous. It's a track at best."

"Ahhh . . ." Duncan rounded the corner and pulled Zeus to a halt as he stared hungrily at his home. The glen stretched away to the left and right, the bottom fertile with fields. The castle stood across the glen from his present position. Located about the middle of the glen, Dunrath had been built on a rugged crag that had made it impregnable for centuries. Late-afternoon sun made the walls and towers glow with sturdy warmth. He wondered how a Sassenach like Gwynne would see it. In his eyes, the castle and glen had matchless beauty. "I've missed this so much."

Gwynne also halted, her gaze avid as she studied her new home. "Dunrath," she said in a hushed voice. "You said the name means Castle of Grace."

He nodded. "Dunrath was named by an early chieftain of our branch of the Macraes. The clan is Highland except for us. We exist here between Highlands and Lowlands, trying to be a model of peace and prosperity."

"An unpretentious task, but you've done well with it." Her gaze swept the length of the valley, lingering on the village north of the castle. "The land looks more productive than much of what we've seen so far." She grinned. "I'll wager you manipulated the clouds and the light to make the place look its very best when I arrived."

He laughed, unabashed. "Of course. What's the point of being a weather worker if you don't give your bride the best possible view of her new home?" His voice softened. "I know the glen is very different from London, but I hope you'll come to love it as I do."

She urged Sheba forward, taking care on the steep road that led down into the glen. "You told me once that the energy of Scotland was splendid and invigorating, and you're right. I feel gloriously alive here. I had no idea what I missed by spending my whole life within a few hours' ride of a great ugly city like London."

"Do you know, I think that must be why your powers were so undeveloped," he said thoughtfully as he followed her down the trail. "All of the Families come from the old Celtic fringes of Britain. Even those of us who must spend time in London have homes deep in the country. Because you always lived near the city, your power was overwhelmed by the chaotic energy of so many people. Your talents never had a chance to grow strong enough to notice."

She looked startled. "Good heavens, if I'd paid a long visit to a Guardian family in Wales or Cornwall, I might have seen earlier signs of power even if the enchantress energy wasn't awakened. Think of all the regrets I would have been spared."

"Perhaps you are more disciplined because of the delay," he suggested. "You are well on your way to becoming one of the strongest mages in Britain." He cast a wry glance her way. "Strongest, and most dangerous."

"Dangerous, me?" She threw back her head and laughed in disbelief.

He hoped she continued to be ignorant of just what her power would do. Since the horses had to take this stretch of road slowly, he decided to mention some local customs. "Don't expect to be addressed as Lady Ballister—since the title is English, no one here uses it."

She looked startled. "If you aren't called Lord Ballister, then what?"

"Scots are not fond of titles," he explained. "Since most people in the glen are Macraes and kin, I'm usually called Macrae or maybe Dunrath. More formally, Macrae of Dunrath so I won't be confused with the Highland Macraes."

Her lips curved in a smile. "So what will I be called?"

"Lady Macrae or Lady Dunrath, though members of

the household will mostly just say Mistress. We Scots are not so rigid in our ways as the Sassenachs."

"I think I could learn to enjoy that. What else should I know?"

"Though Gaelic is the main language in this part of Scotland, most people speak the Lowland version of English, so you should have no problems."

She smiled mischievously. "I actually read Gaelic quite well since it's an important language for Guardian scholarship. It will take time to learn to listen and speak it properly, but surely not too much time."

"You are a woman of unceasing marvels," he said, amazed. "That will make you even more popular in the glen." He thought about what else she needed to know. "Scottish women generally keep their own names when they marry. Shall I introduce you as Gwyneth Owens or Gwyneth Harlowe?"

"Too many names! Since I am in Scotland, I shall go by Scottish custom and use my maiden name, Gwyneth Owens." Her expression turned serious. "There's going to be shock when you introduce me as your wife. I wish you had sent a warning message."

He shrugged. "We are arriving almost as quickly as a message would have."

"Lady Bethany could have called a Scottish Council member with her sphere and the news would have reached Dunrath days ago." Gwynne gave him a shrewd glance. "Did you want to prevent your family and household from worrying because you're bringing home an English bride?"

He reminded himself never to underestimate her perception. "I thought it would be best if they meet you without warning. As a real person rather than an abstract, they will love you right away."

"I hope you're right."

"Of course I'm right. After all, you have the power to enchant." The horses reached the bottom of the glen, so Duncan urged Zeus into a canter, no longer able to wait. Gwynne matched his pace and they raced toward the castle. Occasionally a clan member saw them and called out a greeting, but Duncan was too impatient to do more than wave in passing. There would be a *cèilidh* to welcome his return later. For now, after far too long in distant places, he was coming home.

*   *   *

Gwynne arrived at her new home wind-tossed and breathless from the ride. The last stretch was a steep road that zigzagged up to the castle, passing over a deep, narrow ravine on the way. The bridge that spanned the ravine could be easily destroyed if invaders threatened, a remnant of grimmer days. Dunrath was no stately, comfortable palace like Harlowe. It had been built for war.

As she caught her breath, she surveyed Glen Rath. The valley stretched away on both sides, curving into the distance so that it was impossible to know the length. The steep hillsides were dotted with groups of grazing animals. Though most were the dun color of the tough, shaggy, long-horned Highland cattle, smaller gray shapes marked flocks of sheep. A little river ran the length of the valley, with several streams feeding into it from the hills. She should call the streams "burns" now that she was in Scotland.

The castle itself was awe-inspiring, a massive structure of stone and towers. She suspected that the interior was as cold and inconvenient as the exterior was dramatic. She repressed a sigh. Luckily, there would be time before winter to acquire warmer clothing. Though winter might be closer than she thought—there was a distinct touch of autumn in the bright northern air, and even a doting weather-mage husband was unlikely to keep the glen warm all winter for the sake of his thin-blooded southern bride.

Duncan had arrived in the courtyard a dozen lengths ahead of her, his face ablaze with delight. Now that she was in Scotland, she better understood his fierce connection to the land.

The courtyard was empty when they arrived, but as he swung from his saddle, a light voice cried, "Duncan!" A girl raced down the steps and into the yard to hurl herself into the new arrival's arms. "I had a feeling you'd be home today!"

"Jean!" He swept her from her feet in an exuberant hug. "Aye, but you look bonnie!"

So this was Duncan's sister. Good heavens, she was wearing breeches like a boy! Gwynne struggled to control her shock. Since Jean had been acting as the steward of Dunrath, it was probably more convenient to wear male dress and ride astride. This wasn't England, after all.

With their laughing faces together, there was a distinct family resemblance between brother and sister, yet at first glance they looked very different. Gwynne had expected Duncan's sister to be like him—tall and dark and forceful.

Instead, Jean was inches shorter than Gwynne and had bright red hair that fell past her waist in a thick braid. Freckle-faced and green-eyed, she sparkled like a dragonfly. Gwynne was intrigued to realize that she could sense the girl's power, though it was less intense and focused than Duncan's. He'd said that she had never taken the time to develop her gifts. Perhaps Jean and Gwynne could learn together.

Duncan ended the embrace and turned to assist Gwynne from her mount. His warm hands were strong on her waist as he lowered her to the ground. With a private smile, he said, "Gwynne, allow me to present my sister, Jean, the merry minx of Dunrath. Jean, this is my wife, Gwynne Owens."

Jean gasped and fell back a step, her eyes wide with shock. "Your wife?"

Gwynne mentally cursed Duncan for not warning his sister that he'd married. Poor Jean had been running Dunrath for years, and now she must defer not only to her brother, but to a new mistress of the household. Acting on instinct, Gwynne caught both of Jean's hands. "I'm so happy to meet you. I've always wanted a sister."

"So . . . so have I." Jean's expression suggested that if she'd had a choice of sisters, this tall Englishwoman wouldn't be on the list.

Gwynne released the smaller woman's hands. "I'm sorry you had no warning of my arrival. Duncan and I decided to marry very suddenly, and we started north right after the ceremony, so there was no point in writing."

Rallying, Jean said, "It's time my brother took a wife. I . . . I only wish that I had known to prepare the mistress's chambers for you." The lilting Scottish burr in her voice was more pronounced than in Duncan's speech.

"I'm sure there will be no problem." Gwynne decided to exercise some enchantress charm. "Duncan said that you are the heart and soul of Dunrath."

"He did?" Jean looked pleased but skeptical. "That sounds too poetical for my blunt brother."

Gwynne smiled. "Those aren't the words he used, but it's what he meant."

More members of the household were pouring into the

courtyard, calling to Duncan and studying Gwynne with unabashed frankness. Remembering Duncan's lecture on differences between their nations, she schooled herself not to feel embarrassed. There was no English deference visible, only curiosity, and she must become accustomed to it.

As the babble of voices rose, Duncan took Gwynne's hand and led her up half a dozen of the steps that led into the castle. "Friends and kinsmen," he called out in his deep voice, "allow me present to you the new mistress of Dunrath, Gwyneth Owens. She comes of a fine Welsh family, and has made me the most fortunate man in Britain."

Gwynne guessed that Welsh blood was more acceptable than English, for applause and congratulations echoed noisily off the stone walls of the courtyard. She smiled and waved at the people who were still streaming up to the castle.

When the noise died down, Duncan continued, "There will be time to become acquainted later, but my lady wife has had a very long ride so I'll ask Jean to show her Dunrath while I greet you."

Jean moved to Gwynne's side. "A good idea. Come with me. . . ." She hesitated, apparently unsure what to call this new person who had crashed into her life.

"Please, call me Gwynne. There are only a few years between us, and we are family now."

"Very well, Gwynne. Now to escape before the kinfolk catch up with you. Once people start talking, it will be hours until you can get away, and you must be fatigued."

Actually, Gwynne wasn't tired at all, but she was willing to defer her introduction to the extended family until later. She followed Jean up the steps and through broad oak doors into the entry hall.

"The housekeeper is visiting her daughter, so I'll take

you to your rooms." Jean set a brisk pace through the hall, heading toward a steep stone staircase.

Gwynne examined the huge entry hall with amazement. Easily thirty feet high, it felt cold as December even on this sunny day, and there was a noticeable draft blowing through. The stone walls were covered with massed displays of old weapons: circles of swords, fan-shaped arrays of daggers, and crisscrossed pairs of battleaxes. "That's a great deal of iron to see in the home of Britain's strongest weather mages."

"The family's weapons all have brass hilts." Jean gave her a sharp glance. "You're a Guardian?"

"Yes. Did you think your brother would marry a mundane?"

"I wouldn't have thought so, but he might have taken one look at you and forgotten everything he owed to his blood."

Gwynne assumed it was a compliment, if a trifle backhanded. "He was not that lost to duty. Though it's true that until quite recently I thought I had no power to speak of, I'm a scholar of Guardian lore."

"How did you discover that you had power at your age?" Jean seemed more relaxed now that she knew Gwynne was of the Families.

"I got married. Several days ago, Duncan informed me that I'm an enchantress, who didn't come into my powers until I was wed."

"Really?" Jean started up the stairs. "Enchantresses are rare, aren't they? How wonderful it must be to attract men without even trying!"

"That's what I would have thought until a silly boy abducted me in Northumberland. It was not an enjoyable experience," Gwynne said dryly. "I'm still learning to manage my power, so I hope you'll be patient while I learn."

Jean's eyes could shift through shades of green in the same way her brother's changed shades of gray. Now they were a bright, feline shade. "You are going to be much more interesting than I thought when Duncan first introduced you."

Gwynne blinked. Duncan had mentioned that Scotswomen were plainspoken, and he hadn't exaggerated.

Jean opened the door to a sitting room, then stepped back so that Gwynne could enter. "The mistress's suite. Your bedroom is to the left, while the door to the right connects with the master's rooms."

Gwynne scanned the spacious chamber, startled by the plaster walls, handsome furniture, and thick oriental carpets. The sitting room was in the corner of the keep, so windows on two walls admitted a flood of light, while a pair of fireplaces promised warmth in the iciest depths of winter. "This is lovely, and far more comfortable than I expected."

"Thank Isabel de Cortes. With her Spanish blood she loved the sun, so Adam Macrae built this solar as a wedding present. Every generation since has made more improvements to the private apartments."

"I owe Isabel a debt of gratitude." Gwynne brushed her fingertips over a silk-clad wall, so much warmer than raw stone. What a tangible act of love this bright room was. "Despite all the Guardian history I've read, I didn't know that Adam had created such a luxurious nest for his bride."

"Family legend says they loved greatly, and fought greatly. Isabel and Adam both had such power that it must have been like two swords sharpening against each other. Will you and Duncan be like that?"

"I have no blade to sharpen against Duncan's." Gwynne crossed to a window and looked out. Above the fields of Glen Rath loomed the Highlands, dark and haunting. A place of magic and violence. "An enchantress's power is rather passive—I have some ability to attract, but that is nothing like the active power of a great mage like Isabel."

She shifted her gaze to the courtyard below. A keg had appeared and men were standing around with tankards of ale, Duncan in the middle. He was alive in a way she had not seen him in England. "Duncan said that you hadn't taken the time to develop your power. The thought amazed me—when I was growing up, I longed desperately to have magic."

Understanding the implied question, Jean said tartly, "Someone in this family had to be practical. My father and Duncan were always out rattling the hills with storms, and my mother was a great healer who was often away from home. It was left to me to learn the mundane skills of sheep and farming and accounts."

"So you had to take responsibility from an early age. Have you ever wished for more time to train your power?"

Jean flushed. "Are you saying that you will take over my duties, so I must find something else to amuse myself?"

"Not at all," Gwynne said mildly. "I'm saying that your family has taken shameless advantage of your willingness to do the necessary but unglamorous work, and that you should be allowed the time to pursue your own interests if you wish. While I know how to run a household, my passion is for my scholarly work. I will happily leave the management to you if you like, but I think you deserve more."

Jean glanced out the other window. "I'm sorry for flaring up. I . . . I have been taken by surprise. I don't know what my place here is."

"This is your home, of course. Now it is mine as well, but I hope that we will work together as friends, not as opponents."

Jean's gaze met hers. "You are gracious. I see that Duncan did not choose you only for your beauty."

"I hope not. Beauty fades. Character is forever." Gwynne opened the door to her bedroom. It was also a handsome chamber, with a massive curtained bed to keep the warmth in. "Please don't think I'm trying to push you out the door, but surely a girl as lovely as you has suitors?"

Jean shrugged, but looked pleased at the compliment. "There are not so many men to choose from here."

"Then you can go to Edinburgh or even London if you like, now that you no longer have to carry the weight of the whole estate on your shoulders."

"A season in London would be . . . interesting," Jean agreed. "But I think that Robbie Mackenzie from the next glen and I will make a match of it."

Gwynne studied her sister-in-law's expression. "You don't seem too excited by the prospect."

"Robbie is a braw fine lad, but I must wait until he returns from the prince's army." Jean smiled ruefully. "Truth to tell, I'm angry that he wouldn't take me with him. Perhaps Duncan will."

Confused, Gwynne asked, "You think Duncan will join the rebellion?"

"Here we call it the rising." Jean's expression flattened. "Of course you're English and probably a Whig."

"I'm not much for politics, but I favor peace over war." Guessing that Jean didn't know her brother's views, Gwynne continued cautiously, "I believe that Duncan feels the same way. War is a horror with few benefits."

"This rising is about justice, and it will benefit Scotland," Jean said calmly. "Prince Charles Edward has right on his side. Men of Glen Rath have already joined him, while the others are waiting for Duncan to lead them out."

Jean's confidence was unnerving. "And if Duncan doesn't support the prince?"

"Then I'll lead Glen Rath out myself!" Jean retorted. "Jenny Cameron of Glendessary raised over three hundred men for the prince and brought them at Glenfinnan when he raised his standard. I could lead out our men as well as she did, but there will be no need. Duncan will join the rising, I promise you."

Gwynne felt a deep chill that began in her heart and spread through her whole being. With a certainty beyond doubt, she knew that her destiny was bound to Duncan's role in this looming civil war.

t took Duncan time to escape the impromptu celebration in the courtyard and go in search of his
wife. He found her on the family floor, heading toward
the library with a purposeful stride.

"*Mo cridhe!*" He spun her around and kissed her with
ale-soaked exuberance. "I'm sorry to have abandoned
you for so long."

"No matter." She kissed him back, her mouth as sweet
as Highland honey. "Jean and I had a chance to get acquainted, and she pointed me toward the library before
going off. Have I time to explore it, or am I needed elsewhere?"

"The library must wait, for you are very much
needed." As the kiss deepened, his original purpose began to vanish. His hands moved down her back, kneading her curves. "We need to investigate your new
bedroom to see if changes are needed."

She gave a husky laugh. "A likely story. But I'm sure
you had something less . . . intimate in mind when you
sought me out."

Recalled to a sense of duty, he said, "There's a *céilidh*
forming in the courtyard and we should both be there."

"A kaylee?" she asked doubtfully.

"It's a grand welcome-home celebration that will last until the wee hours." He heard the first wailing notes rise from the courtyard. "The music is starting now."

She cocked her head. "The sound like a creature being butchered alive is music?"

He grinned. "Aye, 'tis. The great pipes take some getting used to, but no other instrument can get the blood pounding the same way." His blood was already pounding, and not from the music. He looped an arm around her shoulders and guided her back toward her rooms.

She slid her arm around his waist, her long stride matching his. "How can there be many guests on such short notice?"

"News of my return has already spread through the glen and the surrounding hills and everyone knows that means a clan gathering. Many people will bring food since the Dunrath kitchens haven't had time to cook." Though a sheep had been quickly slaughtered and it was already roasting over a fire in the courtyard. "All will want to see the grand beauty who is the new lady of the glen."

She glanced down at her dusty riding habit. "The carriage hasn't arrived with our baggage yet, has it? I only have this habit and one plain, wrinkled gown packed in my saddlebags. Neither are exactly grand and beautiful."

"I asked Jean to retrieve the gown and have it brushed out for you. It's just as well that you'll be dressed simply. This is no gentry ball, but a celebration for everyone in Glen Rath." He bent to trace the delectable rim of her ear with his tongue. "Even if you wear sacking, you'll be the loveliest woman in Dunrath. And you're loveliest of all without a stitch on."

"You're getting more Scottish and more bawdy by the minute," she said demurely, but her eyes sparked in a way he recognized.

They were nearing her bedroom door when a thin, middle-aged woman appeared around the corner, Gwynne's other gown draped over her arm. "Ah, there you are. Here's your gown, Lady Dunrath."

"Mistress Maggie!" Duncan caught the woman up in an affectionate embrace. "Gwynne, have you met Dunrath's housekeeper, Margaret Macrae?"

"Thank you so much for taking care of my gown." Gwynne advanced with her beautiful warm smile and an extended hand. "I'm pleased to meet you. I hope all is well at your daughter's house?"

"I'm sorry I wasn't here when you arrived," Maggie said stiffly as she took Gwynne's hand. "Aye, she and her bairns are well, and thank you for asking."

"Perhaps tomorrow you can explain the workings of the household to me. I do hope you plan on staying here at the castle? You have it running so smoothly now."

Duncan watched Maggie's tension fade under Gwynne's soothing words. It was natural for Maggie to be concerned for her position, and perceptive of Gwynne to recognize that, and disarm Maggie's fears immediately. Enchantress charm in action, with a dose of power that made Gwynne irresistible. By the end of the *céilidh*, everyone in Glen Rath would be eating from her hand.

After Gwynne had accepted the gown and Maggie left, Duncan opened the door that led into the mistress's bedroom. "We have a few minutes before we need go down. Now, where was I? Here, I think." He resumed kissing his wife, starting below her ear and working his way south. Her skin had the delectable smoothness of cream.

"*Definitely* more bawdy," she said breathlessly. "You seem almost a different man here."

"One that you like, I hope?"

"Oh, yes." She pressed against him, her lower body

pulsing gently. "In England, you were the Lord of Thunder. Here you're the Laird of Sunshine, at least today."

"I've never been so happy, *mo càran.*" Mo càran, beloved. "I'm home again, this time to stay, and I have you. What more could any man want?"

"Peace and safety would be good." Her eyes darkened for a moment as she draped her spare gown over a chair.

He refused to allow the shadow of the rebellion to dim this moment. Turning her toward him, he unfastened the top buttons of her waistcoat, then went to work on the shirt beneath. "This riding habit covers up far too much of you. Let me help you change your dress." He exhaled soft, warm breath into the tantalizing cleavage he uncovered.

"I thought we are supposed to go to the *céilidh,*" she gasped, running her hand down his torso. Outside, the pipers finished their practice and had joined together to play a reel that rattled the ancient stones around them.

"The *céilidh* can wait," he said hoarsely. The bed was only a few steps away, but if he took her there, they'd want to spend the rest of the evening entwined. "This will take only a few minutes."

He moved her against the wall and kissed the base of her throat. The pounding of her pulse was the drumbeat of desire, heady and intoxicating. Part of her magic was the ability to make a man feel passionately wanted, utterly virile.

He lifted her skirt and petticoat, trailing his fingertips up the satin length of her inner thighs before he delved into moist, heated readiness. She gasped, her eyes widening into blind passion.

Her hand slid into his breeches, and he no longer cared if the whole pipe band marched through the bedroom skirling to raise the dead. He fumbled with the fall of his breeches, yanking a button off in his haste.

Too aroused for subtlety, he thrust urgently into her eager body. For an instant they were both still, paralyzed by the exquisite pleasure of union. She began rolling her hips, her breath an aching moan. Her movements drove him deeper and deeper into madness as the wail of the pipes echoed his uncanny flight into unknown realms.

Even more than the physical joining, he was aware that their emotions meshed in a new and intricate way. He was home, she was his wife, and they were close in ways beyond anything he had ever experienced.

Though he wished this searing harmony could last forever, he knew he was within moments of culmination. Sliding his hand between them, he touched her intimately. She dissolved into frantic convulsions that triggered his own shattering release. They clung together, supported by the wall, until she breathed, "Oh, myyyyy . . ."

He laughed a little. "Words don't exist that can describe such pleasure, my enchantress." Tenderly he pressed small kisses along her brow and temple.

She tilted her head, eyes dreamy. "I'll never hear the bagpipes again without thinking of this."

"Then I'll hire a castle piper," he said promptly.

She chuckled as she disengaged from him. "You were right—that took only a few minutes, but now I don't have the strength to meet the whole of Glen Rath."

"You'll manage admirably, *mo càran*." Since he was drained himself, he used a technique for channeling energy to help refresh them both. He started by searching the skies for weather energy until he found strong winds in the Hebrides. Drawing some of that energy into himself, he tamed the essence of the winds until they were safely aligned with his own nature. Then he clasped her hand and sent power to her in an invisible current. Physical touch wasn't essential, but it made the transfer easier.

"Intriguing!" Revitalized, she released his hand and began to remove her riding habit. "A fortnight ago, I wouldn't have known what you're doing. Now I can sense how you shape the energy and pass the result to me."

"You learn like lightning." He glanced in the mirror and decided that with a little straightening, his appearance would do, though he'd need a pin to substitute for the button he'd ripped off his breeches. "I wonder how far you'll go? Perhaps you'll rival Isabel de Cortes before you're done."

"Nonsense!" Gwynne dropped her refurbished gown over her head. She'd chosen to pack the pretty green sack dress in her saddlebags because it was easy to don, and its simplicity was perfect for the night's entertainment. "She was a sorceress almost from the cradle. I'll never have such power. I don't think I would want it."

He understood her sentiment. Great power was exhilarating but also a vast and demanding responsibility. There were times when he wished that he had been less blessed, yet power was what defined him. He could not imagine himself as a mundane, or even as an averagely gifted Guardian. Though Gwynne had longed for power, she was now recognizing how magic brought worry and responsibility as well as joy. It would take time for her to find the balance within herself.

Gwynne sat at her dressing table and began fixing her hair. "Though you said that everyone here is kin, surely not everyone in the glen is a Guardian."

"No, but there has been enough intermarriage, so that a touch of power isn't uncommon. In the Highlands, second sight is accepted even among mundanes."

"What about Jean's sweetheart, Robbie Mackenzie? I know of no Guardians of that name, but does he have at least some power?"

"Robbie is her sweetheart?" he asked, startled. "It's the first I've heard of that."

"Perhaps that's the wrong word, but she said that she thought they'd make a match of it even though she's angry with him for following the prince and not taking her along. Do you know Mr. Mackenzie?"

Though Gwynne seemed to be studying her reflection, he realized that she was watching him intently. "Aye, I know Robbie and his family. They live just over the hills to the north." He frowned. "He's a decent-enough lad, I suppose. In worldly terms it would be a respectable match and Macraes and Mackenzies have always been allies, but as far as I know he hasn't a particle of magic. I'd hoped for better for my sister."

"Jean thinks you'll join the rebellion."

He recognized that they had come to the heart of this apparently casual conversation. "Absurd. I've given her no reason to think that."

Gwynne relaxed. "I'm glad to hear that. Since she's known you all her life, while I've known you only weeks, I wasn't sure."

He approached the dressing table and wrapped his arms around her from behind. "The young are apt to see glamour in war. In my travels I saw the aftermath of battles on the Continent. There was no glamour there, only pain. I have no desire to support a Pretender to the throne. The Stuarts had their chances, and wasted them all."

"I hope to God this rebellion dies out quickly." She glanced up into Duncan's rugged face. She loved the way he looked after they made love, his soul in his eyes and his energy radiant as the sun. His strength made her feel safe. May God grant that his strength would always be used for protection, not destruction.

$\mathcal{W}$hen Gwynne and her husband looked respectable again, they went down to the *céilidh*. On the stairs, she held his arm a little more tightly than strictly necessary. "Don't worry," he said quietly. "Even without your enchantress charm, you would be loved by my people."

"I hope you're right." She smiled wryly. "I'm trying to dampen my energy so that I'll be liked, but not liked too much. Being abducted here would be most awkward. Am I suitably restrained?"

He gazed at her askance, his eyes unfocused as he evaluated what she was doing. "If you can maintain this level, you should have no trouble. You're appealing enough that both men and women will be delighted to have you among them, but not so much as to cause unbalanced passions." He grinned. "Now your energy is flaring like a bonfire and you look so delectable that I want to take you upstairs again. What happened?"

She smiled ruefully. "One compliment from you and my control disintegrates." Thinking about going back upstairs with him didn't help, either. Deliberately she looked away from Duncan, breathing slowly until she was balanced again.

She had practiced many techniques in the days since she came into her power, but she was still far from the fluid mastery that she needed to live a comfortable life. As soon as possible, she would start researching the lives of earlier enchantresses to learn how they had handled their dangerous gift.

It occurred to her that she knew of no existing essays on the subject. Perhaps she would write one herself when she better understood how to control this particular power. The prospect of research and analysis gave her a warm scholarly glow.

They reached the bottom of the stairs and entered the front hall, which was crowded with people and trestle tables loaded with food. Mercifully the musicians were in the courtyard playing for the dancers. Even so, their music was loud enough to sour milk.

As soon as Gwynne and Duncan appeared, a crowd formed around them. "My wife will not remember all your names tonight," Duncan called out, "so be sure to introduce yourselves again when next you meet."

" 'Tis simple to remember us, Lady Dunrath," a male voice called out. "We're all named Macrae!"

That caused a roar of laughter, but it was true enough; nine out of ten people who were introduced to Gwynne were indeed Macraes. She concentrated on given names, then tried to tie the name to the "flavor" of that person's energy. Sensing an individual's unique inner nature was another new talent.

Maggie Macrae, the housekeeper, moved forward with a wide-eyed youth beside her. "Mistress, allow me to present my son, Diarmid."

Brown-haired and blue-eyed, Diarmid bobbed his

head, then gazed at her with budding adoration. Gwynne realized that her control over the enchantress energy was slipping, so she clamped down on it again. William Montague had taught her how susceptible the young could be. "Good evening, Diarmid. I'm pleased to meet you."

" 'Tis good that Duncan Macrae has brought a wife to the glen," he blurted out.

" 'Tis glad I am to be here." She made sure her smile had only social friendliness.

Duncan said, "Gwynne, meet Donald Macrae, the most valuable man in the glen. Auld Donald is the steward of Dunrath."

The grizzle-haired steward studied Gwynne shrewdly before giving a small nod of approval. There was a hint of power in his aura that he'd probably inherited from a Macrae ancestor. He would be a good ally and a formidable foe.

As she and Auld Donald chatted, there was a break in the music. "Will you dance with me, *mo cridhe*?" Duncan asked. " 'Tis the best way to learn to love the pipes."

She rolled her eyes in mock disbelief, but accepted his invitation willingly. After meeting half of Glen Rath, she wanted to relax with her husband.

They descended into the courtyard, where the cool evening air was rich with scents of wood smoke, roasting mutton, and tangy ale. She and Duncan joined the dancers who were lining up opposite each other in parallel lines. She smiled when she thought of their meeting at New Spring Gardens. "Remember our first dance?"

"How could I forget, milady?" he said with the husky French accent he'd used that night. "That was a dance between strangers. Now we know each other's mysteries."

She smiled a little sadly as she thought of how she had

come to marry him. "Does one ever know all of another person's mysteries?"

The pipes began to wail and conversation became impossible. The dance was similar enough to ones Gwynne knew that she was able to follow the steps easily. Duncan, blast him, had been right. Dancing to the wild, siren call of the bagpipes was exhilarating. This was music that could lead a man—or a woman—to hell and back.

The set ended, leaving her flushed and panting. "We must dance again later, my lord husband," she purred with a provocative narrowing of her eyes.

"Given our long ride, perhaps we should retire early," he said with equal provocation.

"Soon, then." She took his arm, letting her fingers stroke sensuously down his powerful forearm to his wrist. Was this fierce mutual passion because they were newly wed, or did enchantress magic intensify their desire? She suppressed a smile, thinking of how pleasurable the research for her intended essay would be.

The musicians took a break, so Gwynne and Duncan went inside to find some food. They were just finishing their supper when Jean skipped up, eyes shining and a tall young man's hand clasped in hers. "Look who has come! Duncan, you remember Robbie Mackenzie. Gwynne, this is the lad I spoke of."

"Lord Dunrath, 'tis good you're home." Robbie shook Duncan's hand, then bowed to Gwynne with the practiced grace of the wellborn. Living with the rebel army had left his clothing rather the worse for wear, but his accent was educated. "Welcome to Scotland, Lady Dunrath. Glen Rath is a bonnie place to live. Almost as bonnie as Glen Fannach, which is my family's home." He slid a sidelong glance at Jean.

Gwynne could sense no power in him, but he was a

handsome youth with a friendly smile, and she felt no
shadows in his nature. "I'm so pleased to meet you," she
said warmly as she wondered how often she had repeated
that phrase this evening. "Jean spoke of you earlier."

"Did she, now?" he said with obvious pleasure. He
tucked a hand in Jean's elbow. "The lass has been much
on my mind."

Gwynne fervently hoped that Jean wouldn't follow
Robbie to the prince's army. With her new power, she
sensed that was a very real possibility.

"Come along, Robbie," Jean said. "After we sup, will
you dance with me?"

He raised her hand and kissed her fingertips lingeringly
in a clear announcement of his feelings. "It would be my
delight, *mo cridhe*."

After the young couple left for the trestle tables,
Gwynne asked under her breath, "What do you think?"

Duncan frowned. "I can't dislike the lad, but I'm still
not enthusiastic about the match. Not that I can forbid it
if Jean wants him. She's of age and a stubborn wench."

Gwynne studied the girl, who was laughing up at her
sweetheart. "She likes him very well, but from what she
said earlier, I'm not sure she loves him. Perhaps when the
rebellion is over we can take her to London. She showed
some interest in the possibility. At the least, she would
have the chance to meet a wider range of men."

Her husband's frown lightened. "I like that idea. Let us
hope for a swift conclusion to this rebellion."

He took her arm and returned to the task of introduc-
ing more Macraes. There certainly were a lot of them,
but all were welcoming. Even the least educated had a
natural courtesy that Gwynne found very appealing.

As the evening advanced, she began to think that retiring early was a good idea even if all she did was sleep. She

was covering a yawn when the dance music outside cut off in the middle of a phrase, the pipes squealing weirdly at the abrupt halt. Curious, she followed Duncan to the castle door.

Half a dozen well-dressed men were riding into the courtyard. As they pulled to a halt and dismounted, a babble of voices rose and many of the *céilidh* guests dropped down on one knee. Her questioning gaze went to the man in the center of the group of newcomers. She caught her breath with shocked realization. Tall and richly dressed, the young man had the compelling magnetism of a king—or a would-be king.

Recognizing him at the same moment, Duncan said in a steady voice, "Prince Charles. I bid you welcome to my home."

"Lord Ballister?" The prince strode forward, at ease with having every eye on him. An Italian lilt in his voice, he said, "I heard that you have just returned from travels on the Continent, sir. Since I was near, I decided it was time we met."

The Young Pretender had good information sources. Gwynne noted that unlike the Macraes, he used Duncan's English title. His accent was a legacy of being raised in Rome. This was his first trip to his "homeland"—and he'd come to start a war.

That was why he was here, of course—to raise support. What was the protocol when greeting a rebel against one's king? Gwynne decided to err on the side of respect, so she curtsied when he joined her and Duncan at the entrance to the hall. He acknowledged her with a practiced smile. "You must be Lady Ballister. I had heard you were a rare beauty, but the description pales next to the reality."

He was handsome, with brown eyes that contrasted with his fair skin and powdered hair. She understood why females of all ages sighed over him, but curiously, she sensed that unlike most men, he had no interest in her. Behind that easy smile was an icy resolve that had no time for flirtation.

Duncan bowed, though not deeply. "Will you and your companions join us for food and drink?"

"That would be our pleasure." The prince beckoned to his followers and they entered the castle. An eager young girl from the hills approached and swept a deep curtsey, her smile adoring. " 'Tis blessed I am to see you with my own eyes, Your Majesty!"

Charles nodded at the girl graciously. "After I have greeted these good people, Ballister, I would speak with you privately."

Duncan's lips tightened, but he said, "Of course. We can talk in my study."

Gwynne caught her breath, sensing deep, dangerous undercurrents swirling through the hall. Great forces were present, and the results would be significant.

Charles spent a few minutes circling the room and greeting admirers. The prince and his party were here to charm and they did it with some success, particularly among the younger Macraes. Gwynne was glad to see that many of the older, more responsible people held back, their expressions carefully blank. Except for Auld Donald, who made no attempt to hide his scowl.

Having completed his circuit, the prince asked, "Your study, sir?"

"Up these stairs." Gwynne released her enchantress energy, knowing that the allure would make it hard for a man to say no to her. Plucking a lantern from the nearest trestle table, she continued, "Let me light your way, my lords."

As she headed for the stairs, she realized that not only were the prince and Duncan following, but that every man in the hall was gazing after her hungrily. Unnerved, she swiftly damped her energy down again, wishing that she had a measuring stick for magic. Controlling sexual allure was like trying to bake bread using black powder—too much would cause an explosion.

Once they reached the next floor, Duncan led the way to his study. Though the study was clean and comfortably furnished with a desk, chairs, and a bookcase crowded with ledgers, it had the neglected air of a place long unused. Gwynne made a show of lighting the candles, then poured two glasses of claret when she found a tray and decanter on a side table. Duncan didn't comment, but he raised an ironic eyebrow at his wife's unnatural demureness.

The prince frowned when it became clear that she intended to stay. "Lady Ballister, your husband and I will be discussing tedious political matters. Surely you will not deprive my companions of the opportunity to dance with you."

She offered her most wide-eyed smile, along with a strong dose of allure so that he would accept her presence. "I would not deprive myself of the opportunity to hear you speak, sire."

His frown vanished, though she wasn't sure whether it was because of her magic or because he thought she would be an ally in the task of persuading her husband to join the rebellion. Accepting the claret, he chose the most comfortable chair and gestured for his hosts to sit.

Gwynne sat to one side, where she could be unobtrusive while seeing both men clearly. They were a study in contrasts. Youthful and well dressed, the prince had the bone-deep confidence of a man who had been told he was royal from the moment he was born. There was also more than a touch of magic in his nature. She suspected that he had the dangerous ability to inspire deep loyalty—whether he deserved it or not.

Duncan was dressed more casually in worn riding garments and his dark, unpowdered hair was escaping from the riband at his nape. But it was he who drew the eye first, for he radiated strength, power, and hard-won wisdom. Prince Charles Edward Stuart was a boy. Duncan Macrae was a man.

"Your castle is most impressive, Ballister," the prince observed. "I see why it has never been conquered."

"My ancestors chose the site well." Duncan sipped at his claret before setting his goblet on the desk. "Let me speak frankly. You seek support for your rebellion. You will not receive it from me. Scotland has shed enough blood for the Stuarts."

Charles's smile was unperturbed. "There are others of your clan who have decided differently."

"The Macraes of Kintail choose their own path. The Macraes of Dunrath are a distant connection. Though we bear Highland blood, we also have Lowland practicality. You cannot win this rebellion, Your Highness."

"You think not? In the first encounter between Jacobites and Hanoverians, a dozen of my men drove off two companies of royal troops."

Duncan made a dismissive gesture. "The government garrisons in Scotland are undermanned and most of the seasoned troops are in Flanders, so that's a pale victory."

"Perhaps, but I also have the support of the French. Once my army starts winning victories in the north,

France will invade from the south. The Hanoverian king will run back to the Continent, squealing for sanctuary."

He's lying, Gwynne realized. But he lied well.

Equally perceptive, Duncan said, "I've heard that the French refused to put an army behind you so you came on your own, hoping your boldness would raise enough support to convince King Louis that you are worthy of his men and money."

Charles's eyes narrowed. "The French were delayed, but they will come. The Jacobite response here has been even stronger than I hoped for. Every day more men flock to my banner."

"Most of whom haven't a shred of military experience."

"The fierce charge of the Highlanders is legendary," the prince retorted. "A troop of clansmen, shouting and brandishing claymores, can terrify even seasoned troops."

"After which the Highlanders will be ripped to bloody shreds by government artillery," Duncan said icily. "These are my people, and I will not see them die in a hopeless cause."

"The Stuart cause is *not* hopeless," Charles said vehemently. "Within the next few days, I will capture Edinburgh. When we face the Hanoverians in open battle we will win, and tens of thousands of English Jacobites will rise up and join us. I will restore my father to his rightful throne, Ballister. You would be wise to ensure that you are on the right side."

It disturbed Gwynne to know that he might be right, since even the Guardian Council had been unable to determine the outcome of this rebellion. With sufficient luck and boldness, Charles might well carry the day. So far, he'd had plenty of both.

"All things are possible," Duncan said peaceably. "But my first responsibility is to the people of Glen Rath, and I'll not lead them on a fool's crusade."

The prince drank deeply of the claret. "You are a blunt man, Lord Ballister."

"If you didn't want plain speaking," Duncan said with a faint smile, "you should not have come to Scotland."

"Britain has always been my destiny." Charles leaned forward in his chair, his coolness replaced by blazing, charismatic passion. "At the age of six, I could shoot a gun or a crossbow with the skill of a man. As a boy, I built model fortifications. At fourteen, I walked the Spanish trenches at the siege of Gaeta. The earlier Jacobite risings failed because of poor planning and insufficient will, but I have the will, and I will succeed."

Gwynne drew an unsteady breath, feeling the man's power even though she was English, female, and against this rebellion. Striving for detachment, she used her inner vision in an attempt to read his character.

The Young Pretender joined the magic of leadership with absolute belief in his destiny—and in truly royal fashion, he assumed that he was granting men a favor by allowing them to die for him. That fierce confidence in his goals gave him the ability to accomplish great and terrible things. But she could see that his character was also shot through with arrogance, inflexibility, and a weakness for drink. Though he would be a strong leader in success, she guessed that he would falter in adversity.

Yet he had the personal magnetism to create a vision men would follow to the death. Even Duncan was vulnerable to it. Gwynne sensed his barriers going up, protecting his deepest thoughts. "You are resolute and you have the ability to bind men's hearts," he said calmly. "If you had been the Stuart heir when William or Anne died, I don't doubt that you could have restored your dynasty to the throne. But that time has passed. Britain is a different place now than it was then."

Charles's brows arched. "Yes, Britain has changed. Can you honestly say that you are happy with the Acts of Union that turned Scotland into a mere province of England that exists only to be taxed and bullied? This has always been a free nation—until her own leaders sold her for English gold."

Duncan's expression tightened. "Parliament has not treated Scotland well, but even so, the union is better than endless conflict. The economic arguments are also valid. My country is poor. Union with England is beginning to change that. In time, the inequities will disappear and the two countries will be true partners."

"Perhaps, but at what cost?" Charles sat back in his chair, more controlled. "I can free Scotland from this odious union, but to make that happen I need the support of respected men like you. I'm told that over the years, the Macraes of Dunrath have had an uncanny knack for choosing the right side. Which means you belong with me."

Duncan rested his unfocused gaze on his goblet. Gwynne suspected that he was scrying the blood-red wine, trying to part the veil of the future to see what lay ahead for his homeland. "Will you be content with Scotland, Prince Charles?" he said softly. "Or is this but the first step in a campaign to take the throne of England as well?"

"What would be wrong with that?" the prince said with cool arrogance. "The House of Stuart was divinely chosen to rule. It was madness for the English Parliament to hand the crown to those coarse, stupid Germans. Britons deserve better than that."

Duncan looked weary, as if the days of travel and resuming his responsibilities weighed heavily on him. "Most nations deserve better leaders than they are granted, but we must work with what we have. The Hanoverians are the devils we know and if they lack charm, at least they don't cause much trouble."

"That's poor praise for a king," Charles said sarcastically.

Duncan shrugged. "Rivers of blood have been shed in religious wars, so there is great value in having Protestant rulers for a mostly Protestant nation. If your father or grandfather had been willing to swear allegiance to the Church of England, the House of Stuart would rule today."

The prince leaped to his feet, his expression outraged. "What right has Parliament to dictate a sovereign's religion? The Stuarts are faithful followers of the True Church, and so we shall remain!"

"Which is why you shall not win this rebellion. The model in this matter was Henry of Navarre, who said, 'Paris is well worth a mass,' when he renounced his Protestant faith to become a Catholic king of France." Duncan also rose. "I am not saying what is right or wrong in these matters, Your Highness. Only what is. Raising your standard here will bring death and destruction on Scots and Englishmen alike."

The prince made a visible effort to master his temper. "You will think differently after I prove my mettle in battle. You're a stubborn man, Ballister, but I admire your honesty. Know that you will always be welcome at my side."

He pivoted on his heel and opened the door, waving off Duncan when his host started to follow him. "I will find my own way down, Ballister. My men and I will take full measure of your hospitality before we leave."

Duncan bowed. "As Charles Edward Stuart, a gentleman of Scottish blood, you are always welcome in my home."

Gwynne thought the prince snorted before he left. After the door closed, she sank back into her seat. "That was—interesting," she said faintly as she tried to evaluate what had happened, not only the words but also the antagonistic energies that had crackled through the chamber as the men spoke.

Duncan paced to the window and looked out over the darkened glen. The cool composure he had shown the prince was gone, replaced by gray fatigue. "The devil of it is that much of what Prince Charles said is true. Many will follow him, and it won't be only the Highland clans. Even I can feel the power of his call for freedom and independence."

Gwynne stared at her husband, aghast. She had been sure he would stand with the council against the bloodthirsty rebellion that was beginning, yet now he seemed dangerously ambivalent. A single visit with the prince was causing him to waver. How would he react when his sister and others demanded that he lead them out in the Jacobite cause? A man of his enormous power might change the outcome of this rebellion.

This is why she had been asked to marry him. He was her destiny, not because of what pleasure and companionship they might find together, but so that she could influence him in larger issues.

No one ever said that destiny was easy.

uncan turned around when he heard Gwynne gasp. Staring at him with huge, shocked eyes, she said, "How can you agree with the prince? He's a usurper come to sow disaster in pursuit of his own selfish ends. Though he's a compelling man, he has all the faults of his house."

"And the virtues, too. His courage and charisma will rally men to his cause." He wondered if an English-woman, no matter how learned, could understand the depth of Charles's appeal. Scotland's ancient tradition of freedom and independence had been betrayed by the na-tion's own leaders, and the Young Pretender represented a way out. "The Acts of Union were an abomination that all true Scots hate, and the English have done little to make them more palatable in the years since they were signed."

"You said the union will make Scotland wealthier in time. Isn't it worth putting up with some irritations in or-der to ease the kind of poverty we saw on our ride north?"

"Perhaps." He rubbed his temples wearily. "But some-times I wonder if prosperity will come at too high a price. A nation's belly matters, but so does its soul."

"The fact that the prince knows how to woo a Scottish mind doesn't make him fit to rule," she said tartly. "As you said, the Stuarts had their chance, and most of them did badly. A man doesn't deserve to become king simply because he's better looking and and better dressed than his rival."

"The prince's personal attractions are undeniably an asset. He looks royal. George II looks like a critical, mean-spirited shopkeeper."

Gwynne didn't try to deny it. "Nonetheless, war is not the answer. That's a basic Guardian principle. Defending oneself is a man or woman's right. Killing people who disagree with you is not."

"A pity more people don't accept that," he said dryly. "It would make the work of the Guardians easier. The last battle of the Fifteen was at Sherrifmuir. Afterward a song was sung that said, *'There's some say that we won. Some say that they won. And some say that nane won at a'.'*"

"Isn't that true for most wars?"

"That battle might have seemed as if it had no winner, but the rising itself failed. This time could be different."

She frowned. "It's hard to imagine how the Jacobites can win with few weapons, no real army, and no foreign support."

"The matter is balanced on a knife's edge. A few victories and men will flock to the prince. Though the French did not support this adventure, they could easily change their minds if Charles shows signs of success. France came within a hair's breadth of mounting an invasion just last year, and they will be quick to try again if the Hanoverian government is sufficiently weakened."

Gwynne cocked her head. "I heard that last year's invasion threat ended when a storm struck the French fleet at Dunkirk. Did you do that?"

He thought back to the night when he had stood on a French headland and conjured up a mighty tempest. It was not the equal of Adam Macrae's great gale, but it had sufficed. And on that occasion, there had been no question in his mind what was right. "The Macrae weather mages have a long tradition of keeping invaders from Britain's shores. It's the advantage of our island being protected by the sea. One good storm can scatter a whole invasion force."

"Surely you can do that again if the French decide to send troops in support of the Jacobites."

"Aye, I can." He sighed. "If that's the right thing to do."

"Do you truly doubt it?" Gwynne said quietly. "The Guardian Council, even the Scottish members, have feared the prospect of another Jacobite rebellion for years. Now it is here, and there will be terrible bloodshed."

"That will be true no matter what the outcome. Have you considered the possibility that a Jacobite victory will spill less blood and that a restored House of Stuart might be better for Britain than the Hanoverians?" He spoke the words hesitantly, because until tonight he had not considered that possibility himself. Now it would not leave his mind. "James II was a fool, but James I and Charles II ruled long and well. Perhaps Charles Edward has the same gifts of leadership."

To her credit, Gwynne considered his words rather than rejecting them instantly. "It's possible that a Jacobite victory would benefit Britain, yet my instincts say no."

With deep disquiet, he recognized that a breach could easily separate them over this issue. Not only was she English, but she had been raised in the heart of the Guardian establishment. The world did not always look the same out here on the wild edges of Britain. "Enough of politics." Shaking off his grim mood, he sat down at his desk. "I have something for you."

"Something indecent, I hope?" she said with forced brightness. He guessed that she found disagreement on this subject as upsetting as he did.

"That can be arranged later." He traced a swift pattern in the air with his fingertip, the glowing lines fading an instant later. Then he twisted a piece of decorative carving and his secret drawer slid open. The contents included a small, lacquered box. He handed her the box, wondering if she was adept enough to open it. "Now that you are Mistress of Dunrath, this is yours."

She frowned when the box wouldn't open, then realized that it was sealed by magic, as the drawer had been. She took a deep breath, her eyes slipping out of focus for a moment, and the lid of the box popped up.

"Well done!" he said. Her progress was remarkable.

"Isabel de Cortes's ring," she breathed as she lifted the gold circlet reverently from its velvet nest. A brilliant ruby was set in the heart of a gold Tudor rose, the emblem of Queen Elizabeth's house. The ring was a feminine version of the one Duncan wore. She slid it onto her third finger, next to her simple gold wedding band. "It fits perfectly!" she said with surprise.

"They always do." He held up his left hand so that the sapphire of his ring glowed in the candlelight. "Both rings were enchanted by John Dee at the queen's request. Not only were they a reward for the destruction of the Armada. They are also a kind of connection to the rulers of England."

"That I didn't know. The great queen was shrewd." She spread her fingers and smiled at the ring with delight. "I can feel the energies of the women who have worn this. It's like ... layers on an onion. The most recent would have been your mother?"

"Aye. Her energy was soft. Very different from Isabel's." His mother had been gentle—and as formidable as a storm at sea.

"The ring has belonged to six women before me?"

He counted the owners down from Isabel. "Only five."

"There is a sixth." Gwynne's eyes narrowed. "Queen Elizabeth herself wore this for several days before sending it to Isabel. She must have wanted to strengthen the connection to the royal house."

Duncan glanced at his ring, and wondered how he would have reacted to Prince Charles if he hadn't been wearing it. Might he have been more inclined to the prince's arguments? Better not to find out.

Yawning, Gwynne rose from her chair. Shadows of weariness darkened her eyes. "I'm so tired that I can barely keep my eyes open. Do you think anyone will notice if I don't return to the *céilidh*? Your people seem quite capable of entertaining themselves."

"Go and rest. If anyone notices, they'll understand." He smiled a little. "Since you're a dazzling enchantress, they'll forgive you anything."

She laughed. "I wonder if I'll ever be able to believe such a thing. It still seems like a joke that my mere presence can affect men so strongly."

"Never think it a joke." He studied his wife, who was tired, rumpled, and utterly irresistible. What would he do if she ever returned another man's interest? The thought was so horrifying that he couldn't bear to imagine it. Lightly he kissed her on the forehead. "I'll join you later."

She trailed fingers along the sensitive inside of his wrist, leaving fire in their wake, before she withdrew. He was tempted to follow her to her bedchamber and dissolve the tension between them with passion. Instead he returned to the window, gazing sightlessly over the moon-touched hills. Scotland was in his bones, and he hadn't fully recognized how much he missed it until he was home again.

To be a Guardian was to swear to support what was good for the largest number of people. Yet what if the best path wasn't clear? Might his love for his native land distort his judgment so that he would support the wrong outcome? He shuddered at the thought. Partisanship was antithetical to the principles that had been drilled into him since he was an infant.

Yet what if the Stuarts *were* the best rulers for Britain? The Hanoverians were Protestant but pigheaded, and the Crown Prince, Frederick, was weak, extravagant, and deceitful. His own parents called him "the Nauseous Beast." By comparison, Charles Edward Stuart was a model of strength and virtue. Just as Duncan should not choose to support Charles only because of their shared Scottish blood, he should not blindly support the House of Hanover as the council was doing.

With great power came responsibility—and he had a disturbing premonition that the fate of this uprising might end up on his shoulders. Weather was very important in military campaigns. It would be easy to change the outcome of a battle. . . .

Another Guardian principle was, never interfere unnecessarily. Partly this was because meddling with the free will of a person or nation was inherently wrong, and partly it was because excessive interference increased the risk of the Guardians being identified as a dangerous minority.

The Families had survived as long as they had because

of their discretion, supported by spells that kept their children from casually revealing power to mundanes. When necessary, spells of forgetting were laid on mundanes who saw things that might make them suspicious. Even such small enchantments were discouraged unless absolutely necessary.

Duncan prayed that the rising would play itself out without his needing to pick a side. If he was forced to choose, he couldn't guarantee he would make the right choice.

* * *

It was well past midnight when Duncan retired. Most people had gone home under the light of a waxing moon. Others snored quietly in corners of the hall, and one last happy quartet was singing, badly, around a keg of ale. It had been a jolly good party.

Because of the late hour he considered going to his own bedchamber, but he and Gwynne had slept together every night since their marriage. He needed to be with her.

Her room was pitch-dark, so he touched the wick of a candle into soft light. His heart tightened unbearably as he studied her soft sleeping features. Did other men feel this same anguished need whenever they looked at her, or was it worse for him because they were wedded and bedded? If all men found her so enchanting, no wonder young William had felt compelled to abduct her.

He stripped off his garments and slid into the bed beside her. He had intended only sleep, but when she instinctively shifted toward him, his resolve faltered. She was tired and deserved her rest, and yet . . .

He rested his hand on her breast. Under the muslin of her nightdress, it was soft and perfectly rounded. Slowly he moved his thumb, stroking the nub until it hardened. She made a purring sound and moved closer yet.

A gentleman wouldn't wake a sleeping lady to demand intimacy, but if she awoke with pleasure she could decide for herself. Her pulse was slow as the beat of a seabird's wing, until he licked the silky skin of her throat and the tempo quickened.

She was all sensuality as she molded herself against him, her hand exploring with sleepy finesse. Unsure if she was waking or sleeping, he continued a gentle lovemaking, each advance on his part met by a response on hers.

"You are mine, *mo càran,*" he whispered. "Now and forever, only mine."

Perhaps she agreed, because she drew him to her with welcoming arms. Restraint exploded into frantic need and he buried himself in the lush haven of her body. She responded with the passion that could bring a man to his knees. This was the essence of enchantment—a woman who could supply pleasure and fulfillment so intoxicating that it was impossible to imagine life without her.

They were joined by fate. Surely mere politics could not separate them. . . .

Twenty

The next morning Gwynne behaved as a dutiful bride and gravely inspected the inner workings of the household with Maggie Macrae as her guide. After a thorough tour of the kitchens, laundry, dairy, brew house, and other functions, she said frankly, "Mistress Maggie, Dunrath ticks like a fine clock in your capable hands. I truly hope you will continue to manage the household. I need to know what is going on and important decisions should be discussed, but I'll be happiest if I have time every day for my own work."

Maggie said with equal frankness, "It's glad I'll be to continue as I have before. What is your work?"

"I'm a scholar. I read, I take notes, I make translations, sometimes I write." Gwynne smiled disarmingly. "The results are of interest only to other scholars, but it matters to me. When Duncan proposed, he said that Dunrath has a fine library. I look forward to seeing it."

The older woman grinned. "And you're perishing to go there now that you've done your duty. Be off with you, Mistress. I think we shall deal well together."

Gwynne needed no further permission. She had woken that morning knowing that her honeymoon was over.

The magical interlude of travel had given way to the reality of daily life. Now it was time to lay the foundation for the rest of her life, and she saw no reason to take on any more domestic work than was absolutely necessary.

She hadn't seen Duncan since they breakfasted. He had gone off with Jean and Auld Donald to ride through the glen and see how the land and people were faring. She would see none of them till the day was done, she suspected. His attitude this morning had been brisk, and she had been unsure if it was because his thoughts were on the day ahead or if he was withdrawn because of the political tensions between them the evening before. She wasn't too worried, though. Any man who came to bed as passionately as Duncan wasn't withdrawing very far.

She was beginning to appreciate the mixed blessing of enchantress power. It would be very easy to use it to manipulate others, which would be wrong in all kinds of ways, both human and Guardian. Yet—very easy. Fortunately Duncan was not the sort to be manipulated.

Now to find if he had exaggerated the size of the Dunrath library. She entered and took stock of the contents. The room faced south so the light was excellent, always an advantage when reading old texts, and lush Persian carpets softened the floor. A long table, a desk, and half a dozen straight chairs were scattered about, while a pair of wing chairs and ottomans sat cozily by the fireplace.

But when she scanned the book titles, she was dismayed to find no arcane texts at all. Though it was a very fine gentleman's library, there was no Guardian lore.

There had to be more. Perhaps there was a second room housing the secret texts, as was the case at Harlowe?

Frowning, she scanned the library with her inner eye and immediately discovered a door in the corner. It was shaped and painted to fit into the molded wall panels. More important, it was bespelled so that a mundane eye would pass over it unseeing.

She moved a chair that partially blocked access and placed her hand on the flat knob. As soon as she touched it, she recognized that another spell was involved. Frowning, she felt her way through the spell as if walking a garden maze. Ah, it was a repulsion spell. Even if a mundane with a touch of wild magic happened to notice the faint outlines of the door, he would be uninterested in learning more.

Feeling vastly pleased with her ability to navigate the library's defenses, she opened the door and found a second, smaller room furnished in a similar fashion to the main library. But where was it in terms of the castle layout? It was strange to have space to hide a whole room.

Heavens, there was another spell! A very clever one that made people incurious about how the space was arranged. No one would notice that a room-size area was unaccounted for unless they took careful measurements of the whole floor. She hadn't noticed herself, until she had penetrated the arcane library's magical barriers.

This time when she crossed the room to the bookshelves, she recognized texts that could be found in any Guardian library. There was plenty of space for new bookcases, too. Duncan had said she was free to expand the collection. If she were a cat, she'd be licking her chops.

Many of the volumes were deliciously unfamiliar. Much Guardian lore was in journals and workbooks since the information could not be distributed publicly and printing was too expensive when only a handful of copies were needed. Wondering if the library contained any information on enchantresses, she decided to try a technique her father had used.

Concentrating hard on the desired subject, she moved her open hand along the nearest bookshelf, her palm a few inches from the spines of the books. Nothing. The next shelf. Again, nothing.

Unsure whether she was doing this wrong or if there simply wasn't any material on enchantresses, she tried the bottom shelf. Halfway along, she felt warmth emanating from a slim volume. She pulled it from the shelf and found that it was a treatise on powers most often found in females. A quick scan suggested that there was little on enchantresses, but she set the book on the table for closer study.

She returned to her search, and struck gold when one narrow, faded volume almost scorched her palm. The book was the journal of a French enchantress of the previous century. This was exactly what Gwynne had hoped for. It was written in a French regional dialect, but she could understand it reasonably well.

Book in hand, she headed toward one of the chairs by the fireplace—then stopped in her tracks when she saw the portrait hanging over the mantel. It was an oil painting of Isabel and Adam Macrae. Though Gwynne had once seen an engraving of the couple, that had been pale and lifeless in comparison.

She stepped forward to study the portrait more closely. Isabel de Cortes had been her heroine when she was a girl. She still was.

To a half-Guardian child with no power, Isabel had been a shining example of what a woman could be. Gifted with wild magic, she had no Guardians in her ancestry and she'd been raised by a mundane family that loved but didn't understand her. A student of John Dee, Queen Elizabeth's own sorcerer, she had become a great mage through her fierce determination and discipline.

Gwynne had thought it was ironic that she was Isabel's opposite: raised with every Guardian advantage, but no innate ability.

In the painting, the couple were in their middle years and Adam's dark hair had silvered at the temples. Beside him an open window revealed a turbulent Scottish sky as a symbol of his weather mastery. Underneath his Elizabethan beard, his features were very like Duncan's. The Macraes bred true. His hand rested on the head of a tall dog that resembled dogs that lived in the castle now, so it wasn't only the humans that passed down their resemblance.

But it was Isabel who drew most of Gwynne's attention. She was no beauty. Her dark face was too narrow and exotically un-English, her features too angular. Yet the intelligence and humor in her gaze were vividly compelling. On her lap was a large tabby cat, and in her right hand she held the famous obsidian scrying glass.

Last night Gwynne had sensed Isabel's energy on the ruby ring, and today she saw Isabel's face. The combination brought her heroine alive as never before.

Curious what else she might have missed when she made her beeline for the books, she examined the room more carefully. A cluster of miniatures hung on the wall behind the wide desk. She could identify none of the people portrayed, though the men were clearly all Macraes.

Clothing style allowed her to guess which woman was probably Duncan and Jean's mother. She had a lovely, enigmatic smile. The late Lady of Dunrath, who had died about six years earlier, had been a Macleod from the Isle of Skye. In fact, she had been the sister of council member Sir Ian Macleod. They had the same misty gray eyes.

Next Gwynne investigated a glass curio case full of interesting objects from around the world. The dragon figurine was surely Chinese, and there was a mask from somewhere in Asia that she could only guess at. The Dutch East Indies, perhaps. There was also a silver box that looked like a turreted tower, perhaps from Spain or Italy. Other objects were less identifiable, but all possessed a faint glow of magical power.

She knelt to look at the lower shelves, and caught her breath when she saw what was surely Isabel's scrying glass. Duncan had said it was among the treasures of Dunrath even though the obsidian lens had gone blank after Isabel's death. It sat quietly on top of a small padded velvet drawstring bag, the smoky stone giving no hint of its significance.

Surely no one would mind if the new mistress touched it. Reverently Gwynne opened the glass door, hoping that she would feel Isabel's energy more strongly than in the ring, where it had been overlaid with other energies.

She lifted the scrying glass from the cabinet, the translucent stone cool against her palm—and was blasted by a wave of energy that knocked her onto her backside.

Her heart was pounding and she must have blacked out for a moment, but as she retrieved her scattered wits she found that she still held the scrying glass. Glad for the thickness of the carpet, she got to her feet and sat in one of the wing chairs. Isabel's vibrant energy had been deeply imprinted in the obsidian, along with a background chord of powerful masculinity.

Gwynne glanced at the portrait, knowing that the male energy was from Adam Macrae. Strange how the force and individuality of their personalities lived on so many years after their bodies had been laid to rest in the cool green Scottish soil. It was said that they had died within an hour of each other. Gwynne felt a tightness in her throat, and wasn't sure if it was grief for the fact that Isabel and Adam were no more, or regret that her marriage to Duncan was not rooted in such powerful love. Perhaps in time they would develop that—if the Jacobite rebellion didn't tear them apart.

Her eyes a little misty, she looked down at the scrying glass—and found that the long-dormant obsidian had come alive.

Twenty-One

*I*t was late afternoon when Duncan returned to the castle, having called on as many of the glen homesteads as possible. The familiar hills and faces had soothed his tension of the evening before. He was home, where he belonged.

He was unsurprised to learn that his bride had disappeared into the library hours earlier. Guessing that she might be hungry, he ordered a tray with hot tea and shortbread and took it upstairs. She had managed to find and enter the private library. Mentally he was already beginning to think of her as a fully trained mage. He must be careful of that. Remarkable though her progress was, she was still a neophyte in many ways.

"Gwynne?" Balancing the tray on one hand, he opened the door to the inner library. "You must be starving."

She sat at the long table, books scattered about and a tablet full of notes under her right hand. At his entrance she looked up, blinking as if not quite sure where she was. "You were right, this is a fine library, and I look forward to making it finer yet."

He glanced at the books on the table. "What are you researching?"

"Enchantresses. I found a journal by a French woman who had the gift, but she doesn't talk much about how she experienced it." Gwynne made a face. "I think she enjoyed her power a bit too much."

"One can see that would be a temptation." He set the tray down and leaned over for a firm kiss. Her lips were cool, probably a sign of hunger. He poured two steaming cups of tea and placed one beside her, then lifted a knee rug from the back of a wing chair and draped it around her shoulders. "Drink," he ordered as he sat down on the opposite side of the table and helped himself to shortbread.

"Yes, my lord," she said with suspicious meekness.

He recognized the velvet bag sitting on the table near her tablet. "I see you found Isabel de Cortes's scrying glass."

She nodded. "I did. And . . . and it works for me."

"Really!" He leaned forward. "How remarkable. Almost as if the glass has been waiting here for you."

"I think it was," Gwynne said soberly. She touched the velvet bag. "I assume no one will mind if I take possession of this."

"Of course not. The fact that the glass speaks to you says that it's yours." He eyed her thoughtfully. "Scrying and use of the talking spheres are closely related abilities. You may end up on the council."

She looked startled. "I will never have that kind of power!"

"It appears to me that you already have. Now drink your tea and have some shortbread before you faint from hunger. Then you can tell me what you've seen."

After washing down two pieces of shortbread with the tea, she slid the scrying stone from the velvet bag. Her gaze searched the depths, as if not quite believing that it was truly hers. "I saw the Jacobite forces enter Edinburgh, and take the city without a drop of blood being shed."

He caught his breath. "That happened today? If so, Charles made good speed between here and Edinburgh."

"Not today. I think the city will be taken two days from now. But it's quite clear and definite-looking—a sure event, not a mere possibility. Prince Charles will ride into the city at midday wearing Highland dress. Red breeches and a green velvet bonnet with the white Jacobite cockade."

"You can really see that kind of detail?" he asked, amazed.

"It's the stone." Her fingers tightened around it. "It holds immense power and the images are very clear. The prince will have his father proclaimed James III, King of Scotland, England, France, and Ireland."

"It's time England gave up pretending it has authority over France." Duncan said dryly. "What else did you see?"

"He'll declare that the Acts of Union are annulled."

Duncan was unable to suppress a flare of pleasure at the news. "That will certainly win him more support. Can you see the outcome of the rising?"

"That was one of the first things I looked for. As the council says, the result has not yet been decided." She grimaced. "Only blood and death were certain. The first battle will be fought very soon—within the next week, I think."

"Can you see how that will turn out?"

She returned the stone to its bag. "The Jacobites will win in a matter of minutes."

He felt a rush of pleasure at the news. The sun broke through the afternoon clouds and light poured into the library, taking off the autumn chill. "An easy victory will have men and foreign support flocking to his standard."

"It's not an easy victory for the hundreds of men who

will be killed or wounded or captured," she snapped. "Most will be government troops, but their lives matter. A good number will even be Scots."

"I regret that, of course, but if there is going to be a battle, a quick victory will mean fewer casualties on both sides."

Gwynne's eyes narrowed. "You look far too pleased with the news of Jacobite successes. You are supposed to support the cause of humanity, not take sides as if this war is a horse race."

His mouth tightened. "I've not interfered unlawfully, nor do I intend to, but surely I have a right to my private emotions."

"You do *not*!" she exclaimed. "You are a mage and your emotions change the world. When you exulted over the Jacobite victory, the sun came out. If I'd said the prince did badly, thunder would have rocked the glen. You must control yourself, Duncan. Unbridled power flaring around this rebellion is too dangerous. You know the Family rules. We cannot allow ourselves to behave as irrationally as mundanes."

He flushed, knowing there was truth to her words but resenting her reprimand. "Do not give me lessons on the control of power, my lady. I have been a mage these last two decades, while a month ago you were powerless as an infant."

"Because power is new to me, I haven't had the chance to become complacent or arrogant." Her voice could have chipped ice, yet her anger was paradoxically alluring. With her red gold hair tied back simply and her eyes flashing, she was so desirable that he clenched his hands to keep from touching her.

"If you're not arrogant, it's only because you haven't had power long enough to start misusing it," he retorted.

"Soon you'll be manipulating every man in sight! You're damnably close to that now. Stop using your sexual magic to try to influence me!"

"I am *not* using power on you!" she sputtered. "The fact that you're always randy doesn't mean that I'm trying to enchant you."

He jumped to his feet and leaned forward, hands braced on the table. "At least I'm aware of what I'm doing! Don't pretend that you don't know the effect of your power!"

As she drew back instinctively, anger and desire flared into a scarlet energy that swirled through the room. Above the castle, thunder crashed with window-rattling force. Horrified, he recognized how far out of control they were.

Rounding the table, he caught her in his arms, desperate to end their conflict. "Gwynne, *mo càran*, we mustn't let this happen!"

After an instant's resistance, she hugged him back, hard, as if trying to melt into his body. She was shaking, on the verge of tears.

He spun his anger into one of the Celtic knot patterns that helped dissipate unbalanced emotions. Aching with tenderness, he whispered, "We're tearing each other apart, *mo cridhe*. We must never let this happen again."

Raising her head, she kissed him with devouring need. The raging forces they had released flared into frantic physical passion. As her fingers clawed into his back, he lifted her onto the edge of the table and stepped between her legs, raising her skirts so they foamed around his thighs. He was her Lord of Storms, the irresistible force whose power could sweep her mind from her body.

She gasped when his deft fingers touched her intimately, and waves of sensation dizzied her. No matter how their minds disagreed, their bodies were in perfect accord. As soon as he released himself from his breeches, she guided him into her, thrusting against him. They both cried out as they came together with fierce urgency.

Their mating was swift and violent, but it transmuted anger into a searing harmony that left them both drained and panting for breath. As she clung to him, shaking, he repeated in a strained whisper, "We must not fight like this again, Gwynne. It frightens me how my control vanishes where you are concerned."

She nodded, her face buried against his shoulder. "This is the dark side of power, isn't it? When we fight, we risk damaging more than each other. Perhaps we should avoid discussing the rebellion until it is ended."

"That would be impossible, but we must not allow ourselves to become so partisan that we lose our detachment." He stepped away, leaving her bereft. "Try to believe that I know my duty, Gwynne. If the circumstances are right I might intervene to save lives, but I won't try to change the course of the rising."

"Fair enough." She stepped down to the floor and poured two more cups of cooling tea with a hand that was still unsteady. When had he started calling the rebellion the "rising," as the Jacobites did? Telling herself that that subtle shift in language didn't mean he had turned rebel, she offered a tentative smile. "I was impressed at how well you faced down the prince. He is very compelling."

"Worse, he may be right." Duncan sat and stretched out his long legs as he sipped wearily at his tea. "I've pondered this all day, and I believe there is a strong possibility that a Stuart restoration might benefit all of Britain. Lord knows the Hanoverians seem to have no great love of our island. The Prince of Wales is sly, weak, and deceitful. If he becomes king, he could be a disaster far worse than Prince Charles Edward."

"Perhaps, but a Stuart on the throne feels . . . alarming

to me. If only the scrying glass could tell me more!" she said with frustration.

"We must be patient. Events will reveal themselves in time."

The caution was simple to say. Almost impossible to live by.

*   *
*

Tired by the emotional demands of the day, Gwynne retreated to her room for a late-afternoon nap. Discovering Isabel's scrying glass had been all the excitement she needed her first full day at Dunrath. She could have done without the raging fight and reconciliation with Duncan, though she supposed the argument was inevitable and had done much to clear the air. On the positive side, if all arguments with her husband ended in such spectacular passion, at least there were compensations. . . .

She dozed off with a smile on her face, and woke at a knock on her door and Jean calling, "Gwynne, may I come in?"

Gwynne sat up and yawned as she pushed the coverlet aside. "Please do."

Jean entered, face rosy with fresh air and happiness. Today she wore a proper green riding habit that complemented her bright hair and fair complexion. "I've been riding with Robbie. He has to return to the army tomorrow, but he can stay here tonight."

"Good. I'd like to get to know him better." Gwynne's gaze was caught by a lithe creature that followed on Jean's heels. The beast leaped onto the bed a mere yard from Gwynne and regarded her with baleful green eyes. Sleek and striped, it was definitely feline, but like no cat she had ever seen.

Evaluation finished, the cat butted her ribs in a blatant bid for attention. She automatically scratched behind the tufted ears. "Is this a typical Scottish cat? He's enormous!"

"Lionel seems taken with you." Jean perched in the chair by the dressing table. "His papa was a wildcat, which explains the size and arrogance. He comes and goes as he pleases, but until now, he hasn't shown much interest in people."

"A wildcat? I've never seen one. Not even a half wild-cat. What a very bushy tail you have, Lionel." Gwynne stroked down his back. He began to purr, his claws kneading her thigh.

Jean grinned. "I think you have a pet. Crossbreeds have a reputation for attaching themselves to one person. Isabel de Cortes had one."

"Ouch! Impressive claws." Gwynne removed his paws from her leg. Now that Jean mentioned it, Lionel did re-semble Isabel's cat in the library portrait. "How does one detach from an overenthusiastic wildcat?"

"One doesn't. If you were a witch, Lionel would be considered your familiar."

"Guardians don't have familiars."

Lionel reached out a paw and curved his claws into her skirt as if to say, "Mine." Gwynne began to laugh. "I had to leave my sweet old tabby behind. I planned to find an-other, but I didn't expect a brute like this to adopt me."

"You belong here, Gwynne. Lionel is just another sign of that. But the reason I stopped by was to tell you about our traditional Dunrath Friday night dinner. Has anyone mentioned that to you?"

Gwynne glanced out the window at the setting sun. "No, and since it's Friday and almost dinnertime, I'd bet-ter learn."

"Family, staff, and a rotating group of crofters dine together in the great hall," Jean explained. "There's a bit of ritual led by the mistress of the household. I've been doing it, but after tonight it will be your responsibility."

So much for Gwynne's vague idea of having a quiet supper in her room after the full day. "Very well, I shall watch closely."

"When I first saw you, I thought you would be a terrifying London lady," Jean said shyly. "I'm so glad you're not."

"No wonder you looked horrified when we met. The most London thing about me is my wardrobe, Jean. I'm used to a quiet life with books and horses." A heavy paw batted her thigh. "And cats." She frowned at Lionel, who looked remarkably possessive. "Do you think he understands English?"

"It wouldn't surprise me if he did. Crossbreed cats are very bright, and very loyal to their chosen humans." Jean got to her feet. "We dine in half an hour. I'll send your maid up to help you dress."

Jean left. Lionel didn't. Instead, he rolled on his back with his large paws in the air so Gwynne could scratch his striped tummy. As she obliged, she wondered how the cat and Duncan would get on. A castle had room for only one king. . . .

*   *   *

There were easily twenty people in the great hall when Gwynne arrived, with more coming in the front door. Fires roared in both fireplaces and the trestle tables usually set against the walls had been pulled out and placed end to end to create one long table. Four massive silver candelabra were set along the tabletop.

She had vaguely thought this would be a formal occasion, but the atmosphere was warm and relaxed. Duncan crossed the hall to join Gwynne when he saw her. The expression on his dark face was wary. Though they had settled their disagreement earlier, it was impossible not to remember their argument. "I just realized that I didn't tell you about the Friday night dinners."

"Jean did." Gwynne glanced around the hall. People were chatting casually, many of them sipping tankards of ale. "This is so different from England. Servants at Harlowe were treated well, but they never dined with the family."

"Since everyone at Dunrath is more or less related, this *is* a family gathering. Isabel de Cortes began the custom. She thought we should take time every week to celebrate our blessings, not solemnly the way we do in the kirk, but joyfully."

A deep musical sound boomed through the hall, echoes resonating from the ancient stone walls. Gwynne jumped. "What was *that*?"

"A gong from China." Duncan grinned and offered his arm. "We enjoy the eclectic at Dunrath. May I show you to your seat, my lady?"

With a smile, she took his arm. His seat was at one end of the table, and he placed her beside him in another mark of the evening's informality. After everyone was seated, Jean entered the hall carrying a slender burning taper. As she lit the candles on the table, the talking stopped and people settled into comfortable silence.

When the candelabra were radiating warm light, Jean moved to her chair at the opposite end of the table from Duncan. Before sitting, she said in a clear voice, "This is the last time I shall act as Mistress of Dunrath. Welcome to Glen Rath, Gwyneth Owens." She beckoned to her sister-in-law with both arms, her palms facing up.

"Welcome, family and friends." Another beckoning gesture as her gaze moved over the assembled group. "And welcome to any visitors who may be joining us tonight." She smiled warmly at Robbie Mackenzie beside her and gestured once more before sitting. "Now let us offer thanks for the blessings of family, food, and fellowship." She covered her eyes with her hands, as did the assembled guests.

Gwynne followed Jean's lead, but she didn't pray, because her thoughts were full of wonder. When the moment of prayer ended, she leaned over to Duncan and whispered, "Do you know the origin of this ceremony?"

He looked puzzled. "As I said, Isabel de Cortes started the custom."

"Once my lord Brecon took me to dine at the home of a friend of his, a Jewish scholar. It was Friday night, and the lady of the household led a ritual very like this one to welcome the Sabbath." Gwynne smiled. "Even though Isabel and her family had converted to Christianity, they kept some of their ancient traditions."

Duncan's face lit up. "And those traditions live on here in the wilds of Scotland. I'm glad to know that." He took her hand, and they shared a moment of perfect accord.

Gwynne knew there was more conflict ahead of them, but she also knew beyond doubt that she was in the right place—and with the right man.

Twenty-Two

*J*ean was so immersed in a letter that she didn't notice when Gwynne entered the breakfast room. The letter was from Robbie Mackenzie, Gwynne assumed. He wrote at least twice a week, and the letters were fat. So were Jean's replies.

In the weeks since the Jacobites occupied Edinburgh, there had been little action except for the Battle of Prestonpans. As Gwynne had predicted, it was a swift triumph for the prince's forces. Since then, the rebels had been drilling and gathering strength for the next move.

Gwynne took a seat, Lionel leaping into the chair beside her. His manners were excellent and he wouldn't climb on the table, but he did expect to be rewarded for his forbearance. She gave him a bit of cheese, then leaned forward to top up Jean's cup with fresh steaming tea. Her sister-in-law looked up, blinking. "Oh, sorry, Gwynne, I didn't know you were there."

"I'm practicing invisibility," Gwynne said with mock seriousness.

Jean grinned. "As a child, I always thought it would be lovely to be invisible. Think of the mischief one could get away with!"

"It's hard to be invisible with red hair." They shared a laughing glance of commiseration.

Gwynne tucked into her breakfast, thinking that Duncan had been right to say that she would soon find a place at Dunrath. The new mistress's lack of snobbery, acceptance of existing household customs, and progress with spoken Gaelic had endeared her to everyone in the castle. The Scottish-looking red hair hadn't hurt, either. Auld Donald had commended Gwynne on her tact. She hadn't explained that her motive was not tact but sloth. Why wrest control of the household from the hands of those who enjoyed managing it, when her own interests lay elsewhere?

She spread berry preserves on a piece of bread. "Does Robbie say anything about the situation with the rebel army, or is it all sweet words for his lady's ears alone?"

Jean blushed and folded the letter. "The latest news is that several French ships managed to slip through the English blockade with arms and supplies and money."

Gwynne's bread tasted suddenly dry. "How fortunate for the prince."

"Though you wish Charles Edward at Hades," Jean observed, "the rising is growing more powerful every day. The Jacobites can win all, Gwynne. How I would love to be with the army! But Robbie says I would only be in the way."

Gwynne was grateful for Robbie's good sense in keeping his impetuous sweetheart in a safe place, though Jean did not appreciate his consideration. She had a warrior heart and would have joined the rebellion in a heartbeat if she were male. Several young men from Glen Rath had gone to the prince. Their absence was not discussed.

Thinking it time to change the subject, Gwynne said,

"This morning I'm going to be working on some interesting spells. Would you like to join me?"

"No thanks, I've work to do."

It was the answer Jean always gave to Gwynne's invitations to work together, but today Gwynne succumbed to curiosity. "I can't help wondering why you choose not to develop your power."

Jean hesitated before answering. "Having Duncan for a brother was rather overwhelming. I'm a dozen years younger, so he was already a mage by the time I was old enough to notice the world. My parents and other Guardians were always raving about his power—how he was going to be the greatest weather mage since the sainted Adam, and maybe even better. I couldn't begin to compete with that. My potential is average at best, so I decided to concentrate on mundane matters which I could do well."

"I can see how it would be difficult having such a talented older brother," Gwynne agreed. "But aren't you interested in the magic itself? Wielding power is marvelous. When I get it right, I feel a . . . a oneness with creation that is the most exciting thing I've ever known." Except, of course, for her marriage to Duncan.

Face a little wistful, Jean shook her head. "Mostly I found it terribly frustrating. I know it was difficult for you to grow up without power, but when your magic came, it arrived in a great rush. You never went through the awkward, difficult phase. For me, trying to master power was like cutting stone with a dull knife. I might manage to scratch the surface, but the results weren't worth the effort involved."

"Perhaps your power has strengthened with time."

"I suppose that might have happened, but to be honest, I don't really have the desire to concentrate on boring books when the world is such an exciting place. There's a new day dawning, and I want to be part of it. Perhaps I shall travel to Edinburgh to stay with our cousins." Jean finished her tea and rose, taking her leave with a nod.

Gwynne refreshed her tea, hoping Jean wouldn't follow through on her idea of visiting Edinburgh. Though the rebellion was quiet now, the capital would be an obvious focus of conflict if the government forces counterattacked.

Sometimes she had trouble remembering there was a war in progress not far away. Gwynne had ample time to read and study, and while she hadn't learned much about other enchantresses, the day before she had received a promising bundle of books from the library at Harlowe. Life would be idyllic if not for the danger she felt hanging over Scotland, and the tension in her marriage.

After the explosion in the library, she and Duncan stopped discussing politics. That prevented more arguments, but it had also put a barrier between them. They were courteous and affectionate with each other, but the intimacy that had been developing had frozen solid. Marital relations, no matter how amazing—and they were!—couldn't compensate for emotional wariness. She mourned their loss of closeness. When this damnable rebellion ended, perhaps they could find their way to true intimacy.

She was about to leave the breakfast room when Duncan swept in the door wearing riding dress and a mischievous smile. Lionel ostentatiously changed position, turning his back on Duncan and tucking his nose under his tail.

Duncan raised her chin and gave her a thorough kiss. "Come, my lady. It's a beautiful day, I have no pressing duties at the castle, and it's time you abandoned your books for a good ride."

"I've been riding every day," she protested.

"But you haven't been outside of Glen Rath. Today we'll visit a place you'll enjoy, I think. Change into your habit while I find us some food for the journey."

She glanced out the window at the bright, windswept sky. "You're being high-handed, my lord, but I shall overlook it because an excursion on a bright autumn day does sound appealing."

"I'll meet you in twenty minutes at the stables." He vanished again.

Smiling, Gwynne headed upstairs to change. Should she check the scrying glass to see if she could determine their destination? She tried to turn every aspect of daily life into another lesson. But this time, she decided, she would rather be surprised.

*   *   *

"Isn't this view worth a steep ride?" Duncan gestured at the vista before them. The day was windy and the Highland sky was crystal clear. A little below them, an eagle glided through the sky as it watched for prey in the glen below.

Laughing, Gwynne pulled off her bonnet so the wind could pull at her hair. "It is indeed. I'm amazed the horses can manage these trails."

He patted Zeus's sleek neck. "The Montagues breed tough mounts well suited to our hills."

"I suppose that's worth an attempted abduction." Gwynne's gaze swept the rugged landscape. Though some trees had lost their leaves, others still blazed with color. "This may be the last day that's so warm and pretty until next spring." She slanted him a teasing glance. "Unless you intend to give Glen Rath a mild winter?"

When she looked at him like that, he was tempted to turn the glen into a tropical paradise, but he shook his head. "I give my glen more sunshine than most of Scotland receives, but doing too much would be conspicuous. A pity we don't live on a small island, where weather patterns can be very individual. Iona, a holy island in the Hebrides, will be sunny yet have rain falling all around it."

Gwynne frowned charmingly. "How is that possible?"

"I suspect that when St. Columba brought his Celtic monks to Iona, there was a weather mage in the group who set such a powerful spell on the island that even today the rain clouds keep their distance."

"That sounds lovely. Can we visit it someday?"

"It will be my pleasure to take you." After the rising was over—that was an unstated condition that applied to everything in their lives. He felt as if they were in limbo, waiting for a great and terrible storm to strike. "I have another sight for you."

He led the way along the narrow trail that crested the ridge, then descended into a small wooded hollow halfway down the hill. He dismounted and tethered his horse, then helped Gwynne down. The feel of her slim waist under his hands gave him ideas about how to take advantage of the sunny day after their picnic.

She studied the glen below, where a road and a river were visible. On the hills opposite a single lonely cottage could be seen, but the road was well traveled, arching across the narrow river on a stone bridge. "Is this the road to Fort Augustus?"

"Yes." He shaded his eyes. "Look, a company of government soldiers. They must be marching north to reinforce the fort." The scarlet coats looked brave against the green glen, but he noticed that the marching was ragged.

Probably they were inexperienced new recruits. The forces on both sides were ill-equipped and ill-trained.

That would change if—no, when—the Hanoverian government brought experienced regiments back from Flanders, where they were serving now. If the prince had faced seasoned troops at Prestonpans, the result would have been very different, and much more damaging to the Jacobite army.

Wondering how long the prince's good luck would last, he said, "I didn't bring you here to see the view, lovely though it is." Taking her hand, he guided her into the grove of small trees.

"There's great power here." Gwynne studied the grove with unfocused eyes. "I see the glow of two—no, three—ley lines."

He nodded. The ancients knew how to detect the earth's patterns of power, and they built their holy places where ley lines converged. "Can you sense anything else?"

She frowned. "There's something else that's powerful but not as old."

"My lady is most perceptive."

They entered a glade and almost walked into a flat, irregularly shaped stone that had been set into the earth so that it stood upright almost as tall as a man. Half a dozen similar stones stood sentinel around the clearing.

"A Druid circle!" Reverently Gwynne touched the lichened surface of the stone.

"This site has something I've not seen in any other circle." He gestured toward the rectangular stone shape that jutted from the middle of the meadow.

"A carved cross! What exquisite workmanship." Gwynne moved into the center of the clearing and pressed her palm to the cross. "I can feel the energy of the man who carved it. He was a monk, and he carved his faith into the stone." She traced the interlaced patterns that covered the raised surface of the cross. "This was placed here much later than the standing stones. Centuries later."

"Your monk and his friends must have decided to use the energies of the ley lines and the Druid circle to amplify Christian power." Like Gwynne, he traced the sinuously twining patterns that decorated the cross, feeling the serenity that had created them. "The world is so large and we are so small. Belief in something greater is a basic human need, I think."

"A pity that believers can be so quick to kill others who don't believe in quite the same way," Gwynne said wryly. She jerked her head up as a ragged series of booms echoed through the hills. "Gunshots?"

"The soldiers!" Cursing himself for enjoying the day with Gwynne so much that he wasn't paying attention to the world, Duncan raced back through the grove until he could look down into the glen. Gwynne arrived moments later as another volley of shots rattled through the noon air, smoke clouding the pristine glen.

Together they stared in horror at what had been a peaceful green valley. The distant war had arrived on their doorstep.

amnation!" Duncan swore as a screaming company of Highlanders swept down on the government troops. A handful of Hanoverians were standing their ground, and several attackers fell under the musket fire. But most of the raw government soldiers had panicked and they were bolting across the narrow stone bridge, elbowing their fellows in their desperate attempt to escape their attackers.

The rebels didn't even slow when some of their number fell. They continued their charge, waving broadswords and howling for blood. The few Hanoverians who had tried to hold their ground gave up and joined the panicky retreat.

Even high on Duncan and Gwynne's hill, the acrid scent of the black powder was sharply noticeable. Seeing that the horses were disturbed by the noise and smell, Duncan went to Zeus, using power to sooth his mount.

Gwynne did the same with Sheba. "Can the battle be stopped before there's a massacre?" she asked tensely. "The Jacobites are running wild. They'll chop the royal troops into bloody pieces."

She was right—soldiers in retreat were at their most vulnerable, which was why experienced troops knew it

was safer to stand and fight. Duncan could feel the
Hanoverians' fear and terror as vividly as he could hear
the cries of the inflamed, triumphant Highlanders.

A massive rainstorm would quench the muskets and
spirits of the combatants. He reached into the sky for a
swift inventory of clouds and winds. He was always sub-
liminally aware of the weather for many miles around,
and his search confirmed that there was no rain close
enough to drown this battle.

But the wind was powerful over the hills. Enough to
create a whirlwind? Perhaps. In Britain such storms were
rare and weak, but he had seen a full-blown tornado in
Spain and been awed by the majesty and power of
weather at its most violent.

He had never tried to conjure a whirlwind—they were
considered far too dangerous even for a seasoned
weather mage. But if he could create a small one down in
the glen, it might break up the fight before casualties became serious. "Gwynne, take the horses into the Druid
circle and stay with them."

Silently she took both sets of reins and led their mounts
into the protection of the grove. With her safe, Duncan
concentrated on the wind patterns. Pull together what
clouds were available. Find cold dry air, then warmer
moist currents above a loch. Spin them together until a
violent updraft was created.

He poured his own energy into the developing vortex
until the winds reached a savage speed. The sky took on
a greenish hue and a menacing funnel formed—a roar-
ing, raging beast that fought to escape his control. His
power stretched to the breaking point as he tried to con-
tain the whirlwind and move it in the right direction.

He had just forced the funnel to move toward the floor
of the glen when he realized that Gwynne had returned to

his side. The distraction caused him to lose focus, and the tornado exploded from his control. He fell to his knees, head pounding with pain. Howling like the damned, the vortex blasted across the glen, ripping up trees, smashing the distant stone cottage into jagged pieces, and causing shudders in the earth itself.

"Get down!" He grabbed Gwynne's hand and pulled her to the turf beside him. The whirlwind would first strike the government troops, then the Highlanders. Men on both sides were running away in the desperate hope of escaping the devastation. Several Highlanders slowed long enough to help their wounded fellows toward safety, while one Hanoverian dropped to his knees in terrified prayer.

With horror, Duncan recognized that his whirlwind might kill more men than the swords and muskets. Grimly he marshaled his remaining energy, then fought the lethal winds until they were under control again. Head pounding with strain, he wrenched the funnel into a new path that ran along the course of the river, between the warring groups.

The whirlwind swept over the river, sucking up water and howling ever louder. It struck the arched bridge and shattered it, stones flying in all directions. Mercifully the funnel passed between the two groups of soldiers without striking anyone. But now it was heading up the hill—straight at Duncan and Gwynne.

As a gale-force wind struck them, tearing at hair and clothing, Duncan threw himself across his wife to protect her. Too depleted to deflect the tornado himself, he reached into Gwynne's energy field, ruthlessly drawing on her power to bolster his fraying strength. He had only an instant, but how . . . ?

Whirlwinds had a very short life— *Yes,* that was the key to destroying it. He slammed the vortex, blocking the swirling pattern with brute strength. The winds fell apart and suddenly the glen was silent.

Duncan allowed himself to slide into dazed exhaustion. No wonder weather mages were taught never to conjure tornadoes. . . .

*   *   *

Shakily Gwynne pushed her husband's weight to one side and struggled to a sitting position. "Duncan, are you all right?"

"I'm . . . well enough." His eyes opened. They were the color of ash. "You didn't stay with the horses."

"Of course not. Hiding wasn't going to help anything." She didn't feel much better than he looked. Rubbing her aching head, she asked, "What did you do?"

"I'm sorry." He levered himself up and drew a shuddering breath. "I didn't have enough power left to dissolve the whirlwind before it struck us, so I drew on yours."

Though it was a violation of Guardian rules to tap into someone else's power without permission, the Families were always reasonable about emergencies. His sudden assault on her energy body had been disturbing and very intrusive, almost a mind rape, but the situation had been dire. "If I hadn't distracted you at a critical moment, you wouldn't have had to do it."

He grimaced. "It would have been easier if we'd had time to prepare. Transferring power needn't be painful if the connection is established gently."

In an odd way, she was glad for the pain Duncan's energy tap had caused because it had made her part of his life-saving intervention. "It is written that when Adam and Isabel stopped the Armada, he borrowed her strength as you just borrowed mine. I had read about that, but I didn't really understand what it is like to share power."

"I'm sorry," he said again.

"If you hadn't done what was necessary," she said wryly, "we'd have been blown to Glasgow. Probably in pieces."

He brushed back his hair, which had been blown loose around his shoulders. "I feel like a spike has been driven through my head."

"Given the huge amount of power you just burned, that's not surprising." Moving slowly, she got to her feet. The ground swayed only a little. "I'll get your saddlebags. We both need something to eat."

Burning large amounts of power created ravenous hunger. Gwynne could have eaten a loaf of fresh bread all by herself without even trying, so Duncan must feel as if he'd been starved for a month.

She found the horses peacefully cropping grass in the stone circle. Before tethering them earlier, she had used a calming spell similar to the one Duncan had tried on William Montague and his servant. The horses were better subjects than William, for they seemed unperturbed by the nearby battle and whirlwind.

She took the saddlebags back to Duncan, who had fortunately brought enough food to feed a family of six. Even before she spread the picnic cloth, she gave him two bannocks, the Scottish oatcake. He wolfed them down as she laid out more bannocks, cheese, smoked fish, and mutton pies. A jug of ale and two cups had been provided, so she poured drinks before falling on the meal as avidly as Duncan.

By the time he demolished two-thirds of the food, Duncan was looking almost normal. "It's amazing how food restores strength. I felt like I was ninety years old. If I'm

tempted to conjure a whirlwind in the future, remind me
how difficult it is."

Gwynne gestured toward the glen below. The
Hanoverian officer was forming up his demoralized men
to resume their march north, while the Jacobites were
clustered in small groups, patching up wounds and discussing their miraculous survival. "Though it was difficult, you succeeded. The forces have been separated and
the bridge is gone. Even if the Highlanders want to ford
the river, by the time they do the government troops will
have had time to escape."

"It appears that the fight has gone out of everyone." He
studied the remains of the bridge. Apart from a few
stones marking the foundations on each bank, nothing
was left. "I've never worked with such challenging
weather. It's fortunate whirlwinds are so rare in Britain.
Can you imagine the devastation if one struck Edinburgh
or London? The damage would be horrific. I hope no one
was in that cottage."

Gwynne had wondered the same, so she visualized the
vanished structure, then focused to see if there were recent signs of habitation. "The cottage was empty, thank
God. You saved many lives and injured no one in the
process, except yourself."

"Are you surprised that I took so much effort to protect Hanoverian troops despite my Jacobite leanings?" he
said with a touch of dryness.

"Not at all," she said immediately. "The soldiers on
both sides are mostly boys, some no older than Maggie's
son, Diarmid. Of course you wanted to protect them."
She looked at Duncan quizzically. "Mages are trained to
use their best judgment in critical situations, but this
happened so quickly. How did you decide what to do, or

whether to act at all? Did you worry about changing the course of the rebellion?"

"So many considerations raced through my mind that the final decision seemed more instinct than logic." He frowned. "Interfering with events must not be done lightly, but a clash like this means nothing in terms of the overall rising. The only ones affected would be the boys who were killed and their families, so I couldn't stand by and not at least try to break up the skirmish."

She thought of the fear she had felt radiating from the terrified young soldiers, and shuddered. "War is insanity, there is no other explanation. Most of the soldiers on both sides are Scots. They could even be brothers. Yet because some have red coats and others wear a white cockade, they tried to kill each other."

"*Dulce et decorum est pro patria mori,*" he murmured.

"Don't quote Horace at me!" she retorted. "There is nothing sweet and proper about young men dying for old men's ambitions. If battle is necessary, let the Old Pretender and King George settle the matter in single combat. And if they killed each other in the process, I wouldn't weep."

"War isn't only about old men's ambition," Duncan said seriously. "There are causes worth dying for. Freedom. Justice. To defend the vulnerable."

"Show me the freedom and justice in that little battle!" She gestured at the glen. "Show me anyone other than you who was defending the vulnerable."

"Some Highlanders are fighting because their chieftains command it, but others fight because they believe the prince's claim to the throne is just." He hesitated. "There is also a . . . a kind of Highland madness that a sensible

Englishwoman like you might not be able to understand. A fierce willingness to pay any price, even death, for one's principles and loyalties. We all die eventually. There is grandeur in dying for a cause that is noble."

She shook her head vehemently. "That is a man's thinking."

His mouth quirked wryly. "Guilty."

She sighed. "Perhaps this is an unbreachable difference between men and women. Very well, I'll admit there are principles and people worth dying for. But what is worth killing for?"

"I would kill to protect you," he said gravely. "Just as I would die for you."

She felt the blood drain from her face at his blunt statement. *You will betray him.* That harsh mental voice was with her every day. How could she bear to betray a man who was willing to die for her? A man who held her heart in his hands? Yet she could feel a gulf widening between them, and she could dimly sense the kind of dilemma that would force her to make such an agonizing choice.

"I would like to think," she said unevenly, "that I would have the courage to die for you, or for someone else I love, or for innocents in peril. But I would rather by far live with you than die for you."

Desperate to bury all thoughts of betrayal, she leaned forward and kissed him fiercely, burying her hands in his hair. The passion between them was life and truth, the very opposite of what she feared. The future wasn't written yet. Perhaps, with love and loyalty, betrayal might never be necessary.

Duncan's fervent response to her kiss revealed his matching need to bury conflict in desire. But even as they mated with passion's fury, she could not convince herself that they were not on the road to calamity.

he wind blew harshly from the Irish Sea as Duncan rode north into the hills. He let his horse find the best path while he pondered the rising. After he and Gwynne had witnessed the clash of opposing forces, he had been unable to deny that the conflict was on his doorstep. Not only did he have the usual concerns for survival of anyone in a potential war zone, but he also carried the burden of discerning where the best interests of his nation lay. If his opinion differed from the council, he would be forced to make a terrible choice.

The night before he had woken shaking from a nightmare about turning renegade. By birth and training, Guardians were generally more objective and selfless than most people. But Guardians were human, and prone to the same weaknesses. Occasionally a mage would fall in love with power and defy his oath, using magic for selfish, even destructive, purposes.

Such renegades were wickedly dangerous, and the council wasted no time in dealing with them. If Duncan felt called to oppose the council on behalf of Scotland, would he be declared renegade? Though any such action on his part would not be from personal selfishness, he still risked exile from the Families, which was the first level of punishment. All members would be ordered to have nothing to do with him.

Not everyone would obey, given that Guardians were an independent lot. But the safety of the Families lay in unity, and most would comply with the council's edict. He would be cut off emotionally and spiritually from the only people who truly understood what it was like to hold power.

Jean would probably stand by him, but what about Gwynne? He could hardly bear to consider that she might leave him. Despite her sometimes maddening reserve, she was at least half in love with him, and loyalty was at the core of her nature. But what if she had to choose between her husband and her Guardian oath? He had no idea what she would choose—and he feared the worst.

There was a second level of punishment if the council thought a mage was a threat to others: suppressing a mage's power by magical force. Enforcing the council's edicts was traditionally a job for the most powerful mages in Britain—and this council's enforcer was Simon, Lord Falconer.

Despite their many years of friendship, Simon would be pitiless in doing his duty as he saw it. If there was a conflict of power between them, who would win? Duncan wasn't sure—but at least one of them would end up dead.

Telling himself not to borrow trouble, he wrenched his thoughts back to the simpler topic of whirlwinds. He now understood why weather mages were warned not to meddle with them, for they were fiendishly difficult and destructive phenomena. But might it be possible to create a small, more easily controlled version?

In the past week he had read what information the Dunrath library contained on the subject, and he had developed a theory of how to create and handle whirlwinds. Today he intended to put theory into practice, which was why he was on his way to Glen Creag, an area so rocky and desolate that even sheep disdained it. For his purpose it was perfect: flat, hidden among hills, and with scant chance of witnesses.

He tethered Zeus outside Glen Creag, hiking over the last steep hill alone with a knapsack of food to refresh himself in case of exhaustion. If his theory was correct, this attempt should be less draining than his emergency conjuration the week before. The trick was to balance the heat and cold, dry and moist, cloud and wind. How much of each was required to create the vicious updraft needed? How slowly could the winds spin before a funnel collapsed?

For that first frantic conjuration, he had worked from instinct and desperation. The result was a double miracle: first, that he had managed to create a tornado. The even greater miracle was that he hadn't killed anyone. Today he would approach the task in a more orderly fashion.

He worked with the elements of a whirlwind one at a time until he could control each precisely. Then he experimented with finding the best balance of elements. Periodically he paused for food to keep his strength up; this was the most challenging work he'd ever done. Britain's climate and terrain were not well suited to whirlwinds, which meant he had to use large amounts of his own energy to create even a small one.

Despite his fatigue, the afternoon was exhilarating. Developing new magic always was. His practice culminated when he carefully conjured a tornado. Though weak by the standards of its kind, it was still powerful enough to disrupt a small battle. He even managed a fair degree of control, though the blasted bundle of wind still showed an alarming tendency to escape.

After dissolving his creation, he headed back to Dunrath tired but satisfied. He needed more practice to attain real mastery, and it was hard to imagine wielding such a destructive force for anything less than ending a massacre. But since there was a war in progress, the more tools he had available, the better.

*　＊　*

Gwynne gasped at the image that suddenly appeared in her scrying glass: Duncan and a whirlwind. Her husband stood in a barren, rocky landscape, his fierce concentration palpable as he struggled to control his creation.

Though she'd had no intention of looking for him, energy followed thought, and she thought of her husband often. For that reason, it wasn't uncommon for an image of him to appear when she practiced scrying and her focus was uncertain. Like most scrying glasses, hers was spelled so it wouldn't casually pick up scenes that would invade the privacy of others, so usually she would see an image of Duncan riding or talking with people in the glen. She would smile at him fondly, then return to her practice.

This time, the scene had significance. She bit her lip, wondering if he would tell her about his experimentation. If he didn't mention the subject voluntarily, she shouldn't raise it herself, since she didn't want to be accused of spying.

Why was he doing this? For the pure joy of magic? A perfectionist's desire to master a new skill? Intellectual curiosity? All of those things could be true. But it was also true that a tornado was a weapon without equal. If he chose to use his power in the service of the rebellion . . .

With a low rumble, Lionel flowed from the library table onto her lap, then stood on his hind legs and nuzzled her with his whiskery cheek. She stroked him gratefully. His ability to sense her moods was uncanny; maybe he really was her familiar. She had sometimes wondered if he could walk through walls, though there must be a mundane explanation for his ability to appear when she wanted company.

She rubbed her face against soft feline fur as she reminded herself that Duncan had given her no reason to doubt his loyalty. Yes, he had some sympathy with the rebel cause, but that was a long way from treason. She must hope that it was far enough.

The door to the arcane library swung open and Jean bounced in. Gwynne blinked and Lionel left her lap for shelter under the table. "This is the first time I've seen you in here. I wasn't sure you knew the way."

"I had to come here to find you," Jean said with irrefutable logic. She dropped into a chair. "I've heard the Jacobite army is marching south to Carlisle. Is it true?"

Gwynne opened her hand, which still held the scrying glass. She felt uncomfortable tracking the rebellion to satisfy Jean's curiosity, but couldn't think of a good reason to refuse. She inhaled and exhaled slowly, then concentrated on Jean's question. "Yes, the army is on the move south. They've met no opposition so far, and I don't think any is imminent."

"Splendid!" Jean rose and began pacing the room. "I've had the feeling that they will continue into England without opposition, but I wasn't sure of my own prediction, so I hoped you could confirm it. You have."

Gwynne sighed. "For the immediate future, there will be no battles, but many lives will be lost before this rebellion is done. I guarantee it." The images of violence she had been seeing since she'd met—and kissed—Duncan were utterly convincing.

"War happens," Jean said flatly. "I don't like it, either, but some causes are worth fighting and dying for. Men who become soldiers know the risks they are taking. Men die every day, of disease and accident and drunken brawls. Isn't it better to pledge one's life to something noble?"

Duncan was right, Gwynne decided. There really was a Highland madness when it came to war. "Fine words, Jean, but war sends ripples in all directions, affecting not only noble soldiers but wives and children, and fields neglected because their owners are dead. Which is why Guardians almost always support the cause of peace."

"The Families support what is good for the most people over time," Jean retorted. "But disagreement over the long-term good isn't uncommon. Even Duncan, who has done his best to accept conservative council thinking, isn't convinced that the Hanoverians are good for the country. There will be war. There will be deaths. We must hope that the blood that is shed is for the right reasons."

"On that, at least, we can agree." Gwynne tilted her head to one side. "I'm surprised that you didn't go to Edinburgh, as you considered doing."

"I liked the idea of being with other Jacobites," Jean admitted, "but I knew the army would be leaving the area soon. With your scrying ability, I'll know more here about what's happening than I would in Edinburgh." Her face sobered. "Is Robbie going to die in the rebellion?"

A wave of profound sorrow engulfed Gwynne. It took her a moment to reply. "I'm better at seeing what is happening elsewhere at this moment than I am at predicting the future."

Jean's mobile face became still. "You think he's going to die."

"I truly don't know. He is in great danger," Gwynne said truthfully. "I fear for him, but I don't think that dying in battle is inevitable."

"I wish I was a man so I could go to war!" her sister-in-law said passionately. "Better yet, I should have developed my powers to the point where I could aid the prince's cause."

Gwynne gasped, truly shocked. "You would risk being ostracized by the Families?"

"For this, yes!" Jean glared at her sister-in-law, her green eyes as feral as a cat's. "We swear oaths, but we are also trained to listen to our hearts and souls. The House of Hanover is weak, unfit to rule England, much less Scotland. I will do my duty as I see it—and I only wish I had more power to use in the prince's service!"

For the first time, Gwynne was glad that the younger woman had shirked her powers. Though Guardian studies tended to steady one's character, and Jean would have benefited by that. "Why not work on your scrying? Because you are deeply concerned with the rebellion, you might find that you can tune in on events effectively."

Jean stopped her pacing and made a comical face. "You're using this as an attempt to make me study, aren't you? But it's not a bad idea."

Wordlessly Gwynne offered Isabel's glass.

"This has never worked for me." Jean held it in her palm, her eyes narrowing. "Interesting. I see nothing, yet the stone feels alive now. Before it didn't. You've restored it to life after a long sleep." She handed it back.

Gwynne chuckled as she accepted the glass. "I never thought I'd be glad that a stone likes me. You must have received a scrying glass when you came of age." When Jean nodded, Gwynne continued, "Do you want to get it so we can practice together? Since I'm so new at this and still learning, I might remember some useful tidbits for improving technique that experienced scryers have long since forgotten."

"I'll get my stone and come back. And bring a tea tray with some fresh scones and marmalade." One hand on the doorknob, she added, "I do hope that we can stay friends even if we are on opposing sides, Gwynne."

"I'm on the side of peace, Jean. I think that few women are on the side of war." Jean hesitated, then gave a brief nod before she left the library.

The world would be a better place, Gwynne decided, if women were in charge.

Twenty-Five

Gwynne made a hasty attempt to straighten her hair as she rushed from the library to the main hall. A good thing the Friday night dinners weren't formal. She and Jean had become so absorbed in scrying that they had lost track of the time. Jean had done very well. She claimed it was because she had a good teacher, but Gwynne suspected that now that the girl had a compelling reason, she was working harder than in her unwanted lessons when she was younger. She certainly didn't lack talent.

At the base of the stairs, Gwynne paused to take a slow breath. She had quickly developed a deep fondness for the weekly gathering. The warm, relaxed atmosphere made her feel that she was part of this extended family in a way she had never quite managed at Harlowe. There she had been the old earl's child bride, indulged but not very important in the life of the household. Here she felt safe and accepted—the latter particularly welcome given her English origins.

She circulated through the hall, chatting with people who were becoming friends and wondering where Duncan was. Surely he hadn't been so careless as to allow himself to be carried off by his own whirlwind. As she debated whether to ring the dinner gong in spite of his absence, she noticed an apparent argument between Maggie Macrae and her son. As she watched, Diarmid stalked off, leaving his mother frowning.

Gwynne would have joined the housekeeper to offer any comfort required, but Duncan chose that moment to stride in the front doors, drawing the attention of everyone present with his dramatic, windswept energy. She moved toward him with a smile. "You look as if you've been rushing, my dear. Did you lose track of the time?"

"I'm afraid so, *mo càran.*" He kissed her cheek, his lips warm with promise. "A farmer's work is never done."

He wasn't going to tell her about his whirlwind practice, she realized. Not now, and not later. Reminding herself that his silence on the subject didn't necessarily mean sinister intent, she said quietly, "The prince's army is marching south to Carlisle."

Brows furrowed, Duncan evaluated the news. "With November on us, it's a poor season for campaigning, but that might work to the rebels' advantage. I wonder . . ." He stopped. "We can speculate later. Now it's time to break bread with friends and family."

Silently she took his arm and they moved to the small table where the dinner gong sat. Like most men, Duncan liked making noise, so he ceremoniously lifted the wooden hammer and struck a pure, quivering note.

Talking and laughing, guests found places at the table. Duncan and Gwynne had the only assigned seats; now that she was in charge of the ritual, she sat at the head of the table. As the head of the household, Duncan took the foot. No more sitting next to each other.

She lit her taper at the nearest fireplace, then solemnly touched the candles in the massive candelabra to flickering life. As always, the ritual produced peaceful silence. Taking her place at the head of the table, she performed the first beckoning gesture. "Welcome, family and friends."

After finishing the welcome ritual, she lifted her fork to signal the beginning of the meal. Before people could start eating, a young man near the center of the table rose to his feet. *Trouble!* Gwynne recognized him as Fergus Macrae. In his early twenties, he had a vibrant energy that made him charming, but now made her feel deeply uneasy.

Like William Montague, Fergus raised his glass and called out, "A toast to the king over the water!"

It was an invitation and a challenge. Gwynne was acutely aware of Duncan's indecision as to how to handle this. Then three more young men stood and lifted their glasses. One was Diarmid Macrae, who was sitting at Gwynne's left hand. "To the king over the water!" they chorused.

As tension swirled through the hall, Duncan rose, his presence dominating the company. "These are difficult times. I wish good health to the House of Stuart, which led Scotland for centuries, but my toast is to King George, ruler of all Great Britain."

A babel of voices broke out. Half the men present stood and drank toasts, though the conflicting words made it clear that they were divided between Jacobite and Hanoverian sympathies. Fergus raised his voice to cut through the clamor. "Duncan Macrae, 'tis time for you to act as Laird of Dunrath and lead us out in support of our true king. I hear that the prince is marching for England, and all Scots belong at his side!"

"I will do no such thing," Duncan said, his deep voice filling the room effortlessly. "The Stuarts had their chances and they failed. Every attempt to reclaim the throne has cost Scottish lives. I will not lead the Macraes of Glen Rath to certain defeat."

Diarmid said hotly, "If all Scots support the prince, he will not fail!"

"But all Scots do not support the Stuart cause, and even fewer Englishmen do. The government has the soldiers, the training, the weapons, the materials." The faintest of tremors sounded in Duncan's voice. "What do the Jacobites have but the courage and loyalty of too few brave men?"

Gwynne gave him credit for holding his ground, yet she could sense his deep ambivalence on the subject. Could others detect that also?

Jean leaped to her feet, her red hair blazing in the candlelight. "If you will not lead the men of Glen Rath to the prince, Duncan, then *I* will!"

A collective gasp echoed through the chamber. Gwynne was suddenly struck by the sheer barbarism of the scene: the harsh stone walls, the high-ceilinged, drafty hall, flickering torches and candlelight playing off the massed displays of swords and dirks. Earlier she had felt a part of this place. Now, as the heirs of Dunrath fought about war, she was an outlander.

"Jeannie, no," Duncan said, his voice anguished.

"I must, Duncan. I am not the first Scotswoman to lead warriors, and I will surely not be the last." Jean's gaze swept the room, lingering on those who had expressed support for the prince. "We shall march out at midmorning tomorrow. Bring supplies and what weapons you have, and pass the word to others who would join us."

A cheer rose from the Jacobites, most of them young, not all of them male. Gwynne estimated that the rebel sympathizers were about a third of the total group. Virtually all of the older people present looked grim or horrified, except for one old shepherd who had lost his leg in the Fifteen. He had been waiting for another Stuart uprising ever since, and now he cackled with toothless glee.

"I will follow you, Mistress!" Diarmid called.

"And I!" cried Fergus. At least half a dozen other voices joined in.

"Well done!" Jean smiled at her small troop. "If you will excuse me, I must prepare for departure. Unless you propose to lock me and the rest of our rebels in the dungeon, Duncan Macrae?"

His hands clenched, but his voice was steady. " 'Tis not my place to imprison my sister, or others who truly believe in this cause. Dunrath is the castle of grace, and all who dwell in the glen are always welcome under my roof. I shall pray for your safety."

Gwynne stood. "As shall I. We are friends and family here. Never forget that."

Jean flushed a little. "You are both gracious. I will not disgrace the name of Macrae, I promise you."

"I know you won't," Duncan said quietly. "Don't leave yet, Jeannie, nor any of the rest of you. If you begin a long journey tomorrow, you should eat well tonight."

Jean nodded and sat down. The painful knowledge that this might be the last time all these people would gather together hung heavy in the air. A woman sobbed quietly, unable to suppress her tears.

Gwynne thought of the spell of protection she had studied. Perhaps that would be useful here? "Let us all join hands and pray for safety, and for the good of the lands and people we love."

She reached out to her neighbors, taking the hands of Diarmid on her left—dear God, he was so young!—and

Annie Mackenzie, an older woman, on her right. At first
uncertain, all of the guests followed her example.

With everyone around the long table connected,
Gwynne could feel a powerful current of energy flowing
around the circle. With time, she could identify each individual thread. With no effort at all, she could identify Diarmid's exultation, his mother's fear, Fergus's fierce,
bloody determination.

As Gwynne prayed aloud, she also sent the spell of
protection pulsing through the circle of joined hands. She
envisioned each person present sheathed in light so that
neither sword nor bullet could cause harm.

A moment later the light blazed brighter as Duncan
added his deep, powerful energy to her working. A surprised note could be felt from Auld Donald, who had
enough Guardian blood to sense magic in use.

Then Jean joined in, her power a little ragged but intensely felt. Perhaps with three mages joining in, the
rebels of Glen Rath would survive to come home.

As Gwynne whispered, "So be it," at the end of her
prayer, she thought that she felt another Guardian
nearby, one who was contributing to the protection spell.
But surely that couldn't be. . . .

*   *
*

Though everyone stayed through the dinner, the mood
was somber and guests left as quickly as possible. When
Jean rose, Duncan stood and followed her, his long legs
overtaking her before she reached the stairs. Knowing he
must keep his temper under control, he said, "Jean, it's
not too late to change your mind."

Her brows arched. "The moment I said publicly that
I'd lead our men to the prince, there was no turning back.

A Scotswoman has as much pride as a Scotsman, Duncan."

"You won't be allowed to lead our men into battle. Charles Edward is very conventional in his thinking. If you appear before him in breeches, he'll be horrified."

She made a face. "I suppose that means I must use my sidesaddle. I want to stay with the army as long as I can, but I don't expect to be allowed in battle. Which is just as well—I don't think I would much enjoy it. My plan is to take our men to Robbie, who can be trusted to look after them."

"It's a good plan." He thought of the clash he and Gwynne had witnessed. "But for God's sake, be careful! When two armies stalk each other, there are many skirmishes that can kill even though they aren't true battles."

"I'll be safe. Gwynne casts a powerful spell of protection." She laid a hand on his arm. "Don't try to deny that you aren't tempted to do what I'm doing, Duncan. But you're too responsible to follow your heart in this matter."

He sighed, his gaze going across the rapidly emptying hall. People weren't lingering to talk tonight. "There's truth to what you say. My head knows that the prince has his share of weaknesses, but he's a born leader, and my Highland soul wants to raise a sword and shout to hell with the Sassenach."

"Whichever side wins, Dunrath is protected, Duncan." Jean grinned mischievously. "If the government forces triumph, you get credit for loyalty. If the Jacobites carry the day, I'll say that you told me to take our men to the prince."

He smiled reluctantly. "You're right, of course. But it's hard to think politics when my only sister's life might be on the line."

"Danger can be anywhere. You be careful, too." She gave him a swift hug, then turned and walked away, an indomitable Highland lady.

As his sister disappeared up the stairs, a slender arm wrapped around his waist. He turned and embraced his wife. Apart from several servants clearing the table, they were the last two left in the hall. "I had hoped it wouldn't come to this," he said bleakly.

She rested her head against his shoulder, her soft hair tickling his chin. "We're fortunate that the breach wasn't angrier. Jean will be all right, I think."

"Physically, she will be unhurt," he said with a touch of foreknowledge. "But this rebellion will change her."

"Life is change. She may be bruised, but she will not be broken." Breaking away from Duncan, she said, "Time to dowse the candles and go to bed."

"Before you retire, may I beg a bed for the night?" a new voice asked.

Duncan spun around, startled. "Dammit, Simon, you're too blasted good at stealth! Why the devil are you here?"

Lord Falconer grinned, debonair even in travel-stained riding clothes. He was a master at the spells that made mundanes look past him, plus the shields that made it hard even for Guardians to sense his presence. Impossible, if they didn't know he was around. It was one of the reasons he was the council's chief enforcer. "I was sent to talk to you, and carry you off on a mission, if you're willing."

"Simon!" Gwynne swept forward and gave him a joyful hug. "What a marvelous surprise!"

"God's breath, Gwynne, you've changed!" He almost shoved her away. "An enchantress?" He drew a slow breath, then smiled crookedly. "It's wonderful to see you, my dear girl, and I'm sure you have an exciting story to tell of how you discovered your power, but please shield it or I fear for the consequences."

"I'm so sorry!" Gwynne blushed and stepped back, muting her allure. "I haven't yet acquired the habit of always shielding."

Despite Simon's joking tone, Duncan saw that his friend had been badly rattled by Gwynne's unthinking embrace. As a Guardian, he was particularly susceptible to her powers of attraction. Wanting to ease the other man's embarrassment, he said, "Let's get you some food, and then we can talk."

"Am I allowed to listen, or is this one of those male-only meetings?" Gwynne asked with a touch of tartness.

"Your presence is not only acceptable, but necessary," Simon said. "You are not unaffected by my mission. But no need for food—I've already eaten."

"Then we'll go to my study for a claret." As they headed up the stairs, Duncan asked over his shoulder, "When did you arrive?"

"Just before your Jacobite hothead proposed his toast. Under the circumstances, I thought it best not to inflame the situation with my very English presence. So I wandered down to the kitchen and helped myself."

Being Simon, he had been able to do that with no one noticing. Though given the drama at the dining table, a platoon of Highlanders could have marched through with bagpipes playing and no one would have noticed. "Did you see what Jean did?"

"I did indeed. Your little sister has grown up." There was a mixture of amusement, respect, and concern in his voice.

They spoke no more until they entered Duncan's study. As Gwynne poured claret for all three of them, Simon's head came up and he turned slowly, like a hound scenting the wind. "The Pretender has been here."

Falconer was very, very good. "So he has," Duncan agreed. "The night we arrived at Dunrath, he walked into the middle of a *céilidh* and introduced himself. We came up here and he attempted to enlist me in his cause."

"Bold of him. And your answer?"

Gwynne replied as she brought the men their wine. "Duncan said that the prince couldn't win, and he wished the blasted fellow would go home."

Simon laughed. "Surely you didn't call the prince a blasted fellow to his face."

"No, but it was implied," Duncan said as they seated themselves. "He's a compelling and dangerous man, Simon."

"That's why I'm here. As you must know, the Jacobite forces are marching into England."

"And?" Duncan arched his brows when Simon hesitated. "What has that to do with me?"

"The council would like you and me to shadow the prince's army. Not join it, but stay nearby so we can monitor events and be available if our powers are needed."

Duncan's gaze went involuntarily to Gwynne. The thought of leaving his bride was almost unbearable. She looked no happier than he, but she gave a slight nod of acceptance. Duty must always come first.

"Why both of us? So that you can curb any dangerous Jacobite tendencies I might have?" he asked dryly.

"If necessary. And equally so that you can curb my dangerous English tendencies. I despise the Stuarts for their arrogance and bloody-minded belief in their divine mission to rule. Between the two of us, we should achieve balance."

Duncan's irritation faded. Balance was always a Guardian goal, and it made sense for the council to ask the two of them to work together. Presumably their long friendship would help them bridge their political differences. "What is our aim—to reduce loss of life?"

One side of Simon's mouth quirked up. "Yes, while naturally not altering the overall course of events."

"How is it possible to do both?" Gwynne asked. "You may save the life of a man for mercy's sake, and later he could shoot one of the commanding officers on the other side and completely change the outcome of the rebellion."

"Therein lies the problem," Simon agreed. "This is art, not science. War is the most difficult situation to balance. We must hope that we do more good than harm."

"While knowing we can never be sure of that." Duncan had made a study of Guardian attempts to mitigate the effects of war in the past. Given mankind's tendency toward violence there was no shortage of material, but also no coherent theory of how best to proceed. Every situation must be muddled through one step at a time.

"When will you leave?" Gwynne asked.

"Tomorrow," Simon replied. "The prince's force is nearly at Carlisle. There may be a siege. Plus, the government is starting to mobilize troops to come north and engage the Jacobites. Some kind of action is likely."

So soon? Yet Simon was right. Distance made a difference for most forms of magic, and they needed to be close enough to evaluate the situation as it developed. "Very well." Duncan rose. "Gwynne, do we have a guest room ready?"

"I'll show Simon to his room."

Falconer stood, his face showing weariness now that he had achieved his aim. "Gwynne, even with your shields up, you radiate power like a bonfire. It's hard to believe all this developed since I saw you at your wedding, but the proof shines around you. Have you discovered other exceptional powers beyond what most Guardians can do?"

"She a better scryer than you, and Isabel's glass awoke at her touch," Duncan said with a touch of mischief. "I await further developments with alarmed fascination."

Gwynne smiled. "I love that I have power now, but I'm not at all alarming. My talents are the quiet, feminine variety. I read people's energy well, am tolerably good at farseeing with the help of Isabel's glass, and I've learned to shield well enough that I've only been abducted once."

Simon's brows arched. "Fascinating indeed. I look forward to learning more." He covered a yawn. "Tomorrow."

Gwynne led him to the guest room while Duncan stayed in his study and jotted a list of matters to be addressed before he left. A good thing he had caught up with his affairs since returning to Dunrath.

The hardest part would be leaving Gwynne. The thought constricted his lungs and made breathing difficult. They shared her bedroom, and as he headed there his mind repeated, *"The last night, last night, last night."* He told himself that he wouldn't be gone long, perhaps no more than a fortnight, but he was already missing his wife and he wasn't even gone yet.

As soon as Gwynne entered the bedroom, she went straight into his arms. "I hate that you're leaving," she said, her voice muffled against his shoulder.

"So do I, *mo cridhe.*" He kissed her, desperation thrumming through him. How could he bear not having her in his arms every night? "I shall miss you as I would miss my right hand if it were cut off. But I won't be gone for long."

"A day would be too long." She stepped away and loosened her hair so that it fell free, catching bright highlights in the candle glow.

She turned so he could unfasten her gown with impatient fingers. After unlacing her stays, he slid his hands under the quilted fabric to cup her magnificent breasts. She shivered and arched her back before gliding away. "Not yet."

Dropping her shields, she allowed the full force of her allure to blaze free. Awed that her incredible sensuality was only for him, he stepped forward to embrace her. Again she gracefully eluded him. "Wait."

With Eve's instinct, she slowly removed her clothing, garment by garment. He was riveted as each new visual delight was revealed. The lithe bend of her waist when she shimmied out of her gown. The delicious hollow between her breasts. Her shapely legs and ankles as she peeled off her stockings. With every move she made, the erotically charged atmosphere intensified, causing his pulse to accelerate and his breath to catch.

When she was down to the sheer fabric of her shift, he breathed, "Gwynne, *mo càran,* enough of waiting."

"You haven't waited nearly long enough." Smiling wickedly, she began to undress him, her light touches maddeningly provocative as she undid buttons, loosened fabric, tugged off garments.

He thought he would burst into flames from anticipation. When he tried again to embrace her, she laughed and pushed his shoulders so that he sat back on the bed. She swung his legs up on the coverlet, then knelt over him, her shift-covered breasts brushing his bare chest as she kissed his throat. "We must make this a night to remember, my dear," she murmured. "For all the nights we are apart."

He groaned as her lips moved down his torso, sucking

and licking ever lower. There would be little sleep for either of them tonight, he knew. They would make love until both were exhausted, trying to fill the well of passion so that it would sustain them until they were together again.

And yet he already knew that he would feel empty as he rode out of Glen Rath.

Twenty-Six

Gwynne stepped into the courtyard, and found it clattering with life as Jean's rebels assembled. She joined her sister-in-law, who stood on the steps, where she could overlook the activity. "It looks like you'll have a good turnout, Jean."

The younger woman turned, vivid with excitement. Her riding habit was trimmed with military-style gold braid and augmented by a bright tartan wrap, while a white cockade bobbed in her bonnet. She even had one of the family's brass-hilted swords in a scabbard slung around her slender waist. The complete woman warrior. "It looks like about three dozen men will ride out with me—not just from the glen, but from the hills beyond. The eagerness to serve is there."

Gwynne tried not to look too anxious. "Since your mother isn't here to say it, I will. Take care, Jean, for yourself and for the men you lead."

"I'll not do anything reckless, but one cannot join a rebellion with perfect safety." Jean scanned the castle, disappointment showing in her face. "Is Duncan not coming to see me off? I'd hoped . . ." She bit her lip.

Gwynne's voice lowered so that it was under the clatter

and shouting of excited young males. "He isn't showing disapproval. He left at dawn this morning with Lord Falconer, who arrived late last night."

Jean's brows arched. "It will have something to do with the rising. I'm sorry Duncan isn't here, but I can't regret missing Falconer. The man terrifies me."

"Simon?" Gwynne said with surprise. "I always think of him as the perfect gentleman."

"There's nothing wrong with his manners, but he has too much power. Except for Duncan, I find most powerful male mages intimidating."

Gwynne wondered if that was why the girl's sweetheart was not a Guardian. "I felt the same way about Duncan. So much concentrated power is alarming."

"But now you have the ability to bewitch men. To turn the lions into lambs." Jean grinned. "I'm more likely to infuriate lambs and turn them into lions."

"Develop your own power so you can stand up to men like Simon."

Jean hesitated. "Perhaps when I return, I will put more time into lessons. I've enjoyed the work I've done with you. You're a good teacher."

The ranks of would-be soldiers were forming up, so Gwynne gave her sister-in-law a quick hug. "You're a good student. Come home soon, Jeannie."

"This is the adventure of a lifetime, and I'll ride the whirlwind as far as it will take me. We can win this, Gwynne, and free Scotland from English tyranny!" Glowing with youth and confidence, Jean turned to face the man climbing the steps to her. He was older than most of the volunteers, and Gwynne recalled that he'd served with the army. She was glad that someone in this motley crew had experience.

He saluted Jean. "Captain Jeannie, your men are ready to march."

She gave a regal nod. "Well done, Sergeant Macrae." Raising her gaze, she scanned the men standing in slightly ragged lines before her. "We are Scots, brave and free! This small band may make the difference between the success or failure of Prince Charles Edward. I salute you. Now—let's march!"

The sergeant assisted her onto her horse. Though only Jean would ride, several pack animals were being taken for supplies. She looked magnificent—brave, beautiful, and heartbreakingly young. It was all Gwynne could do not to weep.

She had wept that morning after the last fevered kiss between her and Duncan, though she had managed to keep the tears from her eyes until the men left. In some ways, this was worse. Duncan and Simon could take care of themselves in almost any circumstances, but Jean and her troops seemed vulnerable and hopelessly naïve.

"May God preserve you," Gwynne whispered. Though she surrounded the marchers with protection, without other Guardians she feared she was having little effect.

The volunteers saluted her as the representative of Dunrath. She and the other household members who had come to see the rebels off stood erect as they marched out to the beat of a drum and the jubilant skirling of a piper. Maggie Macrae had silent tears running down her cheeks.

Gwynne managed better. Only when the pipes had faded from hearing did she go inside and weep.

*   *
   *

Pulling his horse to a halt at the top of the hill, Simon paused to study the misty, saturated hills. He tugged his hat lower to protect his face from the bitter rain. "If they had to have a war, a pity they didn't choose a better season to invade England." He glanced at Duncan. "You're the weather mage. Can't you do something about this?"

Duncan was equally uncomfortable after days of riding through cold winds and icy drizzle, but he only shrugged. "This weather system is huge and it covers most of the North Atlantic and Northern Europe. If you like I can stop the rain in the area around us, but it will take a large amount of energy and perhaps be conspicuous."

His friend groaned. "And we are not supposed to be conspicuous. Ah, well, it will soon be time to look for an inn."

"There's an inn about a mile along this road," Duncan said. "Small but snug and clean. We might as well stop there for the night."

Simon set his horse moving again. "A pity the Pretender didn't listen to his Scottish advisers and stay in Scotland. Even I will concede that an argument can be made for allowing Scotland to regain her independence under a Stuart king. God knows the country has been a great expense to England with little return. But no, the Pretender must listen to French and Irish advisers who say he should invade England."

"Since the prince's personal desire is to invade, of course he'll listen to those who encourage him," Duncan said. "I wish he'd stayed in Edinburgh and waited for French reinforcements. He could have turned Scotland into a fortress that wouldn't have been worth King George's effort to recapture."

Instead, the Jacobites were invading England with a mere five thousand mostly untrained men. The Hanoverians could muster ten times as many troops, all better trained and better equipped. The farther south the prince moved, the more he risked the rising. He was a fool, and yet there was a part of Duncan that admired the blazing courage of

Charles's action: a lone prince with a small army taking on the English lion. Doomed, perhaps, but magnificent.

It was almost dark when they reached the Border Lord. They were the only guests; wise travelers avoided the paths of armies. The foul weather meant that even locals hadn't come to the taproom for the evening.

As they finished a plain supper of boiled ham and turnips, Simon opened his watch to look at the scrying stone. He swore under his breath. "General Wade, who has twice the men of the Pretender, has decided to leave Newcastle to come to the relief of Carlisle. Instead of sitting tight, your idiot prince wants to engage Wade in hilly country, so he's marching a good part of his army east to some place called Brampton."

Duncan uttered a curse of his own. "So far there really hasn't been much fighting. A pitched battle here and now will have many casualties." Including, surely, men from Glen Rath. He'd been keeping track of his sister through scrying, and knew that she had joined with the main Jacobite army. She was staying with them, too, instead of heading for home. The pigheaded wench. As with the prince, he both admired her courage and wanted to wring her neck.

Mouth tight, Simon snapped his watch case shut. "I'm ready for sleep. The morning is early enough to decide what, if anything, we should do."

They both retired for the night. Duncan was glad to have the privacy of his own room to think about Gwynne. Every day they were apart increased his physical and emotional ache.

Before disrobing, he drew out his scrying glass and looked for Gwynne. As was the case most evenings, she was reading with Lionel draped across her. Watching the way she stroked the cat's heavy head made him wish he was the one in her lap. She looked tired. Missing him as he missed her, he guessed. She looked up, almost as if able to see him through the glass. He smiled involuntarily, then released the image.

Having indulged himself by viewing Gwynne, he scanned more widely. General Wade and his army had made camp for the night. His men were huddled morosely around fires, or in tents that didn't manage to keep out all the rain. It would take two to three days for them to reach Brampton, where the prince waited. Unless . . .

He opened his window and stared into the wet, bitter night as he thought about the bloody battle that would result if the two armies came together.

What if the armies didn't meet? At this time of year, it would be easy to conjure snow that would block Wade's advance. If Duncan did that, his action would preserve life, which was always a Guardian goal.

It could also be considered partisan aid to the Jacobite cause. Would halting Wade be considered too great an interference in worldly affairs? Or was it an opportunity to save many lives?

He frowned, remembering that even Simon thought there was merit in the idea of the Stuarts reclaiming the throne of Scotland. Such a goal could be achieved with relatively little blood spilled. Scotland would be a free nation again. Though Scotland and England had been uneasy neighbors for centuries, gradually they were becoming more peaceable. There was no need for them to be ruled by the same king.

Framed in such terms, a minor intervention began to seem reasonable. If weather problems encouraged the prince to withdraw to Scotland, everyone would benefit.

Even so, Duncan shielded himself before he started work. He didn't want a single shred of stray magic to alert Simon to what was happening. He also slid off the enchanted sapphire ring of Adam Macrae that created a bond with the British throne. He didn't want his concentration undermined by ancient history.

Stopping the rain entirely would have been difficult. Changing the rain to snow over the highland spine of Northern England was relatively simple at this season. He closed his eyes and found Arctic air north of the British Isles. Instead of allowing it to move directly into Scandinavia, he shaped winds to push the icy mass farther south. When the freezing air met the rain sometime before dawn, snow would start falling on the high country. Wade's men and artillery would be bogged down hopelessly.

He was tense with fatigue when he finished, less from the weather-working than from the effort of keeping all traces of magic from Simon. But he felt relieved when he crawled into his cold and lonely bed. A battle had been headed off. Not only had lives been saved, but he might have altered the course of the rising in a positive way.

Had Duncan interfered too much? He didn't think so—but others might disagree.

* * *

Gwynne awoke gasping from renewed nightmares of death and destruction, and recognized with bleak anguish that her world was tumbling toward a sea of blood.

* * *

Northern England was pristine under a blanket of snow the next morning. Duncan joined Simon in the taproom. Sounds from the kitchen indicated that breakfast was on the way. Simon was frowning at the still-falling snow. On this mission he had abandoned his London finery and was plainly dressed in blue, his blond hair unpowdered and pulled back in a queue. His efforts at simplicity did not make him look like an ordinary man.

He glanced at Duncan. "Interesting coincidence that the weather has turned so unsuitable for military operations."

From the coolness of his eyes, Duncan knew that the previous night's magic had not gone undetected. Well, he had never intended to lie about his actions. He was no good at that, even if it was possible to lie to Simon, which it probably wasn't. "Not a coincidence. Events were moving toward a bloody battle with thousands of casualties. Wounded men would have died of exposure before they could be treated. I decided that it was worth intervening to preserve life."

Simon still watched with narrowed eyes. "You probably saved many lives, but you also aided the Jacobite cause. Perhaps you helped it too much."

"My actions weren't taken lightly. If the weather persuades the Jacobite army to withdraw, the rising might end quickly with the Stuarts restored to the Scottish throne and England willing to accept the situation."

"That's a wildly optimistic reading of the possibilities."

"Probably," Duncan admitted. "But where is the line drawn? When does the legitimate saving of lives become unacceptable interference? When does private sympathy for a cause slide over into forbidden partisanship?"

Simon's eyes softened. "Damned if I know. But Duncan . . . be careful. The line is likely to be very clear after you've crossed it." His unspoken message was, *Don't make me fight you.*

Duncan couldn't agree more. But he must follow his conscience. Simon would do the same—and may God spare them from becoming enemies.

Part Three

Destiny

Twenty-Seven

With Duncan and Jean and many of the young men gone, Dunrath waited in an uneasy limbo. Gwynne was acting head of the castle and the clan, which she found strange since she was so new to Glen Rath. Luckily, her authority was accepted without question, for everyone in the glen waited with her.

She spent some of her time writing to Lady Bethany and other English friends. Given the distances and bad roads, replies were slow in coming, yet she didn't feel unpleasantly isolated. The people of this remote valley depended on one another, which created a deeper sense of community than she had known at Harlowe.

With no distractions, her studies prospered. No wonder the Families all maintained homes in the Celtic fringes of Britain. In the pure, wild energy of these Scottish hills, her power continued to grow. As she had told Simon, her abilities tended to be quiet and feminine. Not for her calling the winds or hunting villains, but it no longer seemed impossible that someday she might sit on the council.

Her enchantress allure was now under control. She had developed several levels of shielding, depending on how she wanted to affect those around her. In public, she re-vealed a modest amount of allure to make her seem pleasant and worthy of respect, but not provocative. If she wished to persuade a man, she released enough power to make the fellow willing to listen and consider her point of view, but not so much that he would become a nuisance. As to her full enchantress magic—no one but Duncan would ever see that, and only then when they could act on it.

The combination of practice and using Isabel's obsid-ian glass had sharpened her scrying abilities, particularly in farseeing, the ability to view distant places. She could almost always find what she sought and she usually un-derstood what the images meant. If she saw soldiers, she had only to wonder who they were and what their goal was and answers formed in her mind.

Tracking Duncan and Lord Falconer was harder be-cause of Simon's shielding. Though she had known he was a powerful mage, she had previously lacked the abil-ity to fully appreciate how great his magic was. She guessed that he and Duncan were equals in power, though their special talents were quite different. She hoped that Simon was keeping Duncan's Jacobite lean-ings in check.

Foretelling the future was a separate skill from farsee-ing. Occasionally she had flashes of foreknowledge, as when she sensed the outline of William Montague's life in the West Indies, but she had little control over the process. Even among Guardians, accurate foretelling was very rare because the future was a complex, ever-changing tapestry of possibilities. She was glad that she had no great gift in that area—the future was often not a comfortable place.

Even less comfortable were her blood-drenched nightmares. When she awoke, panicky, she was grateful for Lionel's warm furry presence. She wished there was another Guardian with whom she could discuss her nightmare visions, preferably Lady Bethany. But this was one burden she must carry alone.

Besides cultivating her individual talents, she worked to master the general spells that could be invoked by anyone with power. The look-away spell used to disguise the entrance to the arcane library was such a spell, and Gwynne became quite adept at it. She was particularly proud of concealing a horse in a paddock so that the groom couldn't find it until she released the spell. Luckily, the groom was an incurious sort.

She also practiced personal protection spells, which were particularly useful for females. Though Gwynne refused to learn the spell that could cause an attacker to burst into flames, there were lesser spells that she could use if necessary.

Between household tasks, studying, and starting drafts on three different essays, she stayed busy. Though never too busy to count the long, lonely nights as she waited for Duncan to come home.

From Jean Macrae
Derby, England
4ᵗʰ December 1745

Dearest Gwynne,
Our army has entered the city of Derby! Because of
our cleverness at drawing the enemy away with feints,
we have avoided two English armies and the way lies
open to London, not much more than a hundred miles

*away. Though I know that the prince is disappointed
that more English Jacobites haven't joined us, morale
among the troops is high as the sky. We all feel privi-
leged to be part of such a grand cause. Because of the
swiftness and ease of our progress, there have been
very few casualties on either side.*

*I imagine you are "seeing" that I'm well. I think I
can sense when you check on me—in fact, you might
even be watching me now. My appearance is most
draggled, but don't worry, I'm well and healthy even
though traveling with an army is hard on one's (very
limited) wardrobe.*

*Robbie sends his regards. It is interesting to see him
away from the glen. He seems older. More responsible. He is a good officer, and the men look up to him.*

*Tell Maggie Macrae that Diarmid is well and he
sends his love. He doesn't say that in words, of course,
because at sixteen one doesn't wish to look childish,
but I know that the feeling is in his heart.*

*I must hurry to finish this because the courier who is
taking messages north is anxious to leave, and I
haven't your ability to persuade men to do whatever I
ask!*

Good-bye for now, my dearest sister—

Jean Macrae of Dunrath

Gwynne caught her breath as her scrying glass showed
Jean's small, strong hand writing the words on paper.
Silently the quill moved, was dipped in ink, resumed. By
sheer chance, she had checked on her sister-in-law as the
girl was engaged in writing Gwynne a letter. Watching
the words being formed was a novel experience.

The image shimmered away. Gwynne guessed that the

page was being folded and sealed for the courier. It would take at least a week to reach Dunrath.

Next she looked for Duncan, but she could detect only a faint quicksilver sense of him. She knew that he and Simon were near Derby and healthy, which was much better than nothing. Occasionally she received brief notes from her husband along the lines of "All is well, I miss you, *mo cridhe*." This was reassuring, but hardly satisfying.

Brow furrowed, she put away the scrying glass. Despite Jean's exhilaration at the army's progress, the situation for the Jacobites wasn't good. If they reached London, every porter and fishwife and chimney sweep in the city would join the government troops to defend their homes. The thought of a pitched battle for the city made Gwynne shudder. Casualties on both sides would be enormous. Pray God that didn't happen.

Though perhaps it wasn't God who was making this a relatively bloodless uprising. Quiet Guardian work behind the scenes might be steering the possibilities away from bloody disaster. The thought almost reconciled her to her husband's absence.

At least it did during the day. The nights, when she woke burning with need and loneliness, were another matter.

*　　*　　*

"Interesting," Simon murmured as he contemplated his scrying glass. "Your Jacobite army is going to return to Scotland."

Duncan glanced up from his boiled mutton, concealing his satisfaction at the news. He had improved greatly at keeping his thoughts, and his magic, away from Simon's sharp perception. "So wiser heads have prevailed?"

His friend nodded. "The Pretender wants to march on London and trust that legions of Jacobites will rise in support, but virtually none of his advisers agree. The army will start an orderly withdrawal tomorrow. The Pretender is furious to be thwarted, of course, and swears that he will call no more councils."

Duncan frowned. "I hope he didn't mean that. The prince hasn't the experience to command his army alone."

"I wouldn't count on him to go back on words said in anger," Simon said dryly. "Lethal stubbornness is one of the defining characteristics of the House of Stuart."

Duncan ignored the jibe. There was some truth to it, but the best of the Stuarts also had vision, courage, and the ability to capture men's hearts. Charles Edward would save Scotland with those traits once he relinquished the mad dream of conquering England.

Duncan had been bitterly disappointed when the snowstorm he'd conjured near Carlisle hadn't persuaded the prince to withdraw to Scotland. Instead, the army had marched far south into England. Mercifully they hadn't been attacked, and now they were finally coming home. Surely by the time the spring campaign season arrived, Charles would see the wisdom of consolidating his strength in Scotland.

Thinking of royalty, Duncan pulled out his own scrying stone and looked for King George. Royal actions, related matters . . . It was not hard to locate the energy of a king, for they were thunderstorms among the clouds of normal men.

After a few minutes of seeking, he gave a snort of disgust. "Your noble sovereign has packed the royal yacht with his dearest treasures and stands ready to flee if the rebels come any closer to London. How admirable."

"I never said that I admired the Hanoverians," Simon

said coolly. "It is merely a case of finding their flaws more tolerable than Stuart failings."

Duncan smiled reluctantly. "You're a dreadful cynic, Simon."

"Nonsense. It is impossible to be cynical about royal houses. The most dyspeptic of comments rate as simple truth."

"Perhaps we should try a republic, like the ancient Athenians."

"It would be an amusing experiment, though doomed to failure. Average men are even less capable of governing themselves than kings, who at least are raised to the trade." Simon absently sliced his piece of tough mutton into tiny shreds.

Belatedly recognizing that something was amiss, Duncan asked, "What's wrong?"

Simon frowned at his dinner plate. "I think it is time for us to separate, with you shadowing the Jacobite withdrawal while I track the English armies."

Separation would simplify Duncan's situation, but he was surprised by the suggestion. "We could cover more ground, but I thought the council's purpose was for us to balance each other."

"I'm not sure that's necessary now, since the rebellion is starting to falter." Simon hesitated. "I need to go hunting. I feel that someone—a Guardian, surely—is working quietly behind the scenes to create greater trouble."

"I've felt nothing of that," Duncan said, surprised.

"Your strengths lie elsewhere. Whoever I am sensing must have great power to conceal himself so well. Unless I am imagining this . . . the energies I detect are so subtle that I sometimes question if they are real." A dangerous light showed in Simon's gray eyes. "But I am seldom wrong about such perceptions."

Concealing his disquiet, Duncan asked, "Is this mysterious power aiding the Jacobites or the Hanoverians?"

"Neither, I think. My feeling is that he simply wants to cause trouble. I think of him as Chaos."

Duncan relaxed. Whatever Simon was sensing, it wasn't Duncan's own mild interventions on behalf of the Jacobite cause. "Good hunting. Whoever the fellow is, he sounds like someone who needs to be stopped." A new thought struck, along with a sharp yearning for Gwynne. "If the prince is heading north, I might be home for Christmas."

Simon's smile was wistful. "Very likely. You're a lucky man, Duncan."

He knew that—and hoped that his luck held.

*   *

After the image of Jean's latest letter dissolved in the scrying glass, Gwynne leaned back into her bed pillows and rubbed her aching forehead. She had designed a spell to alert her when Jean was writing a letter home so she could learn what was happening without waiting for days. Looking over Jean's shoulder wasn't easy, but it allowed her to know how the girl felt about what was happening.

Jean seemed to be feeling a touch of disillusionment with the prince, and well she might. Gwynne's scrying showed that every night Charles drank heavily, arising morose and surly the next day after the army was already marching. As she had suspected the one time they'd met, he lacked the steadfastness a leader needed in adversity.

The hour was late and the castle silent, so she set aside her scrying glass and finished her cup of cooling herbal tea. When she dowsed the candles, Lionel emerged from some hidden place and joined her under the covers. He had an unerring knack for showing up at the right time to soothe her to sleep with his rumbling purr.

Toward morning her sleep lightened, and in the hazy state between dream and waking she saw Duncan in her mind. She smiled in her slumber, her hands stroking down her body because in this in-between time she could almost feel that he shared her bed, his kisses igniting her blood. She could feel his hands on her breasts and taste the salt of his skin. Body pulsing, she held out her arms. . . .

The dream Duncan stepped away, anguish on his face. He stood alone on a barren mountain and when she tried to approach, lightning crackled from the sky to form a burning barrier between them.

Dimly she recognized that the members of the council stood in a circle around her husband's position, their expressions grim as he held them at bay with the lightning. She tried to call his name but no sound emerged from her throat. He turned away and raised his arms. As the dark funnel of a tornado appeared above him, the world exploded into storm and blood.

She snapped into full wakefulness, heart pounding and sweat dampening her face. *Dear God, Duncan, what have you done?*

Twenty-Eight

*E*arly afternoon, the day before Christmas. Though the New Year celebration called Hogmanay was more important in Scotland, Gwynne had suggested having a Christmas Eve feast for residents of the glen. As an Englishwoman, she wanted it, plus she thought a party would also raise people's spirits when so many men were away.

She glanced out the window, her hands resting on the spicy fruited cake she had been decorating with marzipan. Outside, snowflakes fell with ethereal stillness. The kitchen was a noisy contrast as every female in the Dunrath household and others from the glen prepared food. The cheerful equality of the process was another strong contrast to Harlowe. There, even when she was merely the librarian's daughter, Gwynne had never worked in the kitchen. She could have held herself apart here, but she enjoyed the feminine bustle and camaraderie of sharing the holiday work.

"They're all well, you know," Maggie Macrae said quietly from across the scrubbed pine table.

Pulled from her reverie, Gwynne smiled at the housekeeper. "I know they are. But it would be fine indeed to

have Duncan and Diarmid and the rest of the men of
Glen Rath home tonight."

"Men will be men, which is to say fools who prefer
war to home and hearth," Maggie said tartly. She cocked
her head. "You have the second sight, don't you? Even
though you're not a Highlander."

Startled by the other woman's casual mention of the
ability to see the future, Gwynne stammered, "A . . . a
touch, perhaps. At least, sometimes I'm very sure of particular things. As now, when I'm sure that Duncan and
Diarmid are well." She had seen Diarmid that morning in
her scrying glass.

"You'll tell me if you have a vision of Diarmid?"

While discussing Guardian power was forbidden,
Gwynne guessed it was safe to speak as if she had the
"sight." "I had a brief dream of him last night. He
looked thinner and tired, but he was well, and helping
another rebel in need of aid. He'll come back to you a
man, not a boy, Maggie Macrae." She smiled inwardly.
The longer she was in Scotland, the more she used
sonorous full names, as those around her did.

Maggie's face eased. Before she could say more, her attention was claimed by her daughter, who had come to
help with the preparations. As Maggie moved away,
Gwynne returned to decorating the cake, an English
recipe she had brought with her.

Keeping busy meant that she didn't think of Duncan
more than a dozen times an hour. His absence was like an
aching tooth, an emptiness that no one else could fill.
They had now been separated longer since their wedding
than they had been together. But at least she knew he was
safe and well, which was more than most women who
waited did.

She was putting the last marzipan star on the cake

when intuition struck hard. *Duncan?* She raised her head and looked around, half expecting to see her husband stride into the kitchen with snowflakes falling from his cloak, but he wasn't there.

Yet he was . . . close. Surely she was not imagining that. Untying her apron, she said to Marie, the head cook, "Can you supervise the rest of the preparations? There is something I must do."

"Of course, Mistress." Marie pinched off a piece of the soft marzipan and popped it into her mouth. "Though of course that means testing the ingredients!"

Smiling abstractedly, Gwynne left the kitchen as quickly as she could. In the back hall, she donned her cloak and gloves, then threw a heavy wool plaid around her shoulders before she darted out to the stables. The gentle snowfall had turned the world to silent white purity. Three or four inches were on the ground and the fall showed no sign of stopping.

Neither of the grooms was in sight so she saddled Sheba herself, unable to bear wasting the time it would take to find help. Bursting with anticipation, she mounted and cantered the mare out into the snow. Luckily her loose morning gown was an adequate substitute for a habit.

Sheba was glad to stretch her legs, though the edge had been taken off her energy by the time they had to slow to climb the steep road that was the glen's only exit to the south. Curbing her impatience, Gwynne allowed Sheba to set her own pace. It wouldn't do to fall and break both their necks.

Incandescent with joy, she headed into the snow, the drumming of Sheba's hooves calling, *Duncan, Duncan, Duncan.*

*   *
    *

Wearily Duncan crested the hill and paused to gaze down into the glen. *Home.* With the familiar hills and fields blanketed in white, the glen was a fairyland. This storm should have been much worse, but he had gentled it to make his ride easier.

Even Zeus seemed to recognize that he was nearing home, because his head lifted and he whickered. But that wasn't a general equine noise, it was the sound Zeus made when he sensed another horse. Wondering who was traveling in this weather on the day before Christmas, Duncan narrowed his eyes and peered into the white air.

Gwynne. Blazing with certainty, he recklessly urged Zeus to go faster. A dark figure began to take shape down the road.

"Duncan!" As reckless as he, she burst into sight from the curtain of snow as he and Zeus reached a broadening of the path. With her hood down and covered in a frosting of icy crystals, she was a fiery-haired angel of storms.

They came headlong together. As they pulled their horses to a halt side by side, Duncan leaped from his mount and reached up to pull her down into his arms. He had just enough wit to cast a stay spell on the horses before he lost himself in her. "Oh, God, Gwynne, I've thought of you every moment of every day!"

"Liar," she laughed. Her cheeks were rosy from the cold, and the shattering power of her enchantress allure made the rest of the world vanish. "You were busy guarding the peace, and surely thought of me no more than once every hour or two."

He stopped her words with his lips and they crushed

together, fervently trying to blend into one being. "I didn't know how much I needed you, *mo cridhe*," he breathed. "If I had let myself miss you, I never could have gone away."

"All that matters is that you are home now." Her hungry mouth and hands maddened him. Beyond thought, he tossed his plaid onto a drift of snow and laid her down, following to warm her with his own body. Her lush curves cushioned him, her softness an invitation to sin.

When she rocked against him, he tugged the folds of her plaid over both of them, then unfastened his breeches, so aroused that his hardened flesh was unaffected by the frigid air. Raising her skirts, he found her hotly ready, whimpering at his intimate touch. He thrust into her, needing union more than he needed the air he breathed.

As she cried out, thunderbolts boomed through the snow, as violent and commanding as the passion they shared. It took only moments for them to explode into shuddering ecstasy. He gasped for breath, lungs stinging from the frigid air, yet profoundly at peace. He felt whole for the first time since they had parted.

Peace shattered when he saw that she was crying, hot tears running across her cold-reddened cheeks. "I'm so sorry, *mo càran*." He kissed her forehead as he moved his weight away from her. "Did I hurt you? It was abominable of me to take you like a crazed beast."

Her eyes opened to reveal not pain but fury. "You've been aiding the Jacobite cause. Damnation, Duncan Macrae, how *dare* you!"

He became very still, wondering if she really knew what he had concealed even from Simon. "What are you talking about?"

She rolled away from him to sit at the end of the plaid,

drawing her knees up and tugging her cloak tightly around her. "Don't try to pretend that you've done nothing wrong. When you are inside me, you can't hide what you have done."

Warily he asked, "What do you mean?"

"Your touch has caused me to see visions since our first kiss, mostly images of blood and chaos and death. That was the chief reason I wanted nothing to do with you." She drew a shuddering breath. "By our wedding night I had learned to shield myself from the images even in the throes of passion. Because I had been missing you so much, today my shields were weak and the images were more vivid than ever. I saw you using your power to protect the rebel forces."

He felt naked. Shocked and ashamed. *Angry.* Struggling with his emotions, he said tightly, "I have been using power to reduce casualties on both sides. There is nothing wrong with that."

She closed her eyes and snowflakes caught in her lashes like stars. "It's a clever rationale, Duncan. But you are interfering in ways that will precipitate disaster."

She was not muting her enchantress power, and she was so achingly desirable that he wanted to prostrate himself on the plaid and beg her forgiveness for anything he'd done wrong. It took a major effort of will to resist the effects of her devastating allure. "Yet you married me despite my evil touch. One wonders why, Gwyneth Owens."

Her eyes opened, her gaze stark. "The Guardian Council asked me to become your balance-mate. They hoped I might prevent you from triggering a catastrophe."

Her words were a dagger in his heart. His wife had lied about their marriage, and the elders of the Families, men and women he knew and respected, had thought him a danger to the world. "So you married me not because Lady Beth thought it a good idea, but by order of the council. How strange." Numbly he got to his feet. "I thought I had taken a wife. Instead I have a spying martyr sacrificing herself in my bed."

"I am your wife, not your enemy. I found you both fearsome and fascinating, and the council's urging made it possible to do what my heart truly desired. We are bound by chains of fate, Duncan. The council's request was merely one link." She also stood, shaking the snow from her plaid before wrapping it around her trembling shoulders.

Duncan pulled his plaid from the crushed snow to protect himself from the bitter cold. Damn, his dismay was causing the temperature to plunge. He forced his mind into the discipline needed to stabilize conditions before they both froze to death, then asked, "What dreadful actions am I accused of?"

"You were using weather magic to keep the armies apart and allow the Jacobites a clear march south," she said wearily. "Perhaps that could be justified as legitimate, but what seared through my mind was your guilt and misgivings. Though you claim you acted for the good of all, in your heart is the knowledge that you are trying to change the outcome of this rebellion. Your doubts betray you."

His eyes narrowed challengingly. "Yes, I have doubts that I am making the right decisions, but only a fool takes such matters lightly. What is undeniable is that my actions have reduced the amount of bloodshed so far. Simon and I both worked to keep the armies from fighting a pitched battle, and he's as loyal a Sassenach as you."

"Intent matters. No matter what you say or how you rationalize your actions, you are defying Guardian principles to support your own desires."

His temper exploded. "Your precious books and principles belong in libraries. I must work in the world as it is! There is a civil war in progress. I didn't start it, but since it's here I'm doing my best to control the damage. My actions have all been aimed at encouraging the prince to withdraw from England. Once that happens, he can reclaim the throne of Scotland which belongs to the Stuarts by right of blood. Scotland and England can be neighbors and equals once more."

Her gaze was unflinching. "It's a pretty dream, but it will not happen. The prince wants to rule all of Britain. He will never settle for Scotland alone."

She was voicing his own private fear—that the prince's ambitions would interfere with a goal that was both better and achievable. Not wanting to admit that, he growled, "What makes you so sure? Did you see that in Isabel's glass?"

She hesitated as if wondering how to explain the inexplicable. "Long before we met, I had one magical talent. On very rare occasions, I have felt an absolute sense that something is true. As I said, this feeling is rare, but so far it has never been wrong. In my bones and soul, I know that a Stuart victory would be a disaster for all of Britain, and that your prince will destroy Scotland as you know it."

Even though he disagreed, her certainty was daunting. "What form will this disaster take? *I* think that a Jacobite victory in Scotland will give us back our freedom for a relatively low price in terms of human suffering. How can that be wrong?"

She shook her head with frustration. "I wish I could say why, but I have the knowledge without the reasons."

His mouth twisted bitterly. "You will have to come up with more persuasive arguments than that, Gwyneth

Owens. You've spent your life surrounded by English council members who had no use for the Jacobites, and that is warping every thought you have on the subject."

"I am not meekly echoing the opinions of the council, Duncan." Shivering, she wrapped her plaid tighter around her. "I had hoped that telling you about my visions would persuade you to reconsider the course you have chosen, but I have failed. I had also hoped that our disagreements would not affect our marriage, but I have failed there also. Failed you, failed myself, and failed our marriage."

His heart seemed to stop. How had they gone from searing passion to estrangement so quickly? "You . . . you will leave and tell the council to censure me?" He reached out a hand in supplication, wanting to hold her.

"No!" She retreated from his hand until she backed up to Sheba. The horses were huddled nose to tail against the biting wind. "I am not leaving you yet. I will return to Dunrath and pray that you come to your senses before it's too late."

Relief was so profound it weakened him. "Perhaps it is you who must come to your senses. Search my heart, Gwynne. You know that I truly desire to help as many people as possible, and that is the essence of being a Guardian."

She swung into the saddle without his aid. "The road to hell is paved with good intentions, Duncan Macrae. What you need is the clarity to see beyond your personal desires for Scotland." Her mouth twisted. "Lady Bethany told me that I would know what to do. I only wish that she was right."

Telling himself that her attitude would soften, he mounted Zeus and followed her down the snowy path into the glen. His wife's enchantress sensuality worked both ways: just as he needed her, she needed him. A few days of shared passion would soften her Sassenach refusal to understand.

He didn't dare believe otherwise.

Twenty-Nine

Gwynne felt a curious calm now that the crisis with her husband had arrived. Though the ride back to the castle was silent, they entered the courtyard side by side. An unperceptive observer might have thought they were in charity with each other.

Duncan welcomed the Christmas Eve celebration, perhaps thinking that the merrymaking—and the free-flowing drink—would soften Gwynne's attitude. She almost wished that would happen, but she could not free herself from bleak despair. Duncan's rationalizations had pushed him perilously close to the point where he might be declared a renegade if the council became aware of his partisanship.

She slipped away from the celebration early, unable to maintain a gay facade any longer. Safe in her rooms, she built up her fire as an icy wind rattled the windows. Nights like this made her particularly grateful for the renovations to the living quarters. If the castle was in its original state, she'd be frozen to the marrow.

Lionel appeared with his usual impeccable timing. She scooped him up gratefully. "Hard times ahead," she whispered into the soft striped fur.

Though she had never lied to Duncan, she had withheld the full truth from him. Today it had seemed right to reveal all in the hope that she could persuade him to turn from the path he was on. She might as well have saved her breath. All she had done was hurt and alienate him, and his pain echoed within her.

Despite her conviction that he was making a terrible mistake, she could understand his position. Guardians were raised to be protectors, and for Duncan the needs of his homeland and countrymen inspired fierce loyalty. No wonder he hoped that Prince Charles Edward would prove a boon to Scotland. But Scotland would not emerge as a free and independent nation again under a restored Stuart dynasty; Gwynne's inner voice was quite sure of that.

Might her inner voice be wrong? In theory, yes, but Gwynne was as sure of its truth as of anything in her life. To Lionel, she murmured, "What can I do to prevent Duncan from being the catalyst of great harm?"

Betray him. The answer was as chilling as the winter wind. Though she could not yet see what form her betrayal would take, it was no longer possible to believe she could avoid it.

Setting Lionel down, she removed her gown. She had deliberately chosen a front-lacing corset and a garment that required no maid. Tonight, she needed privacy.

She slipped her warmest nightgown on, thinking wistfully of Arthurian legends about enchantresses who could hold men in thrall for as long as they wished. But that was legend. If Gwynne tried to persuade her husband to abandon the Jacobite cause by using magic, the effect would be temporary at best—and after his passion had been slaked he would be justly enraged at her attempt to manipulate him.

Passion . . . Sensual memory of their incredible lovemaking up in the hills surged through her with molten power. She had not known that desire could be so earth-shaking. Only in the aftermath of rapture had she sensed Duncan's traitorous behavior and decided it was time for the whole truth.

When and if Duncan left the celebration to join her, would she be able to resist him? Or would she fall on him with wild urgency as she had this afternoon? Afraid to find out, she locked both doors to her room.

She crawled under the covers and cuddled Lionel close. Though Duncan would recognize the message of the locked doors, he would not like it.

*　*　*

The warmth of the Christmas Eve celebration was a grand contrast to the cold, isolated weeks of shadowing the Jacobite army. By his fourth dram of good Scots whiskey, Duncan decided that this gathering should become a regular Dunrath tradition, a gentler prelude to the more riotous Hogmanay celebration.

Now it was time to go to his wife and repair the damage done by their earlier quarrel. She was too blindly faithful to the conservative Guardian Council, but she was also intelligent and adaptable. Once he had explained his position calmly and in greater detail, she would accept his point of view. With luck and passion as a persuader, she might even come to share his views once she discarded her prejudices.

His steps quickened as he climbed the steps. Their coupling earlier had been fiercely satisfying, but now he would make love to her slowly, giving rapt attention to every inch of her exquisite body. Lord above, how he'd missed her! He reached for the doorknob. . . .

Her bedroom was locked. He gazed down in shock, jiggling the fancy porcelain doorknob imported from France. But the door did not open. Still not believing, he stalked into the sitting room they shared and tried that door also.

Locked.

Rage blazed through him, triggering lightning flashes that crashed across the winter sky. Ignoring every tenet of restraint, he blasted the doorknob with thunderous energy. The internal mechanism shattered, releasing the lock.

Furiously he threw the door open and burst into the bedroom. "How *dare* you lock your door against your husband!"

The night candle showed Gwynne jerk herself upright in the bed. The braid of bright hair falling over her shoulder was a garish contrast to her pale face and taut expression. "Whiskey makes your accent more Scottish," she said, her voice not quite steady. "We didn't have a simple argument, Duncan Macrae. You have bent your Guardian oath to the breaking point, and I cannot be your wife while that is true."

He stared at her, incredulous. Gwynne wore a plain nightgown designed for warmth, not seduction, yet she was so desirable that it hurt to look at her. "I don't know how matters are managed in England, but in Scotland a husband and wife settle their disagreements in bed."

A single kiss would begin to melt her stubborn resistance, he knew it. She wanted him as much as he wanted her, and in the melding of their bodies they would be able to breach the abyss that was forming between them. Between rage and desperation, he strode to the bed and reached for her.

As she gasped and pulled back, a screaming fury leaped

from under the covers and attacked him. The beast attached itself to his left arm with vicious claws while its fangs sank through his coat to draw blood. Startled, he knocked the creature from his arm and instinctively retaliated.

"*No!*" Gwynne countered his power with a blast that shoved him away from the bed and neutralized his energy attack. He staggered backward and grabbed at a chair to steady himself, so weak it took most of his strength just to breathe.

As he tried to shake off the effects of her defense spell, his attacker crouched in preparation for another assault. It was Gwynne's damned cat, almost unrecognizable because its fur was fluffed to twice its normal size. Wildcats were the fiercest predators in Britain, and this crouching half-breed looked ready to rip his throat out.

Before the cat could attack again, Gwynne swooped forward and caught the beast in a towel, swiftly wrapping the flailing limbs to prevent being hurt herself. "It's all right, Lionel," she said soothingly. Duncan felt the tingle of magic that meant she was using a calming spell as well as words and touch.

The cat stopped struggling and its fur began to flatten. She cooed to it, "Don't worry, sweeting, my husband won't ravish me." Raising her head, she glared at Duncan. "I won't allow him to."

Dizzily he wondered if he would have taken his wife against her will. Surely not. Yet when he touched her, control vanished. . . . He drew an uneven breath. "I will never harm you, *mo càran*. But don't deny what is between us. Passion is a great gift, and through it we can find common ground."

Face implacable, she cuddled her pet to her soft, provocative breasts. "Sex is not the answer this time,

Duncan. The issues are too large and threaten too many people."

Any remnants of desire he had vanished. "If the council hoped you'd drive me mad, they were right." He sank into the wooden chair that had supported him. Strength was returning, but very slowly. "I should have remembered that enchantresses have a special talent for defense spells since they need protection more than most. I must give thanks that you didn't use a fire spell."

She perched on the edge of the bed, holding the cat like a shield. "I'm sorry if I hurt you, but I was afraid you might kill Lionel by mistake."

"If I do kill him, it won't be by mistake." Seeing her expression, he said, "That was a joke. I won't harm a hair on that vicious moggy's head." He rubbed his throbbing temple, wishing he'd drunk less whiskey. "The beast really is your familiar."

"Guardians don't have familiars. He's just a cat. A loyal cat who thought I might be in danger." Her gaze went to his left hand. "You're not wearing Adam Macrae's ring. Did you take it off so you could deny your clan's connection to the English throne?"

He had intended to put the ring back on before entering Dunrath, but had forgotten when Gwynne met him up in the hills. Pulling the ring from his pocket, he slid it onto his finger and received an unpleasant sting of energy. He stared at the glittering sapphire, wondering if Adam's ghost was chastising him. Silently cursing the whiskey for causing superstitious thoughts, he pulled the ring off and returned it to his pocket.

"We cannot both remain under Dunrath's roof, or we'll drive each other mad," she said quietly. "I shall leave on Boxing Day."

"No!" he exclaimed, horrified by a sense that if she left the glen, she would never come back. "If anyone leaves, it will be me. I only intended to stay until Hogmanay, so I'll be off tomorrow instead."

"I can't drive you from your own home, Duncan. Especially not on Christmas."

"This is your home also, and with Jean and me both gone, Dunrath needs you." He thought of the bleak winter campaign that lay ahead for the armies. "When the rising is over, I'll return and we can . . . make our peace."

She sighed but didn't argue with him. He wondered what horrors she saw in her visions, then decided he'd rather not know.

At least with increased power she should be able to protect the glen and its people if the war came too close. The Jacobite troops had usually treated civilians honorably, but heaven only knew what the Hanoverians might do. Not all the soldiers would make a distinction between rebels and Scots loyal to King George. He thought of Jean, and hoped that she was practicing her own defense spells.

He got shakily to his feet, still feeling the effects of the incredible blast of energy Gwynne had wielded. "I'll be gone in the morning before you wake."

Tears glinted in her eyes. "Stay at least for the church service." Even though she was now shielding her allure, she was infinitely desirable.

His mouth twisted. "As you said, we'll drive each other mad if we are under the same roof yet not mates to each other. Good-bye, *mo càran*."

She set the cat aside and stood as if to come to him, then quivered to a stop as she recognized that touching would be folly. "Be careful, Duncan. In all ways. And if your opinion of this rebellion changes—for God's sake, come home!"

"I learned Guardian principles as a child, but I'm a Scot in my blood and soul," he said with bitter humor. "I'll not abandon my country or my prince." He pivoted and left the room, praying that Charles Edward would lead the rising to a swift and relatively bloodless victory, then be magnanimous to his defeated foes.

Nothing less would bring Duncan and Gwynne together again.

*　*　*

Despite Gwynne's best efforts to read all of Jean's letters when they were being written, this latest message had come the normal way, along wintry roads from Glasgow to Dunrath. Though Jean attempted to sound cheerful, the strain of the campaign was showing. According to her, the rebels were about to withdraw to the north and wait for spring to launch a new offensive.

When would it all end?

Gwynne didn't bother with her scrying glass. Instead, she sat down in her favorite library chair and closed her eyes to see if meditation would help her see the broad shape of events.

As her racing mind gradually stilled, she sensed that an indecisive battle was imminent, and that the crisis would come with the spring. Perhaps in April. From there, the future branched in two main directions. Either way, the repercussions would reverberate down through the years, changing Scotland forever. Though both futures contained wrenching change and tragic violence, one was far, far worse—and that was the future that Duncan might bring into being.

Calm gone, she opened her eyes and reached for her scrying glass to see if she could locate Duncan. As always, she failed. She guessed that he was shielding himself from Guardian eyes, and that meant her as well as the council. She hadn't heard a word from him since he left Dunrath on Christmas Day.

Did he hope that absence would make her heart grow fonder? Impossible—she already loved him with all that was in her even though she had been afraid to say the words aloud. Separating herself from him was the most difficult thing she had ever done.

If she was supposed to save Duncan from destruction by capturing his heart and using her influence to change his mind, she had failed. He was too stubborn to turn from his path even if his heart was breaking.

She wondered if he would be glad to know that hers was, too.

Thirty

*D*ark clouds scudded across the sky as Duncan found a high, unobtrusive vantage point that allowed him to see both Jacobite and Hanoverian forces. He kept the storm at bay, thinking it might be useful during the battle that was on the verge of beginning.

His eyes narrowed as the rebels took position on the Hill of Falkirk, a moor that overlooked the encampment of the Hanoverian army that had been sent to lift the siege of Stirling Castle. Though royal forces outnumbered the rebels by over two thousand men, they were not well positioned and their officers didn't take the rebel threat seriously. The idiot English commander, General Hawley, wasn't even with his troops—he was enjoying a drunken luncheon with the Countess of Kilmarnock. The longer he stayed away, the better chance the rebels had of smashing the government forces.

Besides watching the troop movements, Duncan sometimes checked his scrying glass to see if there were interesting developments elsewhere. His mouth twisted when General Hawley galloped up in a frenzy to join his threatened troops. The man was rumpled and wigless—what had he been doing with the countess? Perhaps that passionate Jacobite lady had decided to contribute her virtue to the task of rendering the general useless.

Since Hawley's artillery was bogged down in mud, the general began to organize regiments of dragoons to storm the hill before the rebels became entrenched at the top. It was a critical moment. If Duncan released the winds he had gathered, it would destroy any chance that the royal dragoons would achieve success.

It would probably also end the battle sooner with fewer casualties. Action on his part could be justified as benefiting both sides, but it would help the Jacobites more.

How far was he from crossing the line into renegade territory? Or was he there already? Each small interference on his part had made the next one easier. Gwynne had been right, damn her cool Sassenach logic. Though he could stand before the council and justify his actions, in his heart he had already crossed the line.

At a signal from the general, the dragoons began their charge up the hill. Duncan watched them, saw their superiority in equipment and numbers and training, and the last of his objectivity splintered. Quickly, before he could think more, he released the winds.

His gale blasted into the faces of the Hanoverian dragoons as they attempted to attack up the steep slope. They were in disarray by the time they reached the top. The rebels held their fire until the last possible moment—then released a shattering volley. Dozens of horses and riders fell, mortally wounded.

Duncan closed his eyes as he tried to slam the door on the pain of the wounded men and their mounts. The fact that he supported one side didn't spare him the other side's agony. Good men were dying, and his stomach twisted at the knowledge that he had made himself part of this battle.

He opened his eyes to a chaotic battlefield. Rain blasted down from the darkened sky, reducing the visibility as Hanoverian troops fled in panic. With muskets made useless by water, combat became a bloody matter of swords and dirks.

In twenty minutes it was over and the Jacobites had won a tremendous victory. Concealed by the pounding rain, Duncan quietly withdrew from the area. Because of the vile weather, the death toll would be relatively low. He had saved lives on both sides, and if the Jacobites followed up aggressively, they would soon be masters of all Scotland.

He hoped to heaven that happened. The sooner this war ended, the sooner he could return home to Gwynne.

* * *

Gwynne sighed over Jean's latest letter. It had taken almost a fortnight to reach her even though Dunrath was not terribly far from Inverness, the current headquarters of the rebel army.

Though Jean's overall mood was weary resignation, she told an amusing story about how five Jacobites had created a great enough ruckus to scare off a whole army of Hanoverians one stormy night. "The Rout of Moy," as it was being called, had allowed the prince and his followers to escape capture. The weather that night had a strong scent of Duncan about it.

Duncan. Still no word from him. All Gwynne could do was wait.

Wait and pray.

* * *

Expression grim, Duncan put away his scrying glass. The Jacobites had squandered their advantage in the days after Falkirk. Instead of pursuing the demoralized enemy or heading east to recapture Edinburgh, they had returned to their futile siege of Stirling Castle. Damned fools!

Scowling, he rose to put more wood on the small fire burning in the mouth of the cave where he had found refuge. Since he could not afford to be traced, he'd been living rough most of the time since leaving Dunrath. The entrance to his cave was high on a hill and not visible from below, so he should be safe enough here.

He impaled a tired piece of black pudding on a stick and held it close to the flames, wanting something hot to eat. When it began to sizzle, he laid it on a crumbling oatcake and began to eat his meager dinner. Was Gwynne missing him?

As soon as the thought formed, he felt her grief and longing as sharply as if he were touching her. But there were no regrets in her mind. She was convinced that he was wrong, and if he returned home he ran the risk of her reporting him to the council.

Thinking of her made him tighten with yearning. Any lapse of his self-control and he'd be on Zeus's back and heading to Dunrath.

He took a sip of the tea he'd made earlier, gloomily thinking how hard it was to change the course of events, or cure stupidity. When younger, he'd read books on military history. The principal lesson drawn from his study was that war was a confused and clumsy affair, and victory often went to whoever made the fewest mistakes. No wonder Guardians were strong supporters of peace.

He was sipping the last of the tea when he froze, his

hackles rising. He was being hunted. Scarcely breathing, he analyzed that faint, questing pulse of power.

Simon. The council's hound had returned to Scotland and was seeking him. He was close, too, within a mile. Duncan had a mental image of Simon riding relentlessly through the cold dusk, all his senses alert as he hunted his prey.

Duncan smothered the fire so not even a tendril of smoke was visible. Zeus was behind him in the cave, lazily munching some hay. The climb up to the cave was difficult for the horse even when Duncan led him, but a Sassenach like Simon, who was used to English mounts, would think it impossible. Duncan rested his hands on the horse's neck and laid a calming spell strong enough to prevent Zeus from being interested in any other horses that might traverse the rough road below the cave.

Then Duncan lay down on his blankets and prepared himself to be overlooked. The cave was shielded with a don't-see spell. He strengthened that, taking care to eliminate any marks of magic that might attract Simon's attention, and triggered the mizzling rain that had been threatening all afternoon.

Lastly, he diminished his own energy to the lowest level possible in which he was still conscious. He lay like a banked fire that should not attract Simon's attention.

Yet the hunter was drawing closer. In the stillness of the hills, Duncan could hear slow hoofbeats and sense Simon's approach. Closer . . . closer . . .

The hoofbeats stopped directly below the cave. Duncan had a vivid sense that the other man was probing the energies of the area, frustratingly aware that his quarry had been here at some time, but unable to detect Duncan's present position.

He closed his eyes, not allowing himself to feel satisfaction, since a change in his energy might attract Simon's hypersensitive awareness. Barely breathing, he waited.

After an endless interval, the hoofbeats started again, moving north. He was safe.

At least for now.

Thirty-One

G wynne gazed absently into the darkness, one hand stroking Lionel and the rest of her yearning for her husband. It had been three months since she had seen Duncan, and in that time she'd heard not a word, received not even one of his terse letters, and seen no image of him in her scrying glass. If not for the way her body remembered his, she might start to think she had imagined him.

The one thing he couldn't block was her sense that he was alive and well. She would know if he were dead. Others from Glen Rath had not been so lucky. Two local lads had been killed in skirmishes in the area around Inverness, where small groups of Jacobites and Hanoverians ran afoul of each other regularly.

She was drifting into sleep when a sudden awareness of a presence, male, caused her to sit bolt upright in the bed. "Duncan?" she whispered, feeling the tingle of power.

"Alas, no." A snap of fingers lit a candle, which illuminated the elegant, weary face of Simon, Lord Falconer. "I'm sorry to intrude on you this way, but I prefer to come and go as invisibly as possible."

Simon looked ten years older than on his last visit to

Dunrath. Even his shining blond hair seemed dimmed. "You must be hungry," Gwynne said. "Come down to the kitchens with me."

"With pleasure." Another snap of his fingers and a globe of cool light glowed on his palm.

"I need to learn how to do that," Gwynne said admiringly. "It looks like a very convenient spell."

"It is, especially for people like me who sometimes hunt in dark places, which I've done entirely too much of lately." He sighed. "If you like, I'll show you the trick of it when I'm not so tired."

"Time you were fed." She swung from the bed and donned Duncan's blue velvet banyan, which she used because she took comfort in the imprinted essence of his personality. It was also good protection from the icy drafts in the older parts of the castle.

In the kitchen, a kettle of thick lamb-and-barley soup was steaming gently on the hob, so she dished up a bowl while Simon lit the lamps. She added bread and sliced cheese, along with a glass of the castle's best claret for both of them.

He elegantly wolfed the food down, if wolves were ever elegant. When he finished, he poured them more wine, looking less like a stone effigy than when he had arrived. "Your control at not asking questions is stunning, Gwynne. Now it's your turn. Ask away."

She hesitated, wondering where to start. "I gather that you have not seen Duncan for some time."

"Unfortunately not. It was my idea to separate because I wanted to pursue what felt like a rogue Guardian. I had no success there—I think the rogue felt my search and stopped stirring up trouble. That's fortunate, but once Duncan was on his own, his Jacobite leanings took over." Simon's mouth twisted bitterly. "I should have known better. We were meant to balance each other, but I thought that the crisis had passed when the rebels began to withdraw to Scotland. I was wrong."

Which meant it was Simon's duty to hunt down one of his closest friends. How damnable. "It's not your fault," Gwynne said. "Duncan was already quietly aiding the rebels even before you went your separate ways. I saw him last at Christmas. At that time he was justifying his interventions as preserving life, but I fear that he was well on his way to discarding his rationalizations and committing fully to the rebel cause."

"If I had stayed, I think I could have prevented him from passing the point of no return." Simon tilted his goblet at the lamp, ruby lights sparkling through the wine. "I have been seeking him for weeks without success."

Gwynne pressed her hand to her lips. If the two came face-to-face, with Simon charged to stop Duncan—she shuddered at the thought. "So he can hide even from you?"

"I have found traces of his passing, but haven't been able to locate his living presence." He sighed. "Unless in my heart I don't want to find him and that is undermining my power."

She leaned forward and covered his hand with hers. "Don't torment yourself over this, Simon. He has great power, and a great desire not to be found."

His lean hand tensed under her fingers. "You've become adept at controlling the enchantress power," he said with unnatural calm, "but your touch is not yet harmless."

"Sorry." Blushing, she pulled her hand away. She would have to work on that.

"Do you know where he is?" Simon asked.

She shook her head. "He is able to shield from me very effectively. He is well, and somewhere near Inverness, I think. Beyond that, I know as little as you." Gwynne thought a moment. "Jean is also in Inverness. She writes me, but if she has seen Duncan, she hasn't mentioned it."

"I spoke with Jean. She said she hadn't seen him, and I believe her."

Gwynne studied his drawn face. They had always been friendly, and she now suspected that part of that was because she was a Guardian without power. He could relax with her because she knew what he was but didn't have the ability to see him with the eyes of power. Those who were capable of seeing his full self tended to be wary unless they had equal magical ability, she now realized. He had too much tightly controlled power to be restful. "It must be hard to be so alone," she murmured.

His head came up. For a moment, she thought he would ignore her comment, or brush it aside as if he didn't understand. Instead, he said, "It is. The curse of being a Falconer. One adapts."

And he did not wish to discuss the matter further. She nodded acceptance. "The armies are drawing closer and closer. The crisis is near, isn't it?"

"Very. A fortnight at the most. Probably sooner." He leaned forward, his gray eyes fierce. "You *must* stop Duncan, Gwynne. You are the only one who can. If you don't, I fear for the consequences."

"I would if I could, but how?" She spread her hands helplessly. "If you can't find him, I certainly can't."

"Don't seek him. Bring him to you."

She stared. "How can I make that stubborn Scot do anything?"

"Send out a mental call. Plead with him using every iota of enchantress power," Simon said crisply. "I don't think he will be able to resist you. Use your knowledge of his strengths and weaknesses as ruthlessly as necessary, but *stop him*!"

She bit her lip. "Duncan is so intelligent, with worldly experience far beyond mine. Have you ever wondered if he's right and we're wrong? Might the prince be the best available choice?"

"I've had this conversation with Duncan, and I've done my best to find clarity on the topic." Simon sighed. "There are different levels of truth, and Duncan has found a . . . a short-term truth that speaks to his loyalties. He dreams of Scotland regaining her independence and prospering as a sovereign nation once more.

"But there are larger truths, and in this case Duncan is not seeing them. The dream of the Stuarts restored in Edinburgh has romantic appeal—even I wondered if that might be a good outcome. The more I meditated on the matter, the more I felt the wrongness. If the Stuarts regained the throne of Scotland, how soon until the border wars begin again? An independent Scotland is a potential traitor at England's back door, and England will not allow that to happen again. She has enough enemies. And if the Pretender won England as well . . ." He shook his head, his expression stark.

Different levels of truth—yes, that made sense. Bless Simon for his ability to put the situation into perspective. She was also grateful that a man with Simon's power and worldly experience agreed with her about the dangers of a Jacobite victory.

The hour of betrayal had arrived. Oddly enough, she now knew how to accomplish that if she could bring Duncan close enough for her to work her wiles.

Living with herself after committing her crime was something she would worry about later.

* * *

Simon was reluctant to spend the night, but Gwynne insisted. She put him in a guest room, laid an ignore spell on the door so no maid would disturb him in the morning, then returned to her own chamber.

With the critical battle likely to occur within days, there was no time to waste if she was to bring Duncan to her side. She returned to her bed, closed her eyes, and tuned her senses to her magic. If forced to describe that power, she would say that it was like a fluid that filled her body, lighter than air but sparkling with subtle luminescence. When her power was focused, the light increased and there was a kind of inner tingling, as if she were more alive than usual.

When her magic was as strong as she could make it, she reached out to Duncan, trying to touch his mind with hers. This wasn't just any man, it was her husband. The man she loved, body, mind, and soul. Surely she could find him. . . .

Nothing. She continued to try, unaware of the passing time, until she had to give up in fatigue. She hadn't achieved the faintest sense that they were connecting.

Temples throbbing, she wondered if there was another method than mind-touch. *Body, mind, and soul.* She caught her breath. Hadn't Simon said to use her enchantress power? Her magic was of the body, not the mind. Since she and Duncan were bonded by their mutual passion, that was how she might reach him.

Once again she concentrated her power until she shimmered with magic. Then she visualized Duncan, but this time she concentrated on intimate details rather than worldly ones. The way his whiskers prickled under her fingertips, the smile that showed in his eyes when he looked at her even if his expression was serious. The way he could bring her to arousal with a single passionate glance. . . .

Her heartbeat quickened and she touched her tongue to her lips. *Duncan, my love, please come home, I need you most desperately.*

The provocative pressure of his mouth, the musky scent of sex, the damp clinging of their bodies after passion was spent. The explosion of ecstasy when he thrust into her. As the memories intensified, her hips began to pulse. *My husband, I will try to be the wife you want me to be, if only you come home.*

Her hands moved over her breasts, caressing before they slid lower with urgent pressure. She kneaded her flesh in a feverish attempt to simulate what she wanted from Duncan. As she visualized their joining, tremors ran through her. She could almost feel that he was here, his mouth ravenous, his fierce desire focused on her. *I need you as the earth needs the rain, as a body needs breath. Come home, beloved!*

Ah, God, what could be more sublime than passion shared with one's love? Waves of rapture convulsed her and for an instant she knew that they were joined, in soul if not in body. *I love you, mo càran, I love you. . . .*

Her shudders faded, leaving her drained, satisfied, and embarrassed by her shamelessness. On some intangible level, she and her husband had made love, and she was sure that he had felt her presence as clearly as she had felt his. This time they had connected as they had not when she had tried the mind-touch.

If tonight's plea didn't work to bring him home to her—well, she would try again.

Body and soul.

*   *
    *

Duncan jerked awake as if his flesh were burning. For an instant he had no awareness of where he was; the only certainty was that he'd just had the most extraordinarily passionate dream of his life.

Or was it a dream?

Breathing hard, he propped himself up on one elbow and glanced around the rough cave, which was faintly illuminated by the banked coals of his fire. Gwynne was a Guardian with ways of learning things unavailable to mundanes. She had seemed so real that he wouldn't have been surprised to find her lying on the blankets beside him. Dear God, he wished she were here!

As sweaty and breathless as if they really had just made love, he lay back on the blankets and tried to analyze what had happened. He had had other passionate dreams of his wife—almost nightly, in fact. This had been different. Intensely sensual, but also embodying what seemed like a message.

Mentally he went over the essence of his dream experience. It had been like mind-touch, but profoundly physical. A summoning of the body. *My husband, I will try to be the wife you want me to be, if only you come home.* Had Gwynne changed her mind about the rebellion? Or was her call a product of loneliness?

Surely it was the latter, for he felt the same. He wanted her with a fever that never cooled. He had left Dunrath abruptly because she wouldn't be a wife to him while he supported the rising. But the summoning, if that's what it was, was not the call of a woman who would refuse her husband her bed.

Dare he answer her call and return to Dunrath? He

ied to think of all the objections. A major battle was
rawing near, but it was still several days away. Time
ough to go home, which wasn't much more than a
ay's ride.

Might she be trying to lure him back to be arrested by
e Hanoverian authorities? No, she would not betray
im like that.

Might she turn him over to the council? Several coun-
llors waiting at Dunrath would be able to overpower
im. But that would be an explosive and dangerous situa-
ion with a strong chance of casualties. He couldn't
nagine Gwynne condoning that, no matter how much
e disapproved of her husband's politics.

Disapproval was not what she had expressed in the
ream. . . .

Wearily he rolled over. It would be worth taking a risk
ist to go home and take a proper bath. And if Gwynne
elcomed him with open arms, that would justify almost
ny danger.

Another, darker thought entered his mind. Though he
adn't been endangered at Falkirk, being in a battle zone
ould be lethal even for a mage. It was quite possible that
e would not survive the upcoming hostilities. If so, a
isit to Gwynne might be the last time he would see her.

Flopping onto his back again, he decided to make his
ecision when he was less distracted by the aftermath of
hantom lovemaking. If that's what it had been . . .

*G*wynne made the necessary preparations for he plan, then spent two more nights using er chantress power to summon her husband before she gav up. Despite her sense that they were connecting, eithe she had failed or he was resisting her invitation. Sinc time was running out, on the third night she simply bur rowed into her pillows and ordered her dream mind t come up with another technique while she slept.

She was jerked awake by the sharp knowledge that sh was not alone. Rather crossly she thought that a disad vantage of Guardian life was the way members of th Families sneaked around and scared a person out of he skin. With a snap of her fingers, she lit a candle. Usin small magics in daily life was becoming routine. "Dur can?"

The candle flared, illuminating the figure of a massiv bearded Highlander by the door. She caught her breath i alarm before she identified her long-absent husband.

"My lady wife." He stepped forward into the light a she lit another candle. In the months since Christmas h had produced a dark, auburn-tinted beard that maske his expression. He must have collected his Highland kil and plaid and brass-hilted weapons during his Christmas visit. He looked barbaric, intimidating—and so compellingly masculine that her breathing roughened.

He glanced at a lump in the bed. "Have you told your familiar to behave?"

Lionel oozed out from under the covers, eyeing Duncan with interest but no hostility. Gwynne said, "He's a mild little moggy, as long as he senses no threat." She stroked the soft fur, mentally saying, *Go.* The cat vanished soundlessly into the darkness.

She slid from the bed, very aware that her carefully chosen nightgown clung alluringly. Her nipples tightened from his heated gaze, becoming rudely visible under the thin fabric. The atmosphere was thick with sexual tension and mutual wariness.

Keeping his distance, he asked, "Dare I hope that you have summoned me because you have come around to my way of thinking?"

She debated lying, but decided against it. She was a poor liar at best, and she could never fool a mage like Duncan. Which meant that everything she said to him at this critical meeting must be the truth, if not the whole truth.

"I still believe that Prince Charles Edward should go back where he came from, but I can no longer let that come between us." Her voice wavered. "I fear for you, Duncan, as I fear for Scotland and England. If . . . the worst happens, I don't want to live with the fact that our last meeting was in anger. I would rather it would be with passion."

His dark brows arched. "After the way you condemned me, do you think I can be so easily seduced back to your bed?"

For an instant she was dismayed. Then she saw the

glint of humor in his eyes. "Yes," she said with a tentative smile. "I do."

"You're right." A pulse throbbed in his throat, but still he didn't move toward her. "But don't think that you can enchant me into a different point of view."

She smiled with rueful honesty. "I know better."

"Passion is enough for you to be willing to consort with the enemy?"

"You are my husband, not my enemy." If he wanted more reasons, she had them. "I want your child, Duncan. If disaster lies ahead, I want something of you to last the rest of my life." Consciously pouring energy into her enchantress allure, she stepped toward him, her arms raised in supplication.

His resistance collapsed. "Ah, Gwynne, sweet Gwynne," he breathed as he tilted her face up. "No man could resist you. I don't even want to try."

Kiss and betray. The thought lanced through her mind. She instantly suppressed it, fearing he would catch an off note in her response unless she was totally focused on the passion of their reconciliation.

In the snow at Christmas they had come together without reservation. Tonight the hunger was even more desperate, but each movement was slower, more tentative. She felt as if they were relearning each other, not quite certain of the response. As she pressed against him, she felt a hard shape jabbing her. Smiling wryly, she said, "Pray remove the dirk and the sword. You're well enough armed without them."

He laughed and removed his weapons and belts and plaid, tossing them onto a chair. She stopped him before he could remove more garments. "I've thought that a kilt presented certain wicked possibilities."

As she kissed the sensitive skin visible at the throat of

his shirt, she slid her hands up his thighs, under his kilt. The hard muscles turned rigid and he groaned at her caress. "A kilt makes a man far too vulnerable," he said raggedly.

"Should I stop?" She slipped her hand around to the front of his body and clasped the hot, steely length of him.

"Don't you dare, my Sassenach witch!" He swept her onto the bed, raising the hem of her nightgown at the same time. He followed her down in a tangle of bare limbs and breathless laughter. As their lower bodies pressed flesh to flesh, he suckled her breast through the thin gown.

She whimpered, barely able to remember that she had a purpose beyond passion. There was something she should be doing. . . .

But nothing mattered beyond the exquisite satisfaction of receiving him into her, the frantic dance of thrust and retreat, the scalding heat and slick fluids of fevered intimacy until she shattered into rapture. As she returned to the normal world, she began crying soundlessly.

Spent, Duncan rolled to his side and kissed the tears on her cheeks. "Why so sad, *mo cridhe*?" he said softly. "We have just been blessed by the enchantress."

"I can't bear to see you go back into danger," she whispered, throat tight, wondering if she was capable of doing what must be done. "Why can't we always be together like this?"

"Too many such nights and I'd be dead, though with a smile on my face." He stroked back her hair. "The world is a complicated place, and love is only one of the great commandments. Duty and honor must have their day, too. I am a loyal Scot as well as a Guardian, and I must do what is best for my country."

She sighed and closed her eyes, unable to bear looking into his beloved face. "I like the beard. It feels nice."

"And here I thought it made me look savage."

"That also." She burrowed against him. Soon she would do her duty. Until then, she would savor what would be the last happy moments of her marriage. . . .

* * *

Dawn would break soon. Moving carefully so as not to wake Gwynne, Duncan slid toward the edge of the bed. Perhaps his beard didn't make him a savage, but sleeping in his rumpled kilt and shirt was definitely uncivilized.

He bent to kiss Gwynne's forehead, wondering if they had managed to create a child together. He hoped so, and wondered if he would live to see it.

Her eyes opened. Seeing him sitting on the edge of the bed, she reached out to catch his arm. "You can't be going already!"

"I must, *mo càran*. It will be a long ride back." He cradled her warm breast, reluctant to stop touching her. "But this has been worth it. If . . . something happens, remember me with fondness even if you think I'm a damn fool Scot."

"Don't leave yet!" Expression frantic, she reached up and drew him back to bed. With surprising strength, she rolled him onto his back and straddled him. "One last time, Duncan. Please."

The heat of her loins and mouth dissolved his resistance. Even if he was half dead with exhaustion later, he wanted this final mating as much as she did.

Like the enchantress she was, Gwynne teased him with kiss and caress and warm breath till he could hardly bear it. He was on the verge of pulling her under him when she raised herself on her knees, then slowly sheathed herself on him. "Ahhh . . . ," she breathed as she began rolling her hips with a motion that stunned his senses.

Her supple body shimmering with movement, she bent into a kiss, capturing his mouth, then pinning his wrists down in a delicious illusion of captivity. To hell with approaching dawn and the risk of being seen if he left. He gave himself wholly to the wildfire sensations that scorched through him. They were joined in spirit as closely as body, her anguish and her love palpable with every shattering thrust.

Passion exploded into ravishing release. Gwynne cried out and clasped him with intimate power, over and over until the last flame of desire had burned into ash. He gasped for breath, half dead and not caring. How could he walk away from her? How could he live without the feel of her silken form against his?

Weeping again, Gwynne pushed herself up, their bodies still joined. "I'm sorry, my love," she whispered. "So, so sorry."

Scalding tears dropped on his cheek as she braced herself above him, her hands still pinning his wrists to the mattress.

He was about to say something soothing when she released his left wrist. She tugged at the mattress—and then, with a clanking of cold iron, his sweetly passionate wife clamped a manacle around his wrist.

Thirty-Three

*D*uncan's eyes widened with disbelief as he realized what she had done. Then he exploded with rage. "Damn you!"

Frightened, she snapped a manacle cuff onto his right wrist, then scrambled from the bed. On his left wrist was the cuff of a manacle with the opposite end secured to a bedpost, while his right wrist had a cuff without an attached chain. Would the iron bands on his bare skin be enough to weaken him?

He lunged toward her, but the anchored manacle brought him to a halt. "You vicious, betraying whore," he swore, his eyes glittering as he yanked at the chains.

She could see that he was struggling to use magic, but he couldn't. She exhaled with relief. Though she had seen him weakened after the knife wound inflicted by William Montague, she hadn't been sure whether an iron cuff on each wrist would be enough to block his power. Apparently it was.

"Now what, you Sassenach bitch?" he snarled, his anger unable to conceal how weak he was. "Will Cumberland be coming by to collect me? Or the Guardian Council? Or Simon?"

"None of them. I may betray you myself, but I'll not turn you over to your enemies." Blinking back tears, she quickly changed from her nightgown to a plain morning gown. "I'm going to keep you locked up in the dungeons until after the battle."

"You are that sure you are right?" His eyes were the color of sleet.

"I am." She held his gaze steadily. "You are blind to the larger consequences of what you intended to do." She caught her breath as an image formed in her brain. "Dear heaven, if the Jacobites fared badly in the upcoming battle, you were prepared to conjure a tornado to turn the tide!"

"Aye," he ground out. "I've been practicing and become quite adept at managing whirlwinds. It would be an easy matter to halt the government forces till the prince and his men escape to fight another day."

She shook her head in despair. His earlier interventions might be justified as reducing casualties, but now he was planning to use his power to change the outcome of the whole rebellion. His previous actions might be forgiven, but never that. "Then thank God I have stopped you."

"I will kill you if you ever let me go," he snarled, but under his words she felt his anguish at her betrayal.

"I have done what I must, and so will you," she said quietly. "But for now, I will take you to the dungeon before the castle starts stirring. I don't want anyone to learn that you're here and set you free."

She flipped the covers back. He still wore his rumpled kilt and shirt, and his plaid would give warmth, but his feet were bare. She reached under the bed and pulled out warm woolen socks and buckled shoes. She had prepared most carefully for his return.

He kicked at her when she tried to pull the sock on his

left foot. "Don't fight me on this," she said. "It's cold in the dungeons, and your feet might freeze if they're bare."

Gritting his teeth, he allowed her to put the socks and shoes on. He managed another kick when she was done. His foot hit her upper arm, but without enough force to do more than raise a mild bruise.

Watching him warily, she unfastened the left manacle from the bedpost. He tried to go after her again, but she eluded him easily. His speed and strength were so badly compromised that it was like dealing with a young child. She hated doing this to him, but at least he was manageable. Reminding herself that she was acting for the greater good, she said, "Get out of bed."

Eyes blazing, he swung his legs over the edge of the mattress. When he stood, she tossed the plaid over her shoulders, not wanting to get near enough to wrap it around him. The chain around his left wrist was long enough to make a decent leash. Trying not to think of the ignominy of leading him like a farm beast, she said, "We must walk quietly down the back stairs. Are you strong enough to do that without falling?"

He drew himself up as well as he could. "If I fall or jump, perhaps we'll both die at the bottom of the stairs."

"If that happens, I'll release the chain and you'll fall alone. Don't try it, Duncan," she said coolly. "If you die, you lose the opportunity to kill me. And if you don't, you may injure yourself so badly you'll be a cripple the rest of your life."

In his eyes, she saw that his flaring rage was settling down into cold, hard anger. Under the circumstances, that was an improvement. "Come along now."

Reluctantly he followed her when she opened the door, then led the way to the back stairs, the links of the chain clinking ominously. She tried to surround them with a look-away spell, but it was hard to focus her power. Her guilt and fears occupied too much of her mind.

Duncan had to clutch the railing, but they descended to the ground floor without incident. She watched him closely, guessing that great effort was required to keep him steady on his feet.

They were crossing to the stairwell that led to the dungeon level when Maggie Macrae walked into the back hall, clean folded linens heaped in her arms. She halted when she saw them, her eyes widening with shock. "Mistress?"

Before Gwynne could reply, Duncan marshaled his strength and snapped, "My mad Sassenach wife is going to imprison me so I can be turned over to the Duke of Cumberland for execution. Release me, Maggie Macrae!"

When the housekeeper's horrified gaze swung to her mistress, Gwynne said calmly, "He's lying, Maggie. I aim to lock him up in a cell downstairs, but it's to save his life, not to take it. You guessed that I have the second sight, and I do. He intends to join the Jacobite army for the great battle the prince lusts after. I . . . I fear that he will be killed."

The housekeeper's face paled. "You think the rebels will be defeated?"

"I'm sure of it." A frightening burst of prophecy swept through Gwynne and words began tumbling from her mouth. "Men will die either way, Maggie. That is dreadful enough, but there will be worse to come. Jean is well known to have led men to the Jacobite camp and traveled with the army. If Duncan falls while fighting for the prince, Dunrath will be treated as a rebel stronghold. The Hanoverians will claim a bloody reckoning, and even babies like your own sweet grandchildren will not be safe."

"Don't listen to her!" Duncan snapped. "She's a Sassenach spy for the Hanoverians. Her goal is to cripple the Jacobite forces. My presence can make the difference, Maggie Macrae. For Scotland's sake, call for help and free me!"

Gwynne's heart sank. Maggie had served Duncan's parents, had watched him grow up. She would never side with an Englishwoman against the head of her clan.

Mouth tight, Maggie said, "I wish I'd had the courage to lock up my Diarmid, Mistress. Do you need my help?"

Duncan stared at her incredulously. "You will betray me, too? A clan member I've known my whole life?"

Maggie's mouth tightened even more, but she held his gaze. "I am a Macrae, but I am also a woman and a mother. I see no purpose to princes leading boys like Diarmid to their doom for the sake of royal power and pride." She glanced at Gwynne. "Sometimes a touch of the sight shows up in my dreams. Last night I dreamed that Dunrath was razed to the ground, the crofters' homes burned, dead bodies lay whitened in the rain. If imprisoning Duncan Macrae might prevent that, I'll help you and let God be my judge."

Weak with relief, Gwynne uttered a silent prayer of thanks. "I've fitted up one of the cells to hold Duncan. Come with me so you'll know the location. If anything should happen to me, someone else needs to know where he is." She repressed a shiver at the thought of him starving to death in a prison where no one would hear his cries.

From Maggie's expression, she'd had the same thought. She set her load of linens on a table. "It will be best if I take him his meals. Your movements are noticed more."

Gwynne nodded agreement, and the three of them descended the ancient steps to the warren of rooms and passages that comprised the lowest level of the castle. The rooms below the kitchen had a separate stairway and they were now used for household storage, but the oldest section had been a dungeon.

Gwynne had picked the most remote cell and placed a don't-see spell on it. As they approached the end of the dank stone corridor, the housekeeper frowned in puzzlement. Gwynne hastily modified the spell so that Maggie would be unaffected. Other mundanes who came this way would probably turn back, thinking they had found a dead-end passage.

Gwynne swung the door open. The cell was small, with a pair of slit windows that would never allow a man Duncan's size to escape even if they weren't barred with iron. Not that going through a window would mean freedom. The cells had been carved from the sheer cliff that made the castle impregnable, and they looked out into nothingness.

Gwynne had furnished the plain, narrow wooden bed with fresh blankets and pillows. She had also surreptitiously hauled a small table, a chair, and a badly worn little carpet down the steps herself. On the table were books and candles, while a hole in an outside corner provided crude sanitary facilities.

Despite her best efforts, it was still a cold, bleak place. "I'm sorry this isn't better, but your ancestors didn't believe in wasting comforts on prisoners."

Duncan glowered at her. "You take me prisoner in my own home, then worry about my comfort? You're a pair of mad featherbrained females!"

"Be grateful you're being held captive by females," Gwynne said tartly. "There's no point in suffering unnecessarily. Though if you prefer, that can be arranged."

He stepped inside with contempt. "Adam Macrae was imprisoned in the Tower of London with brandy and servants, but a prison is still a prison."

And chains were still chains. From the family histories, Gwynne knew that Adam had been put in shackles to keep him from escaping the Tower. The touch of iron had been most effective.

She followed her husband into the cell. One reason she had chosen this one was the rusted but solid iron ring that was set in the wall. A long chain attached to the ring suggested that this chamber had housed other iron-sensitive mages in the past. Snapping the open end of the left manacle to the chain, she said, "You should have enough length to move around the cell easily."

His brows arched. "What an unnatural wife you are to keep me in chains when I'm going to be locked in a cell that no one has ever escaped from."

His comment was for Maggie's benefit, since the older woman didn't know about Guardians and Duncan's susceptibility to iron. "Think of the chain as my respect for your cleverness, my lord husband."

She took a last look around the bleak cell and made a mental note to bring down a tinderbox, since he wouldn't be able to light his candles by magic. Though there was no fireplace, it was April now and there were plenty of blankets, so his captivity shouldn't be too uncomfortable. It was the best she could do. "Let me know if you have any particular requests."

Taking the plaid from her shoulders, she warily wrapped it around him. Bleak and exhausted, he was beyond striking at her again, but his iron-dark eyes still burned with the fury of betrayal. "How long will you keep me here?"

"Until the rebellion is over. Less than a fortnight, I think." Throat tight, she added, "I'm sorry."

"If you were sorry, you would set me free," he said grimly.

"I'm not that sorry." On the verge of tears, she left the cell. After Maggie joined her in the passage, Gwynne turned the heavy key in the lock. There was a second key that the housekeeper could use to bring food to the cell. There was only one manacle key, and Gwynne would carry that herself until the day Duncan could be released.

As she and the housekeeper made their way through the maze of passages, she said, "Thank you for supporting me, Maggie. I feel ghastly doing this to Duncan, but I don't know what other choice I had."

"A pity more women don't have your courage and resolution." Maggie glanced at her askance. "The lairds of Dunrath have always been an uncanny lot, and you're cut of the same cloth, Gwyneth Owens."

Gwynne tried to conceal her surprise. She should have realized that despite the Guardian spells meant to reduce curiosity among their mundane neighbors, great power would not go wholly unnoticed by people who lived with members of the Families.

As they reached the foot of the steps that led up to the ground floor, Maggie asked haltingly, "My Diarmid . . . can you see if he will survive the battle?"

Gwynne winced, wishing the question hadn't been asked, but since it had been, she must try to answer. After visualizing the boy's youthful face, she mentally moved him forward through time, frowning as she tried to sort out the possibilities.

Maggie made a despairing sound at Gwynne's expression. Quickly Gwynne said, "I don't see him being killed fighting. But remember that the sight is far from perfect."

"Then he'll come home safely?"

Eyes unfocused, Gwynne struggled to clarify her impressions. "I don't know. After the battle, the victorious army will pursue the defeated soldiers with . . . great fierceness." A swift image of a mounted man overtaking a fleeing boy and slicing off his head made her want to vomit. Was the boy Diarmid? She didn't think so—but he would be facing such dangers as he tried to make his way home.

Maggie swallowed hard. "Are you *sure* you're doing the right thing?"

Gwynne swayed a little as she thought of the enormous responsibility she was taking on. Dear God, what if she was wrong? *You will know what to do.* Though Lady Bethany had made it sound simple and logical, now that the crisis was here her choices were neither. "Yes, I am. Perhaps the Young Pretender has the strength and will to win the throne, but he'll have to do it without Duncan's aid."

Maggie sighed. "I don't think the prince can win, so I shall pray that the end comes quickly. The longer this rising lasts, the more lads like Diarmid will die."

Gwynne would be praying just as hard.

* * *

As soon as the key grated in the lock, Duncan stumbled to the narrow bed and collapsed. Never in his life had he been forced to endure the touch of so much iron for so long, and he felt as if he had been beaten to within an inch of his life.

Yet what he felt wasn't really physical pain. It was more like a disruption of his nature that paralyzed the deepest part of him. He felt like a woodland creature that had been struck by lightning and left alive but helpless, prey to any passing beast.

Lying down, he felt a small return of strength. Would he grow accustomed to the iron and regain some of his power? There was nothing in Macrae family archives to suggest that. The most he could hope for was some reduction in the psychic discomfort. Mentally he apologized to Adam Macrae for not properly understanding what his ancestor had suffered during his year and a half in the Tower of London.

From where he lay, he studied the cell, looking for a weak spot, but saw nothing. His bloody Sassenach bride had used his love and trust to entrap him when he was least expecting it, and she had put him in a prison he could not escape.

If fate had brought them together, it was a fate unspeakably cruel.

*　*　*

In a bothy south of Inverness, Simon, Lord Falconer awakened to dawn with a surprising degree of well-being despite a damp, chilling mist. He stretched, his muscles complaining about another night spent on the hard ground with only a blanket for warmth. Yet he felt more optimistic than he had in months. What had changed?

Mentally he searched the landscape of events, and found the answer. Relief rushed through him with giddying intensity. In the chess game of war, Duncan Macrae had been taken from the board.

Gwynne had succeeded.

Thirty-Four

14th April 1746
Inverness

Dearest Gwynne,

I wish that I had not started training my power, because I now have a horrid, uncanny feeling that the end is near, and it will not be a good one. My scrying shows that the Duke of Cumberland and his army are only a few miles east of Inverness, and they look well fed and well rested, not like our men.

The prince's Scottish leaders like Lord George Murray have urged him to disband the army and send everyone home. Rebels who know the country can easily harass the Hanoverians, then fade back into the mountains. Later the army could be gathered again for a new campaign.

But the prince listens only to his Irish and French advisers, who urge him to stand and fight. Can't they see what a disadvantage we'll be at against a larger, better-equipped army? Even I, a mere woman with no military training, can see the dangers in taking the field against a vastly superior opponent. The courage of our men has carried the day against great odds be-

fore, but I feel in my bones that our luck is running out.

I wish I could do something. Anything. If only I had studied my lessons more when I was young! If only I had inherited the Macrae weather-working magic. Though I know that using power for partisan reasons would be a violation of my oath, I am desperate enough that if I could, I might conjure a great storm to allow our men to escape if that becomes necessary. I don't know whether to be glad or sorry that Duncan is made of sterner stuff and will not break his vows.

Be strong, dearest Gwynne. My intuition tells me that you are Dunrath's best, perhaps only, hope. And if this is my last letter, know how blessed I feel that for at least a time, I have had a sister.

Jean Macrae of Dunrath

Gwynne's eyes clouded with tears till she could no longer see the letter in her scrying glass. By the time her vision cleared, the image was gone.

Would her sister-in-law be so affectionate if she knew that Gwynne had imprisoned Duncan to stop him from aiding the Jacobite cause? Probably not. Of course, Jean also assumed that Duncan would never consider breaking his oath. Would she be shocked to know that he had not only aided the rebels in small ways but was preparing to change the very outcome of the rebellion? Or would she be glad to know he shared her partisan convictions?

Thank heaven Jean wasn't a weather mage. Gwynne could not have borne to imprison two Macraes.

*   *
*

Two days after Gwynne watched Jean write her letter, the inevitable battle was fought at a boggy place called Drummossie Moor, a few miles southeast of Inverness. Gwynne monitored the movements of the armies, watched them take their positions.

When she saw the smoke of the first ragged artillery volley, she was tempted to put the scrying glass away so she could not see the battle, but grimly she forced herself to watch. By imprisoning Duncan, she had insured that the rebellion would run its natural course. The least she could do was bear witness.

The starved and exhausted Highlanders fought with a courage that was heartbreaking to watch. Gwynne watched dry-eyed, beyond tears. The fighting ended in less than an hour, leaving the field strewn with the dead and dying. Death filled the air, hammered in her head, saturated her with grief.

The brutal pursuit of the defeated troops was what she had envisioned, and worse. When she could bear no more, Gwynne rose from her library table and headed for the dungeon. In the days since she had locked Duncan up, she had been shamefully glad that Maggie Macrae was tending the prisoner, but this news must come from Gwynne.

When she opened the cell door, Duncan looked up from the table where he was reading. "How gracious of you to visit your prisoner." Before he could make another caustic remark, he saw her expression. He jumped to his feet. "What has happened?"

It took her two tries to say, "The government troops have won a great victory. The Jacobites suffered massive casualties." She drew an unsteady breath. "The rebellion has been crushed."

His face paled. "Is the prince dead? What of my sister? How many men of the glen have died?"

"The prince escaped the field, but other than that, I know few details." She fumbled for words to explain what she had seen. "Battle creates a fog of agony and frantic emotions and bloody images that makes it almost impossible to narrow my focus to individuals. I looked for Jean and Diarmid and others from the glen, but couldn't see them." She wondered if that meant they were dead. Surely not everyone she knew and loved who had fought for the rebel cause could have been killed.

"God *damn* you!" With one tormented sweep of his arm, he knocked the table over, sending books flying and smashing a Chinese porcelain teacup. "I could have saved them! Yet you in your self-righteous bigotry prevented me." He turned to face her, anguish and rage equally visible in his face. "My sister may even now be raped and murdered beside the road."

"Jean should be safe in Inverness." Gwynne prayed that was so.

"You think my sister a coward? Unlike you, she would not hide in safety when there was work to be done. If she dies, it is on your head, Gwyneth Owens." His voice dropped to a menacing whisper. "May you live in guilt and pain for the rest of your life."

Her lips twisted bitterly. "You may take pleasure in the knowledge that there is nothing you can do to me that is worse than the guilt I already bear."

His expression changed and they stared at each other, alone in their private hells. They had each done what they believed right—and it had brought them to this.

Duncan was the one to break the silence. "When will you release me?"

Tiredly she tried to see the shape of coming events. "You'll be freed in a few days, when the chaos from battle dies down. No more than a week."

"So you will have a few days' head start in your flight."
His eyes were like ancient ice. "When I am not bound by
iron, there is nowhere you can go that is far enough away
that I will not find you."

"At the moment, death would not be my enemy."
Gwynne left the cell, carefully locked the door behind
her, then slumped trembling against the rough stone wall
of the corridor. If she had refused the council's wish for
her to marry Duncan, she would still be safe and innocent
in England. She would have deplored the rebellion and
been concerned for the toll in human pain, but that concern would have been distant.

Instead, she'd seized her courage and married Duncan,
discovering power and passion together. They'd been so
happy. . . .

It would have been far easier to stand aside, to be a demure wife who wouldn't dream of opposing her husband. Then she wouldn't feel blood on her hands.

As she wearily climbed the narrow stairs to the main
level of the castle, her inner voice whispered, *You did the
right thing. If Duncan had interfered to allow the rebels
to escape, it would only have prolonged and increased
Scotland's suffering.*

Even that knowledge was no comfort.

Thirty-Five

*G*wynne, help us!"

Gwynne jerked from a dark, exhausted sleep, thinking her name had been called. But that was not a real voice, only part of a tortured dream.

Two and a half days had passed since the battle. News had reached the castle the day after the defeat in the form of a fleeing Jacobite lucky enough to have a horse. Gwynne couldn't bear hearing the horrible tales of the Hanoverian pursuit, which had included the slaughter of anyone wearing Highland dress. She had already seen the images in her scrying glass.

She gave orders that fugitives should be granted food and a brief rest before they moved on. Even that was a risk; if government troops found rebels at Dunrath, the castle and the glen would probably be razed, exactly as Maggie Macrae had dreamed.

"Gwynne, please, in the name of mercy!"

With cold shock, Gwynne recognized that the voice was real—Jean was using mind-touch, and from the clarity of the words, she must be very close. Thank God she was alive—but clearly in desperate trouble.

Gwynne jammed her feet into slippers and threw a

heavy robe around her nightgown before she grabbed a lamp and raced downstairs. Her clumsy fingers fumbled with the latch to the outside door before she managed to fling it open. She stepped outside—and by the ghostly light of a fitfully clouded moon, she saw that the court-yard was full of battered fugitives: several dozen men, and one woman.

Jean's horse carried two slumped figures, wounded men apparently. Jean herself was on foot, at the head of her ragged band. Her beautiful hair was tied back like a man's and she wore breeches as she stumbled forward. "Please, Gwynne. Help us." She swayed, staying upright by sheer will. "The government troops are no more than a few hours behind."

Gwynne darted down the steps and caught Jean in her arms before the girl collapsed. "How did you get this far, Jean? Most of the fugitives were cut down within a few miles of the battlefield."

Trembling, Jean rested her head on Gwynne's shoulder. "I took the wild paths through the hills. Whenever I sensed Butcher Cumberland's men approaching, I or-dered everyone off the road and masked them with don't-see spells. I don't know how I managed it." She looked up, her eyes pleading. "I know coming here is a danger to everyone in the glen, but I didn't know where else to go."

"That you made it this far is a miracle!"

Jean looked around. "Where is Duncan? I can't feel his presence."

"He's not here," Gwynne said vaguely as she scanned the fugitives. They stared at her with varying degrees of hope, exhaustion, and despair. Most seemed to be men of the glen. They knew as well as she the danger to Dunrath if she gave them sanctuary.

What should she do? In rough country, a don't-see spell

would be enough to conceal men that were fairly well hidden to start with. The glen was a very different matter. Even if men returned home and pretended never to have left, a search of the castle and crofts would turn them up quickly. Wounds and blood and ruined garments would make most of the rebels easily identifiable, with disastrous results for everyone else who lived in the glen.

Unless—might it be possible to conceal them in the dungeons with strong don't-see spells on the doors? Other spells would be required as well. Gwynne doubted that one mage had enough power for the work that would be required, and Jean was too exhausted to help. But Duncan's power combined with Gwynne's might be enough.

"Please, Gwynne," Jean whispered. "I canna bear to see more death."

Any lingering doubts vanished from Gwynne's mind. "This is the home of the Macraes of Dunrath. Of course they are welcome here."

"Mistress?"

Auld Donald's incredulous voice sounded from behind Gwynne. She turned to see him staring at the battered rebels.

"Our men have made it home safely, and we are going to hide them in the dungeons," she said calmly.

He frowned. "It's a great risk we'll all be taking."

"Yes, but we cannot turn them away," Gwynne replied. "Is there anyone in the glen who would turn rebels in to the government troops?"

"No," Donald and Jean said simultaneously. The steward added, "There were many that did not approve of the prince, but all will be loyal to our own."

Gwynne hoped the other two were right. After a moment of thinking about what must be done if they were to have a chance of success, she said, "Wake everyone in the castle. We'll need food and drink and blankets, and surely medical help as well. Also, it would help if the tracks can be obliterated so it won't be obvious that a large group of men has come here."

"I'll send a herd of cattle back along the northern road," Donald said. "That should do the job."

"Perfect!" Turning to the massed men, Gwynne raised her voice. "Come inside quickly now! I think we can keep you safe in the oldest section of the castle. Does anyone need help climbing the stairs?"

As weary men started up the front steps, Maggie Macrae called out, "Diarmid!" A plaid thrown around her nightgown and her feet bare, she raced down to the courtyard, risking a broken neck, and unerringly went to a slight figure that was supporting a more seriously wounded man.

Heedless of their filth, she wrapped her arms around both fugitives, tears running down her face. "Thanks be to God!" Forgetting that he was man enough to go to war, Diarmid embraced his mother, his shoulders shaking with sobs.

Allowing them privacy for their reunion, Gwynne began giving crisp orders to the servants and crofters who were pouring into the courtyard. She kept an arm around Jean for support, knowing the girl would not rest until her rebel band was under cover.

In the midst of the clamor of soldiers, Gwynne had a quiet moment to speak to Jean. "What about Robbie Mackenzie?"

Jean's face twisted. "He died leading his men in the final charge while that damned cowardly Italian fled the field!"

"You mean the prince?"

Jean spat. "He was a pretender indeed. He pretended to honor, to loyalty, to courage. All he wanted was power and glory for the Stuarts. I hope Cumberland finds him so he can be drawn and quartered."

Jean's anger burned through her fatigue. Grieving for the harsh shattering of the girl's idealism, Gwynne led her inside and up to the family quarters. "Your men are inside now, and we'll see that all are cared for. Now it's time for you to rest. Be sure to wash up before you go to bed. If government troops arrive, you might have to show yourself and pretend innocence."

Jean smiled without humor. "Gwynne, I carried a sword and rode with the men of Glen Rath on the field of battle. How can I deny that?"

Duncan had been right about his sister's courage. "You can't deny that you traveled with the army, but you can say that you were following your sweetheart, trying to persuade him to abandon the Jacobite madness and come home."

The younger woman hesitated. "I am loath to deny my beliefs and my men. Our loyalty and honor were true even if the Pretender was not worthy of it."

Gwynne caught her gaze. "Courage and honor need no defense—and they should not be the reason brave men are butchered. If I can lie to save their lives, so can you."

"When you put it that way, I suppose I can't refuse." She brushed at her tangled hair with unsteady fingers. "But what if someone recognized me on the battlefield?"

"If anyone claims to have seen you there, we'll laugh at the absurdity of the thought. All you have to do is appear in your most dainty, feminine gown and they'll be ashamed to have even suggested that you might have ridden into battle."

Jean gave the ghost of a laugh. "Though I hate to admit it, you're probably right."

"No man will want to believe that a small female is his equal in courage and skill. Now go." Gwynne gave her sister-in-law a gentle push into her bedroom before retreating to her own chamber to don a morning gown. She would not be getting any more sleep this night.

After changing, she descended to the dungeons and checked on how the fugitives were being settled. Auld Donald had remembered that on the east side of the castle there was a string of cells on the same corridor with a single door providing access. This meant that only that one door needed to be spelled, which improved their chances of success.

At the steward's order, bales of straw had been brought in and laid on the floors of the cells as primitive bedding. There were three or four men cramped into each cell, many of them already deep in the sleep of exhaustion.

As Gwynne inspected the cells, a gray-haired woman appeared in the corridor. "You would be Lady Dunrath. I'm Elizabeth Macrae, the healer." She gestured to a heavily laden young woman behind. "And this be my granddaughter, who assists me. Where are the most severely wounded?"

"Down here." Gwynne led the way to the far end of the corridor, where moans were least likely to be heard if the cellars were searched. "What else do you need?"

"Hot water, soap, and towels, and maybe more bandages." Rolling up her sleeves, Elizabeth Macrae knelt by a young man whose plaid was stiff with dried blood.

Gwynne left the healer and her granddaughter to their work and gave orders for the hot water and other supplies. To Maggie, she said, "We must bring everything into this area and have it sealed off by the time the pursuers arrive."

"Can you prevent the government troops from finding them?" Maggie asked, expression troubled.

"I think so. But I'll need Duncan's help."

"You'll be releasing him, then. That's good—he should not be ignorant of what is happening to his people under his very nose."

That was true, but Gwynne was not looking forward to having to face her husband. "I'm going to him now. I expect that our conversation will take some time, so you're in charge, Maggie Macrae. Make sure there is no trace of mud or dust or footprints in the great hall, and that there are no obvious gaps in the kitchen or linen closet. Also, the people who live to the north end of the glen should be sent home soon. If their crofts are empty, it will look suspicious to the Hanoverians."

Maggie smiled. "You've a good mind for deceit, Mistress."

"I hope it's good enough." Girding herself, Gwynne left the housekeeper and headed for Duncan's cell, which was at the opposite end of the castle from the rebel quarters, and luxurious by comparison.

By imprisoning him, she had sowed the wind. Now she would reap the whirlwind.

* * *

Something was wrong. Even with his power paralyzed, Duncan could feel that wrongness in his marrow. It was the middle of the night, and if he had to wait until Maggie Macrae brought him his bread and tea in the morning, he might go mad.

The key turned in the lock, and he spun around as the door opened to reveal his lady wife with a lamp in her hand. Even plainly dressed and with her enchantress aldure completely shielded, she was heartbreakingly desirable. He hated himself for wanting her. Harshly he asked, "What the hell is happening?"

"So even blocked by iron you can tell that something is wrong." She set the lamp on the table. "Jean has returned with most of the men of Glen Rath, including young Diarmid. She says the Hanoverians are in pursuit, so we're hiding the rebels down here."

He found that knowing what was happening did not make him any happier. "Are you trying to get us all killed? If they're found here, everyone in Glen Rath will be treated as a traitor!"

"I know. That's why I need your help to conceal them." A ghost of a smile showed on her face. "Don't look so shocked at my recklessness. You would not have turned them away, either."

She was right, of course. Damn her.

Gwynne produced the small key to the manacles. "I ask that you refrain from murdering me until Dunrath is safe."

"I'm surprised you're willing to risk your pretty neck for a pack of rebels," he said caustically. "Why not leave them to be butchered by Cumberland?"

She raised his right arm and unfastened the iron cuff. "The rising is over, and I'll not see men die pointlessly." She dropped the cuff onto the table and turned to his left wrist.

Grudgingly he knew that his remark was unfair, but it was hard to control his molten anger. He waited with bare patience as she struggled to unlock the manacle. When she finally removed it, he inhaled sharply as power blasted through him like a river that had shattered its dam. He welcomed the return greedily, but the sensation wasn't pleasant. His body and soul felt as if they had fallen asleep and were now coming back to needle-pointed life.

With impersonal gentleness, Gwynne pressed his shoulders so that he sat on the bed. He buried his head in his hands, shivering with reaction.

When he felt more or less in control of himself again, he raised his head. She was within his reach, but from the wariness in her eyes she would be prepared if he struck out at her. She needn't worry. Whatever revenge he might take could wait until the men of Glen Rath were safe. "What needs to be done?"

"All of the rebels are now in the cells of the eastern corridor. I'm hoping that our combined power can produce a don't-see spell strong enough to prevent the door to that corridor from being discovered even if there's a serious search."

He frowned. "Not enough—that spell just makes people want to look away. If several men are involved in the search, they are unlikely to be equally deceived. It will have to be a full-scale illusion spell, and pray that none of the searchers touches the surface and realizes that it feels like wood, not stone."

"Can you do an illusion spell? I've tried but without much success."

"I'm fairly good at them." Illusions were tiring because the mage needed to maintain them continually or they collapsed. He thought he could manage, though. "An illusion will have to do, since I gather there's no time for anything else. How far away are the Hanoverians? Have they camped for the night?"

"I'm not sure." She rubbed her forehead. "It's been so busy I haven't had time to check my scrying glass for their location."

"Well, check it now!"

She pulled out the glass and settled her mind, then azed into the smoky obsidian with half-focused eyes. They've camped for the night perhaps three miles north f the glen. It's a sizable troop of horse soldiers—at least wo dozen, perhaps more. If Jean and her men hadn't narched through the night, they would have been overaken this morning."

"Rain will slow them down in the morning."

"You have recovered enough strength to conjure a torm?" Gwynne asked, looking hopeful.

Not answering, he turned to one of the slit windows, nhaling the damp night air as he began exploring the ky. In April, rain was never very far away, and he found ain over the Hebrides and a howling storm near the Orkneys. Luxuriating in his ability to shape the winds gain, he called them to him, adding the heavy moisture lready in the sky over Glen Rath. In mere minutes the irst drops of rain began falling, and the weather magic leansed some of the anger from his soul.

Turning from the window, he said, "The rain will increase steadily. By dawn, a major storm will be soaking ur government troopers. The fugitives' tracks should be nostly eliminated."

"Auld Donald sent a herd of cattle along the route. Beween hooves and rain, it will be impossible to track anyne to the castle."

Duncan nodded approval. Clever of Donald to have hought of that. "North of the glen, there are several trails eading in different directions. With luck, the Hanoverins won't be able to tell which way Jean was traveling."

"Even with the weather to slow them down, they'll urely be here by early afternoon." Gwynne frowned. "If 'm pretending to be a good Whig, I'll have to offer them ospitality for the night."

He scowled. "I don't think I can be civil to them."

"You won't have to. I've worked out a few good lies, think."

As Gwynne explained, he had to admit that her pla▶ was good. But nothing she said or did would ever tak◀ away the deep wounds of her betrayal.

Thirty-Six

The maid Annie entered the morning room and bobbed a curtsey. "Mistress, a group of government soldiers has arrived, and the commanding officer, Colonel Ormond, would like to speak with you."

Gwynne tried to steady her accelerating heartbeat as the news she had waited for was delivered. She laid down the quill she had been using to write a letter to Lady Bethany—a letter that contained nothing significant, only the kind of domestic chitchat one would expect two aristocratic ladies to exchange. Quite innocent if a suspicious officer chose to read it.

The fugitives, the healers, and Duncan were hidden safely behind the illusion spell. The rest of the inhabitants of Glen Rath were going about their normal business and ready to claim ignorance about any possible Jacobites in the glen. Keeping a secret among so many people was problematic. It would be nice if there was a spell that could be cast over the glen to remind people what to say and how to seem convincing, but magic had its limits. This situation required the help of a higher force.

Gwynne glanced up with her blandest expression.

"How nice to have a diversion. Pray escort Colonel Ormond here and bring refreshments. If he has been traveling in this dreadful weather, he is surely in need of something warming."

"Indeed, Lady Ballister, I should be most grateful for that." The masculine voice belonged to a scarlet-coated officer in the doorway. He'd followed the maid, perhaps hoping to catch the lady of the household in suspicious activity. Tall and weathered, Colonel Ormond had a long face and ramrod posture despite his saturated leather boots and dripping wig.

Gwynne rose from her dainty inlaid desk. Today she wore a wide panniered gown better suited to a London drawing room than the Highlands, plus an elaborate, heavily curled and powdered wig. She hoped she looked too English to be a Jacobite.

As she glided toward the door, she took a reading on the officer's character. Nearing forty, he was an honorable and experienced soldier who had hated the atrocities against civilians after the battle. He would not flinch from doing his duty, but neither would he look for excuses to make arrests. Good.

"Welcome to Dunrath," she said warmly. "After this long, horrid winter, you cannot imagine how glad I am to see a civilized face."

The colonel bowed politely. As he straightened and looked into her face, he blurted out, "Lady Brecon! What are you doing in Scotland?" His expression showed both recognition and stunned admiration.

She must have met him somewhere in London. Yes, years ago at some grand ball. They had danced, unmemorably, but he must be wellborn to move in such elevated circles. "It's good to see you again, Colonel. I am Lady Ballister now. My dear Brecon died two years ago.

never thought to marry a barbarian Scot, but Ballister quite swept me off my feet last summer." She laughed wryly. "I picked a poor time to move to the north, I fear."

"Yet the north agrees with you, Lady Ballister."

"You flatter me, sir," she said with a hint of reproof in her voice. He needed to think of her as a virtuous woman. The sort who wouldn't hide rebels in her cellar.

A deeper insight into Ormond entered her mind. He was recently married to a young beauty, and he needed to believe that a beautiful wife could be virtuous even when her husband was away for months on end. Instantly Gwynne adjusted her enchantress power so that the colonel would perceive her as a faithful and loving wife— the kind of woman he most approved of.

She could feel his subtle reaction to the change in her energy. He still admired her, but accepted her as a chaste married woman, the kind deserving protection. Glancing around, he said, "Most of the Scottish castles I've seen are stark fortresses, but here in Dunrath's private apartments, I can imagine myself in England."

"I am not the first English bride brought to Dunrath, so the Macraes have created an oasis of civilization." Gwynne hoped that also implied that the family had plenty of English blood and would have no Jacobite leanings.

Glancing past the colonel, Gwynne made a little shooing motion with one hand. "The refreshments, Annie. And make sure the colonel's men are invited into the great hall and served something warm. 'Tis not fit for man nor beast out there."

When the maid was gone, Gwynne sank onto the sofa with a luxurious flounce of silk skirts. "I swear, these local servants are in a fair way to driving me mad. They simply have no concept of their proper place. Pray sit, Colonel, and tell me all the news."

He took a chair opposite her. "The news is good, as I'm sure you've heard."

"This horrid rebellion! I seriously considered returning to London, but I could not bear to be driven from my home by that foolish Italian adventurer." She smoothed a wrinkle from her skirts. "It's such a relief to know that the fighting is over. They say that Cumberland has crushed the Jacobites at a great battle near Inverness. Is that so?"

"He did indeed, Lady Ballister, but the rebellion won't be over until every last Jacobite has been rooted out of the Highlands."

Annie entered with a tea tray that included a small flask of whiskey and food substantial enough to appeal to a hungry soldier. Gwynne poured tea, then raised the flask over the officer's cup. "Colonel Ormond?"

After a moment of hesitation, he said, "That would be most welcome, ma'am."

She added a healthy dose of whiskey before passing him the cup. "If you are rooting out Jacobites, what brings you to Dunrath? We are all good Whigs here."

He swallowed half his tea in two thirsty gulps before bracing himself to say, "Does that include Miss Jean Macrae? It's widely known that she raised a company of rebels and personally led them to the Pretender, and that she stayed with the rebel army till the end. It is even said that she was seen on the battlefield carrying a sword."

"How deliciously the truth can be twisted!" Gwynne said with indulgent amusement. "Yes, Jean did travel to the rebel army despite my pleas for her to stay here in safety. She's a headstrong girl who has been raised here in the wilds, and she won't listen to reason, but she's no Jacobite. Now that the rising has been put down, I really must take her to London so she can acquire some polish."

"Being a woman will not save her from being charged as a rebel," he said bluntly. "If even half the stories about her are true, she will be tried and transported. Or . . . worse."

Gwynne didn't have to pretend to shudder at the thought. "I can't deny that she acted foolishly, but she didn't run away to the rebel army because she was a Jacobite sympathizer. She simply wanted to be with her betrothed, Robbie Mackenzie of Fannach. I only met the boy once. He seemed a pleasant youth except for his foolish politics. I begged Jean to break her betrothal, but she was sure that she could persuade him to abandon the rebels and return home."

"What of the troop of men she raised for the prince?" Ormond said skeptically.

"That must be a rumor created because the truth is uninteresting. A mere girl could hardly journey alone across Scotland, so she traveled with a group of volunteers who were heading to the army." Gwynne bit her lip as if troubled. "Though I hate to admit it, there were two or three men of Glen Rath in that group. My husband and I did our best to stamp out rebellious talk, but there are always a few hotheads."

"Have those hotheads returned to the glen?"

"Not that I know of." She sighed. "Perhaps they died during the campaign. That might be for the best since there would be no future for them here. The Pretender is not popular in Glen Rath, Colonel."

"Yet he called here at the castle, I'm told, not long after he landed in Scotland."

Ormond was dangerously well informed. "The night Ballister and I returned from England, he walked into the middle of the welcome-home celebration and tried to enlist my husband's support. We were amazed, but I suppose that adventurers must be bold. Ballister refused and sent him away, of course."

"It might have been better for all concerned if your husband had taken the prince prisoner," he said dryly.

Gwynne shrugged gracefully. "Hospitality is sacred in the Highlands. It's an ancient custom, necessary in a harsh land. It is unthinkable that Ballister would behave dishonorably to a guest, even an uninvited one. Would you, Colonel?"

Ormond grimaced. "No, I suppose not. At least not all those months ago, before there was a real rebellion. But if I saw the prince now, I'd capture him in a heartbeat. He deserves to pay the price for the havoc he has caused."

"I couldn't agree more." Gwynne could feel that the colonel's skepticism was fading. She glanced at the window and saw that Duncan had stopped the rain and sunshine was breaking through the clouds. With luck, she would feed Ormond a few more lies and he would be ready to go on his way.

"Miss Macrae might not have been a Jacobite when she left Dunrath," Ormond said, "but if she fought in battle with the rebel army, she must have become one."

Gwynne laughed again. "Absurd! Jean is the merest slip of a girl. Besides, she was here during the battle. She returned home five days ago, having finally despaired of changing her betrothed's mind."

"You say she's here at Dunrath?" Ormond said, startled.

"Yes. Tired and very sad, of course, but safe. It's hard

to be angry with her after all she has suffered. Do you wish to speak with her?" After the colonel nodded, Gwynne rang for the maid and gave orders for Jean to be summoned.

While they waited, Ormond said, "What of Ballister? There have also been rumors that he is a Jacobite sympathizer."

Gwynne arched her brows with a hint of contempt. "Is he also supposed to have gone into battle with the Jacobites? I assure you, Colonel Ormond, my husband was nowhere near Inverness."

"Then where was he, ma'am?" Ormond's eyes narrowed. "A man who fit his description was observed in the vicinity of the rebels during their invasion of England. It has been suggested that Ballister was acting as a scout for the rebel troops."

It was time for another major lie. "I will be honest with you, Colonel Ormond. Though a loyal servant of the Crown, it grieved my husband greatly to see his homeland torn by rebellion. At my urging, he did indeed travel to England, though certainly not as a Jacobite scout. He had business there, and being away from Scotland was less painful for him. He also took with him several young men of the glen. Not rebels, you understand, but high-spirited youths who might have been tempted to join in that Jacobite nonsense if not diverted."

"Is that why there seemed to be few young men as we rode through the glen?"

The colonel was perceptive. Gwynne said, "Yes, we packed off as many of them as possible. Several lads from Glen Rath are serving with the government forces." Which was even true. "Better for them to be busy and interested somewhere else than to stay here and be preyed on by troublemakers."

"Ingenious," the colonel said thoughtfully. "Young men are like tinder, and it is well not to expose them to fiery ideas. Has Ballister returned to Dunrath?"

"No, but I hope he will be home soon." Gwynne smiled wistfully. "It was hard for us to separate when we were so newly wed, but people of rank must take responsibility for our dependents." Most of the Macraes of Glen Rath would have been outraged at being called dependents, but the colonel nodded approvingly. With luck, after he spoke with Jean he would be ready to continue his pursuit elsewhere.

Gwynne refreshed their teacups and was urging the colonel to eat more when the door opened and Jean entered the morning room. Gwynne mentally applauded. Hair powdered and wearing a pale silk gown with lacy trailing sleeves, Jean appeared delicate, ladylike, and about sixteen years old.

Eyes downcast, she swept the colonel a deep curtsey as Gwynne performed the introductions. Ormond stared incredulously, obviously unable to reconcile the description of a warrior maiden with this fragile, demure young lady.

"Jean, sit down beside me," Gwynne said soothingly as she poured another cup of tea. "I know this will be difficult, but Colonel Ormond must ask you some questions."

The officer cleared his throat, uncomfortable at asking hard questions of a girl barely out of the schoolroom. "Miss Macrae, you are accused of raising a troop of men from Dunrath and joining the Jacobites. It is even said that you fought on Drummossie Moor and escaped with a group of rebels. These are very grave charges."

Jean raised her head and stared at him with great, startled eyes. "Me, a mere woman, lead a band of soldiers?

What a bizarre thought! I did go to the Jacobites, but that was to join my sweetheart, Robbie Mackenzie. I . . . I had hoped to persuade him to return home and marry me before it was too late."

"Lady Ballister said that you returned home almost a week ago. If so, you might not have heard that your young man died in the battle." Ormond delivered the news gently, but his gaze was shrewd as he watched Jean.

"Dear God in heaven, no!" Jean began to sob. "I dreamed he would be killed but I prayed I was wrong. Oh, Gwynne!" She cast herself into her sister-in-law's embrace, her body shaking with sobs as she channeled her genuine grief into her performance.

"Be strong, my dear," Gwynne said with compassion as real as the girl's misery.

Uncomfortable with making a young lady cry, Ormond said, "Captain Mackenzie fought bravely, Miss Macrae. I hope that is some comfort to you and his family."

Jean raised her head, tears blurring her small face. "It is no comfort at all! He gave his life for that . . . that vile Italian mountebank! My Robbie was worth a thousand Stuarts. If he had to die, I wish he had chosen a cause worthy of his courage."

Her furious words were more convincing than any number of calm disclaimers. Looking shaken, Ormond said gravely, "I . . . see, Miss Macrae. You have my sympathies on your loss. I am sorry if I have upset you with groundless accusations."

Jean pulled a handkerchief from her sleeve to blot her eyes. "You must do your duty, Colonel," she said with a heartbreaking attempt to smile. "Scotland is in chaos now. We must all cooperate to restore peace." That, too, had the ring of truth.

Thinking that the colonel was well and truly convinced of their innocence, Gwynne said, "Have some tea, my dear. It will steady your nerves."

At that moment the door swung open to reveal another red-coated officer, accompanied by a roughly dressed local man. Jean made a barely audible hissing sound when she saw the new arrivals.

Gwynne was more concerned by the officer. Where Ormond was a reasonable, honorable man, this newcomer liked blood. He had wallowed in it recently, too—she could feel a miasma of death and pain around him. He had enjoyed slaughtering fugitives. Worse, he had a faint spark of power and would not be easy to deceive. A good thing he was the subordinate, not the commander, because his glance slid over Gwynne with unmistakable insolence. There was nothing gentlemanly about his admiration.

The colonel rose. "Have the men refreshed themselves, Major Huxley? Now that the rain has stopped, we must be on our way to find that band of Jacobites. Apparently they turned off before entering Glen Rath."

"Not according to this fellow," Huxley said tersely. "Say your piece to the colonel, Geddes."

The shabby man shuffled forward, his bonnet in his hands. "I hear ye be paying for information."

"If the information is good," Ormond replied. "What do you know?"

Gwynne whispered to Jean, "Who is he?"

"A good-for-nothing tinker who wanders through this part of Scotland selling rubbish and stealing when he can get away with it," Jean said grimly. "I should have thought of Geddes when you asked if anyone here would betray our own. He is not one of us, but he comes by often enough. Too often, in this case."

If Geddes was a "foreigner," his accent said he was still a Scot. Whatever his origins, he radiated untrustworthiness and opportunism. To the colonel, he said, "Last night late I saw a band of rebels come into the glen on the north road."

"That's nonsense," Gwynne said calmly. "Ask this creature how much whiskey he put away last night."

Geddes's head swung around to her, his bloodshot eyes gleaming maliciously. "I know what I saw, and it was 'er over there leading 'em." He pointed a filthy finger at Jean. "She's one of Charlie's whores, I hear. I followed 'em, and the whole lot marched right up into this castle, and they ain't come out again."

"I see." Ormond's energy shifted from gentlemanly consideration to flinty soldier. "Some of my men are already searching the glen, and now we must search the castle as well, Lady Ballister." He studied Jean more closely, clearly wondering if she was what she appeared to be.

Biting back her fear and frustration, Gwynne said calmly, "Of course you must investigate any such accusations, Colonel. Even if they're nonsense." Her glance at Geddes was contemptuous. "But I wish my husband were here to teach that creature a lesson for the insult to my sister-in-law. How *dare* he suggest a . . . a liaison between Jean and the Pretender!"

"As you said earlier, rumor sometimes embellishes the boring truth," Ormond said, clearly wishing he were somewhere else.

"Geddes might be confused about some things," the major said, "but he gave an accurate description of a troop of rebels sneaking into the glen. More accurate than one would expect of a drunken sot."

Geddes looked mildly offended, but not enough to

protest when there was money in view. Looking harassed, the colonel said, "I appreciate your cooperation, Lady Ballister. Not everyone would accept this . . . difficult situation with such grace."

"Dunrath has nothing to hide." Gwynne was almost embarrassed at how well she was lying. The desire to protect her own was a powerful motivator. "I shall accompany you on your search, since I know the castle better than you. Though I still do not know it all! This is an ancient and confusing place."

Ormond's brows drew together. "This will be a dirty, tedious business, ma'am. No place for a lady, much less one in such a fine gown."

"Never let it be said I have shirked my duty," she said firmly.

"You are an example to all ladies," Huxley said with what sounded like an undertone of mockery.

As Gwynne had thought, he was not easily fooled, but she inclined her head graciously as if she took his praise at face value. To Jean, she said, "You go and lie down, dear, there is nothing to worry about."

"As you wish, Gwynne." Though Jean's gaze said she wanted to do more, she accepted that it was best for her to be as meek and compliant as possible. She curtsied to the officers. "Gentlemen, I bid you good day."

After Jean withdrew, Gwynne asked, "Do you have a preferred place to begin searching? A good housekeeper starts at the top and works her way down, since that is the direction that dust travels."

The colonel smiled, glad for her good humor. "Then we shall begin in the attics."

As Gwynne led the way, she examined the colonel's emotional energy. He wanted to believe that she and Jean and Dunrath were innocent. They would be safe enough, as long as the government troops found no trace of the rebels.

But heaven help them if Major Huxley found anything suspicious.

Thirty-Seven

A dozen cells lined the dank old corridor. Duncan had commandeered the one closest to the door that led to the rest of the cellars. Nearness made it easier to maintain the illusion that disguised the door so that possible searchers would see only rough stone. For now the illusion took only a modest amount of power. He would strengthen the spell if anyone approached.

The cells were quiet, most of the men still in exhausted sleep as they recovered from their long march through rough country. Jean had pushed them hard, and they had been tired and hungry even before the battle. He was proud that his sister had walked the whole way with her men, using her horse for the most gravely wounded. She had the soul of a warrior.

Yet despite the near-absolute quiet of the corridor, the atmosphere thrummed with tension. There wasn't a single man who didn't know that government troops were in the castle, and what would happen if the rebels were discovered.

As he waited, Duncan had used his restored power and scrying glass to scan the battle and its aftermath. The horror of what he found renewed his rage at his wife. Damn Gwynne for imprisoning him! He could have changed the outcome of the battle and spared the survivors from pointless slaughter. Despite his allegiance to the uprising, he was still Guardian enough that he would have protected the Hanoverians if they had been the ones fleeing in panic. Hundreds, perhaps thousands, of lives would have been saved.

Gwynne would burn in hell for what she had done.

But for now, they were grudging allies in their desire to protect the people of the glen. He monitored her interview with the colonel, and almost laughed aloud when Jean entered looking like a fragile, helpless English girl. Gwynne had been wise to suggest that Jean appear rather than hide in the dungeons. No one who saw his sister in her present garb would believe what a Highland spitfire she was.

The interview seemed to be going well, and with the sunshine Duncan had provided, the colonel looked ready to set off again rather than spend the night. Good. Duncan was still fatigued from his iron bondage, and the combination of weather-working, scrying, and maintaining an illusion were rapidly draining his power. The sooner the soldiers left, the better.

Once they were gone, Duncan would sleep like the weary rebels. The next morning was soon enough to decide what the devil to do with Gwynne.

Even when he was at his most furious, he had known in his heart that he could never bring himself to hurt her, but her betrayal had irrevocably destroyed the fragile trust that was the bedrock of any marriage. Even thinking of how she had lured him home only to imprison him caused his anger to rise.

She must leave Dunrath as soon as possible. A pity that

the legal bonds of matrimony could not be severed as easily as the emotional bonds had been.

He was yawning when the scene in the scrying glass changed. One—no, two—men entered the morning room.

One was an army major, the other—Duncan swore when he recognized Geddes. The filthy tinker would only show up if there was money or trouble to be made, preferably both.

The bastard must have seen Jean and her men the previous night, because the amiable scene in the scrying glass changed to tension. Jean went to her chamber, Geddes was taken to the great hall to be watched under guard, and Gwynne and the officers began searching the castle, starting with the attics. Good, they would be tired by the time they reached the dungeons.

Dozens of rebels couldn't be hidden in a wardrobe, so the search didn't go into every box and drawer, but the Hanoverians kept a sharp eye out for anything suspicious. A good thing Duncan had been able to slow them down with heavy rain. Without those extra hours, Dunrath wouldn't have had time to conceal all traces of the fugitives.

From their postures, Duncan could tell that the colonel liked and respected Gwynne. The major was another matter. He was a hound hot on the chase, and he would show no mercy to any prey he cornered.

When the search party finally approached the stairs, Duncan wearily mustered his remaining power. Conjuring storms was easy for him. Knowing all that stood between Dunrath and disaster was a frail illusion was quite another matter.

* * *

Though Gwynne knew the search was going quickly, every moment seemed an eternity. Playing a charming, frivolous English lady was hard work. Even when she lived in England, she hadn't been much good at this, and today the stakes were frighteningly high.

Once they reached the cellars, she led them through every dusty little chamber and passage and storage room, including numerous dead ends. She hoped that the soldiers would become disoriented enough that they wouldn't realize they had missed a section of this level. When their winding search brought them back to the bottom of the stairs, Gwynne shook dust from her gown with a moue of distaste. "I trust you are satisfied, gentlemen. You've now seen all of Dunrath, and nary a Jacobite to be found."

She was starting up the stairs when Major Huxley said, "I believe we haven't seen all of the cellars yet, Lady Ballister." Though his words were polite, the lamp he held showed a sardonic glint in his eyes. Unlike Ormond, he didn't accept her innocent Whig lady performance at face value.

"Perhaps you are right," Gwynne said indifferently. "A pity my husband isn't here to guide you. I don't pretend to know every twist and turn in this beastly place. Because of the rats, I come down here very seldom."

When she mentioned the rats, a movement in the shadows made her heart jump. She relaxed when she recognized Lionel. Was he hunting vermin, or watching over her like the familiar Duncan jokingly claimed he was? Whatever the reason, she was vaguely comforted by the cat's presence.

"This way, ma'am." The major set off to the far side of the cellars, picking his way through the maze of passages with unnerving sureness. When they reached the junction that led to cells on both sides, he turned right, in the direction where Duncan had been imprisoned. Gwynne followed uneasily, the colonel behind her. Duncan's well-furnished cell would arouse questions, and that couldn't be good.

They walked along the row of cells, the major opening each door and glancing in to see the bleak, empty interiors. Gwynne's pulse accelerated as they approached the end of the passageway. Huxley opened the final door and looked inside. "Interesting."

She moved forward to peer around him, concealing her sigh of relief. The cell still had the wooden cot and it was relatively clean, but the other furniture, books, and carpet had been removed. The major stepped inside and studied the interior closely. "This shows signs of recent occupation."

Gwynne shrugged. "Sometimes a cell is needed to lock up some drunken rascal."

Huxley frowned, his intuition probably telling him there was more to the story, but there were no rebels here now. Impatience in his voice, Colonel Ormond said, "We've searched the castle top to bottom and found nothing. It's time we returned to the road. If we leave soon, we can be out of the glen before nightfall."

"We still haven't seen everything on this level," Huxley said stubbornly. "I have been making a mental map and one area is missing. Back this way."

They retraced their steps to the junction with the passage that led back to the stairs. When they had come through originally, the officers hadn't noticed the short spur of passage ahead because Gwynne had laid a strong don't-see spell on it. Coming from this direction and with the major suspicious, the spell lost its effectiveness.

"This is the way—we missed it earlier," Huxley said, eyes glittering. "There should be another corridor just around this corner. . . ."

"I don't think so," Gwynne remarked. "The castle is built on solid rock, you know, and the cellars are fitted in around the stone. The cellar area is smaller than the floors above, and more irregular in shape."

Ignoring her, Huxley rounded the corner and stopped, the flickering lamp illuminating a stub of corridor less than a dozen feet long. Gwynne caught her breath. Earlier, when Duncan had created the illusion spell, her mage vision had simultaneously showed her both the illusion and the underlying door.

Now all she saw was a grimy stone wall, as crude and ancient as the other walls down here. Only with serious effort could she vaguely sense the door under the illusion. It was easier to feel Duncan. He was standing just on the other side of the door and pouring energy into the illusion spell. She wondered how long he could keep the illusion this strong. Not very, she guessed.

Ormond said brusquely, "We have reached the end of our search, Major. It's time for us to get on with our mission."

The colonel turned and disappeared around the corner, heading to the stairs, but Huxley remained, frowning at the wall, the spark of power in his spirit unsatisfied. "There's something wrong here," he muttered. "Maybe a priest hole."

He stepped forward, and Gwynne realized with sinking fear that he was going to touch the "stone" wall, seeking a hidden lever that would open to a hidden room. When he felt wood, he would no longer see the illusion. She must stop him.

When in doubt, rely on one's most powerful gift, and for Gwynne, that was enchantress power. Softly she said, "Major Huxley?"

When he glanced back at her, she blasted him with every iota of sexual allure she possessed. She was the personification of desire, Eve and Cleopatra, Aphrodite and Morgan le Fay. With a single glance, she could ignite a man's deepest, fiercest desires.

Huxley caught his breath and a pulse began hammering in his throat as lust blazed through him. "Yes . . . ," he breathed. "I knew you weren't the prude you pretended to be. You were just waiting for a chance to be alone with me. You're in luck, my lady. There's just enough time to give you a quick taste of what you want."

Setting his lamp on the floor, he closed the distance between them with a single stride. His embrace slammed her against the wall and his tongue invaded her mouth, gagging her. She panicked at the swift violence of his response, frantic to strike him with a defensive spell, yet knowing if she did she would reveal her power.

He fumbled with his breeches, then yanked her skirts up and groped between her legs, seeking entrance with the skill of a man experienced in swift, illicit lust. With horror, she realized he was so crazed that he had no awareness beyond the moment, no fear of consequences. He could ravish her before Ormond noticed they weren't following.

She felt a blaze of rage behind the disguised door and knew that Duncan had recognized what was happening. As his fury scalded through the passage, the illusion wavered and she heard him jam the key into the lock to open the door from the other side. Dear God, if he came out to attack Huxley they were all doomed!

Praying that a defense spell could be used without alerting Huxley to her power, she mentally cried, *"Don't!"* to Duncan, then began to create a spell that might save her without arousing lethal suspicions.

A crackle of wild energy snapped around her and a feline scream echoed from the stone walls. Lionel leaped on the major's shoulder with snarling fangs and ripping claws. As he sank his teeth into the man's ear, his wildcat claws stabbed into unprotected flesh and dark blood spurted upward.

"Jesus Christ Almighty!" Huxley staggered back, breaking off the obscene kiss.

Gwynne screamed, the terror in her voice heart-stoppingly authentic. In the small sane part of her mind, she saw that the stone wall illusion had stabilized, so Duncan had mastered his instinctive fury.

An instant later the colonel appeared. Appalled, he hurled Huxley to the floor. "God *damn* you, sir! How dare you assault a lady in her own home!" He whipped out his sword and placed the tip at the other man's throat.

Huxley stared up at his commanding officer, shocked and disoriented. He knew what he had done, knew he had been caught in the act, but he could no longer understand why he had behaved as he did. "I . . . I didn't mean . . . *Aiieee!*"

He shrieked as Lionel jumped on his arm, simultaneously biting and kicking with his powerful clawed hindquarters.

"Lionel!" Gwynne swooped the cat into her arms, mentally trying to sooth him before he shredded her. To the officers, she said, "My cat is . . . is very protective. When Major Huxley assaulted me, Lionel jumped on his back."

"A small but fierce defender," the colonel said. "Are you hurt, Lady Ballister?"

She shook her head, her shakiness genuine. "No, Lionel's attack gave me the chance to cry for help. Thank God you were near, Colonel Ormond."

"I didn't attack the bitch!" Huxley said furiously. "She wanted me!"

"Don't lie to me!" The colonel pressed his sword and blood appeared on the major's throat. "I'll see you hanged for this. You're a disgrace to His Majesty's army!"

Gwynne brushed her hair back with a trembling hand. She had distracted attention from the illusory wall, but Duncan would not be able to maintain the illusion at this strength for much longer. She must get the royalist officers away. And what was she to do about Huxley? He was a filthy swine, but Gwynne was too much a Guardian to let him die for an assault she had deliberately provoked.

Voice unsteady, she continued, "I don't think the major would have attacked me if you hadn't all been so hard-pressed for days on end. Perhaps in the poor light, he misinterpreted something I said or did."

Ormond frowned, and she knew he was thinking about his wife and what he would do to any man who assaulted her. "Are you saying that you don't want him punished?" he asked.

She drew a shuddering breath. "I don't want him hanged. Just . . . just get him away from me. And don't allow him alone with any other female of any age."

For a long moment, the colonel's expression reflected his desire to slit Huxley's throat. But he was an honorable man. Reluctantly he sheathed his sword. "You should fall on your knees and thank God for her ladyship's mercy, Huxley."

Sullenly the major got to his feet, keeping a wary eye on Gwynne and the tail-lashing cat in her arms. "This was just a misunderstanding, I swear it, Colonel Ormond."

"I wish I were sure of that." Ormond scowled. "You're a decent officer and I need you. If you get through the rest of this campaign with a blameless record—and that means you won't raise a hand to any woman or child, even if they are wearing Highland dress—I will allow this matter to drop. Is that satisfactory, Lady Ballister?"

She nodded. "If my ordeal spares the life of some poor woman without a man like you nearby to protect her, my suffering will not have been in vain."

Her speech was melodramatic, but the colonel liked the idea of himself as protector as much as he admired Gwynne for her Christian charity. To Huxley, he said, "Apologize to this good lady, and then get out of her sight."

Though the major sensed he had been deceived, he didn't understand how. But he was no fool, and he knew he must take advantage of Gwynne's forbearance before she or the colonel changed their minds. "I'm deeply sorry, Lady Ballister," he said stiffly. "I don't know what came over me. There isn't much light here, and . . . and for a moment I was sure that you wanted me. Wanted me bad, your husband being away and all."

Ormond spat on the floor. "You don't know virtue when you see it, Major." But the explanation was one he could understand, which meant he wouldn't wonder about the incident in the future. "Now come along."

Gwynne glanced over her shoulder as the three of them

left. They were just in time, because the illusion was beginning to shimmer from Duncan's fatigue. Silently she sent the message *We're safe. Rest now, my husband.*

For an instant their minds touched, and she sensed from him despair so deep it shadowed the whole world. His emotions gave her a visceral understanding of how impossible it would be to mend the mortal wound to their marriage.

Aching, she touched his mind for the last time. *I'm sorry,* mo cridhe. *So, so sorry.*

Then she walked away, cradling her cat in her arms and glad she had an excuse for the tears in her eyes.

Thirty-Eight

*A*fter the royalist troops left, Gwynne wanted nothing more than to go to her room and sleep, but that was no longer possible after touching Duncan's mind. The sooner she left Dunrath, the better. Her husband was sleeping in his hidden cell, worn out by his iron imprisonment and all the power he had expended to protect the castle. She must be gone before he woke.

She went to her room, forcing her tired mind to decide what to take. It wouldn't be much since she would go on horseback. She rang for her maid. Annie appeared, beaming but a little wary, as if unsure how grand her mistress would be. "That was a miracle, the way those officers couldn't find our men. You baffled them well, Mistress."

Gwynne pulled off her wig and shook out her own hair. "I had much help. Will you unlace this blasted gown, then bring my saddlebags from the attic?"

Glad to have her familiar mistress back, the girl undid the laces, then sped off to the attics, so excited by the glen's narrow escape that she didn't bother to question why saddlebags were needed. Gwynne changed into her simplest riding habit, then went up to the library to retrieve the projects she had been working on. The half-dozen volumes of notes and essays were the only things at Dunrath that were truly hers.

Back in her room, she packed the books into the waiting saddlebags, adding another gown, a set of undergarments, and basic toiletries in the remaining space. Then she stripped off the ruby ring of Isabel de Cortes and set it on her dressing table. That ring belonged to the mistress of the glen, which Gwynne was no more.

She meant to take nothing from Dunrath but the horse that would carry her away, but when she pulled the scrying glass from its hidden pocket, she found herself unable to set it on the table. Her fingers literally locked around the obsidian disk, refusing to release. Her initial confusion dissolved into a sense of peace. The glass also was hers, and it carried Isabel's blessing.

She was about to pick up her saddlebags when Jean entered, not bothering to knock. Though she still wore her stylish gown and powdered hair, there was nothing fragile or girlish about her. Her expression was as hard as the granite of the Scottish hills. Her gaze flicked to the saddlebags, then back to Gwynne's face. "Well done. You managed to save every rebel in the glen, and probably the glen itself."

"It was all of us working together. You did a splendid turn as a helpless young girl, and Duncan's illusion was amazing."

"Ah, yes, Duncan. My brother who meant to save our troops at Drummrossie Moor, but was imprisoned by his beloved wife. Maggie Macrae told me all about it." Jean's hands clenched into fists. "If you hadn't interfered, Robbie might be alive now."

Gwynne sighed. "Perhaps he would. It's impossible to know."

"Why did you do it, Gwynne?" Jean cried, her voice breaking. "What right did you have to prevent Duncan from helping the rebel soldiers escape?"

"I had the right of a dedicated Guardian charged with stopping a renegade," Gwynne said softly. "Duncan started with small interventions to keep the armies apart. He progressed to open partisanship. Ask him, if you will, what he did to aid the Jacobite victory at Falkirk." She had found a vivid image of that in his mind just before she imprisoned him. "He said that he intended to intervene in the final battle only if necessary to preserve the rebel troops so they could retreat. That was an illegal intervention in itself. Worse was the likelihood that in the heat and rage of battle he might have used his whirlwind to destroy the Hanoverians. Would you have condoned him killing royal soldiers for doing their duty?"

Jean's gaze faltered, but she didn't retreat. "If he had done so, how would that be different from Adam Macrae using his power to devastate the Spanish Armada?"

"Sir Adam's tempest was a defensive action against an invading army. Duncan involved himself in a civil war, which is a very different matter." Gwynne hesitated, then decided Jean needed to hear the whole story. "It wasn't only that Duncan was breaking his Guardian oath. For many months I have been having nightmare visions that showed a Jacobite victory having catastrophic long-term results for all of Britain."

Jean frowned. "What kind of catastrophe?"

"I don't know the details. Only that there were rivers of blood that affected people from Cornwall to the most distant of the Hebrides."

"So on the basis of your opinion, you stopped Duncan from saving his people!"

"He had become more Scot than Guardian, and the price of his partisanship would have been unimaginably high," Gwynne said quietly. "You yourself have lost your faith in Prince Charles Edward. As a Guardian, can you honestly say that Britain would have been better off with a Stuart restoration?"

Jean hesitated, her eyes going out of focus as she sought the answer inwardly. She returned to the present with anguished eyes. "I wish to God that I could slit my wrists and drain every drop of Guardian blood from my veins." Spinning on her heel, she left without saying good-bye.

So Jean, having been disillusioned by the prince, now recognized that the Stuart path would have been wrong. The knowledge afforded Gwynne no pleasure.

Sliding one arm under the saddlebags, she made her way down the back steps, stopping in the kitchen for provisions before she went outside to the stables. The castle was quiet in the wake of the visit by the Hanoverian soldiers, and Gwynne also used a don't-look spell so she would not be noticed. She didn't think she could bear talking to anyone else today.

Sheba was full of energy and ready for a ride. After saddling the mare and strapping on the bags, Gwynne walked the horse outside and mounted. She was about to set off when she heard, *"Mrrowwrrrr!"*

She glanced down to see Lionel crouching in the courtyard by the horse. He had run off after they left the cellars, but now he had found her again. "I'm sorry, I must go, Lionel." She wiped her eyes, thinking how much she would miss him even though he wasn't her familiar.

"*Mrrowp!*" He sprang into the air, landing in her lap, then turning to find a comfortable position within her raised, crooked leg.

She'd never thought of it before, but a sidesaddle did provide a rather good resting spot for a feline. She stroked his silky neck. "I'm going on a very long journey and you can't go with me, darling puss."

She tried to lift him away. His ears went down and his tail started lashing. As their gazes met, she tried to send him an image of a very long ride to a strange place. He snorted and tucked his head down, his tail draping over his nose.

Apparently the scrying glass was not the only thing at Dunrath that was truly hers. With a faint smile at the absurdity, she set Sheba in motion. It would be good to have company on her journey.

She only looked back once, at the crest of the ridge that overlooked the glen. This was where she and Duncan had stopped on her bridal journey. She had been a girl then, her power newly discovered and as exciting as the passion that had triggered it. Though she'd had reservations about how she was to balance Duncan, she had dimly recognized how lucky she was that fate had given her such a husband.

At Dunrath, she had found a home of the spirit in a place of incomparable beauty. It was the life she hadn't even known she wanted until it fell into her hands.

Now she was a woman and a powerful sorceress who had no fear of any possible dangers she might meet on the road. She had upheld her Guardian oath to the best of her abilities, exactly as the council had asked her to do.

Mouth tight, she resumed her journey. There was a saying among the Families that magic always had a price. But she had never dreamed how high that price would be.

* * *

Duncan slept the clock around, not waking until early the morning after the government troops had visited. Muscles stiff, he got to his feet and brushed straw from his kilt. Deliberately he banked his power, not wanting to know anything that was happening beyond the reach of his normal five senses.

When he left his cell, voices called out, "Good morning to you, Macrae!" and " 'Tis good to be home!" and other cheerful greetings.

He waved a reply, trying to look equally cheerful. "You must all stay here another few days for safety's sake, but I'll see that your breakfast is down soon."

"I'd sell my soul for a bowl of hot porridge," someone said mournfully.

"Assuming anyone would want a dirty old soul like yours." The taunts were good-natured. The rebels of Glen Rath were in the exhilarated mood that came when one had escaped certain death. Soon they would be eased back into the life of Glen Rath, and it would be as if they had never left. Duncan envied them.

The kitchen was already busy making breakfast for the rebels, including a great kettle of steaming porridge. He swiped a hunk of bread and climbed to his own bedroom, where he washed up with cold water and changed into fresh, English-style clothing. Now was not a wise time to ride out wearing Highland garb. He tried not to think of his lady wife, who was probably still sleeping the sleep of the virtuous.

He felt aimless today, not sure how to talk to Gwynne. Would she resist leaving? Or would she be delighted at the prospect of returning to her English life? Since divorce was virtually impossible, he supposed that they would each develop discreet liaisons with partners who could never be legal spouses but who would warm their beds at night. He almost retched at the thought.

In the breakfast room, he found tea, toast, and his sister. Jean looked up, then came straight into his arms. He hugged her hard. "Ah, Jeannie, my lass, you've had far too many adventures in the last few months."

"Enough adventures for a lifetime." She stepped from his embrace and poured him a cup of tea. As he drank it thirstily, she said, "This morning, I thought about the Friday night gathering where I announced I'd lead our men to the prince. Remember the spell of protection we made together at the end?"

He nodded. That night seemed eons ago.

"I've just realized that everyone who was present that night survived the campaign, and so did the glen." She drew an unsteady breath. "I only wish that Robbie had been there."

He offered a silent prayer for the soul of Robbie Mackenzie, who had lived and died with valor. "I'm so sorry you lost him, Jean."

"He died without losing his faith in the cause. I'm glad he had that, at least." Jean returned to her tea.

Bracing himself, he asked, "Has Gwynne risen yet?"

His sister glanced up with surprise. "You don't know? She left yesterday. Saddled up Sheba and headed off to England. I don't suppose we'll see her again." Jean sighed. "I don't know whether I'm glad or sorry. I have trouble forgiving what she did to you and the consequences of that, and yet she did so much good for all of us."

Shocked, Duncan scanned the castle. No Gwynne. She had really left.

He should have been relieved that he had been spared an ugly scene. With so much anger and recrimination between them, they wouldn't have been able to talk without hurting each other even more. Yet instead of relief, he felt . . . hollow.

"Are you going after her?" Jean asked, her voice neutral.

"No. The marriage is broken beyond mending." Betrayed beyond forgiveness. And yet . . . "But . . . she left too soon. There are things that must be said between us."

Jean said nothing, only watched with great wide eyes as if she expected more of him. She didn't know how agonizing it would be for him to confront the wife who had betrayed him. Of course, it was equally painful not to talk to her.

Reluctantly he accepted that he really had no choice. "Very well, I suppose I must go after her. Not to bring her back, but to . . . to ask all the unanswered questions. To make an official ending."

"That's wise, I think."

He wondered if his little sister found his words as lame as he did. Probably, but she'd learned tact in the last months, and the beginnings of wisdom.

It was more than he had learned.

* * *

Gwynne woke when hazy sunshine slanted through the empty doorway of the bothy. Yawning sleepily, she wrapped a plaid around her shoulders and ambled outside. Ethereal mists gave the dramatic hills the look of a magical kingdom. Later the sun would burn off the mist and the morning chill. Springtime in Scotland was glorious with burgeoning life, and it soothed her frayed spirit

Her first night on the road she had stayed at a small

inn, but the night before she'd had to settle for this crumbling hut. It offered more the illusion of shelter than real protection from the elements, but it had been good enough.

Two snaps of her fingers were needed to light the kindling under her small tin pot. Candles were easier. As the water heated, Lionel appeared with a still-struggling mouse locked firmly in his jaws. She made a face. "I'd rather you ate that elsewhere."

Obligingly he withdrew a few feet away. Not so far that she couldn't hear the crunch of little mousy bones, but apart from his eating habits, he was a good companion. She hoped he liked England.

She was toasting a piece of cheese on a stick over the fire when Duncan appeared, quiet as an evening zephyr. Tall and dark and pitiless, he was the Lord of Thunder in full dramatic mode. She gasped and dropped her cheese into the fire. How the devil had he come so close without her hearing or feeling him? Damn Guardian stealth! And damn her heart, for surging with joy at the sight of him.

Shaking, she jumped to her feet and backed away, the toasting stick clenched in her hand. Their marriage was supposed to be *over*. Why couldn't he leave her alone? She didn't think he looked murderous, but this interview was going to be very, very difficult. If only she didn't still want him. . . .

"Don't bother poking me with that stick," he said dryly. "You have better weapons."

He was right. She dropped the stick. "Why are you here?"

"Not to murder you." He glanced at Lionel, who had abandoned the mouse and now crouched in hunting position, striped tail lashing. "You can call off your familiar."

"He senses when I am threatened." She locked her shields in place. The last thing they needed was enchantress magic in a situation that was already far too volatile. "Why are you here?"

"We have . . . unsettled business."

"I think we've said all that needed saying, and probably a good deal more. I'm sorry for the pain we caused each other, Duncan, but given the people we are, I don't know how it could have been any different."

"I suppose you're right." The sadness in his voice was vaster than the sky. He started to say more, then stopped, his eyes narrowing. "Ye gods, you're pregnant!"

She should have known this wasn't a secret she could keep from a mage of his power. "I did want your child, but I'm still amazed at how quickly it happened." That had been a blessing, since the night she put him in irons would surely be the last time they would ever make love.

A cascade of emotions showed in Duncan's face. Shock, joy, concern, then determination. "He shall have to be raised at Dunrath."

She had known he would say that. It was one of many reasons for leaving Dunrath. "Impossible. I will raise my own child. He is your heir and he must certainly spend time with you in Scotland, but until he's well grown, he is mine."

Duncan's mouth thinned to a hard line. "If you want him all to yourself, all you need do is turn me over to the government as a Jacobite."

"I went to considerable effort to save you from both the government and the council," she snapped. "I'm not about to betray you now."

"You can't possibly betray me worse than you already have," he said softly.

His words stabbed more painfully than a dagger. "You

put me in the position of having to betray either you or my sworn oath." She sighed. "You should have chosen a more malleable wife."

"I don't think I chose you at all. Fate and the council threw us together. Now that your task has been accomplished, you are running away to your pale, safe Sassenach life." He tossed another branch on the fire. It exploded into sparks.

"Considering that you were threatening murder, it seemed wise to leave Dunrath," she said, trying to match his dry tone.

"Did you believe I would really do that?"

"No," she admitted. "But the fact that you could say such a thing was a measure of your fury." She unconsciously placed a hand on her belly, where there was a faint glow of extra energy. "I would have informed you when the child was born. That would have been soon enough. Why the devil did you follow me, Duncan? Isn't this difficult enough already?"

"As I said, there is unfinished business between us, Gwyneth Owens." His eyes were the color of pale winter ice. "Have you reached any conclusions about why a Stuart victory would be so devastating that you chose to betray your own husband? Or could it be that there were no reasons, and you were merely arrogant in your ignorance?"

"No," she said, aching. "I feel with every particle of my being that I am right, but I have never been able to get beyond a wall of fear and pain that blocks me from seeing more."

"There is a way that might give you the answer."

Not liking his expression, she asked, "What?"

"If we mate with our shields down, we might be able to reach a deeper level of knowledge. If the bond still exists between us—if we can trust each other, even if only for an hour—we might find a deeper understanding than either of us can reach alone."

"No!" She backed up until she ran into the wall of the bothy. "Dear heaven, Duncan, haven't we hurt each other enough?"

He stepped around the fire and halted within arm's length of her. "You hate my touch that much?"

"I have never hated your touch, blast you! But I fear what intimacy with you will do to my heart."

"And here I've wondered if you even have a heart within that wickedly provocative body." He cupped her cheek with surprising gentleness. "Don't you want to know the reason why you destroyed our marriage? I'm curious. More than curious."

She began to weep silently, wishing that he had stayed away, wishing that he had come to forgive her and take her home to Dunrath. Anything but this cool, exquisitely painful dissection of what had separated them.

His lips brushed the tears on her cheeks. "A truce, Gwyneth Owens. And perhaps from that . . . who knows?" His mouth came down on hers, light and controlled.

All the reasons why she should keep her distance vanished as longing blazed through her. She wanted his hard, passionate body, his wry humor, his tenderness, the strength that could be both courage and stubbornness. Most of all, she wanted the heart-deep closeness that had once bound them, even if it was only for a handful of moments.

"Ah, God, Gwynne . . . ," he breathed as she kissed him with fierce urgency. Their arms locked around each other as if passion was their last hope of heaven. In a tangle of limbs, they stumbled into the bothy and sprawled onto her blankets, tearing at the garments that separated them.

She writhed against him, desperate to come together one last time, while bitterly aware that if he wanted to punish her, he had found the perfect way. How could she bear to never know his touch again? He was a drug in her blood, a need great as water and air.

They had mated with every shade of tenderness and scarlet passion, but nothing had ever matched the blaze of power that scalded through them when he entered her. She cried out as his spirit penetrated hers as stunningly as his body.

In the white heat of desire, she barely remembered that he said they must come together with shields down if they were to find a deeper truth. The thought terrified her, but she owed him this. Layer by layer, in instants that seemed like hours, she stripped away the barriers that had protected her secrets, her fears, her deep ambivalence about her marriage.

The process took so much of her splintered concentration that only when she was finished did she realize that his formidable defenses were also gone, and lowering them had been as hard for him as for her. Their naked, vulnerable spirits flowed together, and in that ultimate intimacy she gained visceral understanding of how profoundly her betrayal had wounded him. He had always dared more than she. He had risked love while she had hung back, accepting his love but afraid to admit to her own because of the hazards that surrounded him. He had given her all a man could give a woman—and she had used it against him.

Whether her reasons were good was irrelevant. She had committed a crime against love, and only love might heal the damage she had inflicted. She poured herself into him—her love, her admiration, her apologies and deep, deep regrets. *Forgive me, beloved, forgive me.*

"Ah, Gwynne, my heart . . . ," he whispered. Though he had known he must expose himself as thoroughly as she to find the answers he sought, he had foolishly not anticipated what that meant. In this place of no barriers, only essence, his anger crumbled in the fountain of her anguished, sorrowing love.

It was he who must apologize for putting her in an impossible position. Though he had loved her as much for the pure strength of her spirit as for her stunning sensuality, he hadn't wanted to accept the consequences of her integrity. "I'm sorry, *mo càran*," he said, barely able to say the words before passion swamped his mind. "I was wrong. . . ."

Lightning crashed through the sky as they culminated together, and in that searing flash of earthly and magical energy, the shape and form of Gwynne's nightmares became shockingly clear. He almost blacked out from the combined intensity of passion, fulfillment, and the horror of the future that he might have created with his headstrong acts. He looked into the abyss, and found himself.

As aftershocks tingled through him, he rolled to his side and crushed her close, needing the sweet solace of her body to anchor him. She was shaking, yet strong in ways no mere male could ever match. "You . . . you saw that?" he asked raggedly.

"God help me, I did." She drew a shuddering breath. "A Jacobite victory would have been followed within five years by the new king's attempt to convert the nation to Catholicism, by the sword if necessary. It would have become the worst religious war in Britain's history—worse than Bloody Mary's burnings or the rampages of the Puritans."

He nodded as her words crystallized his understanding. "When the people resisted, King James would have invited French and Spanish and Irish troops into Britain to force conversions. The attempt to return Britain to the Roman Church would have failed, but the price would have been monstrous. Beyond belief."

Her eyes squeezed shut as if that would stop the images. "When I dreamed of rivers of blood, it wasn't a metaphor, but a prediction. Merciful heaven, Duncan, did you see what would have happened in London . . . ?"

"Hush, my love." He stroked her silky hair, awed by the power and compassion beneath those shining red gold tresses. "I saw it all." And those images would appear in his nightmares until the day he died. "Those horrors would have come true if not for you, Gwyneth Owens. You are a heroine."

"If I am a heroine, I am also a fool." She stared at him with dazed eyes. "I should have realized what the ultimate danger would be. The potential for religious conflict was always present. I am a scholar, I know history. Yet I couldn't see it. If I had realized sooner—"

He laid a finger over her lips to stop her self-recriminations. "None of us saw it. Not me nor you nor Simon nor the council. The religious wars of the past left deep scars on our nations' souls, *mo cridhe*. I think we all wanted to believe we had risen above religious violence. Who would believe that a modern ruler would invite such atrocities in God's name?"

Her mouth curved wryly. "We Guardians think we are wise. We try to learn from the past and make judgments with clear, objective minds. We're not very successful, are we?"

"We are only human, my love. Our greater powers give us the opportunity to make greater mistakes, as I did." His mouth twisted. "I used my power to urge Charles

Edward toward the throne of Scotland. Now that I see the greater picture, I realize that if I hadn't interfered, the rising might have ended sooner and with fewer lives lost. There is no way I can ever redeem such misjudgment."

"As you said, we are all too human. If you wish to redeem your mistakes, work to rebuild Scotland, for she will need you desperately in the years ahead." Gwynne's eyes became unfocused. "The remnants of rebellion will be crushed with great and terrible violence, yet from that will flower a true partnership between Scotland and England. In the future, Scots and Englishmen will marry, study, and fight side by side as equals. Together they will build an empire that spans the world."

Her words rang with truth, and he found comfort in them. Silently he pledged himself to do all in his power to bring about that bright vision. "Besides working to heal a wounded nation, we must raise our children the best we know how, and hope they are a little wiser than we." He laid her hand on the gentle curve of her belly. It was far too soon for any change to be visible, but the glow of a new soul offered hope for a better future. "I love you, Gwyneth Owens. Will you come home with me?"

Her eyes crinkled with laughter. "You know the answer to that since our souls have been even more closely twined than our bodies."

"I . . . I need to hear the words." He felt like a fool admitting that, but it was true.

"I love you, Duncan Macrae." She raised her face and kissed him with lingering sweetness. "I will stay with you forever, raise our children, tend to your castle—and disagree with you whenever you're a stubborn, lovable fool."

"Spoken like a true Guardian female. Independent, unmanageable, and utterly irresistible." He laughed and rolled onto his back, pulling her on top of him. "I love you, dearest wife. I will even try to love that evil cat of yours."

"No need to go that far." She bent into another kiss that stole his breath and heart away. "Take me home, Duncan. Take me home *now*."

Epilogue

Gwynne tapped on the door of the best guest room. "Lady Bethany, are you awake?"

The lady herself opened the door, her silvery hair echoing the delicate embroidery on her gown. "Of course I am, and eager to attend this Friday night gathering of yours."

"You're not too tired from your journey? You only just got here two hours ago."

"I'm not made of glass, child. Yes, it was a long ride north, but the carriage was comfortable and we were in no rush." She patted Gwynne's expanding midriff. "You're the one who needs to be pampered, but I won't fuss over you if you won't fuss over me."

"Very well." Gwynne hugged her sister-in-law. "I'm so glad you're here!"

"The feeling is mutual. It's been a difficult year for all Britain. But now that the country is settling down, I wanted to see you. That was no easy task you took on." The older woman searched Gwynne's face. "You're truly happy?"

"Oh, yes," Gwynne said quietly. Taking Lady Bethany's arm, she set a course for the stairway. "I could not have imagined how much I love Scotland. This was always my true home. I just didn't know until I arrived here."

"And your husband?"

Gwynne found herself blushing. She'd heard that some men found women who were increasing to be unattractive. Duncan was not of that number. "I owe the council a grand thank you for encouraging me to do something I was too afraid to do on my own."

Lady Bethany smiled. "I'm so glad. I felt that things would probably turn out well for you, but it was by no means guaranteed."

Side by side, they started down the steps. Now that she was less nimble, Gwynne appreciated the railings Duncan had installed on the stairs. When they reached the entrance to the great hall, both paused. Already dozens of Macraes were circulating, chatting and drinking as they waited for the dinner to begin.

For an instant Gwynne tried to see the gathering as Lady Bethany did. None of the guests were fashionably dressed, and many had the ruddy complexions of those who spent much of their time outdoors. In her panniers and stomacher and dainty slippers, Lady Bethany was from another world.

Gwynne shouldn't have worried. The older woman gave a happy sigh. "I see what you mean, Gwynne. Dunrath radiates warmth and goodwill. I may never leave."

"Nothing could make me happier!"

"I think my own children would have a thing or two to say about that, and I would miss them, too. But I'll certainly be here until after that fine strapping son of yours is born." Bethany's glance touched Jean. "Your other sister-in-law breaks my heart. Even that lovely smile can't hide her sorrow."

Gwynne silently agreed. Once Jean was told of the horrors that might have resulted from Duncan's intervention in the rebellion, she had accepted Gwynne's actions. But the bright-eyed girl of a year ago was gone forever. "She improves, slowly."

Lady Bethany narrowed her eyes thoughtfully. "When she is ready, send her to me in London. There might be a touch of fate in her future as well."

If so, Gwynne hoped it was a simpler fate than her own had been. Not that she could complain about the results. "There's Duncan, and look, Simon is with him!"

The two men moved across the room toward Gwynne and Lady Bethany, their progress slowed by greetings and introductions. Duncan's dark hair was escaping its queue and he was dressed in casual contrast to Simon, who looked like a royal courtier even when he was wearing one of his simplest costumes.

The men had worked closely together to quietly mitigate some of the effects of the government's crushing treatment of the conquered Highlands. They had misdirected troops from small hidden glens, supplied food and livestock to crofters whose homes were burned, and helped rebels and their families escape to the American colonies.

Reaching the women, Duncan draped a warm arm around his wife's shoulders. On his hand the sapphire of Adam Macrae's ring sparkled in the candlelight. "Are you well, *mo cridhe*?"

"I am now." Never better than when her husband was with her.

"Lady Beth!" Simon bent over her hand. "This is an unexpected surprise."

Bethany laughed. "Nonsense. Nothing surprises you, Falconer."

Gwynne wondered if Simon realized the extent of

Duncan's actions. She suspected he did, and that he was grateful he'd never been required to take official action. Now the men were again on the same side, doing their best to preserve and protect. She stretched out her hand to him. "It's good to see you again, Simon."

His tired eyes lit up. "You glow, my lady."

She patted her belly. "You know why. Your godson is full of energy."

"Duncan is a fortunate man." Simon's tone held a hint of wistfulness.

"I know it well!" Duncan's arm tightened around Gwynne. Glancing into her eyes, he said, "It's time to begin, my love."

Gwynne nodded and they separated. As she lit a taper, her husband struck the Chinese gong, the deep, musical tone filling the hall. People ambled to the tables to find seats. Smiling, Jean guided Lady Bethany to the chair at Gwynne's right hand. Gwynne was pleased that the two women had struck up an immediate friendship.

The minor irritations of daily life fell away as she lit the candles in the massive silver candelabra. Peace spread through the hall as the familiar ritual began. Candles lit, Gwynne took her place at the head of the table and made the beckoning gesture of welcome. "Welcome, family and friends."

Another gesture. "Welcome to any visitors who may be joining us tonight." Her gaze went to Lady Bethany, who looked completely at home despite her brocade. Even Simon, usually taut as a polished blade, began to relax.

Gwynne gestured for the third time. "Now let us offer thanks for the blessings of family, food, and friends."

Before covering her eyes with her hands, she looked down the table to her husband. As their gazes met, Duncan gave her the smile that was only for her and reached out to touch her mind. *I love you.*

Warmth flowed through every particle of her being. *I love you, too,* mo cridhe. How had she been so lucky as to find a true mate of body, mind, and soul?

Not luck. Fate.

Author's note

Though my Guardians are fictional, the background they move against is real. The New Spring Gardens where Gwynne and Duncan meet is better known as Vauxhall, the name it acquired in 1785. Frederick, Prince of Wales, the heir to George II, really was called "the Nauseous Beast" by his family; the king tried unsuccessfully to remove him from the succession. There was general relief when Frederick died in 1751. His son became George III, a simple man who reigned for decades and generally restored respect to the throne because of his high moral standards.

The Jacobite rebellion of 1745 is well known and often romanticized. A far more charismatic leader than his father, James, Prince Charles Edward Stuart—"Bonnie Prince Charlie"—came closer to succeeding than any of the earlier risings. It's certainly possible to imagine different circumstances that would have led to success. It's equally possible to imagine a scenario that could have led to disaster.

A Scottish friend of mine says that the Battle of Culloden carries a haunting sorrow for Scots. The sadness is not primarily because of the bloody battle itself—Scotland had known many bloody battles. But the harrowing of the Highlands that followed destroyed an ancient way of life. This is why I kept my story clear of the battles— romance is about hope and healing, not irrevocable tragedy.

Like all writers, I'm intrigued by "What if?" questions, and my Guardian stories allow plenty of room to speculate about possibilities. The first Guardian story was "The Alchemical Marriage" in the *Irresistible Forces* anthology. More stories are on the way! After all, love and magic go together. . . .

Read on for an excerpt from
a thrilling new tale of the Guardians!

STOLEN MAGIC

M. J. Putney

Available from Del Rey Books

$\mathcal{I}$mmobilized by ropes and trapped in a window-less stone building, Simon had done his best to withdraw into the quiet of his own mind. Anger and battering at his bonds were futile. Better to inventory his memories of magic, and perhaps find a store of power to use against Drayton when the time came, for that time would surely be soon.

His drifting consciousness snapped to attention when he suddenly caught the scent of innocence that had enraptured him and led to his capture. Every muscle tensed and he instinctively moved toward the scent, only to be jerked to a halt by the ropes that immobilized him in the center of the shed. He sniffed again, wondering if this was the same sweet female or another like her. The same, he decided. Her fragrance was so intense that she must be just outside the door.

She betrayed me to my doom. But not intentionally. Her cry of anguish when the hunters attacked had been genuine. Even if he knew that she would betray him again, he was unable to resist the sweet lure of her purity. He strained against his bonds, remembering the rapturous moment when he had laid himself at her feet.

The door swung open and a cloaked female silhouette appeared against the lesser dark of the night. "M . . . Meggie is sorry, sweeting," she said in an unsteady voice. "Meggie here to let you go." To his surprise, her words were accompanied by a distinct mental image of her releasing him from his bonds. She could mind-touch?

She stepped forward and banged into the rope that secured him on his right side. The impact jarred the cutting bit of the bridle that had been forced on him, hurting his tender mouth. When he shivered away from the pain, the maiden hissed a word that was not innocent, yet curiously endearing.

She must have brought a knife, for he could feel a blade sawing at the rope, accompanied by a murmuring of soft words. She was treating him as he would treat a nervous horse. He would have smiled wryly if he had been himself.

The line parted and she felt her way round him to find the left line. Once more the cutting. A quaver in her voice, she asked, "C . . . can you forgive Meggie for helping to capture you?"

He replied by rubbing against her affectionately, barely remembering to turn his head so he didn't stab her. He almost knocked her over in his enthusiasm. She laughed breathlessly and stroked his muzzle. The touch of her gentle fingers was exquisite. "N . . . nasty bridle. Will you be good if it comes off?"

He rubbed against her again, trying to indicate that he'd follow her anywhere as docile as a lamb. She must have understood, for she removed the wicked bridle and grasped a handful of his mane. "Must leave without being noticed."

Recalled from the fog of rapture she inspired, he stepped outside. A guard lay on the ground, moaning softly. Had his sweet maiden laid the fellow out? Impressed, Simon accompanied her through the shadows, his steps as light as he could make them. A light drizzle was starting to fall. Maybe that would aid their escape.

They were nearing the postern when the clouds broke and the light of a nearly full moon flooded the courtyard. A man yelled, "A thief is stealing the beast! Stop them!"

The blast of a shotgun pierced the night and a shower of vicious lead shot peppered Simon and his escort. The maiden flinched, then cried, "Go!"

Worried, he tried to see if she was hurt, but she released his mane and took off at a speed that proved she wasn't seriously injured. He followed, trying to place himself between her and the man with the shotgun. More shots blasted through the night, this time from the guard tower above the main gate.

The commotion had woken the castle and several men spilled into the courtyard just as Simon and the maiden reached the postern. She halted and said again, "Go!"

Aghast, he stopped in his tracks, nostrils flaring. She wasn't coming with him?

She made impatient shooing motions with both hands. "Meggie will be safe," she said bitterly. "They won't dare hurt the lord's pet simpleton."

Despite her words, he had no doubt that the approaching men would hurt her, perhaps very badly. He went down on one knee and imagined her mounting him.

She stared, shock on her narrow, angular face. Clearly she'd had no intention of leaving, perhaps couldn't even comprehend doing so.

Frightened for her safety and yearning for her presence, he whinnied and sent the riding image again. There was another ragged volley of musket shots, and this time he felt a searing pain in his left haunch, a wound far more severe than the birdshot.

His maiden bit her lip, radiating fear and confusion. Then she looked back at the approaching men and her expression changed to steely resolve. "Want to *go*."

She swung expertly onto his back. He scrambled to his feet and almost collapsed from the agony that blazed through his left leg. No bones seemed to be broken, so he tried to block out the pain as he bolted through the postern. A shiver of energy from the protective wards tingled his skin but didn't slow him.

The forest was less than a mile away, and they could lose themselves · in its depths. He hardly noticed his maiden's weight, for even without a saddle she balanced lightly as a butterfly. Clouds covered the moon again and rain began falling harder, but his unicorn vision was uncannily sharp even in the dark.

They were halfway to the forest when he heard a thunder of hooves behind him. Some damnable person in the castle had organized a pursuit with wicked speed. If Simon was riderless and unwounded he could easily outrun the pursuers, but in his half-crippled state, they were gaining on him.

As thunder boomed and lightning lit up the sky, he dashed into the dark shelter of the woods. Branches lashed them as he followed an almost invisible track made by deer.

The pursuers followed easily, their speed barely diminished. One of them must have some magical tracking power. They would be on him in minutes, and what would happen to his maiden then? He had a horrible image of her raped and beaten, her sweet courage brutally crushed.

He tried to use his hunter's talent for concealment, but in his present form he couldn't wield his Guardian powers. Only the inherent magic of a unicorn was available.

That gave him speed, strength, and heightened senses, but could not hide them from their pursuers. Frantic, he reached out mentally to his oldest friend, Duncan Macrae, the finest weather mage in Britain, perhaps in the world.

Help me!

Amazingly, he managed to reach Duncan, who was peacefully asleep at his home in Scotland. Jolted into wakefulness, Duncan responded with an incredulous, *Simon?*

Even as himself, it would have been almost impossible for Simon to explain the situation at such a distance. But desperation gave him the power to communicate a sense of where he was. He visualized a map of Britain where his position pulsed like a star. *Pursued! Storm?*

Duncan snapped to full wakefulness. *I'll see what weather you have to work with.* After a pause while he studied the weather patterns of Shropshire, he thought with satisfaction, *Excellent.*

Only moments passed before lightning slashed the sky and thunder shook the earth a bare instant later. The rain tripled in intensity, pounding with the force of a physical blow. Even though Simon was expecting this, for a moment he was thrown off his stride, slipping to his knees on the muddy track. His maiden lurched a little but maintained her seat.

He scrambled to his feet and resumed his flight through the forest, relying on his improved night vision to save him from crashing into a tree. Unfortunately his superior hearing could still hear hooves behind him, albeit at a slower pace. With his waning energy, he called Duncan again. *More?*

He thought he had failed to connect with his friend. Then he heard a faint, *More! Take care, Simon.*

The connection broke as Duncan concentrated all his power into his weather magic. The wind increased to near-hurricane force and trees began crashing to the earth behind Simon. A dead tree plummeted across the track too closely for Simon to swerve. Mustering all his strength, he leaped headlong over it. Scrawny branches scratched at his limbs but he managed to clear the trunk without falling.

Along with the turbulent weather, Simon sensed that Duncan was using Guardian magic to blur the trail. He must have guessed that for some reason Simon couldn't use shielding himself. Simon took advantage of the grace period Duncan had given them to run until his heart seemed nigh to bursting. Despite rain and wind, his precious rider clung like a burr.

When even hypersensitive unicorn hearing couldn't detect pursuit, Simon slowed to a walk, his lungs pumping like a bellows. Now what? He was cold, tired, and hurting, and the maiden must be chilled to the bone. They had to find shelter. In his previous exploration of the forest, he'd found a deep, rocky overhang. It was masked by thick underbrush, so there would be some protection from the still-heavy rain.

As he limped wearily through the night, he hoped his maiden knew something about treating wounds, or they might not be going anywhere in the morning.

* * *

Numb with cold, Meggie almost fell off the unicorn's back when he nosed through some underbrush below a huge overhanging rock and halted in the protected area underneath. She had thought their escape was doomed until the storm struck. Luck had been with them. Though she had been grazed by several shotgun balls, the hurts were small. She would be fine, if she didn't freeze before dawn.

The night was very black, but the unicorn's beautiful white coat made him dimly visible even under the rocks—except that part of him seemed to be missing, Worried, she touched the dark area on his left flank and raised her fingers to her lips, tasting the metallic tang of blood. He must have been wounded by a musket ball, which explained the increasing roughness of his gait during their escape.

The unicorn rubbed against her as if asking for help. The poor beast was trembling with fatigue, his sleek coat steaming from the cold rain that had fallen on his overheated body. "Meggie doesn't know what to do," she whispered, frustrated. "M . . . maybe if there was light."

Wait. She was wearing her cloak, and she usually carried a tinderbox in one pocket. She groped in the cloak and almost wept with relief when she found it. Now if she could find dry wood . . .

Cautiously she felt around in the dark under the deepest area of the overhang, hoping nothing nasty lived there. Once more her luck was in, and she found several dry, broken branches and a drift of leaves. She was responsible for the small fireplace in her castle bedroom, so even working in near-absolute darkness she was able to strike a spark onto the charred fabric from the tinderbox. When it caught, she carefully fed in bits of dried leaves, then twigs and kindling until she had a small fire burning.

She looked up to see the unicorn watching her. Was that worry she sensed from him? Aloud, she said, "N . . . no one will see the fire, and we need it."

Though the unicorn didn't reply, she suspected he understood her. He was far more than a horse. "Meggie will look at your wound after hands warm."

She held her numbed fingers over the fire and discovered that her right middle finger was bleeding, wounded by a ball from the shotgun. She sucked at the scrape to clean it, grateful the shot hadn't done more damage.

Later she could bandage the finger, but her injury was nothing compared to the gory slash on the unicorn's flank. Bending to avoid hitting her head on the stone overhang, she moved to his side. His horn caught the light of the fire, shimmering with rainbow highlights.

He nuzzled her affectionately and made a soft chirping sound. Touched, she hugged his neck for a long moment before examining his wound. It was deep and bleeding sluggishly. Though she'd always tended horses, she'd never seen a musket ball injury. "Ugly. Be still, sweeting, so Meggie can look closer."

She knelt by the unicorn's belly, not wanting to be behind those sharp rear hooves if he kicked. "S . . . steady . . ."

She leaned over and frowned, not liking the looks of the ragged wound. Was the musket ball buried inside?

She touched the gaping flesh—and the world exploded. A rush of heat blasted her backward as the unicorn vanished in a whirlwind of blazing energy and scalding light. The very air was warped, impossible to see through, but Meggie saw dimly that he was *changing*. Strange shapes were dimly visible as they twisted into stomach-churningly different forms. She cringed against the stone, terrified.

The blast of heat faded and the blurred air smoothed out, revealing the sprawled form of a human man. A completely naked man.